She placed her elbows on the table and leaned forward, her gaze so intent Bo felt as if she were somehow peering inside his soul.

"Are you in for a little crime investigation?"

The fresh, slightly floral scent of her perfume wafted across the table as her gaze continued to hold him captive. He had arrived at the high school not knowing what his decision was, whether he intended to try to find the real killer or get out of town as fast as possible.

The light of her belief in him shone from her eyes. He bathed in it and realised he wanted this…his innocence restored among the people who had once been friends and neighbours.

"I'm in," he finally said. He hoped in making that decision he hadn't just made a mistake he would come to regret. Asking questions, talking to people and stirring up everything from the past just might stir up a killer's rage.

SCENE OF
THE CRIME:
KILLER COVE

BY
CARLA CASSIDY

Published in Great Britain 2015
by Mills & Boon, an imprint of Harlequin (UK) Limited,
Eton House, 18-24 Paradise Road, Richmond, Surrey, TW9 1SR

© 2015 Carla Bracale

ISBN: 978-0-263-25304-7

46-0515

Harlequin (UK) Limited's policy is to use papers that are natural, renewable and recyclable products and made from wood grown in sustainable forests. The logging and manufacturing processes conform to the legal environmental regulations of the country of origin.

Printed and bound in Spain
by CPI, Barcelona

Carla Cassidy is a *New York Times* bestselling author who has written more than one hundred books for Mills & Boon. Carla believes the only thing better than curling up with a good book to read is sitting down at the computer with a good story to write. She's looking forward to writing many more books and bringing hours of pleasure to readers.

Chapter One

Bo McBride throttled down, the Harley responding by slowing as he passed the old, faded wooden sign that read Lost Lagoon, Population 705.

His stomach knotted painfully as the scent of the swamp not only surrounded him but invaded his lungs, making it difficult to breathe around the anxiety and anger the scent of home now brought.

As far as almost everyone in town was concerned, it had been two years since he'd been back to Lost Lagoon, Mississippi. Only two people knew about his monthly visits back here to his mother's place, secret visits that had him arriving and leaving under the cover of darkness.

He wouldn't be here now if his mother hadn't passed away unexpectedly two days before. A massive heart attack. His best friend, Jimmy Tambor, who had moved into the house when Bo left town, had given him the grim news.

It had taken Bo an entire day to process the fact that his mother was gone and another day to make arrangements with his employees to leave. The funeral was to be held tomorrow. After that, he figured it would take a couple of days to put his mother's things in order and then get the hell away from the town that had robbed him of the last two years of his mother's life, among other things.

He'd been on the road for hours, leaving his place in Jackson before dawn that morning. He hadn't stopped to eat except snacks picked up at gas station pit stops, and now decided before showing up at his childhood home that he'd grab a quick bite to eat at George's Diner, located just inside the city limits.

George's Diner was more glorified hamburger joint than true diner. Although there were a couple of booths inside, most people either drove through or sat at the wooden counter to be served as quickly as possible.

Bo parked his ride on the side of the building and then pulled off his helmet and hand-combed his thick, shaggy hair. He stretched and headed around the building to the front door, eager to escape the June heat and humidity.

It was after three and few people were inside. The prevalent scent was of fried onions, hot grease and the gamy odor of swamp fish and gator. There was a pretty blonde woman serving a couple at one of the tables.

Bo slid onto the first stool at the counter just as George stepped out of the kitchen. George King was a big man, both tall and weighing in at about three hundred pounds of muscle and fat. He was bald, with thick black eyebrows and dark brown eyes that narrowed the instant he saw Bo. He ambled over to Bo as he wiped his hands on his stained white apron.

"Burger, fries and a sweet tea," Bo said.

"Move along, Bo. I don't serve murderers here," George replied, his deep voice filled with disgust.

His words aroused Bo's anger—the anger of injustice, of things unchanged and memories of the isolation and despair he'd felt when he'd left town two years before.

He wanted to fight for the simple dignity of being served a burger, but instead he slid off the stool and left the building without saying a word.

He certainly hadn't expected to be welcomed back to town with open arms, but he also hadn't expected the same kind of intense animosity that had ultimately forced him to leave.

Sitting on his bike, he tried to school his emotions. Jimmy was meeting him at the house and he didn't want to carry any more anger with him than what already burned in his soul. It had just been a hamburger and fries, after all, and everyone in town knew that George was an ass.

He pulled on his helmet and was just about to start his motorcycle when he heard somebody call out his name. From around the corner of the diner the curly-haired blonde waitress appeared. He had a quick impression of long, shapely legs, big blue eyes and a warm smile that was as surprising as a gator wearing a straw hat.

She tossed him a brown paper bag that he caught with his hands. "Burger and fries. I couldn't do anything about the sweet tea," she said, and then before he could reply she disappeared back around the corner of the building.

Bo sat in stunned surprise for several moments. It had been an unexpected gesture of kindness. He opened the bag and ate the food. At the same time he wondered who the woman was and why she had gone to the trouble.

It was almost four o'clock when he drove slowly down the street that was an outer band. Several blocks over to his left was the business area of Lost Lagoon, and on his right was the swamp side of town with a few small, neat cabins intermixed among weather-faded, neglected shanties. The swamp was an overgrown, tangled bog about twenty feet from the back of these houses and continued until Bo made the left curve that would skirt the edges of the lagoon.

On the right side of the lagoon, the swamp ended and he was on higher ground with larger homes and an aura of better prosperity. He made two turns to take him into the neighborhood where he'd grown up.

It appeared as if nothing had changed in the time he'd been gone. Only when he noticed a lot of new construction at the top of a hill behind his neighborhood did he realize something was about to change in the tiny town.

At the sight of the neat white ranch house with black shutters and a butterfly wind chime hanging off the edge of the small porch, his heart fluttered with grief. He pulled into the driveway and parked and wished that the past two years had been different.

He didn't bother taking anything from his saddlebags. He had plenty of time to unpack what few things he'd brought with him. He climbed off the bike, set his helmet on the seat and then headed for the front door.

As he stepped up on the porch the door swung open and Jimmy Tambor pulled him into a bro hug. "I'm sorry, Bo. I'm so damned sorry," he said and released Bo.

"Thanks," Bo said woodenly.

"If it's any consolation at all, the doctor thinks it happened in her sleep," Jimmy replied. "She just went to bed as usual and I found her in the morning. I don't think she suffered."

Bo hoped that was the case. His mother had suffered enough five years ago when his father had passed away in a car accident. At that time Bo had feared his mother would grieve herself to death.

Jimmy had moved into the house when Bo had left town. Bo had wanted somebody he trusted to be there for his mother while he couldn't be.

"I don't know how to thank you for everything you've done for me and for her since I left town," Bo finally said.

"You know she was like a mother to me, too," Jimmy replied, his brown eyes a perfect match for the thatch of unruly hair on his head. "Come on, let's get out of the heat. I've got a couple of cold beers in the fridge with our names on them."

Bo stepped into the house behind Jimmy, and the first thing he noticed was the lack of scent. Even on the day Bo had left town the house had smelled of freshly baked chocolate chip cookies.

His mother had loved to cook and bake, and never had Bo been in the house when the fragrance of her labors hadn't filled the air. It was then that his true grief began.

The pain stabbed him through his heart, leaving him momentarily breathless. He'd felt pain this deep only once before in his life and that had been on the night two years ago that Shelly Sinclair had been found murdered, her body floating in the lagoon.

He sucked it up and stuffed it down, knowing the time to truly grieve would come later, when he was all alone. He followed Jimmy through the spotlessly clean living room and into the kitchen. Jimmy pulled two bottles of beer from the refrigerator and Bo sat at the round wooden table where he'd spent most of his life eating meals with his mother and father.

When his father died, Bo had moved from his apartment on the third floor of his business and back into the house with his mother. He hadn't wanted her alone with her grief, and the return to his childhood home had gone seamlessly.

Jimmy set one bottle of beer in front of Bo and then sat with his own bottle across from his friend. They unscrewed lids and each took a drink. Jimmy set his bottle on the table and leaned back in his chair.

"There will be a simple graveside service tomorrow at three," he said. "Your mother had all the arrangements already made. When I moved in here she told me where to find her important paperwork and that she'd left a will with Grey Davis. I'm sure he'll want you to get in touch with him."

Bo waved a hand and took another drink of his beer. "I'll get in touch with him sometime after tomorrow's service."

"How long are you planning on staying?"

"As briefly as possible," Bo replied. "I stopped by George's place to get a burger on the way in. He refused to serve me." He tried to keep the bitterness out of his voice.

"You want a sandwich? I've got some ham and cheese." Jimmy started to rise from his chair but Bo waved him back down.

"Actually, I was getting ready to pull away from George's and some pretty blonde woman ran out with a burger and fries for me." Bo thought of the warmth of her smile and figured she must be new to town and didn't know he was the prime suspect in his girlfriend's murder.

"Curly hair?" Jimmy asked.

"And long legs," Bo replied.

"That would be Claire Silver."

"Is she new in town?"

Jimmy shook his head. "No, she's been here all her life. She's three or four years younger than us, so you probably just never noticed her."

Bo took another sip of his beer, mentally acknowledging Jimmy's words. From the time he was seventeen, he hadn't noticed any other girl except Shelly Sinclair. Shelly had been his high school crush, then his girlfriend, then his lover and finally a murder victim.

"I'm assuming things are going well at the bar," Bo said, needing to get thoughts of the past out of his head.

"Business is booming, but you should know that by the profits we're turning. In fact, I should probably get out of here pretty quickly because the dinner rush usually starts soon. I just wanted to be here when you arrived. I didn't want you walking into an empty house."

"I appreciate that," Bo replied.

"I've still got all my things in the guest bedroom. I plan to rent an apartment, but haven't had a chance to get it done yet. If you could give me a couple of days..." Jimmy let his voice trail off.

"There's no reason why you can't continue to stay here. I'll only be here maybe a week at the most. The house is paid for and at this point I don't need to sell it."

"We'll see how you feel about it later," Jimmy replied. He finished his beer and stood. "I'll be back here around three or so. I'll try to be quiet so I don't wake you."

Bo stood to walk his friend to the door. "Hope you have a good night."

Jimmy flashed him a boyish grin. "Every night is a good night at Jimmy's Place. We'll talk more sometime tomorrow." He gave Bo a clap on the shoulder and then left the house.

Bo went into the living room and slumped down on one end of the sofa. Jimmy's Place. It had actually been Bo's Place before the murder. During the late afternoons and early evenings, families had filled the dining room, drawn to the good food, the reasonable prices and the atmosphere of community and goodwill. At ten, the diners had mostly gone and the drinkers and partiers arrived.

It was only after Bo had been named as the number-one suspect in Shelly's murder that the families stopped coming in and even the staunchest alcoholic refused to frequent the place.

Within a week Bo had become a pariah in town with only his mother and Jimmy sticking by his side. There had been no evidence to warrant Bo's arrest, but in the eyes of Lost Lagoon he'd been deemed guilty and judged as such.

A month after Shelly's murder it had been his mother who had urged him to get out of town, to start fresh someplace else.

With his life and business in shambles and the woman he'd loved dead, Bo had finally left Lost Lagoon.

Although he still owned what had once been Bo's Place, as far as everyone in town knew, Jimmy had bought the place, and under the new name, business was once again booming.

Bo snagged a second beer from the refrigerator and then spent the next hour sipping his drink and wandering the house. Little had changed. The bedroom where he had stayed while he'd lived here looked as if he'd just stepped out for a meal rather than been gone for so long. The smaller guest bedroom held signs of Jimmy's takeover. The closet door hung open, displaying a variety of clothing including half a dozen black shirts with the white lettering reading Jimmy's Place on the pocket.

Finally he entered his mother's room with its attached bathroom. Apparently Jimmy had worked hard to remove all traces of the death scene. He sat on the edge of the bed and ran his hand over the patchwork quilt in shades of pink and rose, a lump the size of Mississippi in the back of his throat.

He and his mother had usually spoken on the phone at least once every couple of days. He'd talked to her days ago and while she'd sounded a bit frail and weak, she'd assured him she'd just picked up a bug of some kind and that Jimmy was feeding her chicken soup and she'd be fine.

Dammit, Bo should have been here. He should have taken her to the doctor, he should have eaten dinner with her the night of her death and every night in the last two years.

His occasional visits had been short and bittersweet. He'd arrive in the middle of the night on a Saturday, park his motorcycle in her garage so the neighbors wouldn't know he was there, and then leave again in the middle of the night on Sunday.

He'd known it would be easier on his mom if people in town didn't know he was at her home. She'd carried the stigma of being a murderer's mother although she'd never mentioned her own alienation from friends and neighbors.

Bo wasn't sure how long he sat there. He had no more tears left, having spent them on the day he'd gotten the call from Jimmy that his mother was gone.

He was vaguely surprised that it was almost seven when he finally left his mother's bedroom. He needed to get his things from the motorcycle and settle in for the night. If Jimmy continued to stay here, then all Bo needed to do was bury his mother, meet with the lawyer and pack up his mom's clothing and shoes and other items to donate.

It was Wednesday night. He figured if things went smoothly and he used his time wisely, then by Sunday he could be back on the road to return to the life he'd been forced to build, a new life he'd never wanted.

Bo McBride was back.

Nothing exciting ever happened in Lost Lagoon, not since Shelly Sinclair's murder, and that had been tragic.

Claire Silver had heard about Bo's mother's death and assumed he'd come back to take care of whatever needed to be done. His presence here was sure to stir people up.

George had certainly been stirred up. He'd seen her toss the bag of food to Bo and had fired her. Claire had gone home and spent the late afternoon cleaning house, her thoughts whirling about Bo.

She'd never believed in his guilt. Nothing she'd heard had ever changed her mind about Bo's innocence in Shelly's death. She believed he'd been a victim of an overzealous sheriff with tunnel vision that had zeroed in on Bo as the perpetrator, to the exclusion of anyone else.

She hoped he was back not just to bury his mother, but also to clear his name, because if he was innocent, as Claire believed, then a killer was walking free in the town.

At six thirty she grabbed a can of pepper spray and stuck it in her back pocket. After unlocking her bicycle from the porch, she took off riding. She rode most nights, pedaling at a leisurely pace away from her "swamp home" and to the outer band that would take her around the lagoon.

This was her time to unwind from the day, to wave to neighbors and empty her mind of any stresses, which were few in her life at the moment.

Normally when she reached the edge of the lagoon she turned to head down Main Street, but instead this evening she continued around the outer road and then on impulse turned onto the roads that would take her to Bo McBride's home.

When she reached his house she stopped and got off her bike, leaning it against the white picket fence along the boundary of the yard.

She had no idea what she was doing here. Had no indication of what her intentions might be. Did she want to officially welcome him to the town that had effectively driven him out two years ago? Did she want to extend her sympathies about his mother? She'd scarcely known his mother. She'd been a shy, retiring woman rarely seen around town.

Claire grabbed her bicycle and was about to get back on it when the front door of the house flew open and Bo walked out. His blue eyes narrowed as he slowed his steps. She leaned the bike against the fence one again.

"What are you? My new resident stalker? Are you one of those women who writes to serial murderers in prison? Buy sick memorabilia on the internet from crime scenes?" His voice was rife with distrust.

"Actually, I'm the woman who fed you this afternoon and lost my job in the process," she replied evenly. "I suppose a simple thank-you is too much to ask for."

Bo grimaced and raked a hand through his thick, unruly black hair. "Sorry, I was way out of line." He motioned her closer and frowned. "You lost your job?"

"Don't worry about it. George fires me at least once a week and besides, it's just a job to alleviate some of my boredom during the summers. My real job is teaching second graders. By the way, my name is Claire Silver."

"I'm sure you know who I am. Bo McBride, who, according to everyone in Lost Lagoon, is the man who got away with murder."

"Not everyone," Claire replied. She'd forgotten how utterly sexy Bo was with his broad shoulders and lean hips and long legs. She'd always thought him handsome and she'd always thought of him as belonging to Shelly.

He raised a dark brow at the same time he pulled a duffel from one of his saddlebags. "You think I'm innocent? That's novel. There aren't many in town who share your view."

"I've never been much of a blind follower. I prefer to think for myself and come to my own conclusions," she replied.

Bo pulled another duffel from the opposite saddlebag and dropped it to the concrete driveway. He gazed at her curiously, as if she might be an alien from another planet.

"So, how did you come to the conclusion that I'm innocent?"

A wave of unusual shyness suddenly swept through her. She didn't want to tell him all the reasons she believed he wasn't capable of killing Shelly. It would be like sharing a little piece of her soul, a portrait of a romance that would make her look strange.

"Let's just say it's a long story. I was sorry to hear about your mother," she said in an attempt to change the topic of conversation.

The stark grief that swept over his face was there only a moment and then gone, but it was enough for Claire's heart to respond. She had no memories of her own mother, and she couldn't imagine the pain over the loss of his while he'd been virtually banished from his home…from his mother.

"Thanks. It came as quite a shock." He picked

up his duffel bags. "I'm sorry about your job and I appreciate your kindness this afternoon."

"No big deal." She grabbed her bike and got on it. Darkness came early around the lagoon and on the swamp side of town, and she liked to be inside by nightfall. "I guess I'll see you around," she said and with a wave, she pedaled away from his driveway.

She wasn't sure what had driven her to go to his home and stop other than curiosity. There was no question that he was apparently wary of interacting with anyone, and why wouldn't he be?

He'd always been handsome, but the past two years had added lines to his lean face that gave it new character that only enhanced his sexiness. Not that it mattered to her. In her mind he would always be Shelly's man, part of a couple who for Claire had been a shining example of what love should look like.

She pedaled a little faster as she rounded the lagoon where the June twilight appeared darker, gloomier. As always, when her home came into view a sense of pride swelled up inside her.

Two years ago her home had looked a lot like so many of the other broken, faded shanties that lined the street. It had taken most of her first year's salary as a teacher to almost completely rebuild the one-bedroom hellhole where she'd grown up into a pretty cottage with up-to-date plumbing and newly painted walls and a sense of permanence.

For so many years it had just been a place to survive. Now it was her sanctuary, a place that held no memories of her crummy childhood.

When she reached her porch she lifted her bike up the three stairs and chained it to the railing, at the same time noticing the small vase of flowers that sat just outside her front door.

So, her "secret admirer" had struck again. This was the third time in as many weeks she'd found flowers and a note on her doorstep.

The first time the flowers had appeared with a note that simply read, *From your secret admirer*. Claire had found it a little bit charming and a little bit silly. She'd assumed that the admirer would make himself known to her as she had no idea who it might be.

The second vase of flowers had appeared with a note that indicated he was thinking about her. She thought the flowers might be from Neil Sampson, a city councilman she'd dated for about two months and had broken up with about six months before. Neil hadn't taken the breakup well, and she wondered if the little floral treats were an attempt to win her back.

She grabbed the new vase, unlocked her door and then stepped inside. She set the flowers and the folded note on the table and headed directly to the refrigerator for a cold bottle of water.

She unscrewed the lid and leaned against the nearby cabinet as she sipped the cold liquid. Thoughts of Bo instantly filled her mind. She'd heard rumors that he'd moved to Jackson and had opened a bar and grill there. Had he found love with some new woman?

Two years was a long time to mourn, and he was a healthy, vital twenty-eight-year-old male who would certainly not have any trouble gaining women's interest.

She finished the water, tossed the bottle into the recycle bin in her pantry and then walked back to the table where the vase of flowers and the note awaited her.

The vase was a small clear white glass that could be picked up most places for a dollar or so, and the flowers weren't from a floral shop but rather hand-picked.

It would be difficult to try to track down where it had come from even if she was of the mind to conduct a little investigation, and she wasn't inclined to do so. Whoever it was would eventually stop with the anonymous gestures and show himself.

She opened the note. *You look so pretty in pink*, it read. She glanced down at the pink tank top she wore and frowned, a niggle of unexpected anxiety rushing through her.

Flowers on her porch was one thing, but somebody watching her while she went about her daily business was something else. A chill threatened to walk up her spine as she went to her living room window and peered outside.

She flipped the blinds closed and then chided herself for being silly. She'd had on the pink tank top and had been around town all day. There was no reason to believe there was anything ominous about flowers on her porch or the sender's knowing she'd worn pink.

Still, as she moved away from the window she wondered if there was somebody out there now.

Watching her.

Chapter Two

It was an appropriate day for death and funerals. Bo woke just after eight to gloomy dark clouds obscuring any morning sunshine.

Although he'd been in bed and trying to find sleep, he was still awake when Jimmy came in just after three in the morning. Bo remained in bed, his brain whirling and refusing to shut off.

Memories of his mother had plagued him, and he dreaded both the service that day and the final act of packing up her things and giving them away. At least he didn't have to worry about what to do with the house right away. Jimmy had grown up on the swamp side of town, in one of the shanties that threatened to tumble down beneath a stiff breeze.

He and Bo had become best friends in third grade and Jimmy had spent much of his time at the Mc-Bride house, eating meals, staying as long as he could before he had to return to the shanty where his brutal alcoholic father lived with his verbally and mentally abusive wife.

As soon as Bo had opened Bo's Place, he'd hired

Jimmy to be his manager and Jimmy had finally escaped the swamp, moving into a small apartment in the back of a liquor store in the center of town.

When Bo realized his only chance to survive financially and emotionally was to get out of town, it was only natural that he turned to his best friend to move into the house Jimmy had always thought of as his real home. The benefit to Bo was that he knew Jimmy would take care of his mother so she wouldn't be all alone.

It had been a win-win situation for both of them and Bo was in no hurry to toss out the man who had played the role of son when he couldn't be here.

He now rolled out of bed and pulled on a pair of jeans, and then padded into the kitchen where he made coffee. As he waited for it to brew he remembered that just before he'd finally fallen asleep his thoughts had been filled with Claire Silver.

She'd been the first woman in two years who had caught his attention in any way, who had filled him with a touch of curiosity and an unexpected attraction.

She had eyes the color he'd always imagined the waters of the Caribbean might look like, an azure blue that appeared too beautiful to be real. They also had held a spirit that he wasn't quite sure was confidence or craziness.

He dismissed thoughts of her as he poured himself a cup of coffee and sat at the table. In the distance, through the gloom he could see the top of the ridge where new construction was taking place.

Large equipment had been brought in, indicating that whatever was going to be built up there was going to be big. Bo couldn't imagine what would stand on that property, but it didn't matter to him. He definitely wouldn't be here to see whatever it was completed.

He drank two cups of coffee, disappointed that apparently the sun didn't have the energy to burn off the dark clouds overhead. He only hoped that if it rained, it would wait until after the service that afternoon.

He returned to his bedroom where he made his bed and pulled his black suit from the closet. The last time he'd worn it had been to his father's funeral, and it was still encased in dry-cleaner plastic.

He removed the plastic and wondered how many people would show up at the cemetery. Brenda Mc-Bride had been well liked among her peers in the small town. But that had been before Shelly's murder. He'd hoped that by him leaving town she'd been able to keep her friends and hadn't been stigmatized by his presumed guilt.

By the time he'd laid the suit on the bed, he smelled the scent of bacon frying coming from the kitchen. He returned to the kitchen to find Jimmy standing in front of the stove, clad in a pair of khaki shorts, a white T-shirt and a pair of worn sandals.

"I didn't expect you to be awake yet," Bo said as he sat at the table.

Jimmy flashed him a quick smile. "I'm usually up just before eleven. I guess I don't require as much sleep as most people." He flipped the bacon strips. "Scrambled eggs okay?"

"Since you're cooking, whatever works for you," Bo replied. "I'm really not that hungry anyway."

"It's going to be a stressful day. You need to eat something," Jimmy said.

Bo didn't reply. Within ten minutes Jimmy set a plate of bacon, scrambled eggs and toast in front of him and then sat across from him with a plate of his own.

"What's going on up there?" Bo asked and gestured out the window to the top of the ridge.

Jimmy took a bite of toast and chased it with a swallow of coffee before replying. "Mayor Frank Kean was unseated in the last election and our new mayor is on a mission for Lost Lagoon to be found. The town sold the land on the ridge to some corporation that is putting in an amusement park."

Bo stared at him in surprise. First he was stunned to learn that Frank Kean had been voted out after serving as mayor for the past ten years or so. "An amusement park?" he finally said incredulously.

Jimmy nodded. "Jim Burns was voted in as mayor and you know what a hotshot he's always been. Once he was in office he surrounded himself with like-minded councilmen and then rallied the business owners to push through the sale of the land. There was one heated town meeting before the final vote. As you can imagine most of the old-timers didn't want to see the town overrun with tourists and the like, but there were enough who believed Lost

Lagoon is a dying town and the amusement park was the opportunity to get it prosperous and thriving."

Bo stared at his friend for a long moment, trying to digest what he'd just learned. "Why would anyone choose this place to put in an amusement park?"

Jimmy shrugged. "Rumor is it will be pirate themed to play off the legends of pirates once roaming the area."

Many of the businesses in town had already embraced the pirate theme years ago. There was the Pirate's Inn, rumored to be haunted by pirates who couldn't find their ship; the Treasure Trove sold pirate T-shirts and fake swords along with elaborate costume jewelry and gold-wrapped chocolate coins. On Main Street you couldn't walk ten feet and not see something pirate-related.

"Frank Kean must have been devastated to lose the election," he said.

"Actually, I think he was ready to step down. Besides, he's on a small committee that's working closely both with the city council and the people building the park. There are still some people disgruntled about the whole thing, but it's a done deal and life will definitely change around here when the park is done."

As they finished their breakfast Jimmy continued to fill him in on the happenings in town, who had gotten married and who had gotten divorced and all the rest of the local gossip.

Bo encouraged the conversation, knowing it was much easier to talk about things and people he didn't care about anymore than think about the service for his mother that afternoon.

After cleaning up the kitchen, it seemed all too soon that it was time to shower and get dressed for his final goodbye to his mother.

As he dressed in a white short-sleeved dress shirt and his suit pants, he thought about the fact that he hadn't mentioned to Jimmy his unexpected interaction with Claire Silver the night before.

Maybe he was afraid that Jimmy would tell him that Claire was nice, but was also the town's nutcase, and Bo liked her. He didn't want to hear anything negative about her. Right now she and Jimmy were the only two people in this godforsaken town he liked.

He doubted he'd see her again. Tonight he'd have Jimmy bring home some sturdy boxes from the bar, and tomorrow Bo would pack his mother's things, catch up with the lawyer, and by Saturday or Sunday be back on the road with Lost Lagoon just a distant memory.

Oh, he would forever be bound to this place because of his nearly lifelong friendship with Jimmy and his secret ownership of Jimmy's Place, but there would be no reason to ever come here again.

He carried his suit jacket into the kitchen and placed it across the back of a chair, and then walked to the window and stared outside as he waited for Jimmy.

It was two o'clock and outside the window the dreariness of the day remained unchanged, as if a reflection of Bo's somber mood. He already knew his mother had requested a closed casket and a short grave site service performed by Pastor Ralph Kimmel from the Methodist church she had attended for years.

The cemetery was only a ten-minute drive and Bo didn't see any reason to arrive too early. There was nobody he wanted to visit with and he suspected that few people would attend.

Jimmy walked into the kitchen, clad in a dark gray suit that Bo vaguely remembered once had belonged to him. Thankfully the two were about the same size, and many times over the years Jimmy had been given clothes from Bo.

"Maybe we should go ahead and head out. If we get there early you could at least have a few minutes alone before anyone else arrives," Jimmy suggested.

Bo nodded and grabbed his suit jacket and pulled it on, dread, grief and anxiety all boiling inside his stomach. His mother had grieved long and hard following the death of his father, and there was some consolation that the two of them were now together once again.

Minutes later they were in Jimmy's car and headed toward the Lost Lagoon Cemetery. With each mile Bo's heart grew heavier as emotion pressed tighter and tighter against his chest.

Once they arrived it was easy to see where the ceremony would take place. A small white canopy fluttered in the sultry air over the plain white casket, which was already in place to be lowered into the ground.

Nobody else was there yet, and as Bo got out of the car and walked toward the site the emotion in his chest rose up to blur his vision with tears.

He quickly brushed them away, not wanting anyone to see any weakness, but they appeared once again and he was grateful that Jimmy had hung back, giving him a moment alone.

He stood at the foot of the casket, his brain whirling with memories of his mother. She had been the one who had pushed him after high school to drive back and forth to the bigger city of Hattiesburg to attend college, where he'd received a business degree by the time he was twenty-one.

She'd then encouraged him to open Bo's Place, her and his dad fronting him the money to begin the successful venture. One of his proudest days had been when he'd been able to pay them back every cent of their seed money.

"So, I figured I hadn't seen the last of you." The familiar deep voice coming from behind him tensed every one of Bo's muscles.

He turned to see Sheriff Trey Walker and his deputy, Ray McClure. Both men had been Bo's biggest accusers and both had been extremely frustrated that they hadn't been able to put together a case that would see Bo in prison for Shelly's murder.

"What are you doing here?" Bo asked, unable to hide a hint of hostility.

"We always come out to pay respects to one of

our own," Trey replied, his green eyes narrowed as he held Bo's gaze.

"Maybe you should be spending this time looking for the person who really murdered Shelly," Bo said.

"Already know the answer to that question," Ray said. Ray was a mean little creep, built like a bulldog and as tenacious as one. He had been one of the loudest mouths proclaiming Bo's guilt in Shelly's murder.

Bo was about to tell the two of them to get the hell out of there when he heard a female voice calling his name. He watched as Claire ran toward them. Clad in a pair of slender black slacks and a white blouse, the sight of her immediately diffused some of Bo's anger.

She reached Bo's side and looped an elbow with his, as if presenting a united stance. At the same time Jimmy joined them along with Pastor Kimmel, who immediately took Bo's hand in his.

His faded blue eyes held a kindness that warmed him as much as Claire's surprising nearness and open support. "It's a sorrowful day when we have to say a final goodbye to such a good woman."

Bo nodded, unable to speak around the lump that had risen in his throat. Claire moved closer to his side, as if she sensed the myriad emotions racing through him.

Pastor Kimmel released his hand and stepped back, nodding to the other attendees. "Shall we get started or should we wait to see if others want to come to pay their respects?"

Bo glanced at the road by the cemetery. There

wasn't a car in sight and it was three o'clock. "Let's get this done," he said roughly.

So his mother would be sent off to her final destination by a pastor, a loving son, a surrogate son, two cops who thought her son was guilty of murder and a woman Bo hadn't decided yet if she was completely sane.

CLAIRE HAD A FEELING few people would be here today. Brenda McBride had become a semi-shut-in after Bo left town. She and Jimmy showed up every Sunday morning for church, but other than that she was rarely seen out and about.

The service was short yet emotional, and Bo's face and body radiated a soul-deep sorrow that Claire felt inside her heart. She didn't know what it was like to have a loving, caring mother, nor did she know much about having a decent father, but that didn't stop her from imagining the depth of Bo's loss. She'd felt the same way when Shelly had been murdered, that something precious and beloved had been stolen away from Bo.

When the service was finished, Bo looked hollow-eyed and lost. His jaw clenched as Trey and Ray approached him. "You planning on staying in town?" Trey asked.

"Why? Do you intend to put up posters of my face to warn young women?" Bo retorted. He drew a deep, weary sigh. "Don't worry, I just have a few things to clear up and I should be gone by the weekend."

"That's the best news I've heard all day," Ray said.

Claire saw every muscle in Bo tense as a red flush rose up his neck. "Come on, Bo. I'm taking you home with me," she said. Bo looked at her in surprise. "Jimmy, I'll bring him home later this evening."

She grabbed him by the hand and physically pulled him away from both the lawmen and his friend. He balked for only a moment and then went willingly with her.

They didn't speak as they walked through the cemetery and to her compact car parked in the lot. She got behind the wheel as Bo folded his long legs into the passenger side.

"You have a car," he said, stating the obvious.

Claire started the engine. "My usual mode of transportation around town is my bicycle, but I get the car out for special occasions and when the weather isn't conducive to riding or walking."

She felt his gaze on her. "Thank you for showing up today," he said. "And for stepping in before I punched Ray in his face."

"I figured you could use a stiff drink rather than a night in the jail," she replied. "Besides, Ray McClure isn't worth the effort of an uppercut. He's a weasel who likes to chase anything in a skirt and hand out tickets for looking at him cross-eyed."

"He was one of the loudest voices screaming my guilt all over town before I left," Bo said. Once again she felt his gaze on her, warm and intense. "What am I doing in your car going to your home?"

She flashed him a quick glance and then focused back on the outer road as they rounded the tip of the lagoon. "I figure within an hour or so Jimmy will be leaving to go to work, which means you'll probably be holed up in your house all alone, and nobody should drink alone."

"What makes you think I'm going to drink?"

"Because I would if I were in your shoes. You just buried your mother. I don't think you need to be by yourself right now."

"You're kind of a pushy woman," he replied lightly.

A small laugh released from her. "I'm sure I've been called worse. I hope you're a gin-and-tonic kind of man because that's what I've got at the house."

"Anything is fine," he replied, his voice suddenly weary.

She pulled up in front of her house in the driveway that just barely held the length of her car. "Home, sweet home." She unbuckled her seat belt and got out of the car at the same time as Bo.

"Nice," he said. "I don't remember this place looking like this. You must have put a lot of work into it."

She was acutely aware of his presence just behind her as she walked up the porch and unlocked the door. The hot, sultry air intensified the scent of him...a fragrance of shaving cream and pleasant woodsy cologne. "It took me a full year to get rid of what once stood here and make this a real home."

"Looks like you have a gift."

She turned and looked where he pointed to the edge of the porch, where a vase of flowers sat on a folded note. A wave of irritation swept through her.

If this was some sort of a charming courtship game it had gone on long enough.

She grabbed the vase and note and then ushered Bo inside. "Apparently I've picked up a secret admirer." She set the vase in the center of the table next to the one from the day before. "Take off your jacket and get comfortable." She gestured toward the beige sofa with bright green and turquoise throw pillows.

He took off his jacket and slung it across the back of one of the kitchen chairs. "Do you have any idea who your secret admirer might be?" he asked.

She pulled from a cabinet a large bottle of tonic and a bottle of gin, and then opened the refrigerator door to grab a couple of limes. "Not a clue," she replied. "And honestly I think the whole thing is ridiculous. If some man is interested in me, then he should just step up to the plate and tell me. Lime?"

"Sounds good."

As she cut up the limes he wandered the space, checking out the books on her turquoise-painted ladder bookcase, the green and blue knickknacks that she'd found to give the house a sense of home. He finally landed on the sofa. After handing him his drink, she sat on the opposite side of the sofa with her own.

"Why are you being so nice to me? Aren't you afraid somebody in town will see you with me and you'll be shunned?" he asked, his midnight-blue eyes holding her gaze.

She took a sip of the biting yet refreshing drink and then placed it on the coffee table in front of them. "I don't pay much attention to what people think about me. I'm often on the unpopular side of an issue." She offered him a sympathetic gaze. "You want to talk about your mother?"

He settled back against the cushion and took a long, deep drink from his glass. "Not really. I've had days to do nothing but think about her and now I'd much rather talk about you."

"Me? Trust me, there isn't that much to talk about. I was born and raised here. My mother ran off when I was six and I was left with a neglectful alcoholic father in a shanty that threatened to fall down whenever the wind blew. I went to college on a full scholarship and got my teaching degree. When I returned here my father had disappeared and I haven't seen him since. And that's my story."

She leaned forward and grabbed her glass and then took another sip. She'd made her drink light on gin and heavy on tonic and had made Bo's drink heavy on gin and light on tonic.

"So, your turn. Tell me what you've been doing for the last two years," she asked. "Have you made yourself a new, happy life? Found a new love? I heard through the grapevine that you're living in Jackson now."

He nodded at the same time the sound of rain splattered against the window. "I opened a little bar and grill, Bo's Place, although it's nothing like the original." His dark brows tugged together in a frown as if remembering the highly successful business he'd had here in town before he was ostracized.

He took another big drink and then continued, "There's no new woman in my life. I don't even have friends. Hell, I'm not even sure what I'm doing here with you."

"You're here because I'm a bossy woman," she replied. She got up to refill his glass. "And I thought you could use an extra friend while you're here."

She handed him the fresh drink and then curled back up in the corner of the sofa. The rain fell steadily now. She turned on the end table lamp as the room darkened with the storm.

For a few minutes they remained silent. She could tell by his distant stare toward the opposite wall that he was lost inside his head.

Despite his somber expression, she couldn't help but feel a physical attraction to him that she'd never felt before. Still, that wasn't what had driven her to seek contact with him, to invite him into her home. She had an ulterior motive.

A low rumble of thunder seemed to pull him out of his head. He focused on her and offered her a small smile of apology. "Sorry about that. I got lost in thoughts of everything I need to get done before I leave town."

"I wanted to talk to you about that," she said.

He raised a dark brow. "About all the things I need to take care of?"

"No, about you leaving town."

"What about it?"

She drew a deep breath, knowing she was putting her nose in business that wasn't her own, and yet unable to stop herself. "Doesn't it bother you knowing that Shelly's murderer is still walking these streets, free as a bird?"

His eyes narrowed slightly. "Why are you so sure I'm innocent?" he asked.

Claire had never had a problem speaking her mind or sharing her thoughts, but she found herself reluctant to truly answer his question, afraid that he'd think she was silly, or worse, the loony tune she already suspected he thought she might be.

"I'm three years younger than you and Shelly and I know it sounds crazy, but I was in love with your love for each other. You two were the shining example of what I wanted to find for myself someday. I watched you walking the streets, hand in hand, having ice cream outside the ice cream parlor."

The words tumbled out of her, as if the more she spoke the less he'd think she was nuts. "I saw the way you looked at her, Bo. I know the reputation you had in town as being a caring, gentle soul, a loving son, and I don't believe there was anything Shelly could have done that would have resulted in you hurting her."

Bo stared at her for a long moment, his eyes a darker shade of blue than she'd ever seen them. "Thank you," he finally said. "And of course it bothers me that her killer has never been brought to justice."

"It bothers me so much I carry pepper spray

everywhere I go," she said. "I try to be inside the house with the door locked after dark."

Bo took another drink, his gaze not leaving hers. "What does all this have to do with me leaving town?"

Claire uncurled from her position and moved closer to him. "I don't think you should leave town. I think you should stick around and prove your innocence."

Bo laughed, the sound deep and rusty, as if he hadn't laughed in a very long time. "You are out of your mind."

"I don't think so," she protested. "You know that at the time of Shelly's murder there wasn't really a thorough investigation. Law enforcement focused on you to the exclusion of anyone else."

"Shelly's case is a cold case that nobody is working because they all believe I did the crime. I can't imagine Trey or Ray agreeing to reinvestigate it just because I'm back in town," Bo said.

"You're right," she agreed. "They wouldn't lift a finger to help you with any unofficial investigation, but I would." She saw his dubiousness in his eyes and quickly pressed forward. "Think about it, Bo. We don't even know if the sheriff and his men interviewed any of Shelly's friends after her death. I don't believe they did much of anything, but you and I could talk to people, see what they remember about Shelly's life at that time, who might be a possible killer."

"It's a stupid idea."

"Maybe it is, but isn't it worth giving a little time to see what we might stir up? Wouldn't you like to prove your innocence to all the people who doubted you?"

Bo took a drink and sat forward. He placed his glass on the table and raked a hand through his slightly unruly hair. He glanced toward the window where the rain had stopped.

"I need to go home. You've got me half looped and considering things that shouldn't even enter my mind." He stood and she did the same, wondering what it might take to convince him that staying in town and fighting for his reputation would be worth it.

Of course, she'd spent years trying to convince her father to put down his bottle and be a real dad because she was worth it, and that certainly hadn't worked out.

Chapter Three

"Why not hang around a few weeks and see what you and Claire can dig up?" Jimmy asked. The two men were seated at the kitchen table eating ham and cheese sandwiches for lunch.

Already that morning Bo had met with his mother's lawyer, taken care of what paperwork needed to be done, and then had come back and packed part of the clothes in his mother's closet in the boxes Jimmy had brought home from the bar.

"If I know you, you've hired people at Bo's Place who are perfectly capable of running the business without you being present for a while," Jimmy continued.

Bo released a sigh. "I tossed and turned all night. The idea of staying here and putting myself through it all again isn't exactly appealing, and yet the idea of Shelly's killer still out there has haunted me for the last two years. I want to know who and I want to know why."

What he didn't mention to his best friend was how attracted he was to the woman who had put the idea in his head in the first place. He tried to tell himself that it was merely a combination of grief, gin and her proximity. But he'd wanted to fall into the depths of her amazing blue eyes, reach out and run his fingers through her curly mop of hair to see if the strands were as soft and silky as they appeared.

He had no idea what force had brought her into his life and why she was being so kind to him. Although she'd tried to explain her total belief in his innocence, he wasn't sure he understood her reasons. Still, the fact that he was innocent and she'd shown such belief in him had been a balm to a soul that had been scarred for two long years.

"How did you leave it with Claire last night?" Jimmy asked.

"She told me if I decided to stick around and become a crime investigation duo that she'd be hanging out at the school around two."

Jimmy nodded. "Coach Cantor has a key to the school, and I think once a week or so he and Claire sneak into the school gym and play one-on-one basketball."

"Coach Cantor?"

"Roger Cantor. He moved here about six months after you left. He's your typical jock type, but a nice guy." Jimmy looked over at the rooster clock on the wall. "That gives you about an hour if you intend to meet up with her at the school."

It was two thirty when Bo finally made up his mind and backed his motorcycle out of the driveway to head to the school. He was late so he wasn't even sure Claire would still be there, but if he didn't find her there he knew he'd eventually find her somewhere. Or he had a feeling she'd find him.

It took him only minutes to arrive at the school, which housed students from kindergarten kids to seniors. Divided into two parts separated by a short breezeway, kindergartners through eighth were housed on the left and the right was for freshmen to seniors.

Claire's pink bicycle was locked to an old, rusted bike rack and a car was parked in the lot, letting him know that she and the coach were still here.

He parked his motorcycle next to the car and then headed for the front door of the high school side of the building. Locked.

He made his way around the side of the building to the back where he knew there was a door that would take him into a hallway that led directly to the gym.

This door was unlocked, and as he stepped inside it was to the scents of pine cleaner and floor polish. Once school started again the clean smells would disappear beneath the odors of sweaty bodies and smelly gym clothes.

On either side of the hallway were doors that led to the boys' and girls' locker rooms.

Before he reached the gym he heard the sound of squeaky shoes pounding the floor and a male triumphant shout. He stepped up to the open doors and peered inside to see Claire facing off for a tip-off with a tall, pleasant-looking blond man who had the physique of a coach.

But it was Claire who captured his attention. Clad in a pair of white shorts that showcased shapely athletic legs and a turquoise T-shirt that clung to her feminine curves, she looked sexy as hell even dribbling the basketball, which had tipped to her side of the court.

She saw him and grabbed the ball in her arms, a warm smile curving her lips. She moved closer to him. "Bo, I didn't think you were coming."

"I wasn't sure myself until I got here."

She dropped the ball to the floor as the coach approached where they stood. Claire made the introductions between the two and Roger shook Bo's hand with a firm grasp and a pleasant smile.

"You play?" Roger asked and leaned down to pick up the ball. "I could use a little more competition to keep me in shape." He grinned at Claire as she started to protest. "Face it, Short Stuff, you're good for running me around, but not any real competition."

Bo smiled at the outrage on Claire's face. "Actually, I played a little in high school," he said. "But not since, so I probably wouldn't be any better competition than Claire."

"He wouldn't trade me in for somebody better," Claire replied. "If he had any real competition and got beat he'd go home and cry like a sissy baby. And speaking of going home, I've invited Roger back to my place for a late lunch, and now that you're here, you're coming, too."

"Oh no." Bo took a step backward. "I don't want to intrude."

"Nonsense," Roger replied. "It's an eat-and-run for me. Besides, Claire already told me she made chicken salad and you don't want to miss a chance to taste it. She makes the best."

Claire looped her elbow with Bo's. "No arguments. You're coming to eat and once we're finished you and I will have a chance to talk." Her blue eyes radiated a steely strength.

"You might as well just give in," Roger said. "When Claire makes up her mind about something it's darned near impossible to change it."

"Bossy little thing, isn't she?" Bo replied, making Roger laugh and Claire sputter a protest.

Minutes later as Bo followed Roger's car with Claire's bicycle fastened to a rack on its back bumper and her in his passenger seat, Bo realized Roger was right.

Claire was like a force of nature, a whirling dervish of focused energy. Cyclone Claire, he thought with wry amusement as he pulled up behind Roger's car in front of her house.

The moment they got inside the door, Claire pointed them to the table where the two men sat across from each other and talked about sports while Claire bustled to get plates and drinks on the table.

Bo almost immediately noticed two things about his male lunch partner. Roger appeared to be a nice man, and he seemed to suffer more than a little bit of obsessive-compulsive disorder.

Claire tossed his silverware next to his plate and he carefully lined up spoon, fork and knife and then moved his iced tea glass a half an inch to the right of his plate.

"We're rolling our own," Claire said as she placed first a large bowl of chicken salad in the center of the table and then a plate of soft whole-wheat tortillas next to the bowl. "Eat up," she said and joined them at the table.

Bo grabbed one of the tortillas and globbed the chicken salad onto it and then folded it into a semblance of a sandwich. Roger carefully spooned the salad into equal mounds and then rolled the tortilla into a neat burrito.

While they ate, the conversation remained pleasant. It was obvious Roger and Claire shared the camaraderie of coworkers and an easy friendship.

Once they were finished eating it took Claire only minutes to clear the table. "Have you asked Mary out yet?" Claire asked Roger as he got ready to leave.

He winced. "I haven't quite gotten up my nerve yet."

"You've been saying that for a month now. For goodness' sake, man, ask the woman out. She's a terrific woman and I'm sure you two would have a good time together," Claire said.

"I know, I'm working on it." With a wave of his hand to Bo, Roger thanked Claire for the meal and then left.

Bo sat back down at the table and after offering

him another glass of iced tea, Claire joined him. "He seems like a good guy," Bo said.

"He's a really nice guy," she agreed. "He's got some issues he's working on."

"You mean the OCD stuff?"

She raised a blond eyebrow. "So you noticed?"

"It was a bit obvious."

"Not as much as when he first arrived in Lost Lagoon," she replied. "His illness destroyed his first marriage, it was so out of control. He came here for a new start and he's been working with Mama Baptiste using herbs and meditation techniques to help him."

Everyone who had spent any time in Lost Lagoon knew Mama Baptiste. She and her son, Eric, lived two doors down from Claire and they ran an herb and apothecary shop in the center of town.

"Maybe Roger is your secret admirer," Bo suggested.

Claire laughed, the pleasant sound swirling that crazy warmth through him. "No way, Roger and I are strictly in the friend zone. He's got a major crush on Mary Armstrong, a waitress down at the diner, but as you heard he can't seem to get up the gumption to ask her out."

She waved a hand. "Enough about Roger." She placed her elbows on the table and leaned forward, her gaze so intent he felt as if she were somehow peering inside his soul. "So, are you in for a little crime investigation or are you out?"

The fresh, slightly floral scent of her perfume drifted across the table as her gaze continued to hold him captive. He had arrived at the high school not knowing what his decision was, whether he intended to hang around and buy into Claire's scheme of trying to find the real killer or get out of this town as fast as possible.

The light of her belief in him shone from her eyes. He bathed in it and realized he wanted this…his innocence restored among the people who had once been friends and neighbors.

"I'm in," he finally said. He hoped in making that decision he hadn't just made a mistake he would come to regret. Asking questions, talking to people and stirring up everything from the past also might stir up a killer's rage.

CLAIRE GRINNED AT Bo and popped up from the table to retrieve a pen, a legal pad and a three-ring notebook complete with color tabs from a kitchen drawer. "I hoped that was going to be your answer," she said as she once again sat down.

"What's all this?" Bo asked as he gestured toward the notebook.

"I'm a teacher, Bo. I love lists and notebooks and any kind of office supplies."

"You don't have any flash cards stuck in there, do you?" he asked wryly.

She laughed. "No flash cards, I promise." She was pleased that he'd decided to stick around and do a little digging into the crime that had forced him to leave town under a cloud of suspicion. She was also pleased that he apparently had a sense of humor.

She placed the legal pad in front of her and pushed the notebook to the side. "I figured we'd spend some time this afternoon coming up with a plan, names of people to talk to, the events that led up to Shelly's body being found in the swamp, anything that might provide a clue as to who was responsible for her death."

Bo raked a hand through his hair and leaned back in his chair. "It's a bit overwhelming, trying to go back to a crime that happened two years ago."

"Overwhelming is trying to keep second graders focused enough to learn math and reading," she replied. "This is just a puzzle and we need to start at the beginning and work outward. I know Shelly was murdered around eleven thirty at night. I don't know if I ever heard where you were at that time?"

When the murder had happened Claire had been as horrified as anyone in town, and although she'd tried to stay up on all the developments, she'd heard so many stories it was difficult to discern truth from false gossip.

"I was in my bedroom at my mother's house in bed with a twenty-four-hour flu bug."

"Then your mother was your alibi?" she asked and watched a growing darkness take hold in his eyes.

"An alibi easily dismissed. My mother was an early-to-bed kind of woman and she was also a woman who didn't lie." He raised his chin, obviously proud of his mother. "When Trey Walker asked her if she would know if I left the house that night

after she went to bed, she confessed that she probably wouldn't have known."

"And there was nobody you saw or talked to who
could confirm that you were in bed sick?"

Bo shook his head. "I went to bed a little after
five. I made two calls before I crashed out, one to
Freddie Hannity, who managed the bar at Bo's Place,
to tell him I wouldn't be in that night and to take care
of things for me. The other was a text to Shelly telling her I was sick and wouldn't meet her that night."

He paused a long moment, his eyes no longer dark
blue but rather black and unfathomable. "You know
Shelly was the night manager at the Pirate's Inn and
night was my busiest time at Bo's Place. She started
her shift at midnight so every night around eleven
I'd sneak out of the bar and we'd meet at the bench
down by the lagoon."

Once again he stopped talking and stared outside
the front window, as if reliving each and every moment of that fateful night.

Claire had known that going back in time to the
night of Shelly's death would be difficult for him,
but she hadn't expected the rawness of his emotions.
Even though Shelly had been gone for two years, it
was obvious that love for her, that grief for her, still
filled his heart.

Without giving it any thought, she reached out and
covered his hand with hers. He blinked twice and
then directed his attention to her hand. He turned
his over and grasped her.

"Sorry, I got lost in my head." He gently extricated his hand from hers. "Anyway, the next thing I knew it was five in the morning and Sheriff Walker and Deputy Ray McClure were pounding on the front door.

"They told me Shelly had been killed around midnight and I needed to come into the station and answer some questions. I knew the minute I saw the way they looked at me that they believed I was responsible. I scarcely had time to grieve before I was vehemently defending my innocence."

"What did they tell you about the actual crime scene? I know Shelly was found in the lagoon, but she wasn't killed in the water." Claire picked up her pen, knowing that from this point forward the conversation would contain things she wanted written down. She didn't even want to think about how warm, how right it had felt to momentarily hold his hand.

He sat up straighter in his chair, his eyes once again focused. "The sheriff believed the actual strangulation occurred in the bushes around the bench and then she was put in the water, probably in hopes she wouldn't be found until morning or maybe forever. The bushes were trampled as if a struggle had happened, and they found her necklace tangled up in some of the brush. Her engagement ring was missing and has never been found. A couple of teenagers had gone to the swamp to gig for frogs. They're the ones who found her just after two."

"Why would Shelly have gone down there knowing that you weren't coming?" Claire asked. "Are you sure she got your text?"

"Positive. She texted me back that she'd see me the next day. As far as why she went to the lagoon that night, I have no idea. That question has haunted me for two years. I keep thinking that if I hadn't been sick that night…if I'd shown up as usual…" He allowed his voice to drift off.

"You can't blame yourself for this," Claire protested.

He raised a dark brow. "But apparently a whole town could blame me."

"That's because a real investigation was never done, and that's why we're doing this now," Claire replied. "I'm assuming your phone records were checked. How did Trey explain the fact that the texts were the last communications you two had that night?"

"He figured I'd found Shelly somewhere in town and didn't need to use any other form of communication."

"Did Shelly mention to you anyone who was giving her trouble? Anyone she'd made angry?"

"No, she didn't mention anything like that to me. Shelly wasn't the type to make enemies."

"Maybe it was something she didn't feel comfortable talking to you about. Maybe she'd have been more apt to confide in a girlfriend. Names, I need names of the people Shelly was closest to other than you," she said.

"Definitely Savannah."

Claire knew Savannah was Shelly's sister. She was a year younger than Shelly and the two had appeared very close. She wrote down Savannah's name on the legal pad. "You know she's now working the night shift at the Pirate's Inn. Who else can you remember?"

"Shelly was friendly with Julie Melbourne. I know they often had dinner together at Bo's Place while I was on duty. She also ran around with Valerie Frank and Sally Bernard. I think that's about it as far as her closest friends."

"Talking with Sally and Julie shouldn't be a problem. They're both teachers and I'm friendly with both of them. Valerie works the dinner shift at the diner. We can catch up with her there."

Bo scowled. "None of those women will want to talk to me."

Claire offered him a bright smile. "And that's why you have me. You'll be with me, but I'll do the talking." She looked outside where dusk had begun to fall. "We'll start first thing in the morning and try to get Sally and Julie interviewed. Then we'll catch up with Valerie and Savannah later in the evening."

He tilted his head and gazed at her curiously. "Do you really believe anything will come of all this?"

"All I know is that nothing will come of this if we don't try. I believe in your innocence, Bo, and I hate the fact that somebody got away with murder while you have carried this burden for so long. As far as I'm concerned you have two choices—stay here and work the case to prove your innocence or climb back on that hog of yours and leave town with that same burden weighing you down for the rest of your life."

He picked up his glass and peered inside it. "You didn't drug my drink, did you? Because when I listen to you, when I look into your eyes, I feel hope and I have to admit that scares the hell out of me."

"Embrace your hope, Bo." She desperately wanted to grab his hand again, to feel the warmth of his big grasp around her much smaller hand, but she knew it wasn't her place.

She was his partner in crime-solving, one of few people who believed he had nothing do with Shelly's death. She wasn't his girlfriend. She had a feeling Shelly still occupied that space in his heart, that she might always be there, allowing nobody else in for love.

For the next hour or so they talked about the elements of the crime, and Claire took copious notes that she would later transcribe into neat colored tabs of material in the larger notebook.

It was just after seven when Claire popped a frozen pizza into the oven, and once it was finished baking they continued their conversation while they ate.

They moved on from discussing the crime and Shelly to Bo's life in Jackson. "Bo's Place is small compared to what I had here," he said as he reached for a second piece of the pepperoni pie. "I don't socialize with the customers like I did here in Lost Lagoon. I keep pretty much to myself. I don't want people getting too close. It's easier that way…safer."

And it was the saddest thing Claire had ever

heard. Before the murder Bo had been gregarious and bigger than life. He'd made Bo's Place popular by his mere presence.

"And lonelier," she said softly.

Bo shrugged. "There are things worse than being lonely." He gazed at her curiously. "Why don't you have a boyfriend?"

"You mean other than my secret admirer?" she asked drily and then continued, "I dated Neil Sampson for about two months and then broke up with him six months ago. He's a city councilman and a nice guy, but there weren't any sparks, at least on my end."

"How did he take the breakup?"

"Not particularly well." Claire took a drink and thought about Neil. He'd shown little passion except for town business until she'd broken up with him, and then he'd spent the next month trying to talk her back into his arms.

"Is it possible he's your secret admirer?"

"I suppose it's possible," she replied thoughtfully. "But we've really had very little contact for the last five months or so. He's one of the liaisons between the town and the company putting in the amusement park and we really don't run in the same circles."

"And nobody else since Neil?" he asked.

"No. I'm twenty-five years old and as of yet I just haven't felt the kind of passion or love to bind my life with anyone." Except gazing into Bo's eyes definitely shot a tingling electricity through her that she tried desperately to ignore.

"You and Shelly dated for about ten years or so. Why didn't the two of you ever get married?"

"I asked her three times after we'd finished college and Bo's Place was up and running. Although she told me she was completely committed to me, she also told me each time that she wasn't ready to take the final plunge."

"Do you know what held her back?"

He frowned thoughtfully. "She didn't like her job at the Pirate's Inn. She was trying to figure out what she wanted to do...to be, and I think until she settled that she just wasn't ready to be my wife."

"They say on dark moonless nights her ghost walks along the edge of the lagoon."

Bo raised a brow. "Have you seen this ghost?"

"Not personally, but I know people who swear they've seen her. And some nights there are swamp lights that they believe is her spirit."

"And you believe all this? In ghosts and spirit lights?" There was bemusement in his eyes now, making him all the more attractive.

"I believe anything is possible," she replied. "I believe in angels and aliens, ghosts and goblins, all in both human and otherworldly forms."

"I knew I'd thrown my cards in with a nut," Bo teased.

Claire laughed. "This is Mississippi and we are a superstitious bunch."

They finished up the pizza and by that time darkness had fallen outside and Bo prepared to leave. She walked him to the door. "I know you still have things you're doing at your mother's house. Why don't we plan on me picking you up tomorrow right after lunch and we can start hunting down people and asking questions then?" she suggested.

"Don't you think it would be better if I just stayed home and you asked all the questions and then told me the answers?"

Claire smiled at him, but shook her head negatively. "That's not how partners work. Besides, I think it's important that people see you around town and that they know you're here to clear your name. You might be surprised to find out you still have friends here, people who never believed you were guilty."

"It definitely didn't feel that way when I left town," he replied.

She placed a hand on his strong, muscled forearm. "It's going to be different this time, Bo. We're going to find out the truth." She pulled her hand away, finding the feel of his warm skin far too pleasurable.

He opened the door and with a wave of his hand disappeared into the darkness. The low, guttural growl of his motorcycle filled the air as she turned on her porch light just in time to see him pull away from her house.

She automatically checked her porch, grateful to find no surprise gifts or notes, and then closed and locked her door and turned off her porch light.

She returned to the table and began to transcribe the notes from the legal pad into appropriate tabs in the larger notebook. Behind the red tab she listed all the people they intended to question the next day.

When that was finished, she moved to the sofa and thought about the conversation she and Bo had shared. It was obvious that the experience of being the number-one suspect in Shelly's murder case had changed him.

The old Bo had eyes that always held a wealth of openness, of warmth and welcome. The old Bo had believed that strangers were just friends he hadn't met yet.

This new Bo wore his wariness in the shadows that filled his eyes, in the defensive tension of his body, although she'd seen glimpses of the old Bo in his wry humor and his cautious and surprising trust in her.

Angels and aliens, ghosts and goblins, she knew they weren't looking for anything or anybody supernatural or otherworldly.

She was looking for two men, hopefully one benign and one malevolent. She hoped to discover that her secret admirer was just some shy man in town who had yet to get up his courage to declare his interest in her. There was no reason for her to believe there was anything scary or threatening about flowers on her porch, she told herself.

The other man they sought was a cold-blooded killer, a man who had throttled Shelly Sinclair to death and then had tossed her body into the swampy lagoon like a piece of trash.

There was no question that she and Bo were about

to shake things up. She only hoped they shook out the real killer and saw him behind bars. They had to do this before Bo got discouraged and decided to leave town once again with the burden of his presumed guilt still riding his shoulders like a heavy leather jacket.

Chapter Four

Bo carried a third box of clothing from his mother's bedroom to the garage and tried to clear his mind of the dreams he'd entertained all night long.

For a year following Shelly's murder he'd suffered terrible nightmares, all of them with Shelly screaming his name, begging for him to help her, and him unable to stop her senseless death.

During the past year or so his sleep had been dreamless, but last night it hadn't been Shelly who had haunted his slumber, it had been Claire.

Claire with her tousled golden curls and achingly blue eyes, he'd dreamed of her in his arms, her body warmth heating all the cold places that had filled his for what felt like forever.

He dropped the box on the floor in the garage and told himself the dream had been driven by nothing more than the fact that Claire had offered him a friendly smile and a level of support he hadn't had before. Surely that was the only reason he'd entertained the erotic dream.

They were partners and nothing more, and would

remain partners until he decided to leave town, and this time when he left he would never be back again. Oh, he'd still talk to Jimmy on a regular basis, not only because Jimmy was a lifelong friend, but also due to Bo's silent ownership of Jimmy's Place.

"Need some help?" Jimmy poked his head out of the door that led from the kitchen to the garage.

"No, I think that's it for today." Bo checked his watch. "That gives me time to eat some lunch before Claire comes by to pick me up around one."

He joined Jimmy in the kitchen and headed for the refrigerator to pull out cold cuts for the noon meal. Jimmy sank down at a chair at the table. "Do you really think it's a good idea for you and Claire to go off like the Lone Ranger and Tonto to crime solve?"

Bo finished making his sandwich, knowing that Jimmy had eaten earlier. He sat down across from Jimmy before replying. "I don't know if it's a good idea or not. Hell, I don't even know if I'm the Lone Ranger or Tonto. Claire is running the show at this point. She has a touch of bossy in her, but at this point I'm willing to let her take the lead. I've been gone for two years and she's been here. All I know is that it's easy to get caught up in her optimism and there's no question I want the real killer identified and justice served."

"And I want that, too. But it's been so long. I can't imagine what you two will manage to dig up after all this time," Jimmy replied. "But it would be great if you could finally clear your name and get the real bad guy behind bars."

Justice for Shelly—hopefully if he and Claire could accomplish that then he would finally find some peace as he moved forward with his life. Shelly would always be a painful part of his past, but he knew that some of that pain could be released if her real killer were found.

"I'll say one thing, you've picked a good partner," Jimmy said, interrupting Bo's thoughts. "Claire is not only well liked, but she's also got a reputation as being a straight shooter who doesn't take any crap from anyone."

Bo couldn't help the smile that attempted to take hold of his mouth. "She seems like a bit of a fire-cracker."

Jimmy laughed. "That's Claire."

"I have a favor to ask you," Bo said, thinking ahead. "I know you use Mom's car. Could you park outside from now on? There's plenty of room on the driveway for my motorcycle and the car, and that will give me space to stack all the boxes of Mom's things."

"Not a problem," Jimmy agreed.

Minutes later Jimmy drifted back to his bedroom and Bo finished his sandwich, trying not to think about the woman who had haunted his dreams, a woman he'd found himself drawn to since the moment she'd tossed him a to-go bag of burger and fries.

He didn't want to be attracted to her. He didn't want to be attracted to anyone. Losing Shelly had been devastating, but the aftermath of her murder had been nearly as devastating as he'd watched close friends and good neighbors turn against him.

His trust in people had been shattered and thick defenses had built up around his heart. He'd learned in the past two years that being alone wasn't such a bad thing.

He spent quite a bit of his time at Bo's Place, overseeing the daily operation. In his spare time he often took long drives on his bike, allowing the wind in his face to blow out any thoughts of past, present or future.

In the lonely hours of the night when he might have been making love to a woman, he often read books on business or history, or the occasional adventure novel.

He'd grown comfortable…safe in his loneliness and he wasn't about to let some curly-haired cutie under his skin. Still, at one o'clock when he slid into the passenger seat of her car, a nervous energy twisted in his stomach.

He told himself it had nothing to do with the sky-blue blouse she wore that clung to her breasts and enhanced her eyes. It had nothing to do with the fresh, floral scent of her that filled the car. The jumpy tension was the result of what they were about to begin today…talking to people who believed he'd murdered his girlfriend.

She frowned at him as he settled in. "I should have told you to wear something else."

He looked down at his black jeans and T-shirt and

then gazed back at her. "I didn't know there was a dress code for the day."

"A white or blue shirt might have been better. You look dark and brooding."

"Like a bad guy," he replied.

She flashed him a quick smile. "Ignore me, I'm probably overthinking things."

It was hard to ignore her when a vision of his dream from the night before flashed through his head. He consciously willed it away. "So, who's first on your list to talk to?" he asked and noticed that her yellow legal pad was shoved down in the space next to her seat.

"I thought we'd start with Sally Bernard."

Bo nodded and braced himself for a face-to-face meeting with the tall redhead who wasn't shy about speaking her mind. He'd once considered Sally a friend of his as well as of Shelly's, and Sally and her boyfriend had often come to Bo's Place for their evening meal.

Sally had been one of the first of Shelly's friends to turn on him and he definitely wasn't looking forward to seeing her again.

They passed the street where Shelly had lived. "Are Craig and Margie still living in the same place?" he asked.

"They left town about six months after Shelly's death. I heard they moved someplace up north. Mac and Savannah stayed together in the house until about eight months ago when Mac got married and bought his own place."

Mac was Shelly's older brother. He would be thirty-two years old now, and the last time Bo had seen him Mac had sworn if he got the chance he'd kill Bo.

"Then Savannah lives in the home alone now?" he asked.

Claire nodded. "She doesn't date and pretty much keeps to herself. Of course, working the overnight shift at the Pirate's Inn isn't exactly conducive to dating."

"I always thought of her like a little sister." A wave of sadness swept through him. "With her being just a year younger than Shelly, sometimes it was hard to get the two apart." He looked at Claire. "She's definitely somebody you should talk to alone. I don't want to be there when you question her."

Claire turned into Sally's driveway, cut the engine and took off her seat belt. "We'll try to catch up with Sally, Valerie and Julie as soon as we can, then I'll drop you back at your house and find Savannah and talk to her."

Bo released a small sigh of relief, grateful that she seemed to understand his reluctance to question Savannah. "And after you talk to her, you can head back to my place for dinner and tell me what she had to say," he said.

"Sounds like a plan," she agreed. "Now, are you ready for this?"

Bo unfastened his seat belt and looked at the small house where he and Shelly had visited occasionally for barbecues and card games. "She hasn't gotten married?" he asked, knowing he was stalling for time.

"Hasn't even come close in the last couple of years. She dates occasionally, but nobody in particular." Claire narrowed her eyes slightly. "Do you want to sit out here and discuss Sally's love life or do you want to get out of the car and see what she might know about Shelly's life before she was murdered?"

Bo drew a deep breath and opened the door. "Let's get this done," he stated with a renewed burst of nervous energy.

As they headed up the walkway that led to the front porch, Bo wondered if this all wasn't a fool's errand. He could finish packing up the last of his mother's things in another day and be back on the road to Jackson. He could put all this behind him, but instead here he was, about to pick the scab off old wounds.

As if she read his thoughts, Claire smiled at him, that crazy warm smile that shot heat through him. "You're doing the right thing, Bo. You deserve the truth. We all do, and this is the first step in finding out that truth." She knocked on the door.

The tall, slender redhead answered with a bright smile that immediately fell into a scowl as her blue eyes gazed at Bo. "Claire, what are you doing on my doorstep with this murdering slimeball?"

"Don't worry, Sally. I left all my homicidal tendencies at home this morning," Bo replied drily and then grunted as Claire delivered a sharp elbow to his ribs.

CLAIRE WANTED TO pinch off Bo's ears. She wanted to give him a sobering slap. The last thing she needed from him was defensive sarcasm. "Bo and I would like to ask you some questions about Shelly."

"She's dead. What's to ask?" Sally made no effort to open her door wider to invite them inside.

"Do you want to do this here on your front porch where all of your neighbors can see, or can we come inside? It's important, Sally."

Sally hesitated a moment and then with a deep, audible sigh opened the door to allow them entry. She gestured them toward her sofa and then sat in a chair across from them, her gaze focused solely on Claire.

"I know you believe that Bo is guilty of Shelly's murder, but he's not," Claire began. "He and I are looking for any information that might point to the real killer."

"And why don't you believe it's not Bo? Because he told you so?" Sally asked with a touch of sarcasm.

"He's not in jail. There was never any real evidence to point to his guilt except for the fact that he and Shelly were a couple. There was never really an in-depth investigation into the murder. Bo was the focus and I don't believe anyone in law enforcement looked anywhere else," Claire replied.

Sally crossed her arms, obviously in defensive mode. "So, what do you want from me?"

"You and Shelly were good friends. Was there anyone bothering her or angry with her before her death that she might have mentioned to you?" Claire asked. Bo shifted positions next to her and leaned forward.

"Not that I remember. The only person Shelly told me she ever argued with was Bo."

Claire fought her urge to look at the man seated next to her. Was there something he hadn't told her about his relationship with Shelly? Had they not been the golden couple Claire had always thought them to be?

"Are you sure there wasn't anyone else who had issues with Shelly?"

"Not that she ever mentioned to me." Sally unfolded her arms. "But I'll confess Shelly and I were social buddies, not necessarily heart-to-heart confidantes. You might talk to one of her other girlfriends, or Savannah. They might have known more about stuff that was going on in Shelly's life than me."

"Well, that was a waste," Bo said moments later as they got into Claire's car.

"Not necessarily," Claire countered. "She's a name we can now cross off our list. Besides, she said it was possible some woman closer to Shelly might know more."

Claire backed out of the driveway and headed in the direction of their next stop. "What's this about you and Shelly arguing?"

Bo sighed and leaned his back against the headrest. "Shelly and I never had huge arguments, but we did have an ongoing difference of ideas that grew bigger over the last year before her death." He sat up straighter and ruffled his hand through his hair. "Shelly wanted to leave Lost Lagoon and move to a bigger city. She wanted me to sell Bo's Place and start all over someplace else. Business was booming, I felt like my mother needed me here, and I loved life in Lost Lagoon. I wasn't willing to give it all up. I believed that if Shelly and I got married and had babies, she'd be happy here, and if she needed more than that, I encouraged her to get involved with the city council or to go back to school."

"Is that why she wouldn't marry you?"

"She never actually told me that, but yeah, I think that was the reason." He gave a dry laugh. "It's ironic that only after her death did she get her wish and I left everything behind to move to a bigger city."

It was ironic and it was tragic, Claire thought. "Did you and Shelly have a particularly public argument in the days before her murder?"

"No, nothing like that. In fact, it didn't come up that often. It wasn't like we argued about it every day. It was more like a discussion we had every couple of months. Losing faith in me?"

She cast him a quick glance. "Not at all, I'm just trying to understand all of the dynamics."

"The truth of the matter is I don't think Shelly and I would have ever married," he said, his voice softer. "I think eventually she would have left Lost Lagoon and me behind."

"You're shattering the image I had of your romance with Shelly. During my teenage years I'd see you two together and then go home to my shanty where my father might or might not be there and I'd dream about finding a love like yours and Shelly's.

To be honest, that idea got me through a lot of difficult times."

Her cheeks warmed as she realized she'd shared more than she'd meant to with him. She didn't like to think about her childhood or the loneliness she'd felt as a motherless child whose father was gone more than he was at home.

If it hadn't been for Mama Baptiste she would have never made it to school on time and would have gone to bed hungry on many a night.

"Maybe Julie will have something to tell us," she said to break the silence that had descended between them.

"Let's hope. Somebody had a beef with Shelly, something was happening that I didn't know about. It wasn't a random act. She wasn't robbed except for her engagement ring, and it certainly wasn't anything spectacular. Her purse was on the bench, with her wallet and cell phone inside."

"Do you know if the police checked pawn shops to see if anyone tried to pawn the ring?" she asked.

"I don't know what the police did except crawl all over me and try to find the evidence to put me in jail for her murder," Bo replied. "But as far as I know the ring was never recovered."

"Maybe the murdering creep kept it as a souvenir," she replied and fought a shiver that threatened to crawl up her spine.

"And that sounds like some sick obsession," Bo replied. "The police found nothing on Shelly's cell phone or her laptop that would lead to another suspect, and I never noticed anyone lurking around whenever we were together. My text was the last thing on her phone, no more incoming calls or texts after that."

"Somebody wanted her dead for a reason, or somebody met with her that night and somehow things got out of control. Did you ever consider that the killer might be a woman?"

She sensed Bo's look of surprise. "It would take a strong woman to strangle Shelly."

"Rage can give somebody plenty of strength, and Shelly was a petite, slender woman."

"I just never considered a woman as a suspect. I can't imagine her making that kind of a female enemy. Like I told you before, I can't imagine her making any enemies."

Claire pulled into the driveway of Julie Melbourne's home and then turned to look at Bo. "Did you feel somebody stalking you before Shelly's death? Have any women who were showing an interest in you?"

"And killed Shelly out of some kind of jealousy?" He shook his head. "I don't remember anyone flirting or acting inappropriate with me. Everybody in town knew that Shelly was my fiancée and I was committed to her."

"It was just a thought," Claire said. "Now let's hope Julie has something more tangible for us than Sally had."

Unfortunately, Julie had nothing for them. She was obviously surprised and not particularly happy to see Bo, but she invited them in and the conversation went nowhere. No, Shelly hadn't mentioned anyone bothering her before her murder. She hadn't talked about anyone who was angry with her or making her uncomfortable.

"You're wasting your time on me," Bo said once they were back in the car and headed to his house. "We're not going to find any answers."

"Are you really ready to quit after talking to just two people? I don't know about you, but I'd much rather be doing this than serving up George's greasy burgers," Claire replied. "The pay isn't as great, but the company is definitely better. Besides, maybe Savannah knows something that will move us forward."

"That would be good," he replied. She pulled to the curb in front of his house.

"Let's hope she's home," Claire said as Bo opened his car door. "I'll catch up with her somewhere and be back here in an hour or so. If I run into a snag I'll call you." They exchanged cell phone numbers.

"And I'll have some dinner ready when you get back here."

"Sounds good," she replied. She watched as he got out of the car and headed toward his front door. He looked defeated and she had a feeling it wouldn't take much for him to cut and run.

It was three thirty when she parked her car at her house, deciding to walk to Savannah's place and then on to Bo's. She felt the need to stretch her legs. Her mind always seemed to clear when she walked or rode her bicycle, and she wanted to think about what she wanted, what she hoped to hear from Savannah.

It didn't take her long to reach the Sinclair home, where Savannah answered the door on Claire's first knock. As always when Claire saw Savannah she thought of Shelly. The two sisters looked so much alike with their long dark hair, delicate features and wide brown eyes.

"Sally called me earlier so I've been half expecting you," Savannah said as she gestured Claire into the house. "Bo isn't with you?"

"We thought it would be best if I talked to you alone," Claire said as she sat on the chair Savannah gestured her to in the tidy living room.

"Sally told me you were asking questions about before Shelly's murder." Savannah sat on the sofa and curled her legs beneath her.

"I'll be completely honest with you, Savannah. I never believed that Bo murdered Shelly. I also don't believe an adequate criminal investigation was conducted at the time of her death," Claire said.

Savannah raised her index finger to her mouth and nibbled on her nail, her doe-like gaze never leaving Claire's. She dropped her hand into her lap and released a deep sigh. "I never really believed in Bo's guilt, either."

The confession shocked Claire. She leaned forward in the chair, a sizzle of excitement rushing through her. "Was there somebody else you suspected? Did Shelly mention anyone bothering her in the days or weeks before she was killed?"

"No, nothing specific, although she did tell me she was dealing with a potentially sticky situation and was trying to figure out how to handle it. But she refused to tell me any more than that."

Claire frowned. "A sticky situation? What could that possibly mean?"

"I don't know, but I'm pretty sure it didn't have anything to do with Bo. I know that she and Mac were fighting, but Mac would never hurt Shelly. Trust me, over the past two years I've tried to figure out what she might have been talking about. I wished I'd pressed her for more details, but I didn't, and I don't know if it had anything to do with her murder or not."

"What were Shelly and Mac fighting about?" Claire asked curiously.

"Who knows? They were always fighting about something. Sometimes Mac took his role as protective older brother too far and Shelly got aggravated with him."

"Why did you have doubts about Bo's guilt?" Claire asked, filing away in the back of her mind Mac as a potential suspect.

"Bo had been a part of my life since I was fifteen. I loved him like a brother. I knew how much he loved Shelly, and through their years together I never saw him lose his temper. In fact, Shelly used to complain that Bo didn't like to fight, that he never lost his cool."

"Why didn't you come forward on his behalf after the murder?" Claire asked.

Savannah's eyes darkened. "Everyone around me seemed so certain it was Bo and nobody had an alternative suspect. My parents were devastated, my brother Mac was in a rage and my best friend, my sister, was dead. I was in no condition to say much of anything to anyone. As time went by everyone just seemed to forget it. Bo was gone, Shelly was dead and I thought I just needed to move on with my life until I heard Bo was back and the two of you were asking questions."

"I believe Bo is innocent, and he and I believe somebody got away with murder that night and has never faced justice. We're determined to find out who was really responsible for Shelly's murder."

Claire stood, eager to let Bo know that Savannah had always had doubts about his guilt. She knew the information would lift his spirits.

Savannah walked her to the door. "You'll let me know if you think of anything that might help Bo and me try to find the killer. Needless to say we don't expect to get much help from the local law enforcement."

"I'll call you if I think of anything that might help, but I've been thinking about this for two long years and haven't come up with any answers." Savannah opened the door. "Please tell Bo that I was sorry to hear about his mother's death. She was a wonderful woman."

Minutes later Claire walked the sidewalks that

would eventually lead her back to Bo's house. Despite the fact that she'd learned nothing concrete, she was filled with a new optimism brought on by learning that Savannah had believed Bo was innocent. Other than Shelly, Savannah would have known Bo's character better than anyone.

A sticky situation—what could that mean? What kind of a situation had Shelly been facing in the days before her death? Had she had issues with a coworker at the Pirate's Inn?

Had she become enamored with another man and the sticky situation was that she was conflicted between her love for Bo and a new romantic interest?

As she walked, her mind whirled, darting first in one direction and then another. It was just after four and the hot, humid air wrapped around her like an oppressive blanket, making her wish she was in the air-conditioning of her car.

It was only going to get worse. The summers in Mississippi were brutal, especially in the couple of months to come. By the time July came she wouldn't be walking or riding her bicycle anymore until cooler fall weather set in.

She was almost to Bo's house when a new thought struck her. Had Shelly received a note from a secret admirer? Had she found a little vase of flowers on the porch before her death?

Despite the heat that surrounded her, a shiver slid up her spine. "Don't be silly," she muttered aloud. There was absolutely no reason to tie what had happened to Shelly Sinclair two years ago to the notes and the flowers Claire was receiving now.

Still, she hurried her pace to Bo's, the chill inside her refusing to relinquish its hold.

Chapter Five

As soon as Claire dropped Bo at his house, he pulled a package of steaks out of the freezer, scrubbed a couple of large baking potatoes and then sat at the kitchen table to think.

He'd gone into today not expecting answers, not expecting anything but rather indulging Claire and her crazy idea to clear his name. He'd decided he'd spend a couple of days "investigating" and then head home to Jackson.

Talking with Shelly's friends, Sally and Julie, had only made him more discouraged. After all, it had been two years. Did Claire really expect to solve a crime that the police had probably officially moved to a cold case status, but unofficially had declared solved?

Certainly Bo would like to know who was responsible for Shelly's murder. He wanted to see that person behind bars, but the odds of him and Claire managing to do that after all this time and with no official help were slim to none.

Jimmy was in the bedroom dressing for his night

at Jimmy's Place and Bo took the opportunity of the quiet time to call his manager in Jackson.

The call didn't take long and, as expected, everything was running smoothly. Bo had made a great choice when he'd hired Art Bolling as his manager. The forty-five-year-old man was not only honest and hardworking, but he was also a good leader who all the workers respected. It put his mind at ease that he had good help while he was away.

Jimmy came into the kitchen, his lanky frame clad in black slacks and a black shirt sporting Jimmy's Place in white lettering. He smelled like a bottle of cologne and had his brown hair slicked back with gel. "The chick magnet is ready for duty," he said with a grin.

"Is there any chick in particular in the magnet's sights?" Bo asked in amusement.

"Nah, right now I'm just spreading the wealth of my charms all around." He straightened his collar and frowned. "I was dating Maggie Grimes for a little while. Remember her? She sat in front of me in algebra class when we were sophomores."

Bo had a vague memory of a cute redhead with big green eyes. "What happened?"

"I figured out she was just dating me for the free drinks she could get at the bar. She liked being my girlfriend at Jimmy's Place but she wasn't much into me outside of that." He shrugged. "Plenty of other fish in the sea and I'm in no big hurry." He checked his watch. "And on that note, I'm out of here."

Once Jimmy had left, Bo scrubbed the potatoes,

poked them with a knife, then covered them with aluminum foil and set the oven to preheat. It was funny, he'd thought he'd become accustomed to the relative silence in his life over the past two years. But in the past two days Claire had filled that silence and he found himself looking forward to her arrival no matter what information she had learned.

He was torn between the decision to stick around and move forward with her in an effort to prove his innocence, and just heading out and leaving Lost Lagoon forever behind.

He was still contemplating what he wanted to do when Claire returned. Her energy bounced off the walls as she greeted him and followed him into the kitchen.

"Savannah never really believed in your guilt," she said with a smile before taking a seat at the table.

Bo's knees nearly weakened as he moved across to the oven to put the potatoes inside to bake. Sweet Savannah, she'd always held a special place in his heart as Shelly's younger sister.

"She also said to tell you she's sorry about your mother's passing," Claire continued. Bo joined her at the table.

"Did she have any information that might be useful to us? Anything that might shed some light on things?" he asked.

She filled up the room with her presence, instantly dispelling the oppressive silence, the thrum of loneliness that had beat in his heart moments earlier.

"Nothing specific, but she did say just before

Shelly's murder Shelly had mentioned that she was dealing with some sort of sticky situation."

Bo frowned. "Sticky situation? What does that mean?"

"I have no idea and Savannah didn't know, either, but I think if we can figure it out it's the key to the murder."

"How exactly do we go about figuring out something like that?" Bo asked in exasperation. "It could have been an issue at work or a fight with her brother. It might have been unwanted attention from somebody or an issue with a girlfriend."

"And step by step we'll explore all those things," Claire said, her voice calming the storm of frustration that threatened to erupt inside him.

"Why wouldn't she have told me about something bothering her?" Bo asked, speaking more to himself than to Claire. He'd thought that he and Shelly shared everything with each other, both good things and bad. Had she possessed secrets that led to her death?

Claire seemed to know that his question had been rhetorical and she didn't attempt to answer it. In fact, she changed the subject as he got up to season and then broil the steaks. She chatted about teaching and how much she loved spending time with her second-grade class. "They're old enough to know the school routine, but also have a wonderful innocence and eagerness to learn that's so rewarding."

As she regaled him with stories about some of the funny antics of some of her students, Bo felt himself relaxing…enjoying the sound of her laughter and the fact that she could make him laugh so easily when levity had been missing from his life for so long.

The easy conversation continued throughout their meal. He told her a little bit more about Bo's Place in Jackson and the small rental house he called home. He considered telling her that he still owned Jimmy's Place, but ultimately decided not to. It really didn't matter. He had no plans to remain in Lost Lagoon and publicly reclaim his place at the popular bar and grill.

"Jimmy definitely has taken on his role as owner of Jimmy's Place well," Claire said with a touch of humor. "He was always kind of quiet and introverted, but now he's like you were when you were running the place. He's gregarious and something of a social butterfly."

"I'm just glad he's happy. He had a crappy childhood. He was raised in one of the shanties near where you live. Both his parents were alcoholics who either beat him, verbally abused him or ignored him. But from what little you've told me, it sounds like your childhood was pretty crappy, too."

"It wasn't great," she admitted and dolloped more sour cream on her potato. "My mother left when I was six years old. I went to school one morning and when I got home she was gone and she never came back. My father was already a drinker, but after she left he fell into the bottom of a bottle and never crawled out. He was gone more than he was home and when he was home he was usually passed out."

"How did you survive?" Bo asked, his heart swelling with empathy for a little girl who'd apparently had nobody to nurture her.

"On hopes and dreams and with a lot of help from Mama Baptiste, who stepped in to make sure I made it to school and had a good breakfast before starting the day."

"But she had her store to run—she couldn't be there all the time for you."

"True. I spent a lot of time alone, but I had a wonderful second-grade teacher who taught us all that we decide if we're happy or sad in most situations. She explained that it was okay to be sad, but eventually we each had to find our own happiness."

A dainty frown line appeared across her forehead, not detracting from her prettiness in any way. "I have to confess, it took me a while to understand that the true path to happiness was in acceptance."

"I'm not sure I understand," he replied, holding her gaze for so long he felt as if he could drown in its blue depths.

"When I realized my mother wasn't coming back, that she'd not only left my father but also me behind, I was devastated." Her eyes shimmered and Bo reached across the table to cover one of her hands with his.

Having been raised in a good stable home with both a mother and father, Jimmy's and Claire's backgrounds not only seemed alien, but broke his heart for each of them.

"I couldn't understand how my mother could just leave and start a new life somewhere and not take me with her. It took me almost a year to realize and accept that she was gone and she wasn't coming back and I was strong enough to be happy despite my circumstances."

Bo squeezed her hand and then released it. Even though she appeared to have gotten past her childhood, he knew there had to be some scars left behind.

It was after they'd finished eating and cleaned up the kitchen that the conversation turned back to the investigation.

"I think tomorrow we should head over to the Pirate's Inn and talk to Donnie Albright," Claire said.

Bo knew Donnie was the owner of the Pirate's Inn. With a long beard and wiry thick gray-and-white eyebrows, he looked like one of the pirates who purportedly haunted the hotel.

"After that we'll try to find more of Shelly's friends out and about and talk to them, and then we'll end up at the diner for dinner where Valerie is working and we can speak with her," Claire said.

The task ahead of them felt daunting. "I should have stayed," Bo said and slapped his palms down on the table in frustration. "I should have stayed here after Shelly's murder instead of running away. I should have forced Trey Walker and his men to do a real investigation. Dammit, I should have never left town with my tail between my legs."

Regret and more than a little self-disgust swept through him. It would have been so much easier to find out the truth two years ago.

"If I remember right, you didn't have much of a

choice except to leave town. Your business was virtually boycotted, cutting off your financial support, and you also had no emotional support except from your mother and Jimmy," Claire reminded him.

"Mom was most of the reason I did leave. She encouraged me to get out of town and hoped that eventually the true killer would be found. I finally agreed to leave because I thought life would be easier on her if I wasn't here. I thought maybe she'd be able to continue to live a normal life, that people would support her, but you saw at her funeral that she was obviously ostracized anyway."

He swallowed his bitterness and glanced toward the window, surprised to discover that darkness had fallen. "You'd better get home before it gets any later," he said.

Claire glanced toward the window and frowned, then turned back to look at him. "Would you mind taking me home? I walked here and I really don't feel comfortable walking home alone in the dark."

"Of course I'll take you home," he replied. "I don't want you walking home alone at night. I've got an extra helmet in the garage. Let me grab it and we'll head out."

Minutes later they were on the Harley, Claire's arms wrapped tight around his waist and her thighs pressing intimately against his.

Desire for her heated his blood, a desire he'd had to tamp down every minute he spent with her. He had a feeling she felt the physical chemistry between them, as well.

But he had no intention of pursuing anything romantic or sexual with her. There was no point. He was on a mission to seek a killer, and once that mission was accomplished he would return to Jackson alone.

He was almost sorry when they reached Claire's house and she climbed off the back of the bike. She handed him the helmet and he hung it on a clip near the back of the bike.

"Why don't we plan on me picking you up around ten in the morning?" she suggested.

He nodded, and then noticed a white piece of paper that appeared to be taped to her porch railing. "Looks like you got another note from your secret admirer." He pulled off his helmet and got off the bike. He followed behind her and watched as she pulled the note off the railing, read it and then handed it to him.

In the bright moonlight overhead it was easy to read the bold black block letters. STAY AWAY FROM BO MCBRIDE. "Is it the same writing as your secret admirer?" he asked.

She took the paper back from him with a shrug. "Hard to tell. It could just be from somebody who doesn't like the fact that we're asking questions." She wadded it up and smiled. "Don't worry about it. I'll see you tomorrow at ten."

He waited until she disappeared into her house before getting back on his bike and taking off. Restless energy filled him, an energy that made the idea of going back home unpleasant. On impulse he headed for Jimmy's Place. The dinner crowd would have moved out by now, leaving the place to the social drinkers and partiers.

It was Saturday night and the place was packed. Bo pulled around to the back of the building and parked. He wasn't looking for trouble, he just had a desire to sit and drink a beer in the place he owned.

He went in through the back door, which led him to a storage area that held a set of stairs and metal rows of shelving. He went through to the kitchen where two cooks worked, but neither of them spoke or stopped him as he walked on. He passed down the hall with the restrooms and then into the main area.

The long polished bar was just to his right and a single bar stool sat empty at the edge. It was rarely used as it was separated from the main row of bar stools that lined the front of the bar. The only person who had sat there regularly had been Shelly on nights she came in before work and Bo was behind the bar.

He slid onto that stool now, grateful that, for at least the moment, nobody had noticed his arrival. The bartender, an older man he didn't recognize, worked the opposite end of the bar where a couple of young women sat.

When he'd finished serving them he scanned the bar area and noticed Bo. Bo ordered a beer and once it had been served, he swiveled slightly in his chair to look around.

Jimmy stood at a table where four people were

seated, obviously playing goodwill ambassador as he smiled and clapped one of the men on his back.

It should be me, Bo thought. *I should be the one greeting people and thanking them for coming in.* He turned back around and took another drink of the cold brew.

There was no going back in time. He'd made his decision to leave and put Jimmy in control so that the place would continue to survive. Certainly his ownership allowed him to reap financial benefits, but he mourned the position in his community that he'd lost in the process.

Bo was almost finished with his beer when Eric Baptiste walked by him, apparently headed for the restrooms. He took several steps down the hallway and then turned back and stepped up close to Bo.

Eric was two years older than Bo and while the two had never had any problems, they had not been close friends. Eric leaned a muscular arm on the bar next to Bo and gazed at him with flat black eyes.

"About Claire," he said softly.

"What about her?" Bo asked.

"If you hurt her in any way, I'll kill you." Eric didn't wait for a reply, but turned on his heels and disappeared down the hallway.

Bo drained the last of his beer and threw enough money on the bar to cover it, then got up and left the way he had come. As he drove home he wondered if perhaps Eric was Claire's secret admirer?

All he knew for sure was that he'd felt a malevolence wafting off the muscular dark-haired man.

Was his warning really about Claire or did Eric Baptiste have something deeper to hide…something like murder?

Chapter Six

Claire knew the last place Bo wanted to be on a Sunday night was in the diner where the crowd was thick and they had to wait for a table to be cleared in Valerie Frank's area.

When they were finally seated, she knew he couldn't help but notice the people at most of the tables around them whispering and pointing in their direction.

She was proud of the straight set in Bo's broad shoulders, in the way he carried himself as if he had as much right to be in this town, in this diner, as anyone…which he did.

"I'm starving," Claire said as she picked up the menu on the table in front of her.

"That's the gnaw of frustration you're feeling," Bo replied drily.

It had been a day of frustration. They'd started by visiting with Donnie Albright at the Pirate's Inn. Donnie hadn't been able to shed any light on what was going on in Shelly's life before her murder, nor had anyone else they'd spoken to throughout the afternoon.

"Tomorrow is another day," she replied optimistically. "Right now all I can think about is a big plate of meat loaf, mashed potatoes and a hot buttered roll."

"All I can think about is that treasure chest in the Pirate's Inn lobby that Donnie was painting that tacky gold," Bo replied.

She laughed. "Upgrades for the crowd of tourists he's hoping the new amusement park will eventually bring to town, and he's not the only person who is making changes and updates to their businesses."

"I can't imagine Lost Lagoon being filled with tourists." Bo closed his mouth as Valerie approached their booth, her eyes widening slightly at the sight of him.

"Hi, Valerie, how's it going?" Claire said lightly, as if it were ordinary for her to show up for dinner with the local bad-boy suspected murderer.

"Okay." Her brown eyes slid a quick glance at Bo. "I heard you were back in town."

"Valerie, I didn't kill Shelly and I decided it was finally time for me to come back to find the real killer. Claire has been helping me do the investigation that the cops never did two years ago." Bo held her gaze. "We wondered if you knew about anything or anyone that was bothering Shelly before her murder?"

"Or maybe why she went to the lagoon that night when she knew Bo wasn't meeting her there," Claire added.

"I don't know why she was at the lagoon," Valerie

said. She glanced around, as if worried she was spending too much time at their table. "She seemed preoccupied in the days before that night, but when I asked her if something was bothering her, she told me it was something she had to work through on her own. Look, I need to get to my other tables and that's really all I can tell you. So, what would you like to drink?"

After taking their drink orders, she hurried away from the booth. "I wonder if the sticky situation was me," Bo said. "Maybe she had finally made the decision to leave me and head out of town and was just waiting for the right moment to tell me."

"That possibility doesn't upset you?" Claire asked.

He smiled and warmth shot through her. He had a beautiful smile and she wished she'd see it more often. "During the last six months of our relationship I began to accept the fact that Shelly and I probably weren't going to have a happily-ever-after together. Although we both pretended things were fine, there was a bit of a strain between us, and I knew it was because Shelly wasn't happy here."

"But we can't know for sure that you were her sticky situation. That's just speculation and we can't take it as fact," she replied.

Valerie returned with their sodas, took their meal orders and then disappeared once again from their booth. Claire sipped her soda and tried not to focus on how utterly hot Bo looked.

Riding on the back of his motorcycle last night had filled her with a sexual charge. She'd molded her legs against his muscular ones, wrapping her arms around his taut middle and pressing herself so close to his back, and it had stirred up a desire to yank him off the bike and take him into her bedroom and make love.

Unfortunately, the note that had awaited her had stanched any feelings of lust. Although she'd made light of it in front of Bo, the note had kept her sleepless for half the night.

Had it been from her secret admirer? Was it a warning of some kind? Or had it simply been a concerned friend or neighbor who didn't want her putting herself at risk by hanging out with a "murderer?"

"So, what's our next move?" Bo asked, pulling her from her thoughts.

"It would be nice if we could get the murder book from the sheriff to see exactly what kind of investigation was done before."

Bo laughed, the sound rich and bold and once again stirring a heat inside her. "There is no way Sheriff Trey Walker would even let us get close enough to spit on the files of Shelly's case. Remember, officially it's still an open case."

"Was there anyone working the case who didn't seem to be completely closed-minded about looking at other suspects?"

Bo frowned thoughtfully. "At the time it certainly felt like every deputy on the force was determined to find evidence to put me away, but now that I think about it there were two deputies who seemed open to other possibilities."

"Are they still in town working as deputies?"

"I know one of them is—I saw him in a patrol car yesterday, Deputy Josh Griffin. The other deputy was Daniel Carson. I haven't seen him since I've been back so I don't know if he's still around or not. The little interaction with them that I had was definitely less confrontational, and they appeared to be more open to other alternatives of the crime."

"Then we need to talk to them," Claire replied. The conversation halted as Valerie returned with their dinners.

"I don't think they'll talk to us." Bo picked up the conversation as Valerie once again left them alone. "Sheriff Walker is a tough bully with his favorite sidekick of Ray McClure. I'm sure both Griffin and Carson would be concerned about their jobs if they were to speak to us about the case."

"Enough shop talk," Claire said as she picked up her fork. "Let's talk about something else while I wallow in this mound of mashed potatoes and gravy."

Bo grinned. "Definitely a meat-and-potatoes kind of girl?"

"You've got that right. Leave the rabbit food to the bunnies."

"Shelly ate rabbit food," Bo said as he cut into the chicken-fried steak he'd ordered. "She always ordered salads when we went out and complained if I encouraged her to eat other food or have dessert. I thought all women worried about their weight like she did."

"Not me," Claire replied. "I guess I have a good metabolism and I've never had to worry about gaining too much weight." She spooned a bite full of creamy potatoes into her mouth, swallowed and then continued, "To be honest, I remember far too many nights going to bed hungry, so I enjoy food now whenever I get the chance."

Bo's gaze was soft as he looked at her from across the table. "I hate the thought of your childhood. It breaks my heart that you went to bed hungry and were so alone."

"There were lots of us swamp kids who didn't have the perfect life, but we managed to survive," she replied. "You mentioned to me that Jimmy had a pretty rotten start to life."

"True, but he had me and my family to help him. I gave him clothes and shoes and we fed him when he was hungry and my mother tried to comfort him when he was scared." Bo smiled. "From third grade until now, Jimmy has always been my brother from another mother."

"I hope Jimmy knows how lucky he was," Claire said.

"I consider myself just as lucky. He's been the best friend I could ever have."

They quieted for a few minutes, each focused on their food. Claire glanced around the diner, grateful that the initial stir that had occurred when they'd walked in had died down and nobody seemed to be paying them any attention.

Meanwhile she found herself far too focused on Bo. Despite the savory fragrances that floated in the air, she could also smell the scent of Bo's woodsy cologne.

She knew better than to get emotionally or sexually involved with him. They were partners and had become friends while working on a crime, but it would be foolish to cross over a line into anything more intense.

Her life was here in Lost Lagoon, and she had no idea how long he'd commit to being here. His life was now in Jackson with the new Bo's Place, and there was really nothing to keep him here long-term. She wasn't even sure he'd stay long enough to get the answers to clear his name, although he appeared fairly committed at the moment.

They were halfway through the meal when Neil Sampson walked in with Mayor Jim Burns. The mayor headed for the counter where apparently a take-out order awaited him while Neil stopped at their booth.

"Claire," he said, completely ignoring Bo's presence. "You're looking as lovely as ever."

And you're looking stuffy and pretentious. Thankfully the words flew only in her head and not out of her mouth. "Thanks," she replied. "Have you met Bo?" she asked.

Neil's gaze never left hers. "No, and I don't have

any desire to. I just wanted to stop and say hello to you. I often think of our time together."

"I would think you'd have a lot more important things to think about," she replied, irritated by his rudeness with Bo.

He stepped back. "I just wanted to say hello."

"And so you have," Claire replied.

Thankfully by that time the mayor motioned to him from the door and with a final nod of his head, Neil hurried toward the exit.

"I'm assuming that was your ex. He seems like a nice guy," Bo said drily.

"He's an ass. He wasn't as bad before he became Mayor Burns's number-one lackey, but power and position have definitely transformed him, and not in a good way."

"It sounds like he still cares about you. Maybe he's your secret admirer," Bo suggested.

"Doubtful. That's not really his style, but who knows." She shook her head to rid it of thoughts of her secret admirer. She didn't want to think about that mystery right now. She still believed eventually her admirer would come out of the woodwork and confess his feelings for her.

By the time they finished their meal and lingered over coffee, dusk had fallen outside. "Why don't you go and start the car and get the air-conditioning running while I pay the bill," Bo suggested.

"Sounds like a plan to me," she agreed. Even though the June sun had gone down, it would still be hot and sticky outside.

She stepped out into the thick humidity and pulled her keys from her purse as she focused on her car parked across the street.

She stepped off the curb and had only taken a couple of steps into the street when she heard the roar of an engine and the squeal of tires against hot pavement.

She was halfway across the street when bright headlights flashed on from a car careening toward her. She froze, her mind unable to comprehend that she stood directly in the path of death.

It took Bo an instant to recognize the imminent danger to Claire when he stepped outside. He didn't think, he simply reacted. He leaped from the curb and when he was close enough he lunged at Claire, the momentum of his speed catapulting them to the other side of the street where Claire slid up to the sidewalk one way and he rolled the other way.

He'd felt the heat of the car engine, still smelled the scent of burning rubber and oil in the air. He remained unmoving for a long moment, his breath stolen and his brain frozen by the near-death experience they both had just endured.

His head cleared and mentally screamed Claire's name. He rolled over to see her pulling herself up to a sitting position, a stunned expression on her face.

Ignoring pain in his hip and elbow, he rose to his feet and rushed to her side. "Are you okay?" He crouched down beside her, hoping he hadn't broken any of her bones with his tackle.

Her knees were bleeding and raw, as were the palms of her hands. Still, she got to her feet. "I'm okay. A little bruised and battered, but…" Her voice trailed off and in the waning light of deep twilight, tears suddenly sparkled in her eyes. "What just happened?"

Bo quickly pulled her into his arms, bloody knees and all. She clung to him for a long moment, her body radiating the heat of adrenaline and the coldness of fear.

She pulled back and he reluctantly let her go. "You probably have gravel in your knees and hands. We need to get you to the doctor," he said.

"I don't need a doctor," she replied and quickly swiped away any remnant of tears. "All I need is my purse. I've got some tissue inside that will clean up the blood." She looked around and spied it not far from where she'd fallen.

Once she'd grabbed it, Bo gestured her to the passenger side of her car and he got in behind the steering wheel. "And now we're going directly to the sheriff's station."

"Why? I just want to go home." Her voice held the heaviness of tears ready to be shed.

He hesitated a moment, wondering if he should soft-pedal what had just occurred. Instead he decided to be painfully honest. "We need to talk to Trey because somebody just tried to kill you."

He felt the weight of her stare. "Surely you're mistaken. It had to have been a drunk driver, or somebody who just didn't see me in the road. Why would anyone want to kill me?"

Good question, Bo said to himself. But he couldn't deny the fact that the car didn't swerve in an effort to miss her, that brakes hadn't been applied to stop the terrifying forward movement of the car.

"I'd just feel better if we report what happened to Trey," he said.

She opened her purse and pulled out several tissues and cleaned off her palms and knees as best as she could without the aid of water. "Maybe the driver was on his cell phone and got distracted for a minute," she said, still looking for answers to explain away what had just occurred.

"Maybe." Bo didn't want to push the issue and upset her even more than she already was.

They remained silent for the rest of the short ride to the sheriff's station. The station was a one-story building and as Claire and Bo walked into the small reception area they were greeted by Betsy Rogers, who worked as both receptionist and dispatcher.

"We need to talk to Sheriff Walker," Bo said.

"He's in his office. You can go on back," Betsy replied.

Bo placed an arm around Claire's shoulder as they walked by the desk where Betsy sat and pushed open the door that led to the squad room. There were a total of eight desks and only Deputy Josh Griffin was present at one, apparently doing paperwork.

He glanced up at them as they walked toward the back of the room where Trey's glass-enclosed office was shrouded in secrecy by closed blinds along the front.

Bo didn't bother knocking. He dropped his arm from around Claire's shoulder and opened the door to reveal Trey leaned back in his chair with his feet propped up on his desk and Ray McClure slouched in the chair in front of him.

"What the hell?" Trey pulled his feet off the desk and sat up straight in his chair. Ray remained in place, an obvious show of disrespect to both Bo and Claire.

"Somebody just tried to run over Claire in the middle of Main Street in front of the diner," Bo said. "If you get somebody over there now there should be witnesses."

Trey motioned Ray up. "Take Josh with you and see what you can find out," he said. Once Ray had left the office, Trey gestured Claire into the empty chair. She sank down and Bo stood just behind her, a hand on her shoulder. "Now, tell me again, in detail, what happened."

"Claire and I ate dinner at the diner and when we were finished, while I paid, she went outside and headed for her car, which was parked across the street," Bo said and then continued to explain the car that had seemingly come from nowhere aimed directly at Claire. As he spoke he felt a small shudder move through Claire.

Trey's gaze softened slightly as he looked at Claire. "I can't imagine anyone in this entire town wanting to hurt you, Claire." His gaze hardened and shifted to Bo. "But I can think of plenty of people who might want to run you down. In fact Mac Sinclair was in here just yesterday complaining about your presence back in town. Are you sure that car wasn't aimed at you?"

Had he been farther into the street than he'd thought? Had it been the intention of the driver to swerve at the last moment and strike him? Bo just didn't know.

"Maybe it was some drunk coming from Jimmy's Place, or some stupid teenager drag racing down the street," Trey added. "But I can't imagine Claire being the target of whatever happened out there tonight."

"It doesn't matter who the target was," Bo countered. "That car almost killed Claire."

"What color was the car?" Trey asked.

Claire looked up and back at Bo, and then gazed at Trey. "I have no idea. All I saw were bright headlights."

"It was dark…black I think." Bo frowned. "I was a little busy getting Claire out of the way to pay attention."

"So, I'm guessing you didn't get a plate number," Trey said.

"That would be a good guess," Bo replied. It had been stupid to come here, he realized. They had no real information to give to Trey in order to identify the vehicle and no idea of anyone who might want to harm Claire.

"I'll write up a report and we'll see if Ray and Josh can find a witness who might be able to give us more information. Other than that, there's nothing much else I can do."

"You'll let me know if they find out anything?" Bo asked. "I'll give you my cell phone number." When that was completed, he squeezed Claire's shoulder. "Come on, let's get you home where we can properly clean up your hands and knees."

She didn't hesitate. She popped out of the chair as if she couldn't wait to leave. There was no question she was still shaken up. Her face was unusually pale and her eyes appeared larger than usual.

Once again Bo took the driver's seat while she slid into the passenger side. "We'll take you to my place and get you cleaned up," he said.

"No, just take me home, Bo. I want to be home. You can drive the car back to your place and pick me up tomorrow," she replied. Bo turned around and headed in the direction of her home.

"Maybe it was just some stupid drunk," she said. "Or a reckless teenager racing down the street." Her own words seemed to calm her.

"Or somebody who intended to swerve at the last minute to hit me," he added. "I know I have a target on my back with some of the people here in town, but like Trey said, I can't imagine anyone wanting to hurt you. I've seen the way people react to you. You're a favorite among everyone."

"I don't know about that, but I would be hard-pressed to come up with anyone who would want to see me dead," she replied.

By that time he'd pulled to the curb in front of

her house. He got out of the car, ignoring the fact that with each passing minute his body was radiating with more aches from his violent tumble across the street.

He could only assume that Claire was feeling the same thing. By tomorrow they would both be dead-tired.

He walked with her to her front porch, where she unlocked her door and turned back to him. "Thank you for saving my life, Bo."

"If you think you're getting rid of me that quickly, you're mistaken." He pushed past her and into her living room. "Since you didn't want to go to the hospital to take care of your hands and knees, I'm assuming you must have a first aid kit of some kind around here."

"I can take care of it. It's not necessary for you to do it," she protested.

"I say it's necessary," he said firmly. "I've let you be boss of this partnership long enough."

Her eyes widened. "I haven't been bossy," she exclaimed. He raised one of his brows and her cheeks grew pink. "I've just been organized and had a plan each day."

"Right now I'm the one with the plan. Now, where are your first aid items?"

"Under the cabinet in the bathroom." She closed and locked the front door and led him to the bathroom just off the living area. He went directly to the sink and began to run the hot and cold water, turning the faucets until he was satisfied with the temperature.

He then turned to where she stood just behind him and moved her in front of him, wrapping his arms around her. He took her wrists and held her hands under the running water.

For a moment he was nearly overwhelmed by the feel of her warmth and curves so close to him and the sweet, fresh scent of her hair. He steeled his mind and focused on the task at hand. He was grateful to see that as the dried blood slowly left her palms, there were only minor scrapes that wouldn't even require any bandages.

Once her palms had been cleaned, he motioned her to sit on the commode so he could attend to her bloody knees. He used a warm washcloth to gently remove the blood, once again grateful that he found no grit or gravel embedded in her skin.

After washing both knees, he applied antibiotic cream to them and then topped each with a bandage that sported a happy face. He gently kissed each bandage and then rose to his feet. "Boo-boos not only cleaned but properly kissed," he said lightly.

She looked up at him with new tears shimmering in her eyes. "I've always wondered what it would be like to have somebody kiss my boo-boos," she said at the same time a soft sob escaped her.

In a flash of memories, Bo thought of every night his mother had tucked him into bed with a good-night kiss, how many times she'd fixed a boo-boo with a gentle press of her lips. He'd taken for granted all of it, and the thought that Claire had never had anyone to tenderly tuck her into bed or kiss away the pain of a scratch or scrape broke his heart.

He pulled her to her feet and into his arms, wanting to kiss every wound she'd ever suffered in her life, needing to be her soft place to fall that she'd never had as a child.

She clung to him, and when she raised her head to look at him he slanted his lips against hers. He meant the kiss to be soft and soothing, to comfort and calm after the trauma she'd suffered.

However, the moment he tasted her velvet-soft lips, he was lost. It was impossible to keep the kiss sweet and simple as she tightened her arms around his neck and opened her mouth to him in invitation to deepen the kiss.

He accepted the invitation, his tongue swirling with hers as his blood fired through his veins. The instantaneous desire that flared inside him shocked with its intensity and unexpectedness.

She must have felt it, too. She dropped her arms from around his neck and stumbled back from him, one hand reaching up to touch her own lips. "You should be boss more often," she said.

He'd love to kiss her again. He wanted to kiss her until they were both mindless with desire, eager to fall into bed together, but he didn't.

Despite her light words, she looked exhausted and

battle-weary. Now wasn't the time to do anything but encourage her to get a good night's sleep.

He reached out his hand and took hers and led her out of the bathroom. There was only one door in the house he hadn't been through and it was that door he opened… The door to her bedroom.

"What you need more than anything right now is to get into your pajamas and get some sleep," he said, even as his gaze swept the room that he would have instantly identified as belonging to her.

The walls were a pale gray, but the bedspread was an explosion of electric-blue flowers on a gray background, giving the room vibrancy. A vase of fake blue and yellow flowers sat on the nightstand, along with a yellow-based lamp.

Once again he was struck by the fact that when she'd renovated the old shanty into her home, she'd chosen bright, cheerful colors for every space.

"I'm going to get out of here and I'll lock up on my way out," he said.

"What about tomorrow?" she asked and sank down on the edge of her bed.

"I'll pick you up around eleven."

"But I haven't had a chance to plan what we need to do," she said.

"Don't worry. I'm playing boss again tomorrow and I'll have a plan. Now, get into your jammies and get some sleep." He left the bedroom and had just opened the door to leave the house when she called his name.

She stood in the bedroom doorway. "Just for your information, I don't sleep in jammies. I always sleep naked." With these surprising words, she closed her bedroom door.

Chapter Seven

The car careered toward her, the bright headlights blinding her as the acrid scent of burned rubber and hot oil filled her head. Then she was airborne, knowing that when she fell to earth death awaited her.

Death was her shanty where she shivered beneath her favorite blue blanket on a thin mattress on the floor. Outside the thin plywood walls she heard the slap of a creature in the water and feared that creature would creep in the darkness and through the slats in the wall and eat her.

Claire awoke with a gasp and sat straight up in the queen-size bed. Sunshine poured through the single window, and a glance at her clock told her it was just after nine.

She normally didn't sleep so late, but she'd had trouble going to sleep the night before. First she'd played and replayed through her mind that moment of being frozen as the car had headed directly for her, then she'd been plagued with thoughts of Bo's kiss.

Oh, that kiss. She drew in a tremulous breath and

fell back against her pillow, remembering the fire, the absolute mastery of his lips against hers.

She couldn't lie, she'd wondered what it might be like to be kissed by Bo, but there was no way her imagination had been able to conjure up how hot, how utterly breathtaking it would be.

She shouldn't think about it. She'd watched Shelly and Bo together for years and had dreamed of finding what she believed they'd found in each other. She'd believed they'd been each other's happily-ever-after and they might have been, had Shelly not been murdered.

Claire wanted that happily-ever-after for herself. She wanted that special man who loved her as desperately as she loved him. And she knew in her heart that man wasn't Bo.

Bo would have already been gone from Lost Lagoon if she hadn't talked him into hanging around for a while to try to find the real killer.

She had a feeling that with each day that passed with no answers about the murder, Bo moved closer to heading out of town. She didn't want him leaving behind her broken heart.

She got out of bed, grabbed her robe and pulled it around her, then padded into the bathroom and stared at her reflection in the mirror. It was as if she expected the imprint of Bo's lips to still mark hers.

Her mouth looked normal, no sign of the earth-shattering kiss they'd shared the night before. "It can't happen again," she said aloud to her reflection.

She started the water in the shower stall and once

it was a warm temperature she disrobed and stepped beneath the spray. She could not allow Bo to kiss her again. If he did she'd want more, and then her heart would spiral out of control. She had to keep her physical distance.

After showering she dressed in her usual fare of a pair of shorts and a sleeveless blouse. She took off the bandages on her knees, satisfied to see that the scrapes had already begun to scab over. It wouldn't be the first time in her life that she'd sported scabby knees or elbows.

She ate toast and drank a cup of coffee and scanned the names of the people they'd spoken to so far. She wrote notes and frustration niggled at her as she recognized they had really discovered nothing that moved them any closer to the truth of what had happened at the lagoon two years ago.

The irony wasn't lost on her that she wanted to do everything in her power to help clear Bo's name, but in doing that she was also helping him move on from Lost Lagoon.

At a few minutes before eleven she stood at her front door waiting for Bo to arrive to pick her up. She wondered what he had planned for the day. Although Lost Lagoon was a small town, there were still plenty of people to talk to who might have known something about the murder, somebody who could unravel the mystery of Shelly's "sticky situation."

The one person she didn't want Bo to speak to or have anything to do with was Mac Sinclair. Shelly's older brother was known to have a volatile temper, especially since the murder of his sister. The fact that he'd already contacted Trey to do something to get Bo out of town indicated his continued hatred for the man he believed murdered Shelly.

She hated the way her heart lifted at the sight of her car pulling up front. She hated that as she left her house her head filled with the memory of that damned kiss.

Sliding into the passenger seat she gave him a bright smile and determined not to think about the kiss for the rest of the day. "Good morning," she said.

"Back at you," he replied and pulled away from the curb. "I heard from Trey this morning. Ray and Josh managed to find three eyewitnesses from last night. One said the car was black, another said it was blue and the third person was certain it was dark gray."

"Which basically means we'll probably never know who was behind the wheel," she replied. "I still think it was just some crazy nut speeding down the street who didn't see me. Maybe it was somebody texting while driving. I just don't believe that somebody intentionally tried to run me down. And now, what are the plans for today?"

"I'll let you know when we get to my place," he replied mysteriously.

"We still have a lot of people to talk to," she replied. "Even though we talked to Shelly's closest friends, she had lots of other friends in her life, and she might have confided something to a coworker at the Pirate's Inn."

Bo held a hand up, as if to stop her before she named every person in town. "We'll get there, Claire. How are you feeling? The knees doing okay?"

"The knees are already on the mend, although I have to confess that I'm feeling some aches in muscles I didn't know I had. What about you?"

"I feel a little beat up," he admitted. "We both had a hard landing last night." He pulled into his driveway, shut off the car and unbuckled his seat belt. "And that's why I've made the executive decision that we're taking the day off."

"The day off?" She looked at him blankly.

He offered her a small, sexy smile. "Yeah, you know, a day where we don't talk to anyone, we don't work the case and we just hang out and relax." He frowned suddenly. "Unless there's somebody else you'd rather hang out with for the day."

"No, not at all. I just assumed you'd be eager to push forward on the investigation."

"I am, but just not today." He got out of the car and Claire did the same and followed him into the house. Jimmy was sprawled in a recliner chair in the living room and he greeted her with his usual friendly smile. He grabbed the remote and muted the television, which was tuned to a news station.

"Heard you had an exciting evening last night," he said.

"Way too exciting for my taste," she replied and sat down on the sofa. She'd almost been nervous to spend the day in the house with Bo, afraid that he might try to kiss her again and she might let him. She'd forgotten that Jimmy would be here, too.

"Something to drink?" Bo asked, poised between the living room and kitchen.

As usual he was dressed in a pair of jeans and a dark gray T-shirt and looked hot and sexy. "Something cold, if it's not too much trouble," Claire said.

"Iced tea okay?"

She nodded her assent and he disappeared into the kitchen. "From what Bo tells me so far you haven't had much success in your investigation," Jimmy said.

"We've really only just started," she replied, refusing to be discouraged after a couple of days.

"I wish I could do something to help. Bo's like a brother to me. Without his friendship and support I probably would have become a no-account nasty drunk just like my father."

Claire smiled at him. "I had one of those, too. Although mine was a no-account absent father most of the time." Bo returned with two glasses of iced tea. He handed her one and then sat on the opposite side of the sofa and placed his glass on the coffee table in front of them.

"Bo told me that your mother left town when you were young. Have you ever heard from her?" Jimmy asked.

"No, and at this point in my life I have no desire to hear from her. She made her choice to cut and run and leave me behind and apparently never looked back. She wasn't there when I needed her and now I have no need of her. How's business?" she asked, ready to get the topic of conversation off herself and a childhood she couldn't change.

For the next few minutes Jimmy talked about the business that had once been Bo's. He entertained with stories of picky customers and crazy drunks, making both Claire and Bo laugh.

It felt good to laugh and to hear Bo's deep rumble of laughter. It felt good not to think about the investigation and everything she felt they still needed to do in order to accomplish their mission.

Bo was right. They'd needed a day off. He appeared more relaxed than she'd ever seen him. By one o'clock they had all moved into the kitchen for a late lunch. Jimmy insisted that she and Bo sit and leave the meal to him.

Within twenty minutes he served them hot ham and cheese sandwiches on toasted rye bread and French fries on the side. While they ate Jimmy continued to talk about the bar and grill and Claire found herself wondering if it bothered Bo that his best friend was now reaping the benefits of Bo's defection from town.

After lunch Bo and Jimmy entertained her with stories of their childhood antics. They had tales of sneaking out of the house at midnight to go frog gigging in the swamp and running home after only a few minutes, scared of the dark and the fear of being eaten by gators.

There were stories of building a tent in the backyard and then accidently setting it on fire when they decided to roast marshmallows inside the tent.

After each and every story they argued about who had been the one who had come up with the ideas that had usually gotten them into trouble as Claire laughed at the easy banter between the two friends.

"What about you, Claire? Do you have close girl-friends who do lunch with you or go out for drinks and gossip together?" Jimmy asked.

"I have lots of friendly acquaintances but no close girlfriends," she replied. She frowned thoughtfully, wondering why she had never encouraged any real solid friendships.

She knew that when she was young she'd never wanted anyone to know that she was basically living in a shanty that rarely had electricity on and no parental figure in the place.

"When I was young, I was afraid for anyone to find out that I was basically living alone. I was scared that social services would somehow find out and take me away," she continued. "I guess as I got older that self-protectiveness stuck with me and I just never formed close relationships."

"Then who do you talk to about your deepest, darkest secrets?" Bo asked.

She laughed. "I don't have any deep, dark secrets. What you see is what you get."

Bo's gaze lingered on her, his eyes silently seeming to tell her that he definitely liked what he saw. Warmth leaped into her cheeks and she was grateful when Jimmy began talking once again.

The rest of the afternoon passed pleasantly with the conversation remaining light and easy. About four o'clock Jimmy excused himself to get ready for his night of work, leaving Claire and Bo alone on the sofa.

"Isn't this better than being out in the heat and trying to talk to people who don't particularly want to talk to us?" Bo asked.

"It has been a nice break," she agreed. "But tomorrow I think I need to be boss again and we need to move forward in trying to find some answers."

"I only get to be boss for a day?" he asked in amusement.

"What you should want now more than anything is something that will lead us to Shelly's killer," she replied.

He leaned toward her, the scent of him filling her head and stirring up a tension that was both slightly frightening and exhilarating.

"You know what I want more than anything at this moment?" His blue eyes simmered as they held her gaze hypnotically. "I want a repeat of our kiss last night. In fact, I want more than that. I want you in my bed making love with me."

A soft gasp escaped her at the blatant sensuality of his gaze and the unfiltered words that filled her with an internal fire.

"Bo, we're partners, not lovers." She was appalled by the slightly breathless quiver in her voice.

"We could be both," he replied.

"I don't think that's a line we should cross." She knew her voice lacked conviction and she cursed herself for it.

"You're the boss," he replied and leaned back. "I just want you to know that if you change your mind, I'm open and interested."

Thankfully at that moment Jimmy returned to the living room and halted any further conversation on that subject. It was only when Jimmy left that she grew a bit nervous about how the rest of the evening would unfold.

She needn't have worried. Bo remained a perfect gentleman as they watched a movie together and then shared a pizza. Any talk of the investigation remained off-limits and instead they talked more about their pasts, talked about the changes that would occur in the town when the amusement park finally opened, and their favorite books and movies.

Before she knew it, dusk had fallen with night not too far behind. "I should head home," she said. "And we should figure out what our plans are for tomorrow. No more days off."

"But it has been nice, hasn't it? To spend the day together and not think about who said what, when, and not think about what neighbor or friend might be a cold-blooded killer," he replied.

"It has been nice," she agreed. "Maybe tomorrow we need to just talk to everyone we run into who was about the same age as Shelly. Maybe she had a close friend you didn't know about."

Bo heaved an exaggerated sigh. "Okay, boss. Why don't you pick me up around ten?"

"Sounds good." Claire got up from the sofa, grabbed her purse and headed for the door. Bo followed just behind her. When she reached the door she didn't turn to face him to say good-night. She knew instinctively he was too close behind her, that in turning to face him he might kiss her and she might kiss him back.

She opened the door and then the screen door and stepped out on his porch. Only then did she turn around and wave to him.

Once she was in her car and headed home she thought of last night when she'd told him she slept naked. What a stupid thing it had been for her to confess to a man who was obviously sexually attracted to her...a man she was sexually attracted to.

It was dark by the time she parked her car and went into the house. It was only when she set her purse on the table that she realized she hadn't retrieved her mail since Bo had shown up in town.

She opened her front door and headed for the mailbox near the street. The black of night surrounded her, broken only by a neighbor's porch light that shot a faint beam of illumination.

She reached the mailbox and was about to open it when she felt a sudden rush of air coming from behind her. Before she could turn, a plastic bag was yanked not only over her head, but down the length of her body to trap her arms against her sides, as well.

She screamed and kicked out with her legs. Disoriented and with her heart pounding in terror, her kicks didn't connect with anything or anyone. She tore at the plastic around her with her fingernails, attempting to free her arms.

Panicked screams continued to tear from her throat, rising in volume when she was picked up by strong arms.

It was only then that her brain made the connection that she was being kidnapped and there was nobody around to save her.

CLAIRE HAD BEEN gone for about forty-five minutes when Bo's cell phone rang. "It's Eric Baptiste," the caller's deep voice boomed over the line. "You need to get to Claire's." Without offering any more information, Eric hung up.

Bo stood staring at his phone, wondering if this was some sort of a setup? A prank of some sort? Eric didn't seem the type of man to pull a prank. His heart seemed to stop beating. Something had happened.

He grabbed his keys and within minutes was on his motorcycle speeding to Claire's house, his brain whirling with suppositions. Had she hurt herself? Fallen down and broken a bone? Then why would Eric call him instead of calling for an ambulance?

He didn't pay attention to the speed limit; he only knew he needed to get to Claire as quickly as possible. Why hadn't she called him? What could have possibly happened to her in the past forty-five minutes?

He pulled up in front of her place and parked. Jumping off his bike, he noticed a torn black trash bag in her yard. What the hell?

Not pausing, he raced to Claire's door. Eric answered the knock and the minute Bo stepped inside

Claire flew into his arms. Bo automatically wrapped his arms around her as she cried into his chest. What in the hell had happened?

He looked at Eric quizzically, but the well-built, dark-eyed man shrugged and sat in the chair opposite the sofa. Apparently it was Claire's story to tell.

At least physically she appeared to be fine, although obviously emotionally distraught. She had just begun to gain control and Bo had led her to the sofa where they sat down when a knock fell on the door and Sheriff Trey Walker and Deputy Ray Mc-Clure walked in, followed by Deputies Josh Griffin and Daniel Carson.

Trey looked at the three of them. "What happened?" He turned his attention to Eric. "You called about an attempted kidnapping?"

Bo's insides shuddered and he tightened his arm around Claire. "What happened?" he asked Claire, repeating Trey's words as Bo's blood iced in his veins.

"I left your house and when I got home I realized I hadn't checked my mail for a while." Her voice trembled and her face was paper white. "When I got to the mailbox I sensed somebody behind me but before I could turn around he pulled a garbage bag over me." Her eyes simmered with the terror she'd experienced. "I tried to fight, and I screamed over and over again, but he picked me up in his arms."

"Griffin and Carson, check out the area and see if anyone saw anything," Trey said.

"I was sitting on my porch and heard her screams,"

Eric said as the two men left the house. "I yelled and ran down here, but by that time whoever it was had dropped her to the ground and disappeared into the darkness."

"Eric ripped the bag off me and got me into the house and that's when he called Bo and you," she said to Trey.

"Did you get any idea of a description of the man?" Trey asked Eric.

Eric shook his head. "It was dark and he was dressed all in black. I only got a brief glimpse of him from the back."

"Short...tall...build?" Trey asked.

Eric shrugged helplessly. "It was just too dark for me to get any idea of size or shape. He was just a black form running away."

Trey focused back on Claire. "Did he say anything to you?"

"Nothing," she replied. "I can't tell you anything about him. I didn't see him. He didn't make a sound. I just know he was strong enough to pick me up like I weighed nothing."

Bo listened and even though she was safe and right next to him, his blood refused to warm. There was no way to dismiss this attack on Claire as anything but an intentional act.

This forced him to believe that the speeding car that had nearly hit her hadn't somehow been an attack on him, but on her.

"Can I go?" Eric asked. "I've told you everything I know."

Trey hesitated a moment and then nodded. "We'll be in touch if we have any more questions for you."

Eric left the chair and headed out the door and Trey sat in the newly vacated seat. Ray stood just behind him and spoke for the first time.

"Maybe it would be best if you two weren't spending so much time together," he said. "It's possible somebody is ticked off at you because you're trying to help Bo."

"Maybe it would be best if you'd do your job and find out who has tried to harm me twice now," she retorted, her fear momentarily displaced by a flash of anger.

"We're going to do everything we can to find this perp," Trey assured her with a calm that bordered on patronizing. "And you have every right to fraternize with anyone you want in this town."

"This certainly isn't going to stop me from spending time with Bo," she said and placed a hand on his thigh. It was then that Bo's blood began to warm again.

"Has anyone threatened you? Shown anger toward you?" Trey asked.

"No, nothing like that, although I did have a note taped to my porch railing a couple of nights ago that said 'stay away from Bo McBride.'"

Trey sat up straighter in the chair. "Do you still have the note?"

"No, I threw it away," Claire replied. She frowned. "I should have brought the note to you the minute I found it, but I just figured it was harmless, somebody trying to warn me not to get involved in Bo's issues."

Trey rubbed his forehead as if weary. "I have to look at this as if there have been two attacks on you and we don't have much to go on. We couldn't even get a confirmation on the color of the car that tried to hit you and now I have no description of the person who attacked you tonight."

"There is the garbage bag outside," Bo said.

Trey nodded. "We'll take it and see if we can pull some prints, but I'm not optimistic about it." He looked back at Ray. "Go outside and bag and tag the evidence." Ray immediately left to do his job.

Trey turned his attention back to Claire and Bo. "Is there anything else you can tell me?"

Bo looked at Claire, glad to see that some of the fear had left her eyes and her cheeks had once again filled with natural color. "I can't think of anything," she replied.

By that time Griffin and Carson had returned, indicating that they'd found no witnesses and no sign of the attacker.

Trey stood. "I intend to focus this investigation on people who are particularly upset with Bo. I think it's quite possible that your connection with him is the reason for these attacks. But if you think of anyone else who might have a reason to want to harm you for any reason, give me a call."

"Trust me, you'll be one of the first to know," Claire replied.

Once everyone was gone, Claire leaned against

Bo's side and released a tremulous sigh. She didn't speak, and in the silence Bo's thoughts flew as he tried to figure out what should happen now.

The idea that he was responsible for any threat to Claire was unacceptable. From the moment they'd started spending time together he'd never considered the possibility that he was putting her at risk.

"What a night," she finally said.

Bo tightened his arm around her. "I'm just glad you're okay." The idea of anything bad happening to her caused a huge lump to form in his chest, making it impossible for him to speak for a moment.

He'd already been through the agony of losing three people he loved: his father, his mother and Shelly. Although he wasn't in love with Claire, he cared about her deeply and refused to consider losing her to some nutcase with a grudge against him.

What had been the motive of the person who had attempted to take Claire tonight? Was it possible he'd simply meant to scare her, or had the person had deadly intentions? Was it possible the goal was to kill Claire and leave her body in the swampy lagoon in an effort to somehow frame Bo for another woman's murder? It would definitely shake everything up if Bo returned to town and another young woman was killed and left in the lagoon.

"Bo?"

Claire pulled him from his thoughts. "Sorry, I was just thinking about the next move for us," he replied.

She sat up straighter and he pulled his arm from around her. "What do you mean? The next move for us is that we keep doing what we're doing. We continue to try to find Shelly's killer."

"It's not that easy after what almost happened here tonight." He moved several inches away from her. "I have to consider that you having contact with me has put you in danger."

"If that's the case then I'm now on notice and can be better prepared," she replied with a lift of her chin. "I'm not going to let some creep dictate what I do and with whom."

Bo raked a hand through his hair, knowing that she was stubborn enough to continue the investigation with or without him, still putting her potentially at risk.

"As far as I'm concerned we have three options. The first is that I forget this whole thing and go back to Jackson. The second is that you forget this whole thing and distance yourself from me and anything to do with Shelly's murder."

"I don't like those options," she replied with a touch of petulance.

"The third option is that you move into my house where I can be sure that nobody can get to you again."

She stared at him, her eyes reflecting myriad emotions...apprehension, a touch of residual fear and something else he couldn't identify. "So you'd be like my personal bodyguard?"

"Exactly."

She frowned and looked around the room and

then back at him. "And it would be a strictly platonic roommate arrangement?"

"I would never take advantage of you, Claire," he replied softly.

"I have to admit, I'm more than a little shaken up by what happened, and the idea of being here all alone is a bit scary."

"Then pack a bag and let's get out of here," Bo replied.

As she disappeared into her bedroom, Bo quickly processed the bedroom situation at his place. His mother's bedroom still hadn't been completely cleared. The bed had been stripped and he wasn't sure he was emotionally ready to allow anyone to sleep in there yet.

The easiest thing to do was for Bo to put Claire in his bedroom, and he'd bunk on the sofa. There was a door that connected his room to his mother's bathroom and that would give Claire more privacy in a home where two men lived.

With the arrangements set in his head, he stood from the sofa and walked to the front window. He peered out into the darkness and wondered who in the hell had attacked Claire.

He'd known she wouldn't agree to stop investigating Shelly's murder. At this point he wasn't even sure she'd stop if he went back to Jackson. He was only grateful that she'd agreed to come to his place where he could make sure she stayed safe.

He turned away from the window as she came back into the living room, this time carrying a bulging duffel bag, a rigid set to her shoulders. "I hate that some creep is making me afraid to stay here," she said. "I hate being chased out of my own home."

"Hopefully, Trey and his men will get to the bottom of this quickly and before you know it you'll be back here."

She eyed him dubiously. "I don't have a lot of confidence in Trey and his men finding their way out of a paper bag. Trey is too busy sucking up to Mayor Jim Burns to be a good leader in the department. He doesn't want to solve crimes, he just wants any perks that come with his position."

She drew a deep breath. "Sorry, I'm rambling and being cranky."

"You're allowed to be cranky," he replied gently. "It's late and you've had a traumatic experience. Let's get out of here and get you settled in at my place."

Bo stepped out of the front door and onto the porch first and then froze. He was vaguely aware of Claire moving next to him even as his focus remained solely on the items on the porch.

"What the hell?" he muttered as Claire gasped.

On the porch was a beige doll that looked like a stuffed gingerbread man. Sexless and faceless, the doll sported three redheaded pins stabbed into the area that would be the doll's heart. There was also a note written in bold red lettering big enough to read by the living room light Claire had left on, which flowed through the front window.

YOU BELONG TO ME!!!!! The words screamed from the page and once again Bo's blood chilled.

Chapter Eight

It was just after two and Claire was snuggled beneath sheets that smelled of Bo. She'd been too upset to argue with him even when she'd realized that in giving her his room, he planned on sleeping on the sofa.

All she'd really been able to think about was that her harmless secret admirer was obviously an obsessed stalker who no longer wanted to date her but wanted to kill her.

They hadn't touched the voodoo doll or note but rather had called Trey back to the house where he'd collected the evidence. Then they had followed him to the station where she'd told him about the notes and flowers she'd received from somebody she hadn't given a minute's thought to in the past week or two.

Trey had questioned her for about an hour, forcing her to think about each note she'd received, the kind of vases that had been left and who she thought might be her secret admirer.

She'd had little information to give him. She'd been in a state of shock after realizing the threats against her weren't because of her helping Bo prove his innocence, but rather specifically directed at her and had nothing to do with Bo. She'd gotten her first notes and letters long before Bo had shown up in Lost Lagoon.

She now shivered and pulled the sheet up closer around her neck despite the warmth of the room. Her breathing grew shallow as she remembered those moments of being trapped in the plastic bag, unable to see her assailant and incapable of fighting back.

What would have happened if Eric hadn't been sitting on his front porch, if he hadn't heard her scream? She believed she'd be dead.

What had changed her secret admirer from a person who left her sweet little notes and freshly bloomed flowers to a madman who had tried to run her over with a car and kidnap her?

Ultimately she thought maybe it did come back to Bo. Whoever was after her was jealous and angry that she and Bo had been spending every waking hour together. The creep probably thought she and Bo were lovers and in his warped mind she'd belonged to him and now deserved to die for cheating on him.

She'd seen television shows and documentaries about stalking and obsessive love. The cases didn't always end well. She shivered again, and fear once again rose up inside her. She'd been damned for something that hadn't even happened. Her stalker felt she'd betrayed him with Bo. *But you could make it happen*, a little voice whispered inside her head. *You could make it happen right now.*

She thought of being held in Bo's arms, of his lips taking hers as their bodies melded together. Partners with benefits, he'd joked. But tonight was no joke. She wanted him. She needed him to take her away from her own scary thoughts.

Why not make love with Bo? She knew he wasn't her happily-ever-after, but at the moment that's not what she needed from him. She needed his warmth, his heart beating next to hers. She wanted him to assure her that she'd truly survived the night and that her life wasn't just about fear.

Without giving herself a chance to rethink her desire, she got out of bed and pulled her robe around her. If he was already asleep, then she wouldn't wake him.

She crept down the darkened hallway and paused at the threshold into the living room. "Bo?" she whispered.

By the moonlight drifting through the living room windows she saw him sit straight up. "Claire, is something wrong?"

"I've decided I want to be partners with benefits and I want to explore those benefits right now." Speaking the words out loud only made her more certain that she wanted him.

The physical attraction, the sexual tension between them, was undeniable, and they were both single, consenting adults. She was no starry-eyed romantic who expected anything from him other than the physical pleasure and sense of safety she knew she'd find in his arms tonight.

"Claire, you've had a traumatic night." He didn't move from the sofa. "Maybe now isn't the time to make a decision you'll later regret."

"I don't believe in living with regret," she replied. "Trust me, I know what I'm doing. I want you to make love to me, even if it's just for this one night." She gripped her thin cotton robe closer around her, wondering if she was making a complete fool of herself.

He stood. Clad only in a pair of black boxers and with the moonlight appearing to be drawn as if by magic to shimmer on every muscle and lean structure on his body, Claire's breathing grew shallow once again, only this time it had nothing to do with fear.

She nearly stopped breathing as he advanced toward her. He stopped when he stood inches from her, his body warmth radiating out to engulf her; his mere closeness drove every bad thought and fear out of her head.

"Claire." He raised a hand and placed it on her cheek. "You know I want you, but I also need you to know that I'm not looking for a relationship."

"Neither am I. I'm just looking for tonight." She turned her face into his palm and kissed it. "Just tonight, Bo."

He moved his hand from her face to the back of her head and pulled her against him as his mouth found hers. He tasted of fiery desire and mindless pleasure, exactly what she'd wanted, what she needed from him.

When the kiss finally ended, her knees were almost too weak to lead him down the hallway to his bedroom. The room was completely dark with only a faint sliver of moonlight whispering through the crack in the blinds.

Claire shrugged out of her robe and immediately got into the bed and covered up with the sheet. Bo took a moment longer and she knew he was taking off his boxers.

When he got beneath the covers with her there was nothing between them. They were warm skin and hard muscles and soft curves as he pulled her into his arms and their lips once again found each other.

As he kissed her, his arms moved from around her and his hands began to explore her. He caressed her shoulders, and then glided his palms across her breasts. Her nipples hardened at the brief touch as his hands continued a path down the flat of her stomach and then down the sides of her hips.

It was as if he were a blind man seeking to "see" her through his fingertips. It was also an erotic dance of touch that left her shivering with a desire she'd never felt before.

She reciprocated, running her fingers across his broad shoulders and chest. His stomach was an easy six-pack of taut muscles and before she could caress him any further he rolled over on top of her, his hardness against her as he kissed and tongued first one breast and then the other.

She tangled her hands in his hair, her hips automatically moving beneath him as the fire inside her grew to mammoth proportions.

She felt as if from the moment she'd met him they'd indulged in some form of foreplay that had her ready for him to take her now, this instant.

But he seemed to be in no hurry as he stroked her skin and kissed her lips, her throat, and once again covered one of her breasts with his mouth. A gasp escaped her as he licked and teased the taut pebble. She squeezed his shoulder muscles, mindless with pleasure. He was fire and she was being consumed by his flames.

Wanting to bring him as much pleasure, she reached between them and grasped his hardness. He hissed a swift intake of breath at her intimate touch.

She stroked him slowly, loving the feel of his velvet-soft skin encasing rock-hard and ready muscle. And then he touched her intimately, moving his fingers against her most sensitive spot.

She tried to maintain her focus on pleasuring him, but as his fingers moved more quickly her intentions disappeared beneath the building tide of imminent combustion.

Her climax shuddered through her, first tightening every muscle in her body and then leaving her weak, gasping and boneless.

Before she could catch her breath he positioned himself between her thighs and entered her. She closed her eyes and reveled in the fact that his body surrounded her and filled her.

He whispered her name just before he captured

her lips with his, kissing her with fervency, with passion unleashed. His hips moved against hers and she wrapped her legs around his back to pull him closer, deeper into her.

He stroked faster, finding a rhythm that once again built up a tension inside her that was both tormenting and exhilarating.

Once again he took her over the edge and at the same time she heard him gasp her name as he stiffened against her in his own release.

She unwound her legs from around him and he rolled to his back next to her. The only sound was of them both trying to catch their breath. Although she couldn't see him in the darkness of the room, she felt his movement against the mattress and knew he'd shifted positions. She turned on her side in his direction.

"That was amazing and totally irresponsible." His breath was warm on her face.

She knew immediately what he was talking about. "I'm not promiscuous, and I'm on the pill," she replied.

"Then I'll just go back to the fact that it was amazing," he replied. "And I haven't been with anyone since Shelly."

Claire was surprised and touched by the admission, somehow honored that she'd been the first woman since his lost love. "Thank you, Bo."

He laughed. "Don't thank me for doing something I wanted to do and would do again anytime of the day or night."

Once again she felt the mattress move and saw the faint illumination of him standing next to the bed. "Get some sleep, Claire. It will soon be morning."

Although she was disappointed that he apparently had no intention of staying with her for the rest of the night, the fear that had chilled her before they'd made love was gone, banished by what they'd just shared and the knowledge that she was safe in his home.

"Good night, Bo," she said, already drowsy as the last of her adrenaline seeped away.

"I'll see you in the morning," he said and then he was gone.

Claire curled up on her side and hugged the pillow where his head had just lain to her chest. She definitely wasn't eager to face the morning when she'd have to fully embrace the frightening thought that somebody close to her, somebody who had been her "secret admirer," no longer wanted to date her, but potentially had murder on his mind.

Chapter Nine

Despite the late night, Bo was awake at seven. He remained half tangled in the sheet that covered him as he thought about the events of the night before.

There was no question in his mind that Claire's secret admirer had gone rabid and was now a real and present threat to her safety.

Thinking about what had occurred between them in the darkness of night sent a surge of warmth through him. Making love with her had been everything he'd imagined and more. The scent of her, the taste of her, was now in his blood, and having her once wasn't enough.

But he knew if they made love again it would only be at her bidding. She was in control of that aspect of their "partnership." He had nothing more to offer her than the here and now, and the last thing he wanted was for emotions to get tangled up and messy and lead to heartbreak for either one of them.

There was no question that he cared about her a lot, but that didn't mean he was willing to ever give his heart to any woman or to Lost Lagoon again.

Claire had a good life here. She loved her work and the people, and she would continue to have a good life here long after he was gone. But first they had to figure out who had tried to take her last night; who possessed a twisted love for Claire that had turned into something dangerous?

Thoughts of her safety pulled him up from the sofa and down the hall to the bathroom. Thankfully before he'd turned his bedroom over to Claire the night before he'd grabbed clean clothes for today.

It took him only minutes to shower, dress and then head into the kitchen to get the coffee brewing. Jimmy wouldn't be up for hours and he hoped that Claire slept in, as well.

While waiting for the coffee, he dug around in one of the drawers at the small desk in the corner of the kitchen and found a new notebook. He carried it and a pen to the table and set it in the center.

Starting today they would not be working from Claire's notebook on Shelly's death. They would begin a brand-new investigation to find the identity of her secret admirer.

He finally sat at the table and curled his fingers around a mug of the fresh brew and thought about their second interaction with Trey the night before.

The lawman had appeared to take everything seriously, including the fact that the perp had obviously been watching Claire's house while they'd been there the first time that night.

The doll and note hadn't been on the porch when Bo had initially arrived, nor had they been there when Trey and his men had first shown up. Whoever had placed the items on the porch had waited until the lawmen had left, indicating that he'd been watching the place the whole time.

The only name Claire had mentioned to Trey in the way of suspects was Neil Sampson, the city councilman she'd dated and broken up with months before.

Bo intended to press her this morning to come up with some other potential suspects. Claire was bright and beautiful and he couldn't imagine fewer than several men being attracted to her. She might be too obtuse or too naive to recognize their friendly smiles as some sort of sick romantic interest.

It was just after nine and Bo was sipping on his third cup of coffee when Claire appeared in the kitchen. She wore a pair of denim shorts and a red T-shirt and brought with her the scent of minty soap and fruity shampoo.

"Sleep well?" he asked and watched her beeline to the coffee.

"Surprisingly well, considering everything." She poured herself a cup of coffee and then joined him at the table. She nodded toward the notebook. "What's that?"

"You said you like notebooks, so that's the one for our new investigation. From here on out I'll be the boss of this operation and the investigation into who killed Shelly has once again become a cold case. We need to focus on your secret admirer."

She held up a hand. "Let me have a couple drinks

of coffee and process the shock of you being in charge before we talk about anything else."

Bo grinned, finding her charming. He was grateful that she obviously had no intention of talking about what had happened between them the night before.

She took two sips of her coffee and then set her cup back on the table. "If I don't get to be boss, then can I still be the official note-taker?"

"Absolutely," he replied and reached out to pull the notebook closer to her. "You told Trey last night that the only person you could think of in your life who could potentially be your secret admirer was Neil Sampson."

"He was the only person I could think of, and actually I can't imagine Neil being my admirer. The anonymous notes and flower thing just isn't his style."

"Maybe he stepped out of his comfort zone to get cutesy in an effort to win you back," Bo relied. He motioned toward the notebook. "His name should go on our suspect list."

She reached across the table to grab the pen and then opened up the notebook to the first page. In neat lettering she wrote "Suspects" across the top of the page and then placed Neil's name on the first line.

"What about your coach friend, Roger?" Bo asked.

She shook her head. "Roger is a good friend and coworker, but he has the hots for Mary Armstrong who works at the diner. He has no romantic interest in me."

"Write his name down anyway," Bo said. "Right now we need to view any man who has any interaction with you as a potential suspect."

She took another sip of her coffee and then wrote down Roger's name. "I hate this. I hate to think of one of my friends being a nutcase who wants to kill me."

Bo knew exactly how she felt. He'd felt the same emotion in the months following Shelly's death. He'd hated that he'd looked at everyone with suspicion, that an innocence he hadn't even known he possessed had been shattered and had never been regained.

He took a drink of his coffee, knowing the next name he was going to throw out would shock her. But he'd played and replayed what she'd told Trey had happened the night before and he still had so many questions that he knew she couldn't answer.

"I think you need to add Eric Baptiste," he said and watched her beautiful blue eyes widen and then narrow in disbelief.

"Why would I put him on the list? He's been like a big brother to me. He saved me last night."

"Did he?" Bo countered. "Did you hear him yell at your attacker like he told Trey he did? Did you hear the sound of your attacker running away?"

She slowly shook her head. "I couldn't hear anything in that plastic bag except the terrified beating of my heart and my own screams." She wrapped her slender fingers around her cup, as if seeking warmth as she gazed at him curiously. "Exactly what are you implying?"

"I'm just wondering if maybe Eric was the person who attacked you and then saved you."

"And why on earth would he do something so crazy?"

"To be your hero," Bo replied. "If he's your secret admirer then he obviously has or had a romantic interest in you. He sees you spending all your time with me and he gets worried that we have something romantic going on so he sets up a scenario where he can save you from the bad guy and you'll see him as a hero, and every woman loves a hero."

She stared at him as if he'd dropped to the table from another planet. "I should be worried that you could actually come up with that take on the situation."

"I've had a lot of time and a lot of coffee to fuel all kinds of thoughts. I even wondered about Mac Sinclair potentially being your secret admirer."

"But he's married," she protested.

Bo raised a dark eyebrow. "That doesn't always stop a man from wanting a little on the side. I know that sounds crass, but the fact is some men cheat."

Claire leaned back in her chair and frowned thoughtfully. "If Mac was leaving me love notes and flowers, then he'd be particularly enraged by me hooking up with you, the man he thinks killed his sister."

"You need to write down both of their names and

then we need to call Trey to let him know that you've thought of more people who might guilty."

"There's one thing I'd like to do today," she replied. "I want to stop in at Mama Baptiste's shop. If I remember right the doll last night was from a kit that she sells to tourists in her shop."

"A kit?"

She nodded. "It comes with a couple of markers, some yarn to make hair and the pins to stick into the doll. They're a silly, harmless nod to voodoo that appeal to people who don't live in the South and think voodoo is still alive and well in all the Southern Gulf states."

"She should be selling pirate stuff since the legend of the town is that pirates once used the area as their stronghold."

"Trust me, she has plenty of pirate items to sell, too. Of course her real business is her herbal skills, and there are people in town who depend on her homeopathic remedies."

"I imagine Trey will be investigating where the doll came from and will talk to her."

"I'd still like to talk to her myself. Besides, it's been a while since I've seen her."

"Okay," Bo agreed. "We'll eat breakfast and then go to her shop."

It was an hour later that they left the house in Claire's car and headed to Mama Baptiste's shop on Main Street. They'd called Trey to give him the list of names they'd come up with over coffee and Trey had vowed to check each man's alibi for the night before.

A bell tinkled as they walked into the small shop, which held enough items that it could have used three times the space. The front of the store had shelves and wall displays with a variety of tourist-type items.

Overhead and throughout the entire store, herbs and roots hung over exposed wooden rafters, apparently used in the magical concoctions Mama Baptiste brewed up for her customers.

She stood behind a counter in the center of the store and Claire made a beeline for the woman who had helped her get through her difficult childhood.

Mama Baptiste was a tall plump woman with long black hair shot through with shiny silver strands. She was clad in a bright yellow peasant-style blouse and a long multicolored skirt that gave her a gypsy aura.

She stepped out from around the counter and greeted Claire with a big, long hug. "I heard what happened last night," she said as she finally released Claire. "Thank goodness you're okay."

"I'm fine," Claire replied.

Mama Baptiste's dark eyes turned to focus on Bo. "Only a foolish or an innocent man would come back here and stir up old wounds. Which are you, Bo McBride?"

Her gaze was so intense it was as if she were looking right into the center of his heart, his very soul. He felt as though he were strapped to a lie detector machine. "Innocent," he replied without hesitation.

She held his gaze for another long moment and then nodded, seeming satisfied. She looked back at

Claire. "You rarely come to my shop so I'm assuming this isn't a social stop."

"Actually, I'm here about the voodoo doll kits you sell," Claire replied.

Mama Baptiste motioned toward a wall display toward the front of the store. "There are the kits, but I can't tell you the last time I sold one. As you know, we don't get many tourists coming through town."

Bo followed Claire to the display and immediately recognized the dolls in the kits as the same kind that had been left on Claire's porch the night before.

He turned back to Mama. "Is there any other place in town that sells these?"

"Not that I know of," she replied. "There aren't many places in town that sell tourist items, although I'm sure that will change once the amusement park is up and running and we actually have tourists wandering in and out of the stores."

"You said you don't remember the last time you sold one of the dolls. Do you keep records that you could look at or keep an inventory list that would tell you if perhaps one was stolen?" Bo asked.

"Bookkeeping isn't my strong suit. I don't keep those kind of records except for my apothecary business." She looked at him apologetically. "Unfortunately, I can't help you with the doll."

Bo was disappointed, but he also knew how easy it would be for Eric to take one of the dolls without his mother ever knowing. For that matter, they hung close enough to the door of the shop that anyone could steal one.

Mama Baptiste and Claire visited for a few more minutes and then left, nearly bumping into Mac Sinclair, who was about to enter the shop.

Mac was shorter than Bo, with the Sinclair dark hair and brown eyes… Eyes that narrowed ominously at the same time his hands balled into fists at his side.

"Well, if it isn't the town's newest happy couple," he said with a half sneer as his gaze locked with Bo's. "Come back to town to find another beautiful, innocent woman you can use and then throw away in the lagoon?"

Bo remained silent, refusing to be baited. Mac turned his gaze to Claire and instantly his features softened. "Claire, what are you doing with this scum? Don't you know that there are people who would be happy to see him dead? I'd hate to see you get caught up in any cross fire if and when bad things happen."

He didn't wait for a reply, but shoved past them and into the shop. Bo stared after him and for the first time in his life he wished he had a gun, because he felt that danger was inching closer with every minute that passed.

"Was that a direct threat?" Claire asked as they got back into her car.

"I don't know if it was a threat or a warning," Bo replied. "I wonder how his marriage is going?"

"What does that have to do with anything?" she asked.

"Mac said you were beautiful and there was a

tenderness in his eyes when he looked at you. You've never had any interaction with him?"

"Just the casual kind. He stopped into George's burger joint about once a week and we'd visit but nothing about him ever gave me the heebie-jeebies." She definitely had the heebie-jeebies now, not just about Mac but about every man in town. Who was after her? Who wanted her dead?

"What do you want to do now?" he asked.

She looked at him with a small smile. "I thought you were boss of this operation."

"I am, but I'm open to suggestions."

"Let's go get an ice cream cone," she said impulsively. "It's not quite as hot today and we can sit at one of the umbrella tables outside and people-watch."

"Is this part of a master plan to identify your admirer or an avoidance of the issue altogether?"

"Maybe a little bit of both," she admitted. She'd love to be able to forget that somebody had an unhealthy obsession with her. She'd love to pretend that she and Bo were partners not just in crime, but also in love.

She froze as she realized the dangerous path her thoughts had taken her. She was falling in love with Bo despite all of her wishes to the contrary. Making love with him last night had not only been a physical need, it had been an emotional one, as well.

She'd just been fooling herself into believing she was in complete control of her emotions where he was concerned. With his gentle kisses to her boo-boos, with that slow, sexy grin of his that heated her through and through and the quick wit that either kept her questioning things or laughing, he'd sneaked beneath her defenses.

"Earth to Claire." His deep voice broke through her thoughts and she realized they had parked in front of the ice cream parlor. "You disappeared on me for a moment there." He shut off the car engine.

"I was just trying to decide what kind of ice cream sounded good," she said with a forced lightness.

Minutes later they sat at one of the small colorful umbrella tables on a small patio just outside the parlor. Claire held a chocolate mint ice cream cone while Bo had opted for a peanut butter blend.

As he licked his cone she tried not to think about how his tongue had felt against her skin the night before. Dammit, she was supposed to be thinking about the possible identity of her attacker and instead she couldn't help herself from thinking about a one-night stand with a man who was certain to break her heart.

She looked out at the sidewalk and sat up straighter in her chair as she saw Roger walking toward them, a wide grin on his face.

"Claire…Bo," he greeted them. "Mind if I join you for a moment?"

"Pull up a chair," Bo replied.

Roger grabbed a chair from another table and pulled it up to theirs and sat. "Claire, I stopped by your house earlier to see if you wanted to meet me at the gym and get in a little workout."

She licked the quickly melting ice cream cone

and then replied, "This is the only workout I have in mind for the day."

Roger leaned forward slightly. "I also wanted to tell you that I did it. I asked Mary out."

"Roger, that's great!" She held her hand up for a high five. "When and where?"

"Day after tomorrow," he replied. "She's off that night and I promised her I'd take her someplace where she would be served rather than her doing the serving."

"Not many fine restaurants to pick from in this town," Bo said.

"We decided to do casual at the pizza place. That's good for a first date, isn't it?" He looked at Claire with a touch of concern.

"It's a perfect choice for a first date," Claire assured him.

Roger appeared relieved. He jumped up out of his chair. "Well, I'll just leave you two to enjoy the rest of the afternoon." He moved his chair back to the table where it belonged and carefully aligned it in place, then waved to them and headed on down the sidewalk.

"There's no way he should be on my list of suspects," she said and then popped the last of the cone into her mouth. It was as if that last bite held more than a little bit of discouragement.

She'd been excited to help Bo clear his name and identify a killer, but she wasn't so eager to do anything to try to find her stalker. She couldn't believe that anyone she had written down on her list of potential suspects was guilty, and she didn't know where else to look for a creep.

"What next?" Bo asked as they got back into her car.

"To be honest, I think I'd just like to go back to your place. I think maybe I need some more downtime to process everything that has happened."

"Whatever you need, Claire," he replied gently and it didn't take long for them to be back at his house.

Jimmy was up and in a chair with the television tuned to a talk show. "Did you solve all the mysteries already?"

"No, we just decided to take the rest of the day off," Bo replied.

"Let Trey and his men do the work," Claire said and sank onto the sofa. She felt oddly vulnerable, with the horror of the near-kidnapping the night before and the realization that she was more than half in love with Bo weighing heavily on her mind.

"In fact, if nobody minds I think I'm going to take a nap," she continued. After the short night maybe a nap was just what she needed to get herself into a better frame of mind.

"Are you okay?" Bo asked in obvious concern.

She got up from the sofa. "I'm fine. I'm overtired and maybe a little overwhelmed by everything. A nap will set me right." She offered Bo a reassuring smile and then headed for the bedroom.

Once there she kicked off her shoes and curled

up in the center of the neatly made bed. She closed her eyes but her mind refused to quiet.

Her thoughts didn't race to make sense of her feelings for Bo, but rather what her attacker had intended for her the night before.

The pins in the heart of the voodoo doll definitely indicated somebody who wanted her dead, but why hadn't the attacker simply stabbed her in the yard or shot her as she'd made her way to her mailbox?

The assailant hadn't wanted her dead by her mailbox. His intention had been to carry her off somewhere. And do what with her? Kill her at another location? Chain her up in some cellar or isolated place where he could rape and beat her before finally killing her?

The note she'd received warning her to stay away from Bo McBride she now believed was a warning from her secret admirer and not some note from a concerned friend or neighbor. And that note and her continuing relationship with Bo had transformed obsessed love into mad rage for somebody.

Who? Who had killed Shelly Sinclair two years ago and who wanted Claire dead now? She finally drifted off to sleep and dreamed of being held in a dark, dank cellar with no hope for rescue.

They stayed in Bo's house for the next two days, their only information about the attack on her coming from Trey. There had been no fingerprints found on the doll, the note or the garbage bag.

He'd checked the alibis of the men on the list Claire had provided with a variety of results. Mac

Sinclair had been at home with his wife. Roger had been home alone, as had Neil Sampson. Eric, of course, had been at the scene.

Basically the investigation was going nowhere, but in the two days she and Bo had spent together their relationship had deepened as their close proximity had been conducive to heart-to-heart talks about their past and present.

She'd also learned when they'd played several games of chess that he was as competitive as she was, that his laughter was often contagious and that he had the ability to make her feel like she was the most special woman on the face of the planet.

If she'd been on the verge of being in love with Bo before, the two days had only intensified her love for him. She had no idea what he felt toward her. It was obvious he was physically attracted to her and that he cared about her well-being.

In any case, it didn't matter what he felt for her, as their time together would eventually end and she'd return to her life with only heart scars to show that he'd once been here.

That was if the person tormenting her was caught, when that person was no longer a danger. She couldn't stay with Bo forever and could only hope that Trey and his men found the guilty party so that she could gain some needed distance from Bo.

Each night when she got into bed, she thought about calling to him to join her again, to make love to her once more, but in the end she denied herself the pleasure, knowing that it would only make things harder on her when it came time for him to say goodbye.

She didn't want to leave the safety of his house and yet felt a restless need to escape the confines. She was accustomed to being out and about town during the days, enjoying the leisure of summer before school began again in the fall.

She was particularly restless when she went to bed on the third night of being cooped up. She'd never considered herself a coward before, but her desire to stay inside was definitely built on the roots of fear and the perverse desire for her admirer not to be able to see her, to get close to her in any way.

Although the mattress was comfortable and the last couple of nights' sleep had found her easily, tonight she stared up at the ceiling as slumber refused to come.

There was little moonlight tonight and finally at eleven thirty, still unable to sleep, she got out of bed and moved the curtains aside to peer into the dark night.

Adrenaline filled her and she suddenly knew exactly what she wanted to do.

Chapter Ten

"Bo?"

He sat straight up at the sound of Claire calling his name. Immediately his thoughts went to holding her in his arms, making love to her again. That was almost all he'd been able to think about over the past three days.

"Yeah?" His voice was deeper than usual, husky even to his own ears.

"Get dressed."

He frowned at her unexpected words. "Get dressed? Why?"

"It's a perfect night for ghost hunting," she replied. "I'll be back in just a few minutes." He heard her soft footfalls returning to his bedroom.

He raked a hand through his hair and then reached in the darkness for the jeans at the foot of the sofa. He'd hoped she'd call to him again, wanting... needing him, but certainly not for a night of ghost hunting.

Once he had his jeans pulled up, he turned on the living room light. He pulled on the white T-shirt he'd had on before going to bed and then sat on the sofa to wait for Claire.

This wasn't exactly what he'd had in mind for a Friday night. If he was going to be awakened by her, he'd hoped for something far different.

She appeared in the living room dressed in a pair of denim jean shorts and a peach-colored sleeveless blouse that buttoned up the front. Her blue eyes simmered with an excitement he hadn't seen over the past couple of days.

"Are you dragging me out of the house in the middle of the night on a wild-goose chase?" he asked.

"Probably," she replied with a cheeky grin. "But from the rumors I've heard, tonight seems like the perfect night to catch a sight of Shelly's ghost walking around the edge of the lagoon."

Bo couldn't help a snort of disbelief. "I don't believe in ghosts," he replied.

"Then you don't want to go?" she asked, obviously crestfallen.

"Nah, I'll go. I'll indulge you in your craziness. If nothing else we'll get out of the house for a little while." He was rewarded with one of her beatific smiles that made him feel bigger, stronger and better than he was. Those smiles of hers could become addictive to him if he allowed it.

"We need to walk," she said. "The sound of any vehicle might scare the ghost off."

"I'll grab a flashlight." He left the living room and went into the kitchen, where he not only grabbed a flashlight from the cabinet beneath the sink but also opened one of the desk drawers and pulled out a pocketknife with a wicked blade.

He'd bought the knife off another kid at school when he was fifteen, then had made the mistake of showing it off to his mother. She'd immediately taken the knife from him and had grounded him for a week.

He'd forgotten about the weapon until the day before, when he'd been digging in the drawer to find a paper clip that Claire had wanted for her notebook.

He slipped the knife into his back pocket. There was no way he wanted to be out in the dark with Claire and not have some form of protection. He'd certainly prefer a gun, but the knife would have to do. Besides, he didn't really expect any trouble.

"We have about fifteen minutes to get to the bushes in front of the edge of the lagoon," she said when he returned to the living room. "Supposedly the ghost always walks around midnight."

"Of course she does," he said drily. "At what other time would a ghost walk the night?" He locked the door and they were on their way, the humid night air wrapping around them. "Does she also rattle chains as she walks?"

His sarcastic comment was met with an elbow to his rib. "Laugh now, Mr. Nonbeliever, at least I have an open mind."

The street was dark between the lamps that marked each block and Bo grabbed Claire's hand, not quite trusting what might be lurking in that darkness. They'd already been ambushed twice; he didn't want to be caught unaware again.

They left Bo's street and crossed to another, moving in the direction of the tip of the lagoon and the swampy area that surrounded it.

The night felt ominous, with wisps of low-lying fog appearing as they got closer to the swamp. The houses they passed were dark, the residents asleep in their beds as most sane people should be. A dog barked, breaking the silence.

Claire moved closer to him and he squeezed her hand, wondering what in the hell they'd been thinking of when they'd decided to leave the house in the middle of the night.

"You know I'm probably the only man on the face of the earth who would indulge you in this craziness," he murmured softly.

"I know," she replied and this time she squeezed his hand tight.

When they drew closer to the swamp, the air smelled of fish and rotten vegetation, a scent that Bo knew was familiar to them both. On stagnant, hot summer days the smell of the swamp permeated the whole town.

The silence of the night also filled with noise as they got nearer to the swamp. Bullfrogs croaked, and splashes created by fish jumping or gators slapping their tails could be heard.

A knot of tension balled up in Bo's stomach. He knew just ahead of them was the stone bench where he and Shelly had met on so many nights. Just behind the bench a long row of bushes created a barrier between safe land and the lagoon ten feet beyond. It was in those bushes that Shelly had struggled with somebody to her death.

While he would always grieve the loss of her as a beautiful woman he'd once loved, he'd also come to the realization that they would have never married.

At the time of her death Shelly had one foot with him in Lost Lagoon and her other foot pointed in the direction of a bigger, more exciting future someplace else.

Had there been another man involved? Had that been the sticky situation that had troubled her before her death? And had she fought with that man that fatal night?

If she'd lived, Bo knew that the vision she had of a life outside of Lost Lagoon would have won in the end. Still, knowing that didn't make being at the place of her murder any easier.

He would have rather lost her to another man than to death. Yes, she'd been his first love, and he'd made the decision when she was gone that she would be his last love.

They approached the bushes on the left side of the bench and heard some giggling coming from the bushes to the right side. Bo shone his flashlight in the faces of three teenage girls who were crouched down.

"Shut off that light," one of them said. "You'll scare away the ghost." Her admonishment was followed by a new round of excited giggling.

Bo turned off the flashlight and crouched down beside Claire. "We've got to be out of our minds," he whispered. She grabbed his hand once again.

"At least we're a little bit crazy together," she whispered back.

The moonlight spilled but a mere sliver of illumination and the low-lying fog was thicker here, making it impossible for him to see Claire's features. She was only a dark form next to him, a woman he would know in any depth of darkness by her heady scent and by the familiar heat of her body so close to his.

Part of him wanted to leave town now, to climb on his bike and finally put Lost Lagoon behind him forever. Claire was getting too deep inside his heart, and he wouldn't allow love into his heart again.

He no longer cared about clearing his name. The odds of them finding out the real killer after two years and without law enforcement's help were minimal at best.

However, the danger to Claire was real and present, and he couldn't leave town until he knew she was no longer at risk. Shelly and her murder would always be a piece of his past that would haunt him, but as soon as this issue with Claire was resolved it was time for him to leave and get on with his life in Jackson.

It was ironic that Shelly had wanted to leave Lost Lagoon and Bo had wanted to stay in the small town where his mother lived and his business thrived. With Claire it was the opposite: she loved her life here in Lost Lagoon and had probably never considered moving away from the job she loved and the people she'd always known all of her life.

It was a lose-lose situation for them that only confirmed to him that he was a man meant to live his life alone. Besides, he wasn't in love with Claire, he told himself firmly. He just cared about her and her safety and suffered a healthy dose of lust where she was concerned.

She was the first person in town who had been kind to him. She was one of the few people who believed in his innocence. She was bright and funny and sexy as hell. It was no great mystery that he was drawn to her.

He heard the teenagers begin to squeal. He and Claire raised their heads above the brush and Bo gasped as he saw a figure appear at the right of the grassy area between the bench, the bushes and the swamp.

It was a human figure, clad all in white from shoulders to toes and with long dark hair just like Shelly's. She appeared to be lit from within as she glided gracefully across the area and toward the opposite side of the space.

"Shelly! It's Shelly!" The teenagers squealed in a combination of excitement and terror. "It's her ghost."

It certainly looked like the ghost of Shelly, but Bo noticed that the woman never turned her face toward them and he caught a glimpse of black sneakers on her feet.

Since when did ghosts wear sneakers? He grabbed

his flashlight and leaped over the brush at the same time the "ghost" reached the other side of the open area and disappeared into the overgrown brush near the swamp's edge.

There was no place for her to go without walking back out. He assumed that whenever she made her walks she waited until anyone who had watched the spectacle went home and then left the cover of the wooded area.

She wouldn't have that same luxury tonight. He took the same route she took and crashed through the woods, his flashlight scanning the area for any sign of her.

She'd be trapped between the swamp and a high rise of land that was impossible to climb. It was a relatively small area to search and Bo wanted to know who was playing such a sick game for the entertainment of giggling school girls.

He shone his flashlight from side to side, expecting to see a white-clad teenager who was pretending to play the role of the ghost of a dead young woman. Instead he found nothing. Nobody crouched beneath thick brush, nobody hidden behind a tree...nothing.

There was no way out and yet she was gone... seemingly vanished into thin air just like a ghost.

"I'm telling you that was no ghost," Bo said to Claire as they began the walk home. "That was a real person pretending to be a ghost."

"Then how do you explain the fact that you didn't catch her? That she totally disappeared?" Claire asked.

"I can't," he said, his frustration obvious in his voice. "But somebody is playing a sick game and I don't like it. I'd love to find out who it is and why she's doing it."

"Yet another mystery to add to the growing list," Claire replied. She hadn't been fooled into believing the "apparition" had been the ghost of Shelly. What she couldn't imagine was why somebody would do such a thing. What was there to gain by pretending to be Shelly, dead and walking at the place of her murder?

She and Bo strolled at a leisurely pace as they started the trip back to his house. "There is a person who got away with murder, a crazy stalker after me and now somebody impersonating a dead woman. The whole world seems to have gone crazy," she said.

"Number one on my priority list is making sure you stay safe and sound," he replied, his voice deep with determination.

Her heart warmed and she reached out to grab his hand. She could walk through life's ups and downs with his big, warm hand wrapped around hers.

Still, she couldn't help but wonder how long this cozy safe haven Bo had provided her would last. Trey and his men had come up with nothing. She couldn't imagine who might be after her.

How long was she willing to put her life on hold, hiding away in Bo's house with fear as a constant, simmering companion? How long would Bo continue to live his life this way?

"You know I can't just stay at your house forever," she said.

"So far I'm not complaining," he replied easily. "I wonder if the ghost walker has anything to do with the new amusement park?" he asked, obviously changing the subject.

"No way. The ghost walker started making her appearance long before the amusement park bought the land to build. Besides, if it was somehow tied to the amusement park then it would be a ghost of a pirate in keeping with the theme," she replied.

"I thought all the ghosts of pirates past appeared at the Pirate's Inn," he said with a touch of amusement.

"That's the rumor. Supposedly old Peg Leg walks down the hallway on the second floor and you can hear his wooden leg as he walks. Then there's Pirate Joey, who is drunk on rum and stumbles around trying to find his ship."

Bo laughed. "Shelly worked as night manager there for years and never saw a ghost, although she used to tell me it was kind of creepy to work the night shift."

"Creepy how?"

"She occasionally heard noises like creaking and thumping. I told her it was probably nothing more than the building settling, but she still got freaked out occasionally."

They headed down the street that was one block over from Bo's house when she noticed the odd illumination that filled the night sky. "What's that?" she asked.

"Looks like something is on fire," Bo replied and squeezed her hand tighter as he pulled her into a fast jog. They reached Bo's street, where his house was in the middle of the block, and Claire gasped in horror.

The street was alive with activity. The town's two fire trucks were parked along the curb in front of Bo's house. A large group of nightwear-clad neighbors had clustered on the sidewalk across the street as flames shot out of Bo's house.

Two patrol cars were also parked on the street as she and Bo began to run toward the scene.

What had happened? Claire's mind raced. Had they left the stove on after dinner and had it somehow caught fire? Had there been an electrical weakness somewhere in the walls that had sparked into flames?

The volunteer firefighters, clad in their yellow jackets, trained hoses on the flames but they appeared to be making little progress at containment. Thankfully Bo's motorcycle was far enough down the driveway to not be in any immediate danger of catching fire or blowing up.

As they got close enough to feel the heat, Trey stopped them. "Thank God you two weren't in there," he said. "I was afraid we'd be looking for charred bodies in the morning."

"How did this happen?" Bo asked, his features grim in the unnatural dancing light of the fire and the cherry swirl of lights from on top of the various emergency vehicles and patrol cars.

"I can't answer that yet. Bob has been too busy working to talk to me," Trey replied.

Bob McDonnel was the fire chief and at the moment one of the men manning the hoses. "He'll be able to tell us more once they get a handle on the fire and he gets a spare minute. Right now they're trying to save your bike and make sure the flames don't jump to the houses on either side."

Claire felt Bo's frustration wafting from him as she stared at the burning house. As vicious and hungry as the flames appeared, she feared there would be nothing left when the fire went out. She was watching him lose his last tie to Lost Lagoon, the house where he'd grown up.

"By the way, where have you two been in the middle of the night?" Trey asked.

"We couldn't sleep so we decided to take a walk," Claire said. There was no reason for Trey to know they'd ventured out to see a ghost walk.

"Convenient that both of you just happened to be gone when the house went up in flames," Trey replied.

Bo stiffened. "Are you implying something?"

Trey hesitated a moment. "Not particularly, just looking at all the options. You have to admit that where you go, trouble seems to follow."

"Have you talked to Jimmy?" Bo asked.

"I haven't had time. I figured he was still at work at Jimmy's Place and not inside."

"I need to check in with him and make sure he

is still at work. I don't have my cell phone with me. Can I use yours?"

Again Trey hesitated, as if not wanting to do anything to help ease Bo's obvious worry. Finally he pulled his cell phone from his pocket and handed it to Bo. "Make it fast," he said grudgingly.

Bo took several steps away from Trey and Claire. "You don't think this is some kind of an accident, do you?" she asked Trey.

"Until I talk to Bob I won't know for sure, but my guess is that somebody was hoping to kill you or Bo or both with the fire."

Claire wrapped her arms around herself as icy chills walked up her spine. Thank God she hadn't been able to sleep. Thank God she'd decided to wake Bo and leave the house for a little ghost hunting. If they had been inside the odds were good that they both would have been overwhelmed by smoke and would have died for sure.

Bo walked back to where they stood and handed Trey his phone. "Thanks. Jimmy is fine and will stay in the apartment on the third floor at Jimmy's Place."

The fire had become less intense and Claire figured it would only be a matter of minutes before the firemen finally had it completely out. At least the frame of the house still stood, but that was small consolation as she thought of the damage within.

Bob appeared near the house and motioned to Trey and Bo. "I'll just stay here," Claire said. "There are plenty of people out and about. I'll be fine. Go talk to the fire chief and see what he has to tell you."

Bo looked around as if assessing the situation, and then with a curt nod he and Trey headed in the direction of Bob. Claire stared at the house, which would be smoke- and fire- and water-damaged. There was no question in her mind that it was a total loss.

At least they had her place to crash at. She would feel safe there as long as Bo was with her. Her chest tightened with emotion. Had this been a murder attempt or a tragic accident of some sort?

Had it been directed at Bo, or her, or both of them? A hysterical giggle rose to her lips and she swallowed it. The problem with hooking up with the man who was half the town's nemesis and gaining for herself some crazy nut stalking her was that when a hit came there was no way to predict exactly who it was directed at.

She suddenly realized that most of the crowd had dispersed, returning to their homes and their beds to sleep for what was left of the night.

A sharp sting struck the back of her shoulder. She swatted at it, accustomed to the gigantic mosquitos that ruled the evening and nighttime hours.

Within seconds she started feeling strange. Cotton began to wrap her brain, making it difficult for her to think. She started in the direction of Bo and the other men, but her legs grew wobbly. All of her muscles relaxed and her eyelids grew too heavy to keep open.

Someplace in the very back of her mind, she knew

she was in trouble. She tried again to take a step toward the house, but instead fell into darkness and knew no more.

Chapter Eleven

"It was definitely arson," a smoke-blackened face told Bo and Trey. Bob swiped at the sweat across his forehead with a soot-colored handkerchief. "The accelerant was gasoline. We found three gas cans on the back porch."

Bo felt as if he had fallen into somebody else's nightmare. He knew there was nothing salvageable about the house or its contents.

All traces of his childhood, anything left of his mother, was gone forever. He had insurance, but right now didn't think he had the heart to rebuild. He felt utterly defeated.

Somebody in this town had taken the life of his girlfriend, the town had spit in his face, and now the one thing he had left here was gone, burned by an unknown adversary.

Bob clapped him on the back. "Sorry we didn't get here sooner. If we'd gotten the call quicker we might have been able to save it."

Bo nodded. "I know you all did the best you can and I appreciate it."

"It's too hot to go in tonight, but I'll be here first thing in the morning to investigate thoroughly," Bob said.

"I'll be here, too," Trey said. He looked at Bo. "No matter what I believed happened two years ago I'm determined to find out who is behind this fire and the attacks on Claire. Personal feelings aside, I intend to do my job to the fullest of my ability."

"I appreciate that," Bo replied. The mention of Claire pulled his thoughts away from the house. He looked to the sidewalk across the street and realized it was empty of people.

Claire! His brain flashed with the beginning of panic. Where was she? He gazed over to where the firemen were loading up their equipment, hoping to see her talking to one of them. But she wasn't there, and the seed of his panic exploded into a full-blown alarm.

"I don't see Claire," he said aloud. He looked at Trey, as if the lawman could magically make her appear. "Claire is missing."

"She's got to be around here someplace," Trey replied. He called her name and Bo did the same, his heart beating a frantic rhythm that he heard in the sudden pounding of his head.

He ran across the street, still shouting her name, but there was no answering reply. He raced toward the fire trucks and asked each and every man he met if they'd seen Claire, but nobody had noticed her.

He ran back to where Trey stood in his front yard. Trey finished a call on his cell phone. "I've just called in every member of my team to check out the men who were on the list she gave me and to start a search for her. I'm going to check around back and make sure she didn't just wander around to see the damage and maybe got hurt."

"I'll come with you," Bo said, praying that there was an easy answer for Claire's absence and not the one that horrified him most.

He'd been distracted. He'd left her alone and now he feared that her stalker had taken advantage of the situation and had somehow gotten to her. If that was the case it was all his fault, and the thought of anything bad happening to her nearly brought him to his knees.

They reached the backyard, each of them calling her name. Desperation made Bo feel like everything was happening in slow motion. His backyard was not so big that he couldn't see in the glow of his flashlight that she wasn't there.

Somehow, someway, her stalker had taken her and nobody had any idea who that person might be. Bo's heart ripped in a hundred pieces as he could only imagine her fate at the hands of a monster.

"This is a first," Trey said from the back porch. "I've never seen an arson fire where the arsonist was so neat." He shone his flashlight on three gas cans, a small one, a medium and a larger, all neatly aligned side by side.

"Usually, a fire-starter empties the accelerant on the target, then tosses the empty can aside," Trey said.

Bo stared at the cans, his mind racing. Silverware

neatly aligned next to a plate…a chair placed in precise position under an umbrella table…and now three gas cans neatly arranged in a row.

"I know who it is," he said to Trey. "Claire's stalker is Roger Cantor. It's Roger Cantor," he repeated with urgency.

Trey frowned. "Coach Cantor?"

Wild panic filled Bo. "He set this fire and now he has Claire."

"How do you know?"

"I just do. Where does Roger live?" Every muscle in Bo's body tensed. Trey couldn't get the information to him fast enough. Every moment counted, every second might mean the difference between life and death.

"Over on Cypress Street. I don't know the exact address, but it's midblock between Pirate's Lane and Oak Street. He has a basketball goal in his driveway. Come on, I'll drive you there," Trey said.

The two men raced for his patrol car and once inside Bo fought an overwhelming sense of disaster. Had the fire been set as some sort of diversion? If so he had played right into Roger's hand. He'd taken his eyes off the prize and allowed Claire to be stolen away.

Trey couldn't drive fast enough to suit Bo, who kept his focus out the window checking for signs of somebody hiding or Roger carrying Claire away.

If Roger harmed a hair on her head, Bo would kill him. Trey would finally get his desire to see Bo locked up in prison. Bo didn't care. He had nothing to lose but Claire, and the thought of her gone forever was too much for him to bear.

Trey pulled into the driveway of Roger Cantor's house, a neat ranch that was dark. What if Roger was sound asleep inside and had nothing to do with Claire's disappearance? What if Bo had jumped to the wrong conclusion and they were just wasting precious time by coming here?

A million doubts coupled with a rage of adrenaline filled him as he and Trey approached the front door. Trey knocked as though he meant business, the rapping on the wooden door loud enough to wake the neighbors.

"Roger, open the door," he shouted.

Bo noticed Trey had his hand on the butt of his gun, obviously ready for anything they might face. What they faced was no reply. No lights went on and nobody came to the door.

Trey knocked again and Bo moved to the garage door, where small windows allowed him to see the dark shape of a car parked inside. "His car is here," he called back to Trey.

"He's not answering the door," Trey replied.

"Break it down," Bo exclaimed. His imagination filled with visions of Claire tied up and gagged in the basement or in a bedroom while Roger waited patiently for Trey and Bo to eventually go away.

"I don't have that authority," Trey replied. "I can't break into someplace based on your gut instinct alone. Let's check around back."

The two men raced around the side of the house,

where there was a patio and a sliding glass door, but no indication that anyone stirred inside.

Bo's heart beat so hard it felt as if it could explode out of his chest at any moment. He knew Roger was their man. His proof was in those neatly aligned gas cans.

He looked around and saw a large outdoor vase with flowers. He had to get inside and he understood Trey's being bound by the law, but he wasn't bound by anything except his driving need to find Claire.

He picked up the vase and threw it with all his might at the sliding glass door. The glass shattered and Trey cussed. Bo went in through the busted door, carefully avoiding the last of the shards of glass that clung to the frame.

Trey followed after him, muttering curses as he pulled his gun. They entered the neatest kitchen Bo had ever seen, a sign of the obsessive-compulsive disorder Claire had told him Roger suffered and that he'd seen signs of himself.

Trey motioned for Bo to stay behind him as they left the kitchen and entered the living room. They turned on no lights, using only their flashlights to illuminate their way.

Find Claire. Find Claire. It was a two-word mantra that echoed over and over again in Bo's head as they cleared each room in the house.

It was only when they entered the master bedroom that Bo's calculated guess that the stalker was Roger was definitely realized. Taped to the wall above the neatly made queen-size bed were dozens of photos of Claire.

Claire on her bicycle, Claire sitting on her front porch, there was even a photo of her taken through her bedroom window. Thankfully she'd been wearing a robe. They were slices of her life captured forever to feed a sick mind.

What frightened Bo most was that there were three photos of Claire and him together, eating ice cream, leaving Mama Baptiste's shop and getting into her car. In each of those pictures Claire's face had been x-ed out with a bright red marker.

"Here's your proof," Bo said to Trey. Bo whirled around and tightened his hand on his flashlight. "It's obvious they aren't here. Does Cantor own any other property in town?"

"I don't know. I'll have to check it out. I'll let all my officers know that we're looking for Cantor," Trey said.

There was no basement in the house, but there was an entire town to search. Bo's head screamed in pain and fear. "I'm heading out on my own," he said to Trey when they reached the front door.

Trey took his cell phone out of his pocket. "This is my personal phone. I've got another cell phone that is for official business. Take it so that if you find her you can call me, or if we find her we can get in touch with you."

"Thanks." Bo put the phone in his jean pocket and then with a grim nod to Trey, he took off into the night.

He ran in no particular direction, knowing only the driving need to seek and find, praying that it wasn't already too late. Roger could have her held captive in any old shed, in one of the abandoned shanties on the other side of town. Hell, he could have her stashed away in her own home.

With this thought in mind, he raced in the direction of Claire's place, slowing his pace only when he could scarcely breathe and was stabbed by a stitch in his side.

Claire…Claire… His heart cried out for her. A vision of her face filled his brain. Her beautiful eyes, that crazy mop of golden curls, the smile that made him feel wanted and loved, it all haunted him now.

He should have kept her tight by his side while the fire blazed at his house. He'd provided a perfect opportunity for Cantor to strike by being distracted, by allowing Claire to wander away from him.

My fault, he thought in agony. Just like Shelly's murder had been his fault. He should have gone to meet her that night despite being sick. If he'd just gotten out of bed and gone to the bench at the lagoon's edge, she wouldn't have been murdered.

If he'd just kept hold of Claire's hand, she wouldn't be gone now and in the hands of a man whose obsessive love had transformed into a killing hatred.

When he finally reached Claire's house he was shocked to see Eric Baptiste sitting on the front porch. "Nobody is here," he said to Bo.

"What are you doing here?"

"I ran into Deputy Griffin. He told me Claire was

missing and potentially kidnapped. Claire gave my mother a spare key to this place years ago. I got it and went inside and checked it out. There's no indication that anyone has been here and I'm sitting here all night to make sure nobody else tries to get inside."

It was the longest speech Bo had ever heard Eric make. "Have you checked out any of the abandoned shanties?"

"Not specifically, but I've been here awhile and haven't seen anything unusual. No lights or sounds coming from any of the old places."

Dead end. A new desperation crashed down on Bo. Where to go? Where would Roger go? Was it already too late? Had he already killed Claire? Desperation turned to horror as a new thought filled his head.

He turned and ran, not bothering to say goodbye to Eric. He couldn't speak with the emotion that clogged his throat. Was it possible? Was Roger sick enough to do such a thing?

The sound of his feet hitting against the road surface was the only noise he heard. He was so deep inside his head he heard nothing else, smelled nothing as he focused on getting to the place where Shelly's body had been found floating in the swamp.

Roger had to not only hate Claire, but Bo, as well. Would he have his revenge on both of them by making Bo face losing somebody he cared about and tossing her body in the same place where Shelly had been found?

Pine cleanser.

Claire tried to remember if she'd cleaned the shanty with pine cleanser that day. She usually bought the cleanser with money Mama Baptiste gave her. It was cheap and even though the plywood walls had gaps in them, despite the fact that her mattress was thin as paper and sometimes there was electricity and sometimes there wasn't, she liked to keep things clean when she could.

She couldn't remember the last time she'd seen her father. It had been at least two weeks since he'd shown his face at the shanty.

Mama Baptiste had tried to tell her that her daddy wasn't a bad man, he was a sick man. Alcohol had not only poisoned his body but had addled his brain, making him forget that he had a daughter, forget that somebody might need him.

Her bed felt particularly hard tonight...like concrete. She tried to shift her position and realized she couldn't move her legs. Brain-fogged, she thought she was trapped by the favorite blue blanket she always slept beneath.

She tried to reach a hand down to untangle herself, but her hands were bound together. That's when full consciousness slammed into her.

The fire at Bo's...the sharp sting in her back...and then nothing. She'd been drugged and now she was someplace she shouldn't be, a place that smelled of pine cleanser and a faint, lingering odor of sweaty socks, a place that screamed of danger.

She was afraid to open her eyes, scared of what

she'd see, of who might be in the alien space with her, even though she sensed that she was alone.

She finally worked up the courage to open her eyes. She couldn't begin to formulate a plan of escape unless she knew exactly where she was.

With her brain still slightly fuzzy, she took in the concrete floor beneath her and the concrete walls that surrounded her on three sides. It was only when she saw the round drains in the floor and the row of showerheads that she realized she was in the boys' shower room at the school.

Her ankles were tied together with a strong rope, as were her wrists. Just as she'd sensed, she was alone in the brightly lit room.

She managed to roll to a sitting position and then scooted across the floor until her back was against the farthest wall from the opening, an opening where sooner or later she knew she would meet her "admirer."

The severity of her situation sank fully in and tears sprang to her eyes. She was in trouble...life-threatening danger, and she worked her ankles and wrists, twisting and turning in an effort to get free of the ties that bound her.

However, there was no give to the rope and the knots held tight as a rising panic filled her. She had no idea how long she'd been unconscious and even if everyone in town was searching for her there was no reason for anyone to believe she was being held in a shower in a school that was closed for the summer.

She could scream, but she knew it would be no

help. The school building was surrounded by parking lots and playgrounds and she was in a concrete room. Nobody would hear her scream except the person who had brought her here.

She told herself to stay calm, but a terrifying panic rose up the back of her throat, making her feel nauseous. Under the circumstances she just couldn't help the terror that shuddered through her body.

"Hello, Claire." The familiar voice came from the darkened entrance to the shower.

"Hello, Roger," she replied, somehow unsurprised that it was him. Her brain had subconsciously made the connection when she'd realized she was in the shower room at the school. "What's going on?" She kept her voice calm as if this was all some sort of familiar game they played as they so often played basketball in the gym.

"You ruined everything, Claire. I had it all planned out in my head. It was all going to be so perfect and then you ruined it all and now you have to die."

Claire instantly realized she wasn't dealing with the man she'd played ball with, the man she'd shared so many lunches with both at school and in her home. Gone was the warmth in his eyes, replaced by a fire of simmering rage. His entire body was tensed and his hands balled into fists in a rhythmic pattern of one…two…three and then pause. One…two…three and then pause.

"What did I ruin, Roger?" She knew the only

hope she had of somebody finding them was to try to keep him talking as long as possible.

Time. At the moment time was her best friend. She needed as much of it as she could possibly get to give somebody an opportunity to find her.

"Everything," he screamed, his voice echoing in the shower chamber as the cords of his neck popped out.

Claire fought the terror that ripped through her at the raw hatred in his voice. Calm. She had to stay calm. "You said you had a plan. What was the plan, Roger?"

He swiped his hands down the sides of his face, took several steps into the shower and then leaned with his back against the opposite wall and stared at her. The rage in his eyes dissipated and was replaced with a soft look of dreams to come.

"I've loved you for a long time, Claire, but you know I had some issues I needed to work on. I worked hard to make my OCD manageable, and it was all because I wanted to be a good man for you. I finally got to the point where I felt comfortable starting my courtship."

"You were my secret admirer," she said. "You left the flowers on my porch. Why didn't you just come right out and tell me how you felt?"

"Because I had a plan. I needed to follow the plan," he replied impatiently, as if she were slow-minded. "The flowers and notes were just the beginning. I wanted you to believe your secret admirer was thoughtful and romantic."

"I did," she replied fervently. "I was charmed by the gifts left on my porch. I couldn't wait to meet the wonderful person who left them for me." It was a lie. Maybe she'd been charmed after the first couple of times, but the whole thing had become creepy and stalkerish.

"In my plan the next step was to invite you for pizza one night, just a casual meal that we'd share together."

"Like you'd planned to do with Mary," Claire said.

Roger snorted. "I was never interested in that insipid woman at the diner. She meant nothing to me. It was you. It was always you." He frowned. "I want you to hear the whole plan, so don't interrupt me again or I might lose my temper."

He began to pace, taking three steps in one direction and then three steps in the opposite direction. He didn't look at her when he spoke again.

"We'd have a casual pizza date and you'd start to see me not just as a coach, not just as a friend, but you'd feel a little romantic attraction toward me. After a week or so we'd have another date, this one at Jimmy's Place. We'd order the steak special and laugh and the chemistry would be amazing between us. At the end of that date we'd share our first kiss."

He paused a moment in his pacing and closed his eyes, as if imagining the kiss in his mind. Creepy-crawlies shot through Claire as every nerve inside her recoiled.

She realized she wasn't dealing with obsessive-compulsive disorder, but rather something deeper and darker. Roger was in a place in his head where she didn't want to go.

His eyes shot open once again and he stared at her. "The kiss would be magic and you'd know then that we belonged together. After that it would be you and me sharing ice cream at one of the umbrella tables or walking hand in hand down the sidewalks. On our third official date we'd have dinner at my place and that night we would make love."

He began to pace again. "After that it would be a whirlwind romance. Within two months we'd be engaged and in four months we'd be married and you'd never leave me. That was the plan, Claire. We were supposed to be together forever. Then you screwed it all up by hooking up with a bad boy on a motorcycle."

"Bo and I aren't hooked up," she said desperately. "We're just friends and I've been working with him to find out who killed Shelly Sinclair. He really means nothing to me."

"Liar!" Once again Roger's angry voice bounced off the walls. "I see the way you look at him. I see the way he looks at you. That's not friendship, it's lust and want and it wasn't supposed to be that way. You were supposed to be all mine."

"I didn't know the plan, Roger," she protested. "I didn't know that you were my secret admirer. It's not too late for us. We could have that pizza date and see how things play out."

"It is too late." He drew in a deep breath, his eyes

dead and empty of emotion. "You're tainted and now you need to be killed."

"Did you set the fire at Bo's to kill us both?" *Keep him talking*, she thought in desperation. Surely Bo was tearing up the town in an effort to find her. *Find me, Bo. Please find me*, her heart begged.

Roger nodded. "Do you know how many people die in their sleep from smoke inhalation? That was my first idea, but I had a backup plan. If the two of you managed to escape the fire, I figured there might be enough of a commotion around that I'd be able to grab you." He offered her a self-satisfied smile. "A smart man always has a backup plan."

"What did you give me to knock me out?"

"A little antianxiety medication. Trust me, over the years I've learned a lot about the doses and effects of those kinds of drugs. I should have drugged you that night at your mailbox."

"Why do I have to die?" Tears misted her vision and she consciously willed them away, not wanting him to see any weakness.

"Because I can't live my life and see you every day and be reminded of the plan that was supposed to make me happy for the rest of my life. You would just be a painful reminder of my failure and of your betrayal."

"Roger, you won't get away with this. You were already on a list of suspects after you attacked me at my house. They'll be looking for you and you don't have an alibi."

"I'll make one up," he said easily. "I'll tell them I

often have trouble sleeping and come here to shoot hoops. They won't be able to disprove it."

"If you kill me here, there will be evidence." Her desperation peaked as she realized she was running out of time.

"I don't intend to leave a blood trail. The only evidence they'll find is a damp towel and several loose basketballs in the gym, furthering my alibi."

"Then how do you intend to kill me?" she asked, knowing that despite the ropes she'd fight him in any way possible. Somehow, someway, she wasn't going to make it easy for him.

"I'm going to strangle you, Claire, and then I'm going to carry your limp, dead body to the lagoon and leave you where Shelly was left. I think the sheriff will find it a strange coincidence that Bo McBride came back to town and for a second time was intimately involved with a woman who is found floating in the lagoon."

A mind-numbing horror swept over her, not for herself, but for Bo, who would be forced to relive his traumatic past. He wasn't in love with her as he'd been with Shelly, but Claire knew he cared about her.

"I'm going to the gym now to set things up to substantiate my alibi. When I come back, then it's time…time to rid myself of you."

As he left the shower room the tears Claire had fought so hard to hold back released. She would never hug a little student again. She would never see Bo again, feel his arms wrapped around her, taste his hot, sensual lips.

The happily-ever-after she'd dreamed of with a special man ended here, in a pine-scented boys' shower room with a man who had gone to great lengths to end her dreams and end her life.

Chapter Twelve

Bo reached the lagoon and fell to his knees in relief when he found no body floating in the water. He didn't know how long he remained on the ground, emotions raging out of control and leaching physical strength from him.

The clock that had been ticking so loudly, so frantically in his head since the moment he'd discovered Claire gone had gone silent. His relief at not finding her here was short-lived, for he feared they were too late. She'd been gone too long.

He hadn't heard anything from Trey, letting him know that nobody else had been successful in locating Roger and Claire, and she'd been gone for well over two hours.

He couldn't stanch the emotion that erupted from the depths of him. Tears filled his eyes and raced down his cheeks, tears he couldn't stop as his heart felt her absence.

It wouldn't be long before the morning sun would peek over the horizon, making the search a little easier, but also bringing with it a sense of hopelessness he didn't want to face.

He wanted her found before the sun came up. He needed to hold her in his arms before a new day broke. Where could they be? Apparently Trey had found no record of any other property Roger owned, otherwise he would have called Bo.

He finally managed to pull himself to his feet and walked over to the stone bench and sank down. His brain was in utter chaos, making it impossible for him to think clearly as he swiped away the tears.

Had Roger borrowed or stolen a car? Was it possible the two of them were no longer even in the town of Lost Lagoon? If that was the case then they could be anywhere within a two-hour drive.

Think, Bo demanded of himself. If he were Roger Cantor where would he take Claire? Roger Cantor, seemingly nice guy, battling OCD and beloved coach at the school. Nerves jumped inside him.

The school! Bo knew Roger had a key to the gym door. It would be a familiar place, somewhere he would feel safe. Bo jumped up from the bench, his heart beating so fast he was half dizzy.

He took off running, hoping he was right and that it wasn't already too late. The school was on the opposite side of town, but Bo had no intention of pacing himself.

He ran all out, as if he were a high school athlete trying to make the track team. He ignored cramping calf muscles and the stitch in his side, focused only on getting to the place where Claire might be with her monster.

Although he knew deputies were out searching, he didn't see anyone as he raced to the only place that suddenly made sense. It had to be the school, and if they weren't there, then he was lost and defeated.

Would he be in time or would he find Claire injured or, even more heartbreaking, dead? He couldn't think about that now, for if he did he'd lose it, and he needed to keep it together now more than ever before.

He hadn't been able to save Shelly. He needed to save Claire and that need drove him forward faster than he'd ever run in his entire life.

When the school came into view, it appeared to be a dark, uninhabited fortress. No lights glowed at any of the windows. He finally slowed his pace to catch his breath as he moved from the front of the building to the back.

There were no cars in the parking lot, but Bo knew that Roger was physically fit enough to carry Claire anywhere he wanted her to be.

By the time Bo reached the back door that led into the short hallway and the gym area, his breathing had returned to normal despite the race of his heart and a new adrenaline spike.

He reached out for the door handle and caught his breath as the door clicked open. They were here! He stepped into the dark hallway and looked just ahead where the gymnasium was dark, as well.

Then he heard her scream. Every nerve in his body jumped in response as he tried to discern where the scream had come from. He took several steps forward and peered into the boys' locker room. The main area, where the students had their lockers and changed clothes was dark, but a light shone in the shower area.

Bo surged forward at the same time he heard Claire scream again. He entered the shower to see Claire on the floor and Roger on top of her, apparently trying to strangle her.

Bo roared with rage as he threw himself forward. At the same time Roger turned and rolled to his feet to meet Bo's attack.

She's alive, the words screamed in the back of Bo's head. But he knew she wouldn't be for long if he didn't manage to somehow neutralize Roger.

The two men met in the center of the shower and began throwing punches at each other like a couple of bar brawlers. Bo was taller but Roger was stockier. Roger was driven by self-preservation, but Bo was driven by the need to protect Claire at any cost.

Roger landed a punch to Bo's stomach that momentarily took Bo's breath away, but he recovered by slamming an uppercut into Roger's chin. Roger stepped back and shook his head, but then charged Bo once again, this time using his leg in an effort to sweep Bo's feet out from beneath him.

Bo managed to stay on his feet but Roger slammed him with a fist to the eye. The only sound in the shower was the slap and punch of hits and the grunts and heavy breathing of the two men as they battled.

Bo realized the two of them were evenly matched

when it came to throwing punches, and that was when he remembered the knife he'd tucked into his pocket earlier in the evening.

He managed to gain enough distance from Roger to pull out the knife and open it. But the moment he held it out before him Roger surprised him with a perfectly delivered kick that sent the knife out of his hand and sliding across the concrete floor.

Both men lunged for the weapon. Roger reached it first and threw his body over Bo's. Bo grabbed the hand that held the knife pointed at his heart.

"No!" Claire screamed, making the first sound she'd made since Bo had appeared.

Bo's entire body trembled as he fought to keep the knife from plunging into his body. "You should have stayed away from Lost Lagoon." Roger's breath was hot and fetid on Bo's face. "You should have stayed away from her."

"Roger, your plan was stupid and would have never worked because I secretly thought you were nothing but a creep," Claire said fervently. "I would have never dated you or belonged to you in any way. You're nothing to me, Roger, and no matter what your plan you would have never been anything to me."

Her words had power, for Roger weakened and in a flash Bo managed to grab the knife and roll on top of the man. Bo held the knife to Roger's throat.

Bo had never entertained a homicidal thought in his life until that moment. He wanted to kill Roger. He wanted the man dead for touching Claire in any way, for terrorizing her and trying to take her away forever from Bo.

His hand at Roger's throat shook slightly. Roger's eyes were huge as he stared up at Bo, waiting for death to be delivered.

"Bo." Claire's voice cut through the killing rage that threatened to consume him. "You aren't a killer," she said softly. "Don't become what some people still believe you are."

Bo's hand shook harder as he fought an internal battle, the need to destroy the man who'd sought to destroy Claire and the desire to stay true to the man he believed himself to be.

He finally tossed the knife aside and delivered a punch to Roger's face that rolled Roger's eyes up in the back of his head and rendered him unconscious.

Bo instantly got up, grabbed the knife once again and hurried to where Claire was huddled in the corner. Neither of them spoke as he cut through the rope around her ankles and then through the binds around her wrists.

It was only when she was free that he pulled her up off the floor and into his arms. He held her tightly, as if afraid that somebody might try to rip her away from him again.

She began to cry, her face burrowed against his chest as tremors raced through her. He caressed a hand up and down her back, murmuring soft assurances that she was safe and nobody would ever hurt her again.

At the same time he kept an eye on the unmoving

Roger. He had no idea how long the man might stay unconscious and he didn't want to go another round with the athletic coach.

Claire's tears finally ebbed and he released her. "I need to call Trey, but first I want to make sure that Roger doesn't come to and have more fight left in him."

He picked up the ropes he'd cut off Claire and used them to tie Roger's wrists together. The man still appeared to be completely out.

Once that was done, he grabbed the phone Trey had given to him to use and by searching the contacts found the number to call to reach Trey on his official business cell phone.

With the phone call made, Bo led Claire out of the shower enclosure and into the main locker room, where he turned on the lights and then pulled her to sit next to him on one of the wooden benches between the walls of lockers.

"I didn't think anyone would ever find me," she said, her voice still holding a tremor that spoke of the terror she'd suffered.

"Thank God I figured it was Roger before I left the scene of my house." He explained to her the careful alignment of the gas cans that had been the clue he'd needed.

"Trey and I checked his house first. One wall of his bedroom was filled with pictures of you. He's apparently been stalking you for a long time."

Claire shivered and he wrapped an arm around her shoulders and pulled her closer against him. "When we didn't find you at Roger's place, Trey and I split up," he continued.

He told her about going to her home and finding Eric there, then his mad dash to the lagoon, afraid that history would repeat itself.

"That's what he intended to do with my body," she said. "He was going to strangle me and then take me to the lagoon and leave me floating in the water where Shelly had been found. Thank God you thought about the school."

She shook her head. "I was stupid. I allowed myself to be vulnerable."

"I was the stupid one. I let the fire distract me and left you vulnerable. But it's over now, Claire. You don't have to be afraid anymore."

She looked up at him, her blue eyes filling with tears once again. "But you lost your house because of me."

"No, I lost my house because of Roger," he countered. "Besides, I have insurance and it will all get sorted out."

Trey and several of his men came into the locker room. "Claire, I'm glad to see you're okay," he said and looked around. "Where's Roger?"

"In the shower," Bo replied.

"Did you kill him?"

Bo stood to face the nemesis who had done everything in his power two years ago to see Bo behind bars for the murder of Shelly. "I had a knife at his neck. I had every opportunity, every reason in the world to kill him, but I didn't because that's not who

I am. It's never been who I am. I wasn't a murderer two years ago and I'm still not a killer."

Trey motioned his men to the shower enclosure and then he pulled a notepad and pen from his pocket. "I need to get initial statements from both of you."

Bo gazed at Claire's face. Exhaustion played on her pale features. He looked back at Trey. "Very brief statements," he said. "We can come into the station sometime later this afternoon for complete statements, but right now it's almost dawn and everyone is exhausted."

True to his word, Trey kept his questions brief and few and then re-pocketed the notepad and pen. "We can finish things up later."

Bo gave Trey back his cell phone and then together he and Claire walked out of the school, leaving Trey and his men to deal with Roger and sort out the crime scene.

A faint glow of pinks and oranges lit up the eastern sky as they walked toward Claire's house. Morning birds began their songs as the weight of exhaustion fell on Bo's shoulders.

"You know you're welcome to crash at my place for as long as you need to," Claire said.

"I'll take you up on that offer at least until I figure things out. Right now I'm so tired I can't think."

She grabbed his hand. "I'm glad to be so exhausted. It means I'm still alive. I stared madness in the eyes tonight and I'll never be able to thank you enough for riding to my rescue."

He squeezed her hand. "I just couldn't imagine what would happen if I lost my boss," he said with forced lightness.

"After tonight you get to be the boss all the time," she replied.

He laughed. "I have a feeling after a couple of hours of sleep you'll feel differently about that."

"You're probably right," she agreed.

By that time they had reached Claire's house, where Eric still sat on the front porch. He stood. "You're okay?" he asked Claire.

"I'm okay," she replied.

Eric nodded, handed her the spare key to her house and started to walk down the sidewalk toward Mama Baptiste's place. Claire called after him and he turned to face them. "Thank you," she said.

"No problem," he replied and then turned and continued to walk away.

Claire opened the door and Bo followed her inside, closing and relocking the door behind him. "Do you want anything?" she asked. Her features were drawn and a deep exhaustion showed through the dull shine of her eyes.

"Sleep," he replied. "We both need some sleep."

"There's no reason for you to sleep on the sofa. You can sleep with me in the bedroom."

He knew it was no invitation for anything but rest and perhaps the need of a woman who had been to hell and back and simply wanted the comfort of somebody sleeping next to her, hopefully keeping nightmares at bay.

In the bedroom she pulled the blinds closed and then collapsed on the mattress. He did the same and cuddled her in his arms. She snuggled against him, a perfect fit against his body.

She released a weary sigh and was asleep almost immediately. With the sweet scent of her hair and the smell of her perfume permeating the room, Bo also fell into a deep, dreamless sleep.

CLAIRE WOKE FIRST, with Bo spooned around her backside. She didn't move, not wanting to break the utter peace she felt with his body so close against hers and one of his arms thrown over her.

He had been like an animal protecting his mate last night in the shower stall. He'd fought for her with a ferocity that had awed her.

Love for him swelled up inside her, chasing away any bad memories that might attempt to intrude. She loved his strength of character, his courage in agreeing to remain in town and face the people who had condemned him as a murderer.

She loved his dry sense of humor, the way his lips slowly slid upward into a smile that almost felt like a precious gift. She'd thought herself to be falling in love with Bo, but realized now there was no falling… she was deeply in love with the man. He was everything she wanted for her happily-ever-after and yet she knew deep in her heart it wasn't meant to be.

He had given her no indication that he felt the same way about her. Sure, he'd saved her life, but he'd promised to be her bodyguard.

Partners with fringe benefits, that's the way he thought of them, not lifelong lovers sharing a future together.

She wasn't even sure if he'd stay in town beyond tomorrow. The call to return to his life in Jackson would be stronger now. His home here was gone, the danger to her had been vanquished, and she had a feeling the will to clear his name had been more her idea than his.

A glance at her clock let her know it was just after noon. She should get up but she was reluctant to stir, afraid that she'd awaken Bo. Besides, these moments being held in his arms would someday be precious memories she'd carry with her for the rest of her life. She closed her eyes once again and just existed in the warmth and security of Bo.

"Are you awake?" His warm breath caressed the back of her neck.

"Wide awake," she replied and opened her eyes. He pulled his arm from around her and she sat up. "I've just been thinking about having to go into the station today and relive what happened last night." It was a little white lie, but she couldn't very well tell him she'd been thinking about how much she loved him.

He sat up and swung his legs over the side of the bed at the same time he raked a hand through his hair. "I'll be right beside you and hopefully it won't be too rough on you. At least you lived to tell the tale."

"Thanks to you," she replied.

"Besides going into the station, I've got a ton of things to take care of today, the first being buying some clothes and then getting in touch with my insurance company and figuring out what comes next."

She wanted to ask him what did come next. Was he staying or going? She almost hoped he decided to go back to Jackson. She'd be left with a heart broken in two, but there would be no more opportunity for her love for him to grow even deeper.

"Let's get the interviews with Trey over with first," he said. "Then I can bring you back here and I'll take care of some of my own business."

"Sounds like a plan," she agreed and stood. "I'm going to shower and change clothes and then you can shower. Unfortunately I don't have anything that will fit you for you to change into."

He grinned, that sexy smile that only managed to begin the breaking of her heart. "I'd worry a little if you did have clothes that fit me. I'm fairly open, but I draw the line at hanging out with a cross-dresser."

Claire threw a bed pillow in his direction and then walked to her closet to grab clothes for the day. Bo left the bedroom and headed for the kitchen, where Claire figured he'd have a pot of coffee ready by the time she'd showered.

Minutes later she stood beneath a steamy spray of water and tried not to think about Bo McBride. Instead she forced herself to go back to the night before and the time she'd spent with Roger.

She would have never guessed him to be a stalker...her stalker. They'd shared a great relationship as coworkers and friends, but she'd never dreamed he had become obsessed with her.

Had she missed telling cues? Had she not noticed something that she should have realized was off between them? She'd never felt any odd vibes coming from him.

It didn't matter now. He would be going away for a long time and the danger to her was finally over.

The scent of freshly brewed coffee greeted her as she stepped out of the bathroom. Bo was seated at her table with a cup in front of him.

"The bathroom is all yours," she said and poured herself a cup of coffee.

"I called Trey and told him we'd be in within a half an hour or so. It's a good thing you still have a landline because both our cell phones are probably melted into ash mounds."

"I kept the landline because cell phone reception is a bit spotty in the house," she replied. She sat at the table as he stood.

"It won't take me long and then we can head out and get the interviews over with." He disappeared into the bathroom.

Claire sipped her coffee and tried not to think about Bo naked in her shower. Drat the man anyway and damn her for allowing him to get so deeply into her heart. She certainly hadn't been looking for love when she'd ignored George and thrown a burger and fries to Bo.

True to his word, he showered and re-dressed in a matter of minutes and then they were on their way to talk to Trey. Claire had thought that emotionally she'd handled the ordeal just fine, but when she had to relive the details of the horrendous night she broke down.

It was only Bo's presence, his hand on hers, that allowed her to get through it all. She then listened to Bo give his statement and finally they were finished.

They swung by Bo's house and she was surprised that the outer shell still stood. The windows had been blown or broken out, the paint was dark with soot, but the good news was that his motorcycle, parked in the driveway, appeared to be undamaged.

"Thank God the garage was full of boxes that I was going to give to charity, otherwise I would have parked inside and the bike would be gone," he said.

"What about a key?" she asked.

He turned off the car and smiled at her. "I've got a spare in a combination lockbox I had welded to the inside of the saddlebag just in case of an emergency." He pulled the keys out of the car ignition and handed them to her. "At least I have wheels to take care of some business. Why don't I plan on being back at your house between six and seven?"

"Okay," she agreed. "I've got a few errands I need to run, too, so I'll see you at the house later."

She got out of the car and got into the driver's seat he'd vacated. Only when he had his spare key in the ignition of his motorcycle and she heard the throaty roar of the engine did she drive away.

Her first order of business was to get a new cell phone. She also needed to stop by the bank and get a new credit and debit card. She'd also have to go to the motor vehicle bureau and get a copy of her driver's license.

Her brain spun as she tried to think of everything that had been in her purse…a purse now burned to a crisp in the fire. If she was lucky she could accomplish everything, stop by the grocery store and pick up a few things, then have a good dinner waiting for Bo's return to the house.

It was five o'clock when she finally got home and unloaded the groceries she'd bought. She'd managed to get everything she needed to do done and had planned a meal of a salad, spaghetti with meat sauce and garlic bread for dinner.

She got the meat sauce cooking and made the salad, and it was only as she set the table for two that she realized how difficult it was going to be for her if Bo stayed here for an indeterminate period of time.

Two plates on the table looked right. Her house was a perfect size for her, but would be an intimate setting with Bo sharing it.

He hadn't mentioned a word about leaving town and she could only assume he intended them to pick up where they'd left off before danger had reached out to her. Could she go back to investigating Shelly's death with him at her side, with him staying in her house?

She suddenly felt vulnerable and far too fragile. She'd never even felt this way when she'd been alone as a child and the darkness of night had been a very scary place.

Bo returned at six thirty, carrying a new duffel bag with new clothes and toiletries and with an energy that filled the house, making it immediately shrink to minuscule size.

"Hmm, something smells good," he said. He walked across the room and tossed his duffel bag into the bedroom.

"And your timing is perfect," she replied with a forced lightness. "It's ready to be served."

"Great. I'm starving. Is there anything I can do?"

"No thanks, I've got it."

He sat at the table and while they ate he told her about what he'd accomplished during the afternoon. She shared her afternoon activities with him and while she did she was struck by the domestic scene created.

They were like husband and wife, coming together over a meal to share the events of their day. The domesticity continued when they'd finished eating and Bo helped her clear the table and clean the kitchen.

This was the happily-ever-after she'd dreamed about when she'd been young. The filling in of a loneliness she'd suffered for most of her life, the sharing of both simple and complicated things. But this couldn't be her happily-ever-after. Even though Bo was the right man, she was the wrong woman in the wrong place.

By the time they sat on the sofa Claire's nerves were completely shot. She turned on the television and stared blankly at the screen. Bo sat next to her, close enough that she could smell the scent of a new sexy cologne, feel the heat of his body radiating toward her.

He would just assume that tonight he'd share her bed and why wouldn't he assume that? She'd opened her home to him, opened herself to him in a way she hadn't intended and now knew she couldn't continue with her emotions in such turmoil.

"Are you okay?" he asked gently after several minutes of silence had passed.

She turned to look at him and to her horror she burst into tears. He instantly reached for her, but she scooted back from him and held up her hands to keep him away.

If he held her right now she wouldn't do what she knew had to be done. If he touched her in any way she wouldn't be strong enough.

"I'm sorry, Bo," she managed to say through her tears. "I thought I could do this… I thought I could have you here with me and it would be no big deal. We'd continue on like we were, investigating and spending all our time together. But it is a big deal because…because I'm totally in love with you." She held her breath and watched the stunned expression sweep over his handsome features.

"That wasn't supposed to happen," he finally replied.

She brushed the tears from her cheeks and drew a deep breath. "I didn't exactly plan it. All I know is I can't do this. I can't spend my days and nights with you as if I'm not in love with you. I can't play at being partners in crime when I want to be partners in life forever."

He frowned and scanned the room, as if lost and trying to get his bearings. He finally gazed at her, a wealth of sadness in his eyes. "I'm sorry, Claire. I don't know what to say."

What he hadn't said, said it all. He hadn't proclaimed his love for her. He certainly didn't appear happy at her pronouncement of her feelings for him.

"There's nothing to say," she replied. "I can't change the way I feel, and I certainly can't make you feel something you don't. You were straight with me from the very beginning. I just didn't realize that I wasn't in control of my own emotions."

He stood from the sofa and walked to the bedroom, where he grabbed his duffel bag and then headed for the front door. She watched him covetously, her heart already beginning to splinter.

"I owe you so much, Claire," he said and opened the front door. "I just want you to know that I've appreciated your help and your belief in me."

"You saved my life last night. I figure we're even." She fought back a fresh wave of tears. "Are you planning on sticking around town or heading back to Jackson?" she asked.

"I think it's time I put Lost Lagoon behind me," he replied. "Goodbye, Claire."

He disappeared out the door and it was only when she heard the roar of his motorcycle that her heart completely shattered and she allowed the tears to overwhelm her.

Chapter Thirteen

Bo headed toward Jimmy's Place, knowing that there was plenty of room in the upstairs apartment for him to bunk there until he decided what he was going to do.

Stay or go?

Claire's confession of love for him had shocked him. He hadn't seen it coming, although perhaps he should have. Driving down Main Street he thought of the softness of her gaze when she looked at him and the passion she'd shown him when they'd made love.

The way her hand had so often sought his, how easily she'd smiled at him, he should have realized she was into him, but he'd been completely blind to the depth of her emotions where he was concerned.

The knowledge of her love weighed heavy on his heart. He'd never wanted her to love him. Love had no place in his life. He was a man marked as a murderer, a man who had decided never to allow himself to love again.

Stay or go?

He parked his bike behind Jimmy's Place. Just

inside the back door in the kitchen area was a set of stairs that led up to the apartment on the third floor.

The apartment door was unlocked, as he'd expected it to be, and as he stepped inside the wide-open space of combined living room and kitchen, memories from a different life slammed into him. There were three doors; two led to bedrooms and one to a bath.

This was where he'd lived when his father had been alive and Bo's Place had been a roaring success. He and Shelly had stolen private time here until his father had passed and he'd made the decision to move back with his mother, who he felt needed him at the time.

He opened the door to the smallest bedroom, knowing that Jimmy had taken up residency in the master bedroom. He tossed his duffel bag on the bed and then headed back downstairs.

He needed a drink. Hell, he needed a hundred drinks to erase the vision of Claire's tearstained face from his head. She was in love with him. He'd broken her heart, so why did his heart ache so badly?

He slid onto the stool he'd sat in the last time he'd been here. Jimmy was behind the bar and ambled toward him. "Glad to see you aren't a crispy critter, and I was happy to hear that Claire is okay," Jimmy said and opened a bottle of beer and placed it in front of him.

"Unfortunately the house is a total loss," Bo said. "I'm sorry about your things."

"It was just things," Jimmy replied easily. "I just

can't believe that Coach Cantor was such a nutcase. By the way, where is Claire now? You two have been like Mutt and Jeff since you came back to town."

Pain shot through his heart and he took a sip of his beer before replying. "She told me she's in love with me." Bo hadn't meant to lay it out like that, but the words just slipped from his mouth.

Jimmy didn't look surprised. "I figured you two had a mutual thing going on. It looked to me like you were as much into her as she was into you."

Bo looked at his friend in surprise. "I was into her. She's sexy and smart, amazingly centered, what's not to like?" Bo paused to take a sip of his beer, the icy liquid tasting bitter. "But you know I have no intention of inviting anyone into my life again on a romantic basis."

"Your mother would be disappointed to hear you say that," Jimmy replied. "Her greatest hope for you was that you'd get married, have a family and find real happiness despite what happened to you here. She hoped your bitterness would eventually disappear."

"I'm not bitter," Bo replied wearily. It was true. The bitterness he'd arrived in town with was gone, and he knew much of the reason had been Claire.

"So, how did you leave things with Claire?" Jimmy asked.

"We said goodbye, you have a roommate for the night and tomorrow morning I'm heading back to Jackson." Just that simply he made up his mind. It was time to leave.

"What about sticking around and finding out who killed Shelly?"

A dry laugh released from Bo. "It was a stupid idea. It's been too long, and without any law enforcement backing there's no point in trying to solve a crime."

"And the killer just gets away?"

Bo shrugged. "He's gotten away for the last two years. For all I know the person who killed Shelly isn't even in town anymore. I need to get back to my life in Jackson and put all this behind me forever."

He took another drink of his beer in an effort to banish the vision of Claire that continued to fill his head.

"What are you going to do about your mother's place?" Jimmy asked. "You know I'm good staying upstairs. I was only there for your mother."

"I know, and I appreciate it. To be honest, I don't know what I'm going to do about the house yet," Bo replied. "Probably rebuild and then sell."

"You know I'll be glad to be your point man if that's what you decide to do. You hire the contractor and I'll see that he and his workers stay in line."

Bo smiled at Jimmy. "I don't know what I would have done without you over the last couple of years."

"And I don't know how I would have survived my childhood and be where I am now without you," Jimmy countered. "Will you still be around when I get up tomorrow?"

"I doubt it. I'm planning on taking off around nine, but you know we'll be in touch often." With Bo still the official owner of Jimmy's Place and now the matter of his mother's burned home, he and Jimmy would always have reasons to remain in close contact.

Bo finished his beer and waved off the offer of another. Exhaustion weighed heavily on his shoulders, or perhaps it was the memory of Claire's tears that made him feel like a broken, soulless man.

When he got back upstairs he got into bed and stared at the dark ceiling, wishing he could stanch the visions of Claire that danced in his head.

She'd be fine without him, he told himself. She was a survivor. She had a job she loved and people who loved her here. Eventually she'd forget all about him. He'd become just a bad memory like her childhood.

She was too bright, too beautiful to be alone for long. She was optimistic by nature and deserved a man far better than him. She'd find that man and live the happily-ever-after she'd dreamed about.

The thought brought him small solace as he finally fell asleep.

He AWAKENED JUST after seven and showered and dressed. Jimmy's bedroom door was closed and Bo had no intention of bothering his friend before he took off.

He made a pot of coffee to fuel up for the long ride back to Jackson and then poured himself a cup and sat at the table. He tried to keep his thoughts schooled to the future and not dwell on what would soon be the past.

Still, he had to admit to himself that, despite the danger, it had felt good to be back in Lost Lagoon. This was and always would be home to him, no matter where he decided to live out the rest of his life.

By nine o'clock, juiced up on caffeine, he slung his duffel bag over his shoulder and left the apartment. He stowed the bag and then climbed on the motorcycle and headed down Main Street.

Everything had gone down so fast, so unexpectedly, with Claire the night before. He hadn't really gotten the chance to thank her for being his friend, for wanting to be his partner, and more important, for believing in him.

Her unwavering belief in his innocence had healed some wounds, had given him back his dignity and made him realize it didn't matter what people in Lost Lagoon thought about him; he knew what kind of man he was, and that was enough for him to move forward.

He'd had no intention to see Claire again, but found himself parked outside her house. Just a quick goodbye, he thought as he climbed off the bike.

She opened the door before he knocked, apparently hearing the arrival of his motorcycle. She allowed him inside and then backed away from him. "I figured you'd be halfway to Jackson by now," she said.

"I'm getting a late start and I didn't want to leave town without telling you once again how much I've appreciated your support." His words sounded stiff and he felt tongue-tied.

Maybe this would have been easier if she didn't have on the turquoise T-shirt that so perfectly matched her beautiful eyes. Maybe goodbye would have been easier if she didn't look so beautiful with the morning sunshine glinting in her hair and a look of soft vulnerability on her features.

He laughed suddenly as he realized he hadn't stopped for a final goodbye. He hadn't wanted one last conversation with her before he left town.

Her eyes widened at his laughter and she took a step backward, as if he might be losing his mind. "Bo, what are you doing here?"

He took several steps toward her, his heart beating faster. "I thought I came by here for a final goodbye, but now that I'm here looking at you, I realize I came by to tell you I love you."

She stared at him in disbelief and he took another step toward her, knowing that what he said next would the most important words he would ever say to a woman, that this was a chance at true happiness that so far had been elusive to him.

"I don't want to go back to Jackson. Despite all the odds against me here, Lost Lagoon is where my heart is…and I believe it's because you are here."

She didn't appear happy; rather, she looked confused. "But what about your life, your business in Jackson? How would you live, how would you survive, here in Lost Lagoon?"

"I can break my lease on my rental home and

stay here with you until we rebuild the house. My manager at Bo's Place in Jackson has hinted more than once that he would be interested in buying the business from me if I ever decided to sell." He took another step toward her, pleased that this time she didn't back away.

"As far as making a living here, I still own Jimmy's Place." Her eyes opened wider and he continued, "Nobody in town knows that I didn't sell out to Jimmy. Money isn't an issue if I stay here, but there's only one reason I would decide to stay and you gave that to me last night when you told me you loved me."

"You didn't exactly appear happy when I told you how I felt about you," she replied, her eyes still holding wariness, but also a faint shine of hope.

Bo walked forward until he stood so close to her he could lean forward and take her lips with his. "You shocked and awed me last night when you told me you were in love with me. I'll admit, my first instinct was to run. I'd sworn to myself that I'd never allow anyone deep in my heart again, but somehow, someway, you got in so deep I can't imagine living my life without you. I love you, Claire, and I'd be all kinds of fool not to stay and see if there's a happily-ever-after for us."

The wariness was gone from her eyes and instead he was bathed in the love that poured from her. "Are you going to kiss me now?" she asked impatiently.

He laughed and pulled her into his arms and kissed her with all the love, all the passion that burned in his soul for her. They might not have been able to clear his name yet, but the love that filled his heart was more than enough for him to know true happiness.

"Does this mean I get to be boss again?" she asked once the kiss had ended.

He laughed again. "I think that issue will continue to be one that's negotiated on a regular basis. Right now I'm boss and I'm going to kiss you again."

"Fine with me." She barely got the words out of her mouth before his lips took hers again.

Bo knew it wouldn't be easy to stay and face the people who still believed he was responsible for Shelly's death. But never had Lost Lagoon felt more like home than at this moment, with Claire in his arms.

This was where he belonged, and this was the woman who owned his heart. Hopefully Shelly's murderer would eventually be found, but in the meantime he had a happily-ever-after to give not only to a woman who had earned it, but to a woman who held his own forever happiness in her hands.

* * * * *

"Be careful," Melissa said.

Electricity shot through her hand and up her arm where her fingers connected with James's skin.

"What?" He spun to face her.

Her breath caught in her throat and she struggled to focus on her words. "Be careful. If this man suspects you're back looking for a missing SEAL, you could be in as much danger, if not more."

Before she could withdraw her hand, he captured it in both of his. "Worried about me?"

"Of course. I wouldn't want anyone else to be hurt in the course of this investigation."

"Just anyone?" He drew her into his arms.

Her hands resting on his chest, she sighed. "Okay, yes. I'm worried about you."

"Why? I'm a big boy. I can take care of myself."

"I'm sure our missing friend thought the same."

NAVY SEAL
JUSTICE

BY
ELLE JAMES

MILLS
BOON®

Published in Great Britain 2015
by Mills & Boon, an imprint of Harlequin (UK) Limited,
Eton House, 18-24 Paradise Road, Richmond, Surrey, TW9 1SR

© 2015 Mary Jernigan

ISBN: 978-0-263-25304-7

46-0515

Harlequin (UK) Limited's policy is to use papers that are natural, renewable and recyclable products and made from wood grown in sustainable forests. The logging and manufacturing processes conform to the legal environmental regulations of the country of origin.

Printed and bound in Spain
by CPI, Barcelona

Elle James, a *New York Times* bestselling author, started writing when her sister challenged her to write a romance novel. She has managed a full-time job and raised three wonderful children, and she and her husband even tried ranching exotic birds (ostriches, emus and rheas). Ask her, and she'll tell you what it's like to go toe-to-toe with an angry three-hundred-and-fifty-pound bird! Elle loves to hear from fans at ellejames@earthlink.net or www.ellejames.com.

This book is dedicated to all the brave men and women of our military forces who dedicate their lives to protecting our freedom. A heartfelt *thank you*!

Hooyah!

Chapter One

Cowboy, you're the only person I can trust.

Those words had echoed over and over in James Monahan's head since he'd received the call at two in the morning, thirty hours ago.

He'd been at the Raging Bull Ranch for only three days, getting to know his new boss, billionaire Hank Derringer. He had been familiarizing himself with other members of Covert Cowboys Inc. and the assets available through Hank's elite organization. The billionaire had an extensive arsenal of weapons, a computer system that would make the FBI and CIA green with envy, and some of the most decorated heroes the United States had known working for him.

Hank hired only the best. All of the members of Covert Cowboys Inc. had been raised on farms or ranches, where they'd learned the value of hard work, honesty and caring for people and animals. They'd learned of truth and justice and had proved themselves, each in his or her own career field. Whether risking their lives in the military, FBI or other law enforcement agencies, CCI agents were highly respected and fully capable of defending themselves or others.

Honored to have been recruited by Hank, after having quit the Navy SEALs to spend the past two years working as a ranch hand, he'd been happy to get away from the sadness of living on the ranch where his father had died.

Jim had made the tough choice to leave the Navy and his SEAL brothers to take over his father's responsibilities as a foreman on the Triple Diamond Ranch, while his father fought and ultimately lost the battle against cancer.

Once his father was gone, Jim left the ranch that held so many memories of the only other member of his family. The ranch had been the only home he'd known and a place he felt he could always come back to.

Not anymore. Every day with his dying father had been like ripping another piece of his heart out. When the end finally came, the pain the man had suffered in silence was gone. And so was the last member of his family. After the funeral, Jim severed all ties to his past. He'd received and accepted a job on the other side of the state and determined to insulate himself from caring about anyone.

Three days after being hired by Hank, his first assignment with the Covert Cowboys Inc. had fallen into his lap with the call he'd received from Cord Schafer, or Rip Cord, as his Navy SEAL teammates had nicknamed him. Contact with Rip reminded Jim that he was not truly alone in the world. He had his brothers in the SEALs. Men he cared about and would do anything for.

"I made a mistake," Rip had said. "I got a friend involved in something I'm working on. Now I'm afraid she'll be a target. These people play for keeps. If they suspect she knows anything, they'll kill her. Now that I've contacted her, I can't get hold of her to call her off. I'm supposed to meet her at the Shoot the Bull Bar at ten at night in two days. You remember the place?"

Jim remembered. He'd spent more than one evening drinking with his brothers after a hard day of training on the river. "What do you want me to do?"

"She's picking up a packet at the post office in Biloxi

between nine and ten in the morning in two days. Keep her and the packet safe. I'll contact you both when I can. Things are getting hot. I might have to go dark."

"Rip, what did you get yourself into?"

"Gotta go. It's not safe. I'll contact you as soon as I can." The line went dead and Jim stared at his cell phone.

Jim had gone directly to Hank, requesting time off, feeling bad about asking when he'd just started his job with CCI.

Hank not only granted him the time to pursue his friend's request, but he'd also declared the appeal for help an official CCI assignment and offered the full gamut of CCI technology and human resources for Jim's use.

That had been almost two days and 750 miles ago. Now he stood in the lobby of the Biloxi, Mississippi, post office waiting for a woman to access the box number Rip had given him. When exactly she'd arrive, he didn't know. Nor did he know what she would look like, or what to expect once she showed up.

Jim arrived a few minutes before nine o'clock with a box full of paper and a roll of tape. For a full hour, he pretended to struggle with packing and taping the box. Then he'd fiddled with the automated postal machine printing a shipping label to an old address he hadn't lived at in ten years.

Still the woman hadn't arrived. As ten o'clock rolled around, he'd about given up on her. He could purchase only so many stamps before the staff at the post office or any of the bad guys Rip had alluded to caught on that he was stalling.

As he tucked another sheet of stamps into his back pocket, the door to the post office opened and a woman dressed in a bright floral dress, a wide-brimmed bright red hat and huge, dark sunglasses walked in. Her lips were painted the same shade as the hat, and what he could see of the hair beneath the hat was a silvery shade of gray. She carried a large white satchel-style purse over her arm.

Something about the way she carried herself—her back straight, her shoulders squared and the tilt of her chin—caught his attention. Though a little thick around the middle and bosomy, she was attractive.

In Biloxi, where gambling was legal and a huge boon to the economy, the woman could have been just another tourist there to try her hand at the slot machines. Or she could have been an upper-class Southern lady who lived in one of the plantation-style mansions lining the coast.

For an older woman, she walked with the strength and determination of a younger, athletic one. Jim studied her in his peripheral vision as he stood at a counter, pretending to address an envelope.

If she was an older woman, which he was beginning to doubt, her skin would be more wrinkled and little lines would have formed on her lips. And where were the age spots that went along with the gray hair?

Jim's instincts kicked in and he studied the other people who'd come in shortly after the woman with the red hat had arrived. The post office was bustling with patrons. Many were housewives with children in tow. Others were businessmen or women there to drop off baskets of mail or to stand in line to send mail to other parts of the world.

The woman in the red hat wasn't there to mail a package. She wasn't carrying letters or a box. If Jim wasn't mistaken, that was a key she held in her hand.

MELISSA BRADLEY STEPPED into the Biloxi, Mississippi, post office and paused a moment to let her vision adjust from the bright outdoors to the dim interior. The large round sunglasses she wore to hide her eyes and much of her face didn't help her vision. The interior of the post office appeared darker than it actually was.

The broad-brimmed bright red hat and gray wig covered her deep brown hair. Her outfit was complete with a gaudy floral print, wraparound dress and sensible, low-heeled red shoes. She could be any senior citizen in town to gamble at the casinos.

In her hand, she clutched a key to a post office box. The key had arrived in the mail two days ago at her apartment in San Antonio, Texas.

Melissa had just gotten home from a tiring day of conducting background checks on individuals and looked forward to a long soak in her bathtub. When she'd found the letter among the advertisements for steam cleaning and coupons for pizza, she'd checked the postmark. The only person she knew in Mississippi was Cord, and he never wrote to her. He always called or texted her.

Excited to get any word from the boy she'd grown up with and called her brother, she'd torn the letter open and a key had fallen out onto the floor. With the key had been a single sheet of paper with the words *NEED HELP* written in bold capital letters across the top. Below were instructions to pick up a package at the Biloxi, Mississippi, post office between nine and ten o'clock in two days. She was to arrive in disguise, collect the package and meet him at the Shoot the Bull Bar outside Stennis at 10:00 p.m. the following evening. At the bottom of the page were the initials *C. S.*

Cord never asked for help. For the most part, he rarely contacted her. His life in the Navy SEALs kept him busy and often out of the country on dangerous deployments. For him to reach out to her, he had to be in dire straits.

Between major assignments at her job with the FBI, Melissa had called her boss, told him she had a family crisis and needed to take some time off. She'd hopped in her bright red pickup, driven all night to Biloxi and spent the next day gathering what she thought she might need in the way of a disguise before her rendezvous at the post office.

Now as she stood in the bustling, busy post office, she wondered if her layers of disguise were overkill. Cord had played pranks on her as they'd grown up together on neighboring farms in Ohio. Was this an elaborate hoax? If so, she'd have words for him.

But something inside her told her it wasn't a hoax, and she kept her eyes open for anyone who looked in any way suspicious as she worked her way through the building to the rows of post office boxes.

No one followed her, but there was a man standing at a counter addressing an envelope. He was big, somewhere between six feet two or four, had dark hair that hung down to his collar and wore a Texas Rangers baseball cap. It was the smoldering dark eyes that were at that precise moment following her that made her look at him twice.

The hairs on the back of her neck rose. She located box 1411. As she slipped the key into the lock, she turned her head enough to catch the big guy staring at her.

Committed to opening the box, she twisted the key and pulled open the door. Inside was a large, thick envelope. She took it out, slipped it into her purse and closed the box.

Then she turned and walked by the big man, making note of his face, eye color and the shape of his chin and lips in case she had to have a forensic artist draw a picture of him.

As she stepped out the door into the bright sunlight, a car pulled up in front of the building. Two men, dressed in black jeans and T-shirts, wearing dark sunglasses, hopped out. They hurried toward the entrance, and her, at the exact moment the man she'd passed in the post office exited the building behind her.

Melissa forced a smile, performed an abrupt right turn

and walked quickly away from the door, praying the men weren't actually aiming for her.

Unfortunately they were, and they followed. She'd parked the car she'd rented a block away, just in case. Now she wished she'd parked in front of the building. She'd already be in it and speeding away.

That was, if her stalkers didn't make a grab for her and try to force her into the car that had been easing through the parking lot of the post office, matching her pace.

Melissa walked faster. Knowing she wouldn't make it to the rental car soon enough, she turned right again and headed for the café on the backside of the post office. If she could make it there, she might be able to slip in and get out another way.

A man and woman were walking ahead of her in the same direction. She ran to catch up and clapped a hand on their shoulders. "Oh, there you are," she said. "I thought you were going to wait for me."

They turned with startled looks at her.

The man pulled the woman into the circle of his arm. "I'm sorry, ma'am, do I know you?"

She laughed, glancing over her shoulder.

The two men in black were right behind her and the café was to her right.

"Sorry. I thought you were someone else. My bad." She smiled and shot to the right, making a beeline for the café's front door. As she entered, she yanked off her sunglasses and called out, "Where's your bathroom? It's an emergency."

The waitress at a table pointed to the back of the building. "Back left corner."

The door opened behind her.

Melissa didn't turn to look back, making a run for the bathroom. Once inside, she thanked her lucky stars it had a sliding lock on the main door and a small window at the back. Quickly, she stripped out of the hat, wig and floral dress. Beneath it, she wore a pair of stretchy biker shorts and a thin jacket with a hood. She pulled a small drawstring backpack out of her satchel, along with a pair of tennis shoes. Stuffing the large envelope into the backpack, she traded shoes and climbed up onto the toilet seat. The window was small, but she had fit through smaller.

A loud knock made her bite back a scream. Her pulse hammered against her ears, muffling the next rap on the door. Based on the heavy-handed taps, she'd bet her red shoes the men who'd been following her thought they had her cornered.

Leaving the satchel with the dress and shoes hanging on the back of the stall door, she balanced on the lid of the toilet tank, levered herself through the window and dropped onto a large azalea bush below the window.

Pulling the hood up over her head, she took off at a slow jog, trying to put as much distance as she could between the café and the men inside. Staying close to the shadows of buildings and bushes, she hurried down a secondary street, afraid to go back for her rental car in case the men who'd been chasing her caught up to her.

A shout behind her made her turn back. The two men in black jeans had spotted her and gave chase.

No longer trying to appear casual, she sprinted toward the next street and started to run across when a motorcycle slid to a stop in front of her.

The rider pushed back the facemask on the helmet, exposing the piercing dark eyes of the man she'd seen watching her inside the post office. "Get on if you don't want those guys to catch you."

She bolted around him and kept running down the sidewalk. Thanks to the man on the motorcycle slowing her escape, the men who'd been chasing her on foot were closing the gap.

Motorcycle man revved his engine, bumped up over the curb and drove on the sidewalk, racing up behind her. Melissa ran faster, her lungs burning with the effort.

He kept pace with her, swerving to miss a woman who'd stepped out of a building. "Cord sent me," he called out. "Get on."

Not sure what to do, but quickly running out of steam, Melissa glanced behind her. One of the men stopped running, reached into his jacket and pulled out a pistol.

In that split second, Melissa made her decision. She hopped onto the back of the bike and grabbed the man around the waist. "He's got a gun! Go! Go! Go!"

A loud bang exploded behind her and a bullet pierced the no-parking sign beside Melissa's head. She ducked, pressing herself into the biker's back, hoping the men behind her were really crummy shots.

The motorcyclist jerked the handles to the right, sending the bike off the sidewalk and out onto the street. He swerved to miss an oncoming car and twisted hard on the throttle. The front tire of the bike left the ground and bounced down again. The back tire gripped the road and they shot forward.

The dark sedan that had followed her in the post office parking lot leaped out of a side street, fishtailing around to fall in behind them.

Her arms squeezing around the man's middle, Melissa glanced back. "They're catching up!" she shouted.

"Hold on!" he called out.

Her arms already holding tight around the man, her body moved with his as he leaned low into a swift turn, taking a corner so fast, the back tire skidded sideways.

The vehicle following them tried to take the same corner at the same speed and didn't make it. They started out okay, but once the car started turning, the back end spun around and kept spinning until the vehicle had completed a 180-degree turn, facing back in the opposite direction.

The time it took the car to circle around in the middle of the street gave the biker enough of a head start to turn at the next corner and again at another corner. He doubled back three blocks over, switching in and out of narrow streets until Melissa was sure they'd lost their tail.

Her biker didn't slow until they were deep in the heart of Biloxi. He pulled into a building with a shadowy parking garage before he stopped.

Now that the shooters and the dark sedan weren't chasing her, Melissa had time to rethink her decision to climb onto the back of the motorcycle with a complete stranger. Especially now that he had taken her into a dark, deserted parking garage. He could easily kill her and take the packet she'd gone to all that trouble to retrieve.

As soon as her rescuer stopped, Melissa hopped off the back of the bike and backed away. "Who are you?"

The man swung his long leg over the bike and stood, towering over Melissa. He pulled the helmet off his head, shook his head to clear the dark hair out of his face. He set the helmet on the seat, his intense gaze skimming over her figure. "I'm James Monahan. Cord sent me to look after you."

"How do I know that? You could be another one of the guys trying to kill me."

"You could take me at my word." He shook his head. "I'm guessing that isn't good enough."

She crossed her arms. "Not hardly."

"Cord said you'd be picking up a package and that the possession of what's inside might make you a target."

Her eyes narrowed. "Did he say who would target me?"

"No."

"That still doesn't tell me why you're involved. How do you know Cord?" she shot at him. The man was too damned good-looking, and the way his eyes skimmed over her body made her feel deliciously exposed. Not a feeling she wanted at a moment when she should be hiding from would-be killers.

"Rip and I used to be on the same SEAL team."

She raised her brows. "Used to be?"

"I left active duty two years ago. I haven't had much contact with the team since."

Her shoulders sagging, Melissa adjusted the straps of the backpack on her arms. "So you don't know what this is all about?"

"Not really."

"Well." She glanced around. "Thanks for helping me."

"You're welcome."

Melissa turned and walked down the ramp toward the exit.

"Hey," Jim called out.

Melissa turned.

"You didn't tell me your name."

She smiled. "I didn't, did I?" She resumed her march toward the exit.

The motorcycle revved behind her. Before she reached the street, Monahan pulled up beside her. "Need a lift?"

She shook her head, continuing down the ramp to the entrance. "If it's all the same to you, I'd rather not be seen on that motorcycle. If those guys see it, they'll home in and start shooting again."

"Good point. Where are you staying?"

She twisted her lips into a half smile. "Can't tell you."

"And if you did, you'd have to kill me?"

"Something like that." She waved. "I'll see you around." Melissa stepped out onto the street and walked as fast as she could in what she hoped was the direction of the hotel where she'd left her other clothes. If she was going to meet with Cord the next day, she had work to do to throw others off.

Half a block later, the ex-SEAL was still following her. She stopped and faced him. "Are you going to follow me all the way to my hotel?"

With his visor up, his grin was clearly visible. "Yes, ma'am."

Melissa rolled her eyes. "Fine. You can give me a ride."

"What if I don't want to now?"

"Are you always this aggravating?" she asked.

He nodded. "Only when the girl is pretty." He tipped his head. "Get on. I promise to take all the back roads through town."

She eyed him again. "My instincts tell me you could be as dangerous as those other men."

"I can be, when I need to be." His lips curled in a sexy smile. "You should trust your instincts when I tell you that, though I can be dangerous, I'm one of the good guys."

Tingles of electricity radiated across Melissa's arms as she climbed onto the back of the motorcycle. "If you're one of the good guys, we're all in trouble."

"Damn right," he agreed.

He was far too sexy to be a good guy. And she'd do right to remember that.

Chapter Two

Jim dropped the woman at the hotel she indicated and drove away, circling around to hide behind a bush nearby.

Not five minutes later, a taxi drove up and the woman climbed in.

Jim followed the cab to another hotel five miles away, staying far enough back that his quarry wouldn't detect him. At the second hotel, Rip's female friend got out and went inside.

Jim waited a good fifteen minutes until he was convinced she was at her actual hotel, then he drove the motorcycle back to the dealership where he'd "borrowed" the bike for a test drive. The salesman had a contract ready, but he told the man that, though he liked the bike, he wanted to think about the purchase overnight. He drove off the lot in the bold black truck Hank had given him to use for as long as he needed.

As soon as he was away from the bike dealer, Jim called Hank.

Hank answered on the first ring. "Were you able to make contact with Schafer's friend?"

Jim smiled, recalling the woman in the floral dress and later wearing the bicycle shorts, her arms and legs wrapped around him on the bike. His groin tightened. Those legs had been fit and contoured like a runner's. And her arms had been surprisingly strong. "Yes, I was able to make contact."

"Who is she?"

"I don't know," he answered honestly. "She wouldn't give me her name."

"Where is she now?"

"I left her at her hotel."

"You left her at a hotel?" Hank asked. "If she doesn't trust you enough to tell you her name, do you think she'd trust you to leave her at her hotel?"

"Hank, you hired me. Do you have faith that I know what I'm doing?"

"Of course I do. But she's female. Women can be wily."

Jim chuckled. "I know. I stuck around long enough to see her get into a cab. I followed the cab to the hotel where she's really staying. And, yes, she's wily. I'm on my way back to the same hotel to check in."

"Jim, I have news on my end."

He sobered, stiffening at the tone in Hank's voice.

"Yeah?"

"Got word today that a SEAL from Special Boat Team 22 disappeared today during a routine training exercise on the Pearl River at the Stennis Space Center complex in Mississippi."

Jim's knuckles tightened on the steering wheel. "Did they say who?"

"I'm sorry to say it was Cord Schafer."

"Damn."

"I've had Brandon Pendley, our computer guru, hacking into every system he could access to learn more. There isn't any more information concerning the disappearance.

"Brandon has also been working on another assignment. I had him hack into the SEAL SBT-22 personnel records. He's pulled a few virtual strings, forged some signatures and got you back on active duty with your old team, should you choose to accept the assignment as such."

Jim's chest squeezed hard. The toughest decision he'd made in his life was to leave his SEAL brothers on SBT-22. To go back into the unit would be like a dream come true. "And what assignment is that?"

"Find and help Petty Officer First Class Cord Schafer."

"And when this mission is over?"

"I can pull enough strings to make it permanent, or you can continue to work with CCI." Hank paused. "It'll be your choice."

For a long moment, Jim forgot to breathe. Once he'd been discharged from the Navy, he'd thought he could never go back. In his heart, he'd made the right decision. His father had needed him more than the Navy, and he'd stayed with him to the end.

No regrets.

Now his life was being handed back to him. All he had to do was accept it. Taking a deep breath, he filled his lungs and gave his answer. "I'll do it."

"Good. Now get back to our girl. Learn all there is to know about her and why Cord chose her to retrieve that packet. If you can, find out what's in that packet."

"I'm on it." Jim drove back to the hotel he'd left the woman at, marched up to the desk, gave a description and explained he'd found her cell phone and wanted to return it.

The young man behind the desk tipped his head, his eyes narrowing as Jim described her. "Was she about five foot five or six, with dark brown hair and brown eyes?"

"Yes," Jim said.

"Wearing biker shorts and a jacket?"

He nodded. "That's the one."

The young man shook his head. "Sorry, sir. She came in, called a cab and left fifteen minutes later."

MELISSA WAS STILL congratulating herself for having ditched Jim Monahan at the second hotel. She'd taken another cab back to her actual hotel, changed into cutoff shorts and a T-shirt and then hit the road, driving the hour and a half back the way she'd come toward Stennis Space Center. There in the backwater community of southern Mississippi, Cord and the SBT-22 team of SEALs trained themselves and others on riverine warfare.

That night at ten she was supposed to meet with Cord at the Shoot the Bull Bar and pass the packet of information to him. She wanted to be in place at the bar, not as a patron, but as a waitress. In order to do that, she'd have to convince the owner to hire her.

The night before, she'd swiped a Mississippi license plate from a truck parked outside a building a couple of blocks over from her hotel. She'd installed the plate onto her own truck, replacing the Texas plates.

Using her smartphone's GPS, she located the bar outside Stennis, drove directly there, parked her bright red truck out front and climbed down. At two o'clock in the afternoon, the front door was open, but the bar was empty except for a rotund man in the back, stocking the shelves with bottles of booze.

"Excuse me," she called out.

"Bar's closed until five," the man said without turning around.

"I'm not here for a drink."

Turning, the man stared at her with a frown. "If you're here to sell something, I'm not buying."

"I'm not selling anything." She smiled as she crossed the sticky floor to the bar in the back. "I'm looking for a job."

He turned his back on her. "I got all the waitresses I need," he called over his shoulder as he continued to stock the shelves.

"Yeah, but you don't have me."

The man straightened and wiped a towel over his sweaty brow as he faced her again. "And what makes you so special?"

"I'll work for tips only."

His eyes narrowed. "You think you're good enough you can afford that?"

She tilted her head, letting a smile slide across her face. "I'm that good."

He sucked in a breath and let it out. "I don't need no drama with the waitresses I got. I'm not hirin'."

"One night, that's all I ask. I get along well with others and I don't like drama, either. What will it hurt? I'm strong, a quick learner and I can take care of myself." She held out her hand. "My name's Melissa Bradley. But you can call me Mel. I can even help you finish stocking the shelves, if you like."

For a long moment, the man stared at her and the hand she held out. Finally he took her hand and gave it a firm shake. "There's another box in the storeroom on the floor by the door. Bring it out and set them up on the shelf beneath the counter."

She nodded. "You got a name?"

"Eli Vincent. I'm the owner of this dump."

"Nice to meet you, Mr. Vincent."

"Call me Eli."

Mel nodded. "Eli."

Eli nodded toward the back. "Well, get to it."

"Yes, sir."

Mel spent the rest of the day stocking shelves, cleaning glasses and mugs, and scrubbing the stickiness off the floor and tables. By the time five o'clock rolled around and the first customers trickled in, the place looked and smelled cleaner and Mel's back was sore from pushing a mop for over an hour.

Eli tossed something at her and she caught it neatly in her hand.

"What's this?"

"Waitress uniform," he said and went back to work scrubbing the bar.

Mel held up a skimpy powder-blue tank top with *Shoot the Bull* written across the front. "Seriously?"

"You wanted the job, that's the uniform," he said.

"Okay, then." She marched into the bathroom, pulled her T-shirt over her head and dragged the tank top on. It was a size too small and displayed more cleavage than it covered. Melissa tugged the garment, stretching it as much as it would go, before squaring her shoulders. If it got her the job and the chance to meet with Cord, she couldn't complain. Now all she had to do was wait on customers until Cord showed up at ten that night.

"CHIEF PETTY OFFICER James Monahan reporting for duty, sir." Jim stood at attention in front of Commander Paul Jacobs in his office at the SBT-22 headquarters building on the grounds of Stennis Space Center. He'd stopped at the Air Force Base in Biloxi with the full printout of all his military records he'd spent an hour reproducing at a local office-supply store. With his records, he had the orders Hank had forged to get him back on active duty and assigned to SBT-22. Calling ahead to the offices of his old unit, he'd determined the uniform of the day and he'd gone directly to Keesler Air Force Base Clothing Sales, where he'd purchased the uniforms he'd needed and gave the seamstress a hundred-dollar tip to sew on patches as he waited. Dressed in a brand-new uniform, he'd gone to the personnel office on base and had his ID card made. It had taken hours waiting in lines, but he'd gotten through and left Biloxi headed east by early afternoon.

Driving onto the grounds of Stennis Space Center

brought back many memories, good and bad. One thing he'd learned in all his years on active duty, going back was never the same as your first time there, no matter where you were going back to.

Commander Jacobs was a freshly promoted US Navy commander who'd earned his place on the SBT-22 team by training as a junior officer with SBT-12 in Coronado, California. From what Hank was able to tell him, the man had deployed to the Middle East six times. He was a decorated SEAL, having earned the Navy's Bronze Star for significant achievements in Afghanistan. He led by example and was respected for his hard work, determination and intelligence.

The man tossed Jim's orders on the desk. "Whose butt did you have to kiss to be reassigned to active duty? And why now?"

Jim had expected pushback from the commander. Any SEAL leader worth his salt would question the timing and the selection of a SEAL being transferred onto his team. Especially with one man missing during a live-fire exercise.

"Sir, I chose to leave the Navy for a short time, during which I helped my father through his struggle with cancer. My father passed over a month ago." The pain of his loss still hurt, but Jim refused to let it show. He squared his shoulders and stood at attention in front of the man he'd call Commander, should he be allowed to stay. Commander Jacobs had that call to make. If he chose to fight the assignment, Jacobs could cut Jim off before he had a chance to investigate Cord's disappearance.

Jacobs rose from his chair and walked around the desk. He stopped in front of Jim and looked him square in his eye. "Were you or were you not a friend of Chief Petty Officer Cord Schafer's?"

Jim stared ahead, his back ramrod straight. "Sir, yes, sir."

"Have you or have you not heard that we lost Schafer today during a live-fire exercise?"

"Sir, yes, sir."

"After two long years playing civilian, you show up on the day Schafer disappears. Just how am I supposed to react to having you arrive on my doorstep waving orders to assign you to my unit?"

"Sir, with suspicion and doubt, sir."

"Damn right." Commander Jacobs stuck his face in Jim's. "Monahan, you are officially on a thirty-day probation. If you step one foot out of line during the next thirty days, you will be off my roster and out of my unit so fast you won't know what hit you. If you threaten any of my men, I will take you down." Jacobs stepped up to Jim toe-to-toe. "Do you understand?"

"Sir, yes, sir!" Jim shouted.

"Now get the hell out of here. Report to duty at zero-six-hundred, ready to work the flab off your post-civilian body."

Jim popped a salute, performed an about-face and marched out of the office.

As he exited the commander's office, he passed by the desk of the commander's assistant, Seaman Randall.

"Chief Monahan." The seaman stood and held out his hand. "I'm Seaman Randall. Do you have quarters assigned?"

"Not yet."

"For now, you can stay in a local hotel."

That worked out fine with Jim. He'd have freedom of movement in and out of the facility while he continued to investigate Schafer's disappearance. He prayed Rip hadn't actually been shot during the live-fire exercise but had used it as cover to go black ops. Whatever had him spooked must be bad.

Jim resolved to find out what was in that packet the

woman had collected from the post office in Biloxi. The sooner the better. Hopefully, it would shed light on the trouble Cord Schafer was in before he took a live round... if he hadn't already.

As he walked out of the commander's office, several of SBT-22's personnel entered the building, still wearing the dark green camouflage uniform with the woodland pattern, their faces painted black, tan and green.

At first they all looked alike. Then one of them stepped forward, a toothy grin shining white teeth in the painted face. "Well, damn. Cowboy, is that you?"

Jim's eyes narrowed and he stared at the man in camouflage paint. "Duff?"

"Yeah, it's me." Dutton Callaway stepped forward and wrapped Jim in a bear hug, pounding him on his back. "You ol' son of a bitch. I thought you quit the Navy and went back to ranching."

"I did." Jim hugged his friend. "And you, are you still blowing things up for the Navy?"

"You bet. The bigger the bang, the more I like it." Duff turned to the man beside him. "Lovett, meet CPO Jim Monahan. He used to be a member of our team before your time. We called him Cowboy because he liked to wear a cowboy hat off duty."

"Chief Petty Officer Quentin Lovett." The man held out his hand.

Jim shook it, sizing up the new guy, appreciating the irony that Quentin wasn't the new guy. Jim was. "Nice to meet you."

"You remember Huck, don't you?" Duff reached behind him to grab a man at the rear of the others.

Sawyer Houston had been part of SBT-22 for a year when Jim had processed out. "I remember." Jim held out his hand and shook Sawyer's. "You've been promoted. Congratulations."

Sawyer pulled Jim into a hug. "Good to see you back."

"Yeah, I don't suppose you heard." Duff's voice dropped to little more than a whisper.

"About Rip?" Jim nodded. "I heard."

"Happened this morning during live-fire training. One minute he was there. The next…"

"No one knew he was gone for a good five minutes after it happened," Sawyer added. "We've been out searching the Pearl all day. They finally made us come in and sent out another squad to continue the search."

"Who was with him when he disappeared?"

"Gunny, Hunter and Garza."

"I don't know them."

"All good guys. They were looking forward as they navigated a bend in the river. Tracer rounds were flying overhead. A lot of noise."

"Then he was gone." Duff raised his hands, palms up.

Commander Jacobs stepped out of his office. "We have a team looking for Schafer. Dutton and Houston, you need to get some rest. We'll start the search again at daylight. If he's alive, we'll find him."

"If he's hurt, the alligators will find him sooner," Duff protested. "We need to be out there looking for him."

"And we are. The Coast Guard and the county sheriff's rescue unit are hard at it. Go home."

Duff's jaw tightened and he appeared to be on the verge of arguing with his superior officer. Instead, he nodded. "Yes, sir." He turned to Sawyer and Jim. "Come on."

Once outside, Duff shared with Jim, "A bunch of us are meeting at the Shoot the Bull Bar for drinks."

Jim's pulse picked up. He was familiar with the bar where the SEALs hung out during their off time. It was the bar Cord had wanted to meet his friend at to exchange the packet.

"I know where it is. I need to find a hotel first. I'll meet you there in an hour."

Duff laid a hand on his shoulder. "Glad you're back, Cowboy."

"Glad to be back." Jim could think of better circumstances under which he could return to his old unit. He was thankful Hank had managed to pull the strings he had. With one man missing, he'd be well positioned to discover why and whether it had anything to do with the packet Rip had the woman collect.

Hopefully, Rip had disappeared under his own terms, not because he'd been shot during the live-fire exercise. Rip was a smart man. If he thought himself in imminent danger, he could have manufactured his "disappearance" to get out of harm's way.

Jim prayed his body didn't turn up during the Pearl River search.

Chapter Three

Melissa spent the first couple of hours after the doors officially opened to the Shoot the Bull Bar waiting on the local civilian population of construction workers and good ol' boys stopping in for a beer on their way home.

One other waitress showed up around five-thirty, tucking her tank top into her cutoffs as she strolled through the door.

"You're late, Cora Leigh," Eli said.

"Oh, keep yer pants on, Eli. Ain't hardly no one here anyway." She glanced at Melissa as she cleared a mug off an empty table. "Who's the new chick?"

Melissa smiled across the room at her.

"Your replacement," Eli stated.

"Yeah, like that's gonna happen." Cora Leigh's lips twisted as her gaze swept over Melissa.

Melissa lifted her tray with empty mugs and beer bottles and closed the distance between Cora Leigh and herself. "Hi, I'm Mel Bradley." She set the tray down and held out her hand. "Nice to meet you."

Cora Leigh took her hand and gave her a limp shake. "Yer not from around here, are you?"

"No, I'm from up around Jackson."

Her brows lifted. "Farther than that. You don't sound like no Southerner. What brings you to these parts?"

"You're right. I moved to Jackson from Ohio to be with my boyfriend." Mel gave her a lopsided smile. "Left Jackson to get away from my *ex*-boyfriend."

Cora Leigh grinned. "You picked a good place to hide from him. This piss-hole is as far back in the boonies as you can get and still see daylight. Welcome to the Shoot the Bull."

"I'm not really here to take your job," Mel stated.

Cora Leigh snorted. "I've been workin' here three years. No other waitress has lasted that long. Eli can't afford to fire me."

"Keep pushin' and I'll make a liar out of ya," Eli grumbled.

Cora Leigh stuck out her tongue at the big man. "Love ya too, ya big galoot."

Melissa liked Cora Leigh. She was feisty and didn't seem to take crap from her boss. If she'd lasted for three years at a bar that served the military and local rednecks, she had more gumption than most people would give her credit for.

"Tips must be good," Melissa said.

"Damn right they are. The boys usually pony up as long as I smile and keep bringing the goods." Cora Leigh stared around the place. "The frogmen must be workin' late tonight. They're usually here by now."

Melissa's pulse picked up. "Do we get many SEALs here?"

"Honey, this place is swimming in them most nights. And they're the best tippers." She nodded toward Mel's tank top. "Show enough cleavage and you'll have them eating out of the palm of your hand. Just make sure that's all their eating out of." She winked and hurried off to take a customer's order.

The Navy SEALs from SBT-22 didn't arrive until after seven o'clock in the evening. One minute there weren't any in the bar, the next it filled with a swarm of the men, most of them freshly showered, some of them still wearing some of the camouflage paint from whatever maneuvers they had practiced earlier that day.

All of them seemed subdued. Melissa kept an eye out for Cord, ready to pass on the packet and be done with it.

Cora Leigh stood next to Melissa at the bar. "Something's not right. They're usually shoutin', braggin' or drinkin' each other under the table."

"What do you suppose is wrong?" Melissa asked.

Cora Leigh's eyes narrowed. "I don't know, but I'm gonna find out."

"Hold on to your britches, Cora Leigh," Eli said. "I bet I know what's got 'em all down in the dumps."

Melissa turned toward her new boss. "You do?"

Eli scrubbed the counter with a damp cloth. "Heard it on the police scanner earlier today. They lost one of their own in a live-fire exercise. One minute he was in the back of the boat, the next, he was gone, and where he'd been sittin' was covered in blood."

Melissa's heart skipped several beats and then raced on. She glanced down at the tray she'd been loading with beer bottles and mugs. "Oh, my God. Did they mention a name?"

"One of our regulars," Eli said.

As if she was in a long dark tunnel, where sound was muffled yet echoed, Melissa heard Eli's words.

"Chief Petty Officer Cord Schafer."

Melissa's fingers tightened on the tray to keep it from falling to the floor.

"Rip Cord? No way." Cora Leigh's eyes widened. "He's one of the nicer ones. Never once pinched my butt or propositioned me." She shook her bleached-blond hair. "Now, that's a crying shame."

Hands shaking, Melissa took the tray and its contents

and weaved her way through the tables, depositing the beer in front of men whose faces were drawn and sad. All the while, her mind spun around the news.

Cord Schafer was gone. He'd been her friend for almost as long as she could remember. Whenever she'd had a problem growing up, he'd been there for her to lean on. Once, they'd even kissed. They'd mutually agreed there were no sparks and kept it at friends. Even after he'd gone into the Navy, they'd kept in contact. Once or twice he'd sent her flowers on her birthday. He was her only family. A brother by connection, rather than blood. Her heart ached so badly, she could barely breathe.

"You all right, honey?" Cora Leigh asked.

"No, I think I ate something bad. Can you cover for me while I visit the ladies' room?"

"Sure. Just don't be too long. This place is full and they're still coming in. It's like a freakin' wake."

Melissa spun and ran for the bathroom. Her eyes stung and a knot formed in her throat. By the time she reached the hallway for the restrooms, she was so blinded by the tears welling in her eyes that she hit a wall and would have bounced off it, had arms not reached around her and pulled her close.

The wall was a rock-hard chest of muscles. The arms belonged to a man.

"Let go of me," she said on a sob. "I don't need this right now."

"What *do* you need?" asked a voice that sounded so familiar she blinked back the tears and stared up into James Monahan's blue eyes. He looked different. Gone was the long shaggy hair that hung down to his collar, and he'd shaved the three-day-old beard from his chin. If possible, he was even more handsome than when she'd run into him in Biloxi.

"Are you okay, darlin'?" he asked, his brows furrowed with concern.

Unable to hold back any longer, she fell against him, her fingers curling into his shirt, her tears spilling down her cheeks. "He…he's gone," she said, forcing air past her blocked vocal cords.

Monahan's hand cupped the back of her head and he held her until she stopped shaking. Then he said, "Don't go ordering flowers for the funeral, yet." The sound rumbled in his chest, vibrating against hers where she was pressed against him.

After a good three seconds, his words sank in and she glanced up at him through watery eyes. "What?"

He brushed a strand of her hair away from her damp cheek. "Don't plan the funeral."

"What do you mean?"

"They haven't found a body."

"But it was a live-fire exercise. They reported blood where he'd been sitting."

His brows rose and he cocked his head to one side. "No body."

"He fell into the river. He could float all the way to the gulf before they find him."

"I choose to believe he *wanted* to disappear. What do you choose to believe?" He tipped her chin upward and stared down into her eyes. "Come on, sweetheart. Give your boyfriend the benefit of a doubt."

The knot in her throat eased and she swallowed hard to clear it before speaking. "He's not my boyfriend. Why would he want to disappear?"

"I imagine someone probably did take a shot at him. If so, they wanted him dead. He couldn't very well continue his investigation if he was dead, now, could he?"

Melissa wiped the tears from her cheeks. "What investigation?"

Monahan tucked another strand of her hair back behind her ear and smiled. "That's what we have to figure out if we're going to help him."

"We?"

"He called me and apparently he contacted you. I'd assume that was his plan. My guess is he got into something bigger than he could handle. I understand why he called me, but I don't know why he called you." He chuckled. "But then, I don't know who you are. You never did tell me your name."

Melissa realized she was still standing in the man's arms and her body heated at his nearness, tingling where he touched her, from her breasts to her hips and at the small of her back, where one of his big hands rested. "I didn't, did I?" She paused before continuing, "Why should I trust you? You say Cord sent you. What if you're lying in order to get the packet he had me collect?"

"Sweetheart, if I'd wanted that packet, I would have taken it back in Biloxi. Cord sent *you* to get it. He must trust you to do the right thing with it. He wanted you to meet him here at ten o'clock tonight, didn't he? That's why you're here, right?"

She searched his blue eyes for any sign that he was leading her on, but all she saw were the clear, dark, honest eyes of a very tall, muscular man who could snap her in two if he chose to. "Yes."

"Given that he's disappeared, I doubt seriously he'll be here at ten. If he is, whoever tried to kill him might show up to finish the job."

Melissa shook her head. "He's not coming, is he?"

"One way or another, he can't." Monahan raised his hand. "I'm going with the way that indicates he's in danger and wants to protect you. You did a good job of disguising yourself when you collected the packet. Hopefully, whoever tried to take it from you won't suspect the woman in the red hat and the hooded jacket is the new waitress at the Shoot the Bull Bar. Now, are you going to tell me your name, or are you going to keep me guessing?"

She drew in a deep breath and let it out. "Melissa Bradley."

"Why did he call you?"

She glanced away. "We grew up together in Ohio. I've known Cord since he and I were kids. I'd trust him with my life and he can trust me with his. Who are you to Cord?"

"We served together on SBT-22. I saved his life once, and he saved mine." Monahan sighed. "I think he called me because I wasn't a member of the team anymore. He said I was the only man he could trust."

Melissa snorted. "He told me I was the only *woman* he could trust."

A muscular man with tattoos on his biceps appeared at the end of the hallway.

Melissa tensed and whispered, "Crap. We can't stay here and talk or someone will get suspicious." She grabbed the front of his black T-shirt and pulled him close. "Kiss me."

"But—"

She leaned up on her toes and said between her teeth, "Just do it, damn it."

JIM LOWERED HIS head and brushed his lips across Melissa's. As soon as they connected, a burst of electricity coursed through him. His hands tightened around her and he pulled her closer, his mouth pressing down hard on hers, his tongue tracing the seam of her lips.

She gasped, her lips and teeth parting.

He took advantage and he dived in, his tongue thrusting against hers.

At first she stood stiff in his arms, then her body melted into his and her hands slid up around his neck.

"Hey, hey," said the man at the end of the hallway. "The man's not back one day and he's already staked a claim on the new waitress. Not fair, Cowboy."

Jim broke the kiss, though his gaze remained connected with Melissa's. "Beat it, Duff. This one's mine," he growled.

"Okay, okay. At least let me by. A man drinking beer has to shake the dew off his leg once in a while."

Turning Melissa in his arms, Jim allowed Duff enough room to squeeze past them.

"Mmm. She even smells good. Lucky dog." Duff entered the men's bathroom and closed the door behind him.

Jim gripped her arms, staring at the end of the hallway, while keeping a watch on the bathroom doors. "We do need to talk. But you're right, not here. Where are you staying?"

She hedged. "Where are *you* staying?"

"I haven't actually secured lodging. I had hoped to find something in Slidell."

"Do you have a cell phone?" she asked, holding out her hand.

"I do." He fished it from his back pocket and handed it to her.

She looked at it and then handed it back to him. "Unlock it, please."

He hit the code to unlock it and gave it back to her.

She keyed a number into his contacts list. "This is my cell-phone number." She handed the phone to him. "Call me when you find a place. I'll meet you there."

Jim gave her a wry smile. "Afraid I'll take the packet of information from you if I know where you're staying?"

"No. I know you won't take it from me because I have it well hidden."

"I hope so. Apparently, whatever Rip has gotten himself into, someone is willing to kill to keep it quiet." He tilted his head and frowned down at her. "Are you sure you don't need me to stay with you?"

The men's bathroom door handle wiggled.

Jim gripped Melissa's arms and dragged her against him.

"I don't think it's necess—"

Before she could finish her sentence, Jim covered her mouth with his.

At first, he told himself it was payback for surprising him earlier with a kiss, but when their lips met, he knew he was lying to himself. He liked kissing Melissa. Her lips were soft, full and tasted of cherry ChapStick lip balm. Her mouth opened to him, and he slid his tongue along hers in a lingering caress. The longer the kiss, the more his groin tightened and the world faded into a haze around him.

"Seriously?" Duff's voice cut through the fog, bringing him back to earth. "Is that all I have to do? Take two years off from the Navy and the girls will fall all over me?"

Jim chuckled. "Try a shower and a haircut. I bet that would go a long way toward finding a woman who can tolerate you."

Duff laughed out loud. "Damn, Cowboy, I've missed having you around to keep me humble." He pounded Jim on the back and continued down the hallway. "When you get a minute, we need to talk about Rip."

Jim set Melissa at arm's length. "I gotta go. I'll call you later."

"I'm working until closing. Leave a message. I'll find you."

"You really should consider bringing that packet. Two heads are better than one. Personally, I like Rip, and I'd do anything in my power to bring him out of hiding alive."

"Assuming he's still alive." Melissa's very kissable lips firmed into a line. "And if he's not, I'll find whoever killed him and take him out myself."

"Get in line." Jim left her in the hallway and returned to the barroom, taking his seat amid the members of SBT-22. Many of the men he knew, but so many more were new to him. Young, eager and physically fit. He'd been around the table with introductions and he focused on remembering their names.

Two years was a long time to be out of the Navy. Working a ranch wasn't easy. He'd put in long hours herding cattle, mending fences, training horses and anything else that needed doing. In the evenings he'd wanted to collapse into his bed and just sleep, but he'd spent time with his father and continued to work out to keep in top condition.

Perhaps, in the back of his mind, he'd dreamed of rejoining the SEALs when his father's cancer finally took him. Now he was glad he'd continued to work out.

Jim didn't have to ask what had happened that day on the river. The team was all abuzz, talking in hushed tones, looking around as if wary of someone overhearing their speculation.

"Those live rounds are supposed to be well over our heads," Duff was saying.

"You think one of the guns malfunctioned?" Chief Petty Officer Juan Garza asked.

Petty Officer Benjamin Raines, Montana to his teammates, shook his head. "Rip's been acting funny lately."

"You noticed that? I thought it was just me," Duff said.

"No, he's been punchy since he got back from Honduras," Montana insisted.

"Yeah, that was a bad deal all around," Quentin Lovett muttered.

"What happened? Every surviving member of the team has been super-secretive."

"We aren't allowed to talk about it." Quentin toyed with his longneck bottle.

Duff snorted. "That doesn't stop everyone else who

wasn't on that mission from talking about it. Rumors are all over the board."

Sawyer Houston stared into his beer and said in a low tone only the men at his table could hear, "Suffice it to say the whole operation went south."

"Some think there was an intel leak and that the five-man element walked into a bloodbath," Garza said.

"We lost Lyle on that mission," Montana said and nodded.

The group gave a momentary pause of silence.

"Rip's been nervous ever since," Duff finished.

Jim lifted his beer and pretended to swallow a gulp. He didn't dare drink while on a mission. He needed to think clearly and process all the information he could acquire. "Did Rip show signs of post-traumatic stress disorder?"

Montana's head tilted, his eyes narrowing. "Could have been PTSD, but I think it was something more."

"Doesn't matter now," Sawyer said, his eyes hollow, his voice gloomy.

"You think he's dead?" Jim asked.

"I saw the blood." Duff ran his hand over his face. "If he wasn't dead when he hit the water, and if he isn't found soon, it won't be long before he *is* dead. The alligators will finish him off." Duff slammed his fist on the table. "We should have stayed out there looking."

Quentin set his beer bottle on the table. "We looked until the Coast Guard and the local search and rescue unit took over."

Sawyer's lips thinned. "We should have gone out in our scuba gear."

"You know as well as I do, that river's so muddy, you can't see your hand in front of your face. We'd be bumpin' into alligators. If he's down there, the only way we'll find him is if we drag the river."

Jim's chest tightened. He clung to the assumption Rip

was alive and hiding somewhere until he could figure out who wanted him dead.

In the meantime, he needed to see what was in that packet. Perhaps it would explain everything, or at least give them a starting point in their search.

For the next couple of hours, he stayed at the Shoot the Bull Bar. Tired, but determined to stay as long as he had to in case someone figured out Melissa was the woman who had collected the packet from the post office in Biloxi. As the numbers on his digital watch ticked closer to midnight, the bar patrons thinned until his teammates stood and stretched. "We have PT early in the morning," Duff said. "You better hit the rack."

Jim stood and threw a ten-dollar bill on the table. "I'm going after a visit to the head."

He took his time walking to the back of the bar, giving his teammates ample time to clear the building, all the while searching for Melissa, without finding her.

"If you're looking for Mel—" the waitress called Cora Leigh straightened from wiping a tabletop "—she left five minutes ago."

"Thanks." Jim performed a sharp about-face, marched out of the building and circled the perimeter. She was gone, all right.

Damn. What were the chances she'd show up at his hotel room when he texted her the location?

Hell, he didn't have a hotel room. He hopped into his truck and drove out of the parking lot, hitting the buttons on the navigation system for nearby hotels.

He smacked the steering wheel with the heel of his palm. He needed Melissa and the information she had to help find his friend. How could he have been so stupid?

Damned female. She'd given him the slip yet again.

Chapter Four

Melissa left the bar before it closed. Since learning Cord had gone missing, she'd been champing at the bit to open the packet he'd had her retrieve, but she didn't feel comfortable opening it around the bar or the other SEALs. If Cord couldn't trust his own team, she couldn't trust them.

Tired to the bone from cleaning and serving at the bar for the past ten hours, she slid behind the wheel and pulled out of the parking lot, careful to watch for anyone following her. She hadn't gone two miles before her cell phone rang.

She smiled as she hit the talk button and answered, "Took you long enough to figure out I'd left."

"I'm getting a room in Slidell." James Monahan's voice was warm and rich as he gave her the name of the hotel. "Can you meet me there in twenty minutes?"

"Okay."

"And bring what you've got."

"I'll think about it."

"If we want to find Cord, we have to figure out what made him desperate enough to disappear. That packet might be key to finding him."

"Understood. I reiterate, I'll think about it." She'd stashed the packet in the secret panel she'd had built into the driver's side door of her truck.

The truck had been custom built for her when she'd moved to Texas. As an FBI agent, she had use of the nondescript sedans that blended in with every other car on the road. But when she was on her own time, she liked driving her four-wheel-drive cherry-red pickup. It suited her and her newly adopted Texas lifestyle.

Her goal was to own acreage in the Texas Hill Country. Having grown up in Ohio, she didn't particularly want to shovel snow through another cold winter. She liked Texas, and the people were open and friendly. She'd build a little house on a hill and surround herself with cows, goats and maybe a horse or two.

Melissa sighed. That was her long-term goal. As an FBI agent, she wouldn't always be around to take care of a small ranch. She might be traveling on assignment at any time and have to leave for an undetermined period.

One day, she wanted a home and a family, like most women. With her parents dead and no siblings, she didn't want to be alone all her life. But it would all come in time. When she was ready to settle down. Not a day sooner.

For now, she liked her job and liked being available for any assignment that came her way. Not many men understood so she held them at bay and refused to extend a relationship past one or two dates. Why risk falling in love when she wasn't ready for the long-term commitment?

In the meantime, she had to figure out what happened to Cord and who would want to kill him. Since James had saved her butt and hadn't tried to take the packet from her the first time, he appeared to be the only person she dared trust. He'd said Cord had called him. Mel didn't know if that was true. She had only his word to go on.

She'd meet him, after she took pictures with her cell phone of all the information in the packet. That way, if he did take the information from her, she wouldn't be stuck without a lead to follow.

Which meant she had to find a secluded place to stop, open up the packet and get started. She had at least a five-minute lead on Monahan. That wasn't much, considering how thick the package was.

She made a turn onto a narrow road and parked on what appeared to be a deserted track between some bushes and trees. Once she was certain she couldn't be seen from the road and that there weren't any houses nearby, she hit the latch on the secret panel and removed the packet that had been there all day and evening.

She tore open the top and spilled papers and photographs onto the seat beside her. Sifting through quickly, she snapped pictures of the photos with her cell phone. Because she was in a hurry, she didn't take time to look closely. She clicked one photo after the other until she had all the documents loaded onto her phone.

A quick glance at the time and she yelped. She'd be later than the twenty minutes she'd promised Monahan. Mel shrugged. It would give him more time to check in.

Fifteen minutes later, she arrived in front of the hotel Monahan had indicated and found a parking place in the back behind a large tractor-trailer rig. She sat for a moment, wondering if she should leave the packet in the truck or take it in with her.

A tap on her window made her jump, her heart thumping hard against her chest. When she turned to face the intruder, she let go of the breath lodged in her throat.

"James." Mel shoved open her door and glared at him. "You almost gave me a heart attack."

"Sorry. I waited a minute to see if you'd notice me, but you appeared to be deep in thought." He grinned. "So, did you come to a conclusion? Are you going to show me the packet or not?"

"Yes, I decided to show you the packet." Her cheeks heated and she grabbed the envelope from beneath her seat, where she'd stashed it after photographing the contents. Before he'd tapped on her window she'd still been debating whether or not to share. But in that instant when she thought she might be under attack again, she knew. If she was going to trust anyone, James would be the one.

She slid down out of the truck onto the ground and handed him the envelope. "Let's get inside."

"I'm on the end." He held the packet in one hand and hooked her elbow in the other, leading her toward the corner of the building farthest from the entrance. Once inside the first-floor room, he closed and locked the door.

He tapped the open end of the packet. "What did you find in all this?"

"I really haven't had the time to look through it thoroughly. There are photos and documents. I was about to comb through when you called." It wasn't a lie, but she could feel her cheeks heat anyway. James didn't have to know she had copies of the contents. Until she was 100 percent sure of the man's intentions, she'd keep that little bit of information to herself.

James lifted a sheaf of papers from the pile and read, "Operation Pit Viper." He glanced up at Mel. "This is a top secret after-action report. I wonder if Pit Viper was the operation Cord and a few of the others had gone on that went south."

"What operation are you talking about?" Mel sat on the edge of the bed and flipped through the photographs.

"Some of the guys from the unit were saying Cord hadn't seemed the same since getting back from his last assignment. Six men were on the team. They lost one on that op. Cord must have taken it hard."

"Losing one of your team has to be difficult. It could make anyone second-guess his role in the op."

James nodded. "It's like losing a family member. These men have been through a lot of the toughest training together, and they've gone on missions where they had to rely on each other to stay alive."

"In other words, there has to be a lot of trust between them," Mel concluded.

"Exactly." James shook his head, his gaze returning to the document in his hand. "Which is why it worries me that Cord didn't trust anyone in his unit to help him out of whatever tight spot or situation he got himself into."

"What does the report say?" Mel leaned over James's shoulder, liking the way he smelled. A subtle blend of the outdoors and tangy aftershave. Being so close to him made her want to lean on his big, muscular shoulder. Her logical brain told her hormonal body to resist.

"Pit Viper was an effort to extract DEA agent Dan Greer from deep undercover in a terrorist training camp in Honduras." His voice trailed off as he continued reading. "Apparently they got in fine, found Greer and were on their way out when someone popped off a shot, taking out one of the SEALs. Once he was down, the DEA agent was left exposed and was shot, as well."

"Who were the men on the team?" Mel peered at the paper.

James pointed at the list of personnel. "Petty Officers Quentin Lovett and Lyle Gosling, and Chief Petty Officers Cord Schafer, Sawyer Houston and Benjamin Raines. Gunnery Sergeant Frank Petit was in charge."

"Did each give their account of what happened?"

James tapped the paper. "There are short paragraphs of each individual's account of what occurred."

"Who wrote the after-action report?" Mel asked.

"Gunny, Gunnery Sergeant Frank Petit," James said. "Gosling was the man killed. Gunny carried him out under fire."

"Who carried out the DEA agent?"

"Cord."

A chill fluttered across Mel's skin. "Do you think the agent got a message across to Cord?"

"Hard to say. The report doesn't say if Greer died instantly or if he bled out on their way to the pickup point. He was dead when they reached the riverboat."

Mel chewed on her bottom lip. "I wish we could talk to Cord."

James set the report aside and sifted through the photographs. "These look like they were reproduced recently. They are all crisp and smell like freshly developed prints."

Mel took the ones James handed her. They appeared to be taken of a camp in the jungle, based on the amount of overhanging green foliage in the background. In the pictures were dark-haired, dark-skinned people, either native Hondurans or they could even be Middle Eastern men, unpacking large wooden crates with the World Health Organization logo marked in stencil on the outside. Inside were canned goods and staple products Mel would expect to find in a WHO crate.

"Interesting." James leaned toward her and showed her a photo of one of the crates lying open, the canned goods, clothing and boxes of food halfway removed to expose another layer of items that had nothing to do with food and clothing. It was what was beneath the usual and expected items that caught her attention and made her blood run cold.

"Are those—"

"Rifles and grenade launchers?" Jim's lips thinned. "Yes. And by the look of them, they're American-made." He pointed to one in particular. "That's an AR15."

Mel chewed on her lower lip. "They look new."

"Which leads me to believe that someone's selling weapons to a terrorist group."

"Damn," Mel whispered. "That someone is from the

US." Mel grabbed the envelope and flipped it over, staring down at the postage. "There's no address on this packet."

"Cord could have gotten a copy of the after-action report, but the photos have me stumped," James said.

"Would the SEAL team have had contact with the DEA agent before going in to extract him?"

"Not normally. They'd know nothing about him until just before receiving their orders to perform the extraction."

"And the team wouldn't be there long enough for Cord to snap the photos."

"No." James flipped through the photos. "The agent had to have taken these while undercover in the camp. They appear to be at odd angles, like he was trying to disguise or hide what he was doing."

Mel took a stack of the photos and glanced through them, studying the faces of the people gathered around the boxes. None of them looked familiar. "Do you suppose it's possible the agent slipped Cord a memory card before he bled out?"

"That's my bet. And Cord could have developed them at any instant kiosk without raising suspicion."

"Once he did," Mel continued, "he apparently knew he was in trouble."

"He put himself at risk by stealing a copy of the after-action report." James set the photos aside and returned his attention to the report.

Goose bumps rose on Mel's arms. It was one thing to have the photos, but sneaking into files to make a copy of the after-action report would have put him in danger of being caught stealing top secret documents, a career-ending move for any SEAL. He had to have been desperate. "Whoever discovered he'd gotten the after-action report might have suspected he knew more than he should."

James ran a hand across his short-cropped hair. "So he hid the packet in the post office box."

Mel stepped away from the bed, chewing her bottom lip. "Why ask me to bring it to him? He knew what was in the packet."

"Maybe because he thought his secret was compromised. He might have called you in, someone not from his unit, to safeguard the information."

"Then why have me meet him in a public place?"

"You're a female. You could pretend to be there to see him as his girlfriend. He could talk to you, let you in on his suspicions and let you take it from there."

"Whereas you, an old Navy friend, appearing out of the blue might raise suspicions."

James nodded. "Cord asked me to look out for you while you retrieved the packet from the PO box. He didn't ask me to get the packet. He was concerned about you. And he probably put it there so that you could find it, in case he disappeared. Which he did."

"Damn. He must have known how much trouble he was in."

James grinned. "Great disguises, by the way."

"Thanks." She turned, paced across the room and spun on her heel to face him. "So what's the plan?"

"My boss pulled strings and got me back into my old unit, SBT-22. Cord's unit. I can work this investigation from the inside."

Mel held her hand up. "Whoa, there, Cowboy. What do you mean, your boss got you back on the SEAL team?" She waved her hand in the air. "People don't just get back onto active duty that easily."

Jim's lips twisted. "I work for a pretty influential man, apparently."

"Apparently? Don't you know?"

"I've worked for him for less than a week. He's letting me treat this as my first assignment."

"And you trust him? You tell me Cord is your friend. This man you're working for, do you trust him with Cord's life?" Mel pushed her hair back from her face, shaking her head. "There are too many pieces to this puzzle. Cord, the packet, Operation Pit Viper and you." She reached for the papers, gathering them into a pile before shoving them into the packet. "It's all too much of a coincidence and I don't believe in coincidence. I think we're done here."

He captured her wrist in his grip. "I'm on the up-and-up. I came because Cord asked me to. From what I know about my new boss, he's a good man. My coworkers have told me stories of some of the operations he's backed to help others."

"What's his name?" Mel demanded.

"I'm not certain I have the liberty to say."

"Then I'm done here."

"You haven't told me why you're here and why Cord trusted you."

"We are old friends. I told you that."

"Who do you work for?"

She hedged. This man she knew little about didn't need to know everything about her. "That's my business."

His lips thinned and he squared off with her. "Look, I'll tell you who I work for if you tell me who you work for."

She considered his trade for a long moment and sighed. "I work with the FBI."

His brows rose. "Proof?"

She fished in her bra for a moment and pulled out her credentials, handing them to him. "Satisfied?"

When his hand touched hers, a jolt of pure electricity blasted up her arm and throughout her body. James set her nerve endings on fire. Rather than take the proffered proof from her, he gabbed her hand, credentials and all, and yanked her into his arms.

"Almost satisfied." He dragged her close until her body was flush against his. "Who really sent you?"

"I told you. Cord sent me a key in the mail and asked me to collect the package and deliver it to him."

"Why should I believe you? You're an FBI agent. For all I know, the feds could have sent you."

"And I'm supposed to trust a man who quit the SEALs two years ago and suddenly shows up claiming he got a call from a friend? A man who won't reveal who his boss is?" She pulled hard on her wrist, trying to work free of his grasp. "I told you who I work for. It's your turn."

For a long moment, he stared into her eyes. Then he said, "I just signed on with an organization called Covert Cowboys Inc. CCI was established by Hank Derringer."

"Whoa, wait. *The* Hank Derringer, the Texas billionaire?"

He nodded. "That's the one."

Mel frowned. "We had an FBI agent from the San Antonio office leave the agency to go to work for him."

"What's his name? Maybe I met him while I was at Hank's ranch."

"Not him…her." Mel paused. "Tracy Kosart."

Jim grinned and held up his hand. "About so high with long, straight brown hair?"

Mel nodded.

"I met her. She was brought on board a week before I was. We're the new recruits."

"Just what is Covert Cowboys Inc.?"

"From my orientation with Hank, it's an organization he established to fight for truth and justice."

"Great. All we need is another billionaire dishing out vigilante justice."

"He only wants to help people right wrongs when

the local, state or federal government can't seem to get it done."

Mel nodded. "Sadly, I know what he's talking about. We had one go bad. Regional Director Grant Lehman. He used to be my boss's boss at the regional office in San Antonio. It was all pretty hush-hush when he was removed from his position." Mel's gaze met Jim's. "He had something to do with the disappearance of Derringer's family."

"He had them kidnapped and taken to a location in Mexico where he imprisoned them for two years."

"Damn." Mel stared down at the big hand holding her wrist. "Agent Kosart went to work for him after she escaped from being captured by a drug cartel. I only knew her for a few weeks before all that went down."

"Hank Derringer has a pretty elaborate setup and connections only money can buy."

"So?"

"I say we shoot this packet to him and let his computer genius go through it and the list of names and find out what they can about the shipments."

"Or I could turn it over to the FBI and let them do it."

JAMES STARED INTO her eyes, his gut telling him not to trust anyone but himself and CCI on this investigation. And maybe Melissa. "Pit Viper may have been an operation intended to fail. It appeared that once they got the DEA agent out of the camp, he wasn't supposed to live to share the information he'd acquired."

"Couldn't someone in the camp have taken him out?"

"Based on the after-action report, they were pretty much out of the camp. Someone picked off Greer. Someone who knew who he was."

"Still, it could have been a sentry," Melissa insisted.

"Why only kill Greer? A sentry would have killed all of them." James shook his head. "Whoever did it had to have some pretty good skills to target the DEA agent specifically."

Mel frowned. "Then why kill the SEAL?"

"The SEAL might have stepped in front of the bullet meant for Greer. But back to the packet..." James gave her a pointed look. "Do you really believe Cord asked you to collect the packet to turn it over to the FBI?"

"No. He said I was the only one he could trust." She chewed on her bottom lip.

"He said the same to me." James wished Melissa would stop chewing that bottom lip. It was making him crazy, and his groin tightened. He swallowed hard and tried to focus on the issue at hand. "Which tells me he thinks someone higher up—maybe in his unit, possibly the DEA or some other federal organization—arranged for them to get Greer away from the terrorist training camp so they could kill him and bury any information he might have been gathering to relay. Someone must have figured out the agent passed information to Cord."

"Perhaps the same sharpshooter who killed the agent?" She bit down harder on that bottom lip.

James captured her chin in his hand.

Startled, her teeth released the bottom lip and James brushed his thumb across it.

"I'm worried about you," he said.

Her gaze locked with his.

He cupped her cheek in his hand, his heart fluttering at the feel of her soft skin against his fingertips.

"I'm an FBI agent," she whispered. "I know how to look out for myself."

"And I'll bet you usually have another agent as a partner or backup." When she couldn't refute his statement, he smiled and bent to brush his lips across hers, the move so natural, he couldn't imagine *not* doing it.

Melissa's eyes widened. "Why did you do that?"

"Do what?" His lips twitched at her confused expression. "You mean this?" Again, he kissed her, only this time he swept his tongue along the seam of her mouth. When her lips parted, he dived in to taste her tongue.

Mmm. Just as good as he remembered from earlier that evening.

"Why do you keep kissing me?" Her words breathed against his lips.

"I can't seem to stop," he responded and kissed her again.

When he came up for air, she leaned her forehead against his chest. "This isn't right. Cord is missing." Her fingers curled into his shirt. "He could be in a lot of danger."

James tipped her chin and brushed a strand of hair behind her ear. "Sweetheart, if they figure out you were the woman who retrieved the packet and that you're onto them, you could be in as much danger as Cord."

Chapter Five

Melissa fought the urge to lean into James's grip. His gaze was so compelling and the feel of his body against hers made her forget who she was and what they were up against.

She wanted to stand on her toes and press her lips to his, continuing the kiss he'd initiated. More so, she wanted to strip his clothes and hers and make use of the king-size bed.

Her core heated and she fought mightily to regain control of her baser instincts. With a sigh, she pushed away from him, putting distance between their bodies. "It's obvious—" she squeaked, heat suffusing her cheeks. She smoothed her hair back from her face, cleared her throat and continued, "They didn't want that information to get out. Now it's up to us to maintain our cover and continue Cord's investigation where he left off."

For a long moment, James watched her as he clenched his fists. Then he blinked, the moment passed and he was back to business. "While I'm at the unit, I can dig around and find out more about the personnel involved in Pit Viper."

Glad for the easing of the sexual tension and the return to the task at hand, Melissa nodded. "Good. Since I don't have the advantage of being a SEAL, I'll stick to background checks on the families of those personnel and see if anything spells *motivation*. I'll also keep an ear open for information at the bar."

"In the meantime," James said, "I'll get Hank to work his magic and locate home addresses of those men and get these pictures and the report to him for further study."

"I don't feel comfortable giving Derringer Cord's information." Melissa chewed on her lip. "He specifically said he didn't trust anybody."

"With nothing else to go on and limited resources, Hank's our best bet." He raised his brows. "Unless you're actually willing to bring the FBI into it."

Melissa shook her head. "No."

"Hank's got the technical goods. Really, from what I've learned about him from other members of his team, he's trustworthy. A point in his favor is that he's not affiliated with the government. What information Hank acquires stays with Hank. No leaks."

"For Cord's sake, I hope so."

"I'll find a way to pass the packet to him virtually, then I'll give it back to you, if it makes you feel better."

She nodded. "It would." Her gaze swept the room. "I'd better go find a hotel for the night."

James's brows dipped. "You don't have a hotel?"

"I drove straight to the bar and went to work."

"I'd offer for you to stay with me, but something tells me you'd turn me down." He grinned. "I would suggest that, since we're working this case together, you stay in the same hotel so that we can compare notes at night."

"I don't know. It might be too close."

"We've already established a kissing connection at the bar." His lips twitched. "It wouldn't be a big leap in logic for you to stay in the same place."

"Won't you be expected to move into the barracks or something, now that you're back on active duty?"

"Not necessarily. We can live off post. I planned on claiming that I was apartment hunting and the hotel is only temporary."

"Okay, then. I'll see if they have a room available." She backed toward the door, still pretty sure it was a bad idea to stay in the same hotel as James.

Yes, she could get updates sooner and not have to worry about someone tapping into her phone or overhearing her conversations. But for James to be so close would add an entirely different level of danger to the situation. Based on her immediate attraction to the man, she risked the danger of falling for the big Navy SEAL, when she knew nothing would ever come of a relationship with him. She had her life working with the FBI. He had his, working for Hank Derringer.

With her hand on the doorknob, she stared at the packet to keep from focusing on James. "Let me know what Hank finds. The sooner the better."

"Let me know what room they assign to you."

"Why?"

"In case you run into trouble." His face softened. "I promise not to bother you, if you don't want me to."

"Okay." With that, she left his room and hurried to the front office to check in.

Ten minutes later, key card in hand, she returned to her truck, gathered her suitcase and wheeled it into the hotel and up to her room on the third floor near the stairwell. Before she forgot, she texted her room number to James.

Her pulse fluttered when she realized her room was directly above James's. If she needed to, all she had to do was shout or stomp her feet to get his attention. Not that she'd need him to bail her out of a tight spot again.

She stepped into the shower and washed away all the spilled beer and sweat from the bar. After scrubbing her hair, she turned off the shower, dried and slipped into panties and a softly worn, oversize T-shirt. Tired, but too wound up to sleep, Mel padded barefoot to the window, parted the curtains and stared out at the parking lot.

Where was Cord? Was he alive? If so, would he risk contacting her?

And what was with James Monahan kissing her? God, and she'd kissed him back!

This wasn't the time or place to get involved with anyone, especially someone she wouldn't see ever again once they found Cord. But, dear Lord, the way his chest felt against her fingertips and the strength of his arms when they'd wrapped around her, all hard muscles, spring-loaded for action, were enough to make any woman drool.

Her pulse quickened and her breathing became more erratic. Just the thought of him stirred her body and made her dream of more than a kiss. For that moment in time, she'd mentally moved ahead, shedding her clothes, pressing her breasts to his naked chest. Mel touched a hand to her chest, her heart banging against her ribs. Damn. The man tied her up in knots, with only one way to unwind. And she wouldn't go there.

But he's only one floor below you, the wicked devil on her shoulder urged. Her fingers curled around the curtain. All she had to do was slip down the stairs and knock on his door. If his kiss were any indication, he'd be amenable to a late-night fling.

Mel sucked in a deep breath and let it out slowly, trying to slow the beat of her heart, her pulse pushing red-hot blood throughout her body. *Pull yourself together.*

A shadow moved below between her red truck and the tractor-trailer rig. For a moment Melissa thought it might be her imagination. Then she saw it again. A man, dressed all in black, slipped from between the two vehicles. He wore a hooded jacket, hiding his features in darkness. The man seemed to be studying her truck.

Surely if he were contemplating stealing it he wouldn't be so open and visible. Unless he didn't think he was being observed.

Finally, he jammed his hands into his pockets and walked along the front of the row of vehicles.

Melissa didn't realize she'd been holding her breath until she let it go. Her overactive imagination was getting the better of her and making her jumpy. It was just a man cutting through the parking lot, stopping to admire her red pickup. Lots of men did.

The darkly dressed man stopped and glanced up as if staring straight at her window.

Mel jerked her hand away from the curtain and stepped back, glad she'd left the light off behind her. Her pulse hammered through her veins and she waited—afraid to move again and draw attention to herself.

Unnerved, her first inclination was to fly down the stairs and bang on James's door, demanding to be allowed in. As soon as the thought materialized, she had to remind herself she was an FBI agent, capable of defending herself. All that training at Quantico was in preparation for missions where she might find herself alone and up against a bad guy twice her size or weight.

James wouldn't always be around to protect her as he'd done earlier that day. Once again, she was back to her initial self-discussion about the pros and cons of getting involved with anyone. As long as she was a member of the FBI and responding to assignments that could take her away for long periods, she wasn't good girlfriend material. Past experience proved that. Once bitten and all…

Her former fiancé had dumped her and married another woman within months of their breakup—a woman who promised to be home every night and who would bear and raise his children, as his version of a good little wife should.

Pfsst! Melissa was glad he'd moved on. After a couple of weeks, she was even more thankful. In retrospect, Mel realized, he had been all wrong for her. He'd never truly been supportive of her career. It had also opened her eyes to the fact she couldn't have a steady relationship with a man as long as she worked for the FBI. Not that what she was feeling for Monahan could be construed as leaning toward a steady relationship.

Lust.

That was all it was.

The best she could do now was to go to bed, forget about James, forget about the man in the dark hooded jacket in the parking lot and get some sleep in what was left of the night.

As she padded across the carpeted floor, she glanced at the door one last time before turning her full attention to the bed and the slim possibility of sleep.

A sharp knock on the door made her jump, and her heartbeat skipped into overdrive.

She hurried toward the door and paused with her hand on the knob to peer through the peephole. James stood on the other side wearing a black T-shirt and PT shorts.

Mel let out a shaky breath and yanked open the door. "Thank goodness it's you."

His brows rose. "Who else did you think it might be?"

The man in the parking lot most likely was nothing more than her overactive imagination. Mel shook her head. "No one. Forget it." She stepped back, allowing him to enter, and closed the door behind him.

James gripped her arms. "Were you afraid the men from earlier today had found you?"

"Not necessarily." For heaven's sake, she was a trained FBI agent. She wasn't supposed to be afraid of anything. "I saw a man lurking around the parking lot near my truck. It was probably nothing, just a gut feeling."

"I've dodged deadly situations based on my gut more often than I care to admit. If it'll make you feel better, I'll have a look around the parking area before I call it a night."

"Thanks."

"Which one is your truck?" he asked.

"The bright red one next to the tractor-trailer rig." She frowned. "Speaking of calling it a night. What brings you up to my room?" A thrill of excitement rippled across her skin. She'd been thinking about him and how good it had felt to be in his arms. Had he felt the same draw?

James dropped his hands from her arms and reached into his back pocket. "Hank's computer guru was up and got addresses for all the men on the Pit Viper team. I thought you might want them now rather than at five in the morning when I plan on heading out to PT." He handed her a sheet of paper with four addresses written in broad, bold handwriting.

So, he hadn't come up to her room to pick up where they'd left off on the kiss. Mel took the paper and stared down at the writing rather than up at the man filling her room with his personality and muscles. "Yes, you're right. I'd rather sleep a little longer. Thanks."

"Be careful tomorrow. If one of these guys is connected to Cord's disappearance or the death of the SEAL and the DEA agent in Honduras, he will be dangerous."

"I'll play it low-key and do my snooping during the day when the men should be at their unit, training with you."

"Then I'd better get to bed. It's been two years since I did PT with the team."

When he turned to leave, Mel reached out and touched James's arm. "It goes both ways." Electricity shot through her hand and up her arm where her fingers connected with James's skin.

"What?" He spun to face her.

Her breath caught in her throat and she struggled to

focus on her words. "Be careful. If this man suspects you're back looking for Cord, you could be in as much danger, if not more. There are a lot of opportunities to kill a man or make him disappear on training exercises. Cord's disappearance was just one example."

Before she could withdraw her hand, he captured it in both of his. "Worried about me?"

God, did she look that needy? Mel tugged at her hand. "Of course. I wouldn't want anyone else to be hurt in the course of this investigation."

"Just anyone?" He drew her into his arms.

She tried to remain stiff, but couldn't, melting against him. Her hands resting on his chest, she sighed. "Okay, yes. I'm worried about you."

"Why? I'm a big boy. I can take care of myself."

"I'm sure Cord thought the same."

"You kind of like having me around, don't you?" His arms tightened around her middle.

She snorted softly. "Don't go and get a big head. I find myself somewhat attracted to you. But that doesn't mean I want it to lead anywhere." Mel refused to look into his eyes, knowing that if she did, she might be lost.

"No?" He touched a finger beneath her chin and tipped her face upward until she was forced to meet his gaze. "Not even if it leads to another kiss? Because you see, I'm attracted to you, too."

Her gaze locked with his and her voice deteriorated to a whisper. "Well, now, that will never do. We only just met. It can't go anywhere, and it would be a big mist—"

His lips crashed down on hers, cutting off further protestations. And it was just as well. Mel had run out of steam and resistance. Her hands slipped upward from his chest to lock around the back of his neck. She met his kiss with equal passion, opening her mouth to allow his tongue access to hers. He tasted of minty-fresh toothpaste and smelled like a heady combination of soap, aftershave and male.

When his lips slipped from hers along her jaw, she let her head fall back, giving him better access to the long line of her neck. She curved her calf around his and slipped it up the back of his leg, shocked and titillated when she remembered she wore only a T-shirt and panties. And now those panties rubbed against the top of his thick, muscular thigh, making her even more excited and desperate to feel his skin against hers.

Then he was setting her away from him and backing toward the door, a smile curling his lips. "I'll see you at the bar tomorrow." And he was gone.

JIM BARELY MADE it out of her room. It was all he could do to walk away from the sinfully sexy FBI agent in that T-shirt that barely covered her bottom and only emphasized the beaded tips of her nipples through the thin cotton.

She was right. She had her job; he had his. The duration of anything that might start up between them would be the length of this investigation. But then, that wasn't necessarily a drawback. He wasn't in the market for a long-term relationship. Starting a new life with a new job, working for an eccentric billionaire who could send him to God only knew where, wasn't the time to get tangled up with a female.

If he decided to take Hank up on the offer to continue on with his SEAL team, he definitely wouldn't be in a good place to start a relationship with an FBI agent who lived and worked a few states away.

As much as he wanted to turn around and march back up the stairs to Melissa's room, he didn't. Instead, he stepped outside into the parking lot and made a complete sweep of the lot and the hotel grounds. He stopped next to the bright red truck parked beside a tractor-trailer rig and smiled.

It was a big, in-your-face red truck. Not exactly what he pictured Melissa driving. Then again, it gave him a little more insight into her personality. She was tough, independent and smart. The more he learned about her and the more he was around her, the more he liked her.

The way she made him feel when he touched her was altogether different. Fire burned in his veins and funneled south to his groin. He'd been so busy helping his father through the last days of his life he hadn't had many opportunities to date or be with a woman.

Jim circled Melissa's truck. In the dim glow from the security lights positioned around the corners of the hotel, he couldn't see any tampering. Whoever had been wandering around the parking lot that late had disappeared. Thankfully, the window from his room looked out on the parking lot. He didn't have the bird's-eye view Melissa had, but he would remain aware. And being in the room directly beneath hers, he could hear her if she screamed.

He'd be close enough to keep an eye on her until tomorrow when he'd leave early in the morning for PT with his unit. Then Melissa would be on her own to conduct her investigation into the Pit Viper team's families, while he poked around and asked subtle questions.

He didn't like being away from Melissa. Cord had asked him to look out for her. Assigned to his unit, he wouldn't have the flexibility to take off anytime he liked.

Unable to find anything out of sorts, Jim returned to his room and settled in bed. Morning would be there all too soon and he'd have to be up and ready to work out with the SEALs.

When his head hit the pillow, he forced all thoughts of Melissa out of his mind. At least he tried.

Instead he thought of Cord and where he could be. If he

was injured, he could by lying on the banks of the Pearl River, suffering. No man should be left to die like that.

Jim had to believe Cord was alive.

Chapter Six

The alarm went off all too soon. It was time to get up. Thankfully, Jim was used to rising early, having taken over his father's duties on the ranch where he was foreman during the last two years of his life.

Jim slipped into his PT shirt and shorts and pushed his feet into his tennis shoes. Grabbing his uniform, boots and hat, he headed out for his first full day back as a member of the SEAL unit he'd hated leaving.

Everything about returning to SBT-22 was surreal. Some things about being in Stennis, Mississippi, felt normal, as if he hadn't been gone for two years. Other aspects were different. His father was gone. Jim had changed, matured and grown in the two years, feeling much older than the men on the team. When he lined up in formation for the morning calisthenics, he noted how many of the faces had changed and how many were still the same.

The men he had considered friends were still his friends. What had drawn him to them in the first place hadn't changed. They were two years older and some had gained rank and scars, but they were still the same men he'd called brothers. In that respect, he felt as if he'd come home.

Unfamiliar faces graced the ranks with recruits fresh out of BUD/S. They were young men toughened by the grueling training, still trying to prove themselves worthy of the SEAL designation.

Jim remembered when he'd graduated from the physically demanding rigors of BUD/S. He and Cord had been stationed together on their first assignment and had stayed together when they'd been transferred to SBT-22.

Being back without Cord just didn't feel right. Jim vowed to find his friend and fix whatever had been broken during the Pit Viper mission.

"Hey, Jim!" Duff Dalton fell in beside Jim and clapped him on the back with his big hand. "Ready for a short run? It's a little different from mucking stalls on the ranch."

"Yup." He didn't bother to tell Duff he'd been working out every day since leaving the team. He knew words weren't proof of his stamina. He'd have to show his teammates that he was up to the challenge, even if he had to work twice as hard to prove himself. They'd be watching. His physical abilities might make the difference between life and death for any member of the team. They had to be capable of protecting each other's backs.

Gunny stood in front of the group, called them to attention and led the first round of exercises, including jumping jacks and windmills to warm up. They moved to the pull-up bars, where they performed repetitions until Jim's arms burned. Next were the push-ups and finally the lower-body exercises. By the time they finished the calisthenics, Jim was glad he'd continued his physical fitness routine on the ranch. He'd never have made it through the rigorous morning without it. They formed up and took off at a steady jog for their five-mile run around Stennis, sweating in the humidity and singing cadences all the way.

When they got back to the unit, the men took turns in the showers, rinsing off dirt and sweat. Jim didn't get the chance to talk with the men of Operation Pit Viper until they were dressed in uniform trousers, boots and T-shirts. His first assignment of the day was to help maintain the thirty-three-foot Special Operations Craft-Riverine (SOC-R) used during the previous day's river exercise when Cord had disappeared. He hoped the boat would reveal some clue as to what had happened.

The team who'd been on the boat the day before was quiet as they scrubbed down the craft, broke down the weapons, cleaned and oiled them. The sun beat down on them, the humidity making it even worse. Jim had worked out in the heat of the sun on the ranch, but the weather in Texas was a lot drier than in Mississippi. Before long, he was sweating again.

Petty Officer Benjamin Raines, nicknamed Montana, worked alongside Jim as they scrubbed the sides and floor of the bow. "You and Rip were pretty tight when you were here a couple years back, weren't you?" Montana asked.

Jim nodded. "Yup. I'd hoped to get to see him when I got here."

Montana shook his head. "Things have been…different."

"I noticed. Lots of new faces." He glanced around. Most of the men had moved out of earshot. Lowering his voice, Jim asked, "What do you think happened yesterday?"

Montana's lips tightened. "I don't know. We've never had someone hit in a live-fire exercise."

"You're a sharpshooter, aren't you?" Jim continued to scrub, studying the younger man in his peripheral vision.

Montana straightened, his eyes narrowing. "I was in the boat with Rip. I didn't shoot him."

Jim nodded. "I know. I just wondered if as a sharpshooter you might have a better idea of what it would take to target Rip."

The younger SEAL's shoulders slumped and he dropped down onto the deck to scrub at an already cleaned spot.

"Someone with a little skill could have taken him out easily."

"But why Rip? I know him. He's a good guy. He always had my back and any other man's back on the team."

"Rip's one of the best. I'd give my right arm to figure out who did this to him."

"You and me both," Jim agreed. "The team isn't the same without him."

"Bad enough we lost Gosling," Montana muttered. "Now Rip." He hit the deck with his fist. "It just ain't right."

"Gosling?" Jim played dumb. He knew exactly who Gosling was, but if his story was to be believed, he shouldn't have known.

"Gosling was from the same BUD/S class as me." Montana gazed out across the bow of the boat as if staring into the past. "He'd been so proud to make it through BUD/S. He was on his first real assignment when he was cut down."

"What happened?" James asked.

"Wish I knew. I'd have taken the bullet for him. He left behind a wife with a kid on the way."

"Damn shame." Jim's heart twisted. Yet another reason it wasn't advisable to get involved with a woman or family when you were at risk of being shot or killed in an explosion.

In his gut, Jim didn't think Montana had anything to do with the mission in Honduras going south. Nor did he think the man was responsible for Cord's disappearance. But he might have seen something in either place that could give him a clue as to what really happened.

"How did Gosling die?"

"Sniper." Montana didn't hesitate. "Gosling was picked off."

"Was he the only casualty?"

Montana shoved a hand through his shaggy hair. "No, the sniper got the man we were sent to extract, as well." The young SEAL snorted. "What got me was the fact he didn't shoot any of the rest of us. It was like he was targeting Gosling and the other guy."

"Or was it that Gosling was in the way?"

Montana stared at Jim, his head tilting to the side. "Could have been. Gosling was hit in the right side and went down before our extraction was hit in the same side. Gosling could have been in the way."

"Are you two having a picnic?" Gunnery Sergeant Petit barked from a distance, headed their way.

"No, Gunny." Montana straightened. "Just finishin' up."

"Good, Monahan has some qualifying to do." He jerked his head. "Come with me. Sawyer's gonna take you out to the range to see if you can still shoot straight after your two-year vacation."

Jim didn't bother to correct Gunny on the vacation remark. Ranch work was hard in so many ways. Maybe he wasn't being shot at by the enemy, but he risked his life on many occasions herding highly agitated and resistant cattle into chutes and cattle trailers or through gates. The days were long, hot and grueling. On top of hauling hay, mending fences and clearing brush, he'd made time to work out to keep all his muscles in top physical condition. All this, he kept to himself. As far as Gunny was concerned, Jim was a new kid on the team and had to prove he could still perform up to SEAL standards before he would be accepted.

Gunny led him to the parking lot. A military vehicle waited at the curb, CPO Sawyer Houston behind the wheel. "Get in. We're going to go poke a few holes in some targets and see if you still have what it takes."

Jim glanced at the gunnery sergeant. "Are you coming with us, Gunny?"

Gunny's eyes narrowed so slightly, Jim wouldn't have noticed had he not been paying close attention. "Yeah. I'm going." He claimed shotgun, while Jim slipped into the backseat.

"Two years is a long time to be away from all this." Sawyer shifted into Drive and pulled away from the curb.

"Passed so fast, I hardly feel like I've been gone," Jim commented. Sadly, the time *had* passed far too quickly. Two years didn't seem like nearly enough time to spend with his dying father. Now that he was gone, Jim would give anything to have him back for another two years.

"Firing the M4 is like riding a bicycle." Sawyer tipped a glance his way and grinned. "From what I remember, you used to fire expert when you were here before. I predict you'll be doing the same before you leave the range today."

Jim chuckled. "I don't know if I'd go that far."

Gunny sat in silence throughout their conversation. As they parked on the firing range, he got out and opened the back of the vehicle.

Sawyer removed two M4 carbine rifles, handing one to Jim. "You remember one end from the other?"

With a nod, Jim accepted the weapon, weighing it in his palms. It fit in his grip as if it belonged. During his six years as a Navy SEAL, he'd carried one of these so often, it became like an extension of his arms. His hands wrapped around the stock and barrel, curling with familiarity. "I think I can remember which end is the business end."

Sawyer handed him a magazine and a couple of boxes of bullets.

As Jim loaded bullets into the magazine, Gunny walked away from the two of them and stared out at the range.

"It's good to have you back," Sawyer said. "Though it doesn't feel right with Rip missing. You two were like brothers."

James nodded, his gaze on Gunny. He wanted to question Sawyer about his account of what happened in Honduras and on the boat the day before when Cord disappeared. With Gunny standing nearby, he didn't feel the timing was right. To get open, honest feedback, he preferred to get each of the Pit Viper team members alone. If anyone had a different story, it would become apparent quickly.

Once they had rounds loaded into their magazines, Sawyer and Jim stepped out on the firing range, each carrying his rifle, with his magazine in the opposite hand.

Jim twisted a couple of foam earplugs and jammed them into his ears.

The two men burned through thirty rounds and reloaded for another thirty rounds.

Jim adjusted his sights once and hit his targets dead on every time after that. When they were done, he'd qualified expert as predicted.

Sawyer clapped him on the back. "Damn, Monahan, you'd never know you'd been on vacation for two years."

"What makes you think I was on vacation?" James bent to collect the brass bullet casings scattered around his feet.

Sawyer dropped to his haunches to gather his.

Out of the corner of his eye, Jim noted Gunny had wandered away with a cell phone to his ear. If he wanted to find out any information from Sawyer, now was the time.

"Speaking of vacations, have you been on any particularly exciting missions? After two years on a ranch I could do with something to get my blood flowing."

Sawyer's hand froze over the shell casings he'd reached for. He hesitated for a moment, before scooping up the brass casings and dropping them into his hat. Still, he didn't respond to Jim's question.

"Sorry," Jim said. "I didn't mean to poke a sore spot."

Sawyer glanced over his shoulder at Gunny.

The old sergeant stood with his back to them and his phone to his ear.

"Things didn't go well on our last assignment," CPO Houston said, his voice low.

"What do you mean?" James asked.

"It was supposed to be a hot insertion and extraction. We expected trouble and had practiced the scenario here before we deployed." He sat back on his haunches, staring out across the range and shaking his head. "What we didn't expect was for it to go so easily."

"Easily?"

"Yeah. We found our target, got him out of the compound and were on our way back to our pickup point when it fell apart." He clenched his fist around the casings in his hand. "We shouldn't have lost Gosling. His kid will never know him."

"What happened?" James asked. "Did the team come under fire?"

"That's just it. It was as if someone was gunning at only Gosling and the man we'd gone in to extract."

"Just the two of them? What about the rest of the team?"

Sawyer shook his head. "I was behind Gosling. We were hurrying out with our man intact, little to no resistance. The next thing I know, Gosling moved up alongside the extraction, he was hit, the agent was hit and the rest of us dropped to the ground."

After a short pause, Sawyer continued, "What was weird was that no other shots were fired immediately. Before we hit the dirt, the sniper could have taken out a couple more of us." Sawyer turned to Jim. "But he didn't."

"So Gosling could have been collateral damage," Jim concluded.

Sawyer bowed his head.

"You two done lollygaggin'?" Gunny had finished his call and rejoined them on the range.

Jim straightened, his hat full of empty casings. "Ready when you are."

"Good. I don't have time to babysit the new kid. We have work to do. I'll be glad when they call off the Coast Guard and local rescue units. I want to get our own people on the river to find Schafer's body. Dead or alive."

"How will you justify it with the commander?" Sawyer asked.

Gunny jerked his head toward Jim. "Familiarization exercise for the newbie. I got no argument. He approved."

Jim was glad to know the new commander of SBT-22 felt strongly enough about finding his man that he allowed the team to go out and look again.

Excitement surged through Jim's veins at the thought of getting out on the boat. Nothing felt better than having the wind in your face, other than knowing whether your buddy was still alive.

MELISSA HAD TOSSED and turned through the night, her thoughts bouncing between Cord's disappearance and James's kiss. Sleep had been fleeting. Her dreams, like her waking thoughts, alternated between sniper fire and running through the jungle-like undergrowth of southern Mississippi. In the midst of her flight, she'd been captured by a tall, muscular Navy SEAL. The terrain changed to the inside of a hotel room with a king-size bed. She and James had fallen onto the sheets, naked, making passionate love with the threat of discovery looming over them.

By the time Mel had given up on sleep, showered and dressed, the sun had risen. She grabbed a piece of toast in the breakfast bar on the way out of the hotel. With her list in hand, she planned on visiting each of the addresses Hank Derringer had provided for members of the Pit Viper team.

Hank had gone so far as to list the names of their spouses next to the addresses. If she got caught snooping around, she would come up with some excuse.

First stop, Benjamin Raines's apartment. She set the GPS in her truck and followed the directions, arriving in front of an apartment complex where half the parking lot was empty, most of the residents having left for work. Hank's list didn't specify a spouse, but Raines could have a girlfriend living with him.

Mel found the upstairs apartment, thankful the door wasn't visible from the parking lot. She knocked on the door and waited for someone to answer. When no one did, she knocked again. After the second knock received no response, she dug in her purse for the slim metal tool she carried around with her in case she locked her keys in her apartment. It worked great for picking locks.

A niggle of guilt pulled at her as she jimmied the lock until the locking mechanism turned. With a quick glance over her shoulder, she pushed the door open, stepped inside and closed the door behind her. "Hello," she called out softly. Nothing moved. Lights were off, but sun pushed around the edges of the blinds on the windows, giving her enough illumination to move around the room without switching on the overhead lighting.

A quick glance around Raines's apartment revealed nothing out of the ordinary. A typical male's apartment, it was sparsely furnished with a brown fabric couch and a giant television across from it. Pizza boxes littered a plain wooden coffee table with leftover slices still inside. Empty beer cans stood beside the boxes.

In the corner was a duffel bag filled with what appeared to be clean uniforms and underwear. Probably a bag staged for quick deployments.

Moving on to the bedroom, Mel shook her head. Dirty clothing was piled in a corner. The bed was unmade and the bathroom needed a good cleaning. So much for the military corners and neatly hung clothing you'd expect from a highly trained SEAL.

She went through the dresser, filled with T-shirts, underwear and socks. One drawer held old bills, loose coins and letters from family, based on the last names listed on the return addresses. Mel riffled through the bills and letters, just in case something was stuck between them. Nothing jumped out at her and she moved to the nightstand.

A photo frame stood on the stand with a picture of a bunch of men in full combat gear, less their helmets. Shaggy hair, scruffy chins and grins a mile wide. Melissa recognized Cord in the middle, with the same smile he'd had when they were growing up. What had gone so terribly wrong for this to happen to him?

She understood he had a dangerous job, but he had to be desperate to call her to collect the packet. Based on what had happened when she did get the packet out of the post office box, it had been watched. And Cord had probably been watched or he would have gotten it himself.

Mel lifted the mattress. Nothing. A glance beneath the bed produced only old shoeboxes and dirty socks. The man needed a wife to get him to clean up after himself.

The bathroom provided no more clues than the rest of the apartment. After fifteen minutes of searching, Melissa left the apartment, locking it behind her.

Next address on the list was Quentin Lovett's. Fortunately, he lived in the same complex as Raines and he didn't have a spouse.

A minute later, Mel jimmied the lock on Lovett's door and entered. This apartment wasn't quite as much of a mess.

The living room was neat, no pizza boxes or empty beer cans. In the kitchen, the dishes were all clean and stacked in the cabinets. A junk drawer had organizer baskets in it for batteries, paper clips and keys. A curious array of plastic cards from gambling casinos were arranged in one of the baskets, indicating Lovett had visited six casinos and kept cards for future visits.

Apparently Lovett preferred order in his home and he liked gambling.

Mel passed through the living room. The door to the bedroom was closed part way. She eased it open and peered inside.

Here, the bed was rumpled, the blankets and sheets piled in a lump in the middle.

About the time Mel started forward, the lump moved.

She froze, her heart slamming into her ribs.

"Quentin?" a gravelly female voice called out.

Mel hadn't knocked on this door as she had at Raines's apartment and she could have kicked herself.

The blankets moved again.

Mel tiptoed quietly, backing out of the room, pulling the door closed behind her.

"Is that you, Quentin?" The voice sounded louder, clearer.

Mel hustled back across the living room to the front door and would have made it out if she hadn't tripped on the throw rug in front of the door.

She fell, landing on her knees.

"Stop playing games, Quentin, and come back to bed."

Rolling to her feet, Melissa reached for the door.

"Who the hell are you?" a voice demanded behind her.

Caught, Mel straightened, spun around and faced the blonde with the sheet wrapped around her naked body.

Chapter Seven

Drawing on all the attitude she could muster, Mel squared her shoulders and tipped her chin up. "I should be asking you the same thing."

The blonde with the rumpled bed-hair narrowed her gaze. "I asked first."

"Quentin asked me to come by and clean his apartment." Mel stared down her nose at the blonde. "He didn't bother to tell me it would be occupied. I'll come back when you're not here."

The woman's brows dipped. "Right. You're the maid." She spun and headed back into the bedroom, her voice carrying through into the living room. "I knew I shouldn't have trusted him. He said he wasn't in a relationship. I was the only woman he had eyes for. Well, bull crap on that." When she emerged she wore a sundress and was slipping her feet into a pair of strappy sandals. She curled her lip into a sneer. "As far as I'm concerned, you can have the lying bastard."

"I don't want him. I only came to clean the apartment."

The woman snorted. "Yeah, right." She stormed past Melissa and out the door, slamming it behind her.

Melissa made a quick pass through the apartment, finding nothing that would lead to a clue. She concluded Quentin's apartment was a wasted effort. Worse, she'd been seen by someone after breaking and entering. Not good.

She vowed to be a little more circumspect at the next residence.

Glancing at the list, she noted it was the gunnery sergeant's home address, a little more of a challenge if someone was home.

Mel climbed into her red truck and arrived at Gunny's street as a shiny pearl-white BMW sports car pulled out of the driveway and roared away.

Curious about the expensive, sporty vehicle and who would be driving it away from Gunny's house, she followed the car to a local gym, where the driver of the BMW parked and got out.

A curvaceous platinum blonde climbed out of the car in designer yoga pants and matching sports bra. Instead of looking as if she was going for a workout, she appeared to be going to a cover shoot for a sports magazine. Hair perfect. Makeup perfect. Tennis shoes with little wear on the soles.

Even more curious about the driver of the BMW, Mel parked a couple of rows over and reached into the backseat for the gym bag she kept there in case she ever had time to work out. Her bicycle shorts and a T-shirt would have to suffice in what appeared to be an upscale gym.

She hurried toward the gym behind the woman in the yoga outfit.

"Excuse me," Mel called out.

The blonde stopped, executed a perfect model's turn and raised her brows. "Yes?"

"Are you familiar with this gym?"

"I am." She waited for Mel to catch up.

"Oh, good. I was hoping to join a yoga class or maybe

a jazzercise group. I'm new in the area." Mel held out her hand. "I'm Melissa."

The woman shook her hand. "I'm Lillian. Nice to meet you."

"Same."

Lillian waved in the direction of the building. "I'm headed to a yoga class if you'd like to join me."

"I'd love it."

"You'll probably have to join the gym first. But I'll save a space for you."

"Thank you. It's always so hard to start over in a new place."

"Yes, it is." She pushed through the door and held it for Mel. "Talk to the young lady at the front desk. She'll help you."

"Thank you so much. I'll see you in a few minutes."

Mel made note of the room Lillian entered, then headed for the desk to inquire about membership and the yoga class.

"The free trial to the gym is for use of all the equipment and the courts. You have to pay a registration fee for the class, if there is room available," the young brunette behind the counter said.

Mel paid the full fee for the yoga class, anxious to get inside and find Lillian. A quick stop in the locker room to change and she hit the yoga room.

As promised, Lillian had saved a spot for her on the floor near the back of the room.

The class instructor had assumed the cat pose on her hands and knees, her back arched.

Mel grabbed a spare mat from a stack at the side of the room, laid it out beside Lillian and assumed the same pose.

"Thanks," she whispered to Lillian.

For the next thirty minutes, she worked all the kinks out of her joints and introduced herself to a few muscles she'd forgotten she had. When the class was over, she replaced the mat where she'd found it and hurried to find Lillian tying a ribbon around the mat she'd carried in.

"I'd like to thank you for pointing me in the right direction," Mel said. "Do you have time for a cup of tea or coffee?"

Lillian glanced at the clock on the wall. "I have a hair appointment in an hour. That should be plenty of time. There's a lovely place a couple doors down if you don't mind going there in your workout clothes."

Mel laughed. "I could use some liquid to rehydrate my body. It's been a while since I've done yoga. I'm always amazed at what a workout it is."

"I know. I've never been able to get my husband to understand. He thinks all workouts should include a lot of rolling around in the dirt and sweat."

Mel pushed the exit door open and held it for Lillian. "Sounds like a man who gets into his workouts."

"Oh, it's all part of his job. He's a Navy SEAL." She shrugged and turned left to follow the sidewalk past a florist's shop and a weight loss clinic. "SEALs have a nasty job, if you ask me. They're always covered in mud, dirt and that paint they put on their faces. Do you know how hard it is to get that out of your clothes?" She shook her head. "I wish he'd give it up and go to work for a large corporation."

"I would think that having a SEAL for a husband would be every woman's dream." Mel found the tearoom, opened the door and waited while Lillian entered.

"Not me. I had greater expectations of Frank. He could have been anything, but he chose to be a SEAL."

The disgusted curl of Lillian's lip made Mel grind her teeth together as they stepped up to the counter to order.

Lillian ordered without looking at the menu. "Chai tea."

Mel ordered the same and paid while Lillian found a

seat. The barista whipped up the order and placed it on a tray for Mel to carry to the table and the waiting woman.

Though she wanted to tell Lillian to grow up, she managed to sound sympathetic. "Must be tough as the wife of a SEAL."

"Good Lord, yes," the other woman exclaimed. "I never know when he's going to be home to pay the bills. If it wasn't for me, the yard would be a mess, all overgrown with weeds."

"I like a nice yard, too," Mel agreed. She took pride in getting out once a week to mow her little lawn and edge the sides of the driveway.

"Oh, honey, I have the best lawn service. They take care of mowing, edging and they even plant my annuals the way I want them."

"What do you do for a living, Lillian?"

"Me?" Her eyes widened. "Why, I take care of my husband's wants and needs."

"You don't work outside the home?"

"Good heavens, no."

"You must be one of those good moms who stay home with the kids, then."

Her brows rose even higher. "Does this body look like it's had children?" She waved a hand. "I told Frank a long time ago I'd take care of him as long as he took care of me. My job is to stay in shape and make sure he has a healthy meal on the table when he's home to appreciate it. I manage the housekeeper and the gardener and take the car to have it detailed twice a month."

All on a gunnery sergeant's pay? Melissa smiled and kept her mouth shut.

"It's a miracle we manage. That's why I want Frank to quit and get a real job. One that pays better so that we can live somewhere else besides this sweaty hell called

Mississippi. I can't get a hairstyle to stay long enough for me to get from my house to my car!"

"You poor thing." Mel wanted to laugh out loud, but the woman was serious.

"I know. If I'd only listened to my father, I wouldn't have married an enlisted man." She sat up straight. "My father was a colonel in the Marine Corps. If I'd listened to him, I'd have gone to college, met a man with a business career ahead of him and wouldn't be stuck in this hell."

Now Mel didn't want to laugh—she wanted to reach out and slap the woman for her selfish ways.

"But then that's what love is. You have to make sacrifices for the man you fall in love with, right?" Lillian rolled her eyes and sighed. "What about you? Are you married to a military man?"

"No." Nor could she be. She had a career that didn't give her the option of following her husband around the world.

"Good. My advice to you is, don't marry a military man. They move too much and the pay is dismal. What brought you here?"

Mel smiled. "My boyfriend is a SEAL." Her lips twitched at the lie, knowing it would get the lovely Lillian wound up all over again. And it did.

"Oh, honey." The blonde reached over and touched her hand. "Drop him now and run as fast as you can."

"I'll keep that in mind." Mel sipped her tea. "Does your husband talk about his work?"

"If he does, I pretend to listen. It's all about shooting this and sneaking here and there in the water, through villages. Blah, blah, blah. You hear about one mission, you've heard them all."

"My boyfriend doesn't tell me a whole lot. But he did say something about one of the teams losing a SEAL on their last mission. It scares me to think my sweetie might be shot."

"Oh, that one." Lillian leaned in. "Frank's not supposed to tell me about his secret missions, but a wife knows, and he slips up every once in a while. Apparently one of the young SEALs died on that one. I don't know all the details. I just know that Frank came back all upset and cranky. I couldn't get him to talk to me for two days after it happened. I had to threaten to divorce him to make him speak to me."

"Do you know what happened?"

"Only that it didn't go according to plan. Frank felt responsible for the boy's death. Although, they sign up for the danger. I think those boys get high on adrenaline." Lillian shook her head. "I don't know why Frank should feel like he's at fault." She glanced at the clock over the counter and gasped. "I have to get to my stylist's shop or he'll give my spot to someone else. Then it's off to get a mani-pedi." She rose from her seat. "I enjoyed our little chat. Maybe after our next yoga session we can do this again."

"I'd like that." Mel stood and walked out with Lillian. They parted and Mel waited until Lillian left the parking lot before heading for her own truck.

They were halfway through the day and she felt no closer to finding Cord or the person responsible for shooting him.

Frustrated, she climbed into her truck, pulled out her smartphone and searched for the local marinas. If she could rent a boat and get on that river where Cord was shot, she might have a better chance of finding Cord or finding evidence that he was still alive.

JAMES CLIMBED ABOARD the thirty-three-foot SOC-R water-craft along with eight other SEALs and Gunny. After two years on dry land, it took a moment to get his balance.

"Feels good, doesn't it?" Quentin Lovett smiled.

Sawyer manned the GAU-17/A minigun in its position

on the starboard bow, while Montana affixed his to its stand and stood behind the matching minigun on the opposite side. The weapons weren't loaded, but the men were so conditioned to their positions, they stood in place, on the alert, ready for anything as they'd been trained.

James had been in Montana's position when he'd last been assigned to SBT-22 two years ago. He wasn't sure where to stand until Gunny pointed to the machine gun on the starboard stern of the boat. "Take Schafer's place."

Duff finished fixing the gun into its slot. "It's all yours." The big man stepped up behind the grenade launcher and rested his arms on the weapon.

A chill rippled across James's skin in the hot and humid Mississippi air as he took the position involuntarily vacated by the man he was there to find. He stood behind the gun and braced himself as the engines roared and the boat moved away from the dock.

Seconds later, they blasted down the canals and onto the Pearl River at forty knots, with the wind in their faces.

It felt good to be back on a boat, skimming across the water, every man on board trained, physically fit and focused on his mission. James had missed the camaraderie of being on the team more than anything. Cattle ranching could be solitary, working out in the field, just the cowboy and the cows. On a SEAL team, you knew your buddies had your back.

Except in Cord's case.

With the wind loud in his ears and nothing but his thoughts to occupy him while he searched the underbrush for signs of Cord, he reviewed what he'd learned from Montana and Sawyer. Someone had picked off the DEA agent and Petty Officer Gosling because he'd gotten in the way. The camp they'd extracted him from didn't wake up to the fact they were under attack until after the first two bullets had been fired.

Hampered by two bodies they carried out, the team barely made it back to the pickup point before the terrorists came barreling after them in their vehicles equipped with machine guns.

Since a sniper had picked off the DEA agent, he had to know they were extracting him. A good sniper would have been able to kill more than the two men he'd hit. He could have taken out all seven of them before they really knew they were under attack.

So why hadn't he? The only reason James could come up with was that he hadn't been hired to kill all the SEALs, just the undercover agent.

Someone didn't want it to get out that the agent had evidence that American weapons were being supplied to a terrorist training camp in Honduras. Jim bet the agent had gotten too close to discovering who was supplying the weapons and needed to get out while he could.

What bothered him most was that a sniper had known whom he was supposed to shoot and was in too good a position for it to be an accident. Someone had tipped him off. Someone who'd had access to the information about the operation. Perhaps someone hired by the organization supplying the weapons.

If Cord had information from the DEA agent, he was just as much a target as the agent and wouldn't last long with an expert sniper after him. All the more reason to remain "dead."

Gunny slowed the boat as they neared a narrow bend in the river and brought it to a halt.

"This is it. This is where Rip fell overboard," Lovett said. All the men stood silently scanning the water and the underbrush for any signs of Cord's body.

Jim didn't expect to find Cord here. Had he been wounded severely, the search teams would have found him by now, or his body would have been carried downriver.

If he'd come by himself, James would have liked to search the shoreline for signs of the sniper's location.

He scanned the shoreline from the position Cord would have been standing. A sniper had to have known Cord would be on the starboard side and would have positioned himself on the side of the river that would give him the best shot.

"What did you think we'd find, Gunny?" Montana asked.

Gunny raised binoculars to his eyes and focused on the shoreline on each side of the river. "If he survived long enough to make it to shore, he might have left a blood trail."

"Don't you think the rescue teams would have considered that?" Lovett commented.

"Yes. But we know Rip. If he survived, wouldn't we be better able to find signs?" Gunny steered the boat closer to the shore on one side and trolled slowly. All the men on that side of the boat, including Jim, studied the underbrush and steep muddy banks.

"Anything?" Gunny called out.

"Nothing here," Sawyer responded.

"Should we suit up in our dive gear?" Duff asked, the most eager diver among the crew. He spent his vacations off the coasts of Mexico and Costa Rica, diving. Muddy water didn't bother him. He loved breathing through a regulator. He especially liked setting explosives underwater, and he was the best at it.

Gunny shook his head. "River's too muddy. Besides, they dredged and didn't find anything." He turned the boat and skimmed the other shoreline, moving slowly, raising his binoculars.

They traveled several hundred yards downriver, and Gunny turned the boat and went up the other side again.

"Nothing." Gunny lowered his binoculars.

"What do you think happened?" Montana asked, his face solemn, his hands resting on his minigun.

Gunny's lips thinned. "Wish I knew."

Duff hung his head. "Damn shame. Rip was one of the best."

Jim didn't bow his head with Duff. As far as he was concerned, Cord wasn't dead. He wouldn't stop looking until he found his friend.

At a break in the foliage, Gunny pulled up to the riverbank and ordered Duff and Garza out to check for footprints, blood or broken branches, anything that would indicate whether or not a man had passed through the underbrush.

Both men disappeared into the dense undergrowth only to return a few minutes later, shaking their heads.

Two more passes and four more stops along the side of the river and Gunny called it, turning the boat toward the dock.

Jim searched the riverbanks along with the rest of the crew, but he knew that if Cord had *wanted* to disappear, he'd have gotten a lot farther away before climbing out of the river. He wouldn't swim upstream. Instead, he would have let the current take him a lot farther downstream before he'd attempted to exit the water, and then he would have covered his tracks.

Knowing all that, Jim kept his mouth shut. Cord hadn't trusted his team or someone on his team enough to confide in them. Jim wouldn't redirect Gunny's efforts to find the man. He'd come back when he could do so alone…or with Melissa.

Chapter Eight

Hopefully, Monahan would remember how to get to the area where Cord had disappeared. He had sent Melissa a text message to meet him there at the marina when he got off work.

She'd decided to continue with the waitress job in case she could glean more information from the owner or the clients. She liked Eli and knew he needed the help.

With her hair shoved up into a fisherman's hat and wearing jeans and a bulky life vest, Melissa hoped she appeared to be just another angler taking off from the marina. She settled the cheap fishing pole and bait bucket in the bottom of the little boat she'd rented for the afternoon and waited for Monahan to show up.

Though she'd been fishing many times with her grandfather up in Ohio, she knew it would be easy to get lost among the rivers, bayous and canals in the area. Eli, at the Shoot the Bull Bar, hadn't minded that she called in to say she wouldn't be there until nine that evening. With it being Friday night, he needed the help later in the evening when the band played and things started getting interesting.

Melissa had spent the afternoon calling around for a marina that rented fishing boats. If Monahan didn't show up by six-thirty, she'd set out on her own, armed with tributary maps and the GPS on her smartphone.

She adjusted the bait bucket once more, anxious to get started. With miles of river to navigate, they'd be lucky to get to the location where Cord disappeared and back by the time she had to go to work.

"Where the heck is he?" she grumbled, sweat already sliding down her cheeks.

"Right in front of you."

The deep voice jerked her gaze to the dock. She glanced up from her seat in the boat and shaded her eyes with her hand.

The SEAL hovered over her, wearing shorts, old tennis shoes and a tank top that displayed all the striking tattoos on his arms.

"Thank goodness. I only have a few hours to search since I have to work the bar tonight."

Monahan handed her a fishing pole and stepped into the little pirogue, which was nothing more than a johnboat with a thirty-horsepower motor on it.

She didn't want to get anything bigger in case they had to go in shallow water. Granted, it would take a lot longer to get where they were going with the smaller engine, but it would also slip in and out of tree shadows more easily than a bigger boat with a deeper hull and a louder engine. The idea was to get where they were going unnoticed.

With all his tattoos showing, Monahan would stick out and be remembered. "Do you have a shirt to go over those…arms," she asked, catching herself before she said *lovely muscles*.

He chuckled and shrugged out of the camouflage backpack he had slung over one shoulder. "In the bag."

"Good. Put it on. Your tattoos are too memorable if we're spotted on the river."

"Yes, ma'am." He stripped out of the tank top and stood in front of her, his chest bare and incredibly gorgeous.

Melissa swallowed hard, trying hard to remember her

name and why she was there, when all those muscles and tattoos made her heart flutter and her pulse bang against her veins.

Black Celtic vines ringed his biceps and an eagle spread its wings across his back, the feathers fanning across his shoulders. God, he was beautiful.

Melissa's mouth dried and she ran her tongue across her lips.

James dug in his backpack, his muscles rippling with every movement until he removed a heather-gray T-shirt and slipped it over his head. He turned to face her as he pulled it down over rock-hard abs.

Melissa followed the hem until it completely covered his six-pack and found herself at a complete loss for words.

"Did you want me to steer?" he asked, his lips twitching at the corners as he settled a Texas Rangers ball cap over his head.

"Um, yes!" Melissa stood so fast she nearly fell out of the boat.

James caught her arm and steadied her. "Be careful."

Hell yeah, she needed to be careful. If she wasn't, she might just fall—head over heels for this hulking Navy SEAL in the boat with her.

He's just a man. Those were only muscles, she reminded herself. Muscles she wanted to touch, taste and press her body against. *Holy hell!*

He held on to her as she stepped around him, their bodies brushing against each other, stirring sensations Mel thought had gone dormant in her long dry run on dating. She sucked in her breath and held it until she was settled in the front seat and he was ensconced in the back, his hand on the tiller.

He reached behind him and pulled the rope. The engine started the first time, roaring to life.

Lowering the propeller into the water, he steered the boat into the canal and away from the dock.

Once they were out of earshot of anyone who might overhear their conversation, James asked, "What did you find out today?"

Sitting sideways on the front bench seat, she filled him in on her visits to Lovett's and Raines's apartments.

"You broke into their places?" The SEAL grinned. "Isn't that illegal, even for the FBI?"

Mel pressed her lips together. "Cord is a very good friend of mine. If something happened to me, he'd do whatever it took to help me."

James nodded. "He would. Rip is just that kind of guy."

"Why do the guys call him Rip?"

"It's his nickname. He's pretty good at skydiving. He can maneuver a chute to within a one-foot-square block landing on the ground."

"Rip Cord," she concluded. "Like on a parachute."

"Right."

They'd been traveling along at what felt like a snail's pace for twenty minutes when James spoke again. "We're within a mile of the point at which Rip disappeared. If he was able to get himself out of the water—"

"Which he was." Mel pivoted on her seat to cast a glance back at James. "I prefer to think positive."

James nodded. "He would have stayed in the water longer to throw any search parties off. He wouldn't have gotten out of the river in the area the search party would concentrate."

"Makes sense."

He nodded toward a break in the branches along the shoreline. "The underbrush is pretty dense along this stretch. He might have gotten out at a gap in the branches and bramble. Or he might have found a tributary and swam up in it before getting out of the water."

Mel pointed. "What about that one? Can we get the boat into it to search?"

James swiveled the tiller and the boat altered course to swing into the mouth of the tributary feeding into the Pearl River. As soon as they left the river's current, James shut off the motor and the little boat drifted forward.

The tributary started out wide enough to fit the boat, but quickly narrowed to nothing more than a creek, growing shallower the farther in they drifted.

Mel studied the banks. No sign of footprints, blood or broken branches caught her attention.

"Look." James pointed to a low-hanging branch that cast a dark shadow over the ground. Something moved in the shade.

A thrill of excitement and fear rippled through Mel and she whispered, "What is it?"

"Watch." He lifted a wooden paddle from the bottom of the boat and reached out to the shadowy area with it.

Powerful jaws opened, exposing a wide white mouth lined with wicked rows of razor-sharp teeth. The long snout of an alligator snapped at the paddle with a fierce crunch.

James jerked the paddle back and grinned. "I hope Cord didn't try to get out here. You see that sharp rise in the ground behind her?"

Mel stared past the alligator, noting the hump of dirt behind it. "I see it."

"That's her nest," James said.

A shiver snaked down Mel's spine and she looked at the banks and water with apprehension. "Are there many alligators in this river?"

"Let's put it this way, you don't want to fall in. If you do, you hope you get out at the right spot."

A lead weight settled in Mel's gut. "Do you think Cord…"

"No. I think he's smart enough to know what the odds are and how to get out of the water before he becomes breakfast."

"But if he was in the river for over a mile, any number of alligators could have come after him."

James chuckled. "Thinking positive, remember?" Using the paddle, he pushed off a cypress tree trunk, sending the little boat back out of the tributary and into the river.

He started the engine and sent the skiff skimming through the water, slowly heading upstream.

Mel stared hard at the banks until her eyes burned.

A quarter of a mile farther, James turned the boat, heading toward the bank where a willow tree leaned drunkenly over the water, its branches dangling low, the tiny leaves dragged by the river's current.

As they neared, Mel gripped the sides of the boat. "Aren't you going to stop?"

"No," he said. "Duck."

The bow of the little boat disappeared in the leaves of the willow tree and Mel bent forward and crossed her arms over her head. The supple branches brushed over the back of her head and neck.

"You can sit up now." James killed the engine and the boat drifted through a grotto formed by the overhanging trees. "This one goes back a lot farther." The stream was wide enough and deep enough for the little boat to go at least to the bend in the creek ahead. What lay beyond was hidden in the trees and brush.

Mel turned her head left and right, scanning the shoreline for signs of Cord or alligators. "See anything?"

"If I was Cord, I'd have chosen just such a spot. It would have been hard to see into this area from the river and it appears free of alligators."

The breath she'd been holding while he spoke released from her lungs. "I don't see any footprints."

"You wouldn't. He'd have covered them." James nodded toward a log laying half in the water and half on the muddy banks. "That log would provide good camouflage."

"Can we get closer?"

James lifted the paddle and dug it into the water, sending the boat toward the log.

As they neared the bank, a turtle slipped off the log and plopped into the water, swimming away.

"Just so you know, that was a snapping turtle," James noted calmly.

"Are they dangerous?"

"If you put your finger in its mouth it could take it off."

Mel pulled her fingers away from the edge of the boat. "Anything else I should be afraid of?"

"Snakes."

A shiver shook her from her head to her toes. "That's something we didn't see a whole lot of in Ohio. I admit, I'm a chicken when it comes to snakes. What kinds are there around here?"

"Lots of different kinds. The ones you have to be wary of are the water moccasins. Some people call them cottonmouths."

"How do you tell them apart from the others?"

"You can't really tell because they are a muddy-brown color like a lot of different snakes. But when they open their mouths, they're white inside."

"Great. So I wait until a snake opens its mouth to determine whether or not it's a water moccasin?" Mel shook her head. "What hell have we come to?"

James chuckled. "Southern Mississippi. And wait until we get off the river. You'll want to check all over for ticks and chiggers."

An involuntary reflex had her hand rising to scratch at an imaginary itch. "Cord better be alive, because I want to kill him for putting me out here in this nasty jungle."

"Shh." James raised a hand to his lips. "Did you hear that?"

Voices sounded through the trees around the shrouded bend and hacking sounds like someone clearing brush away.

"Who do you think it is?" Mel said, barely breaking the silence.

James's eyes narrowed as he stared into the trees and branches. "I don't know, but I should check it out."

"What if we're trespassing on someone's private property?"

"This area is a wildlife refuge. Likely, *they're* trespassing."

"And they won't want to be caught." Mel nodded. "Let's get a look, then. I'll be quiet." She pointed at the water. "But I'm not getting in the water."

"We'll go by land."

That option didn't much appeal to her, either. Alligators, snakes, snapping turtles and ticks weren't her idea of a picnic in the park. She'd have to remember to request assignments in the city, where all she had to contend with were guns, gangs and vehicular homicide.

James paddled toward a low spot on the shore, running the front end up onto the mud. Mel leaped out and grabbed the tie-off line and held it while James climbed out of the boat.

He dragged the boat farther up the bank into the trees. "Just don't think about the animal critters. They might be the least of our worries." With a wink, he led the way through the brush, pushing aside limbs and briar vines.

Mel was glad she'd worn a long-sleeved shirt and jeans. Her tennis shoes would be a mess by the time she got back to the marina.

They moved quietly, the spongy ground absorbing the sound of their footsteps.

Whacking, slicing sounds grew louder the closer they got and the voices sounded angry.

"Don't know why you're botherin'. No one comes out here," someone said with a deep Southern accent.

"I paid you to lead me into the bayou." The second voice was deeper, gravelly and brusque. "Shut up and keep moving."

"You paid me to take you to the cabin in the bayou. I did. It was empty. I'm done."

"You're done when I say you're done."

"I'm leaving."

"Not yet, you aren't." The deeper voice took on a sinister quality.

James carefully brushed the branch of a scrubby tree aside and Mel gasped.

A muscular man wearing a lightweight black jacket, black jeans, a dark ball cap and sunglasses stood in front of another man, blocking his path.

"I didn't sign up for trail blazin'. No, sir." The man whose path the black-jacketed man blocked wore torn, stained blue jeans, a faded T-shirt with the picture of a fish on the front, gumboots and a fisherman's hat. Sweating, his face beet red, the man carried a long machete. "I could cut you down with my knife."

The man in black pulled a gun out of his pocket and pointed it at him. "I can pull the trigger faster than you can swing that. Care to test the theory?"

Mel's heart slammed into her ribs and she muttered beneath her breath, "Crap."

YEAH, CRAP, JIM THOUGHT. A gun was a definite game changer. He froze with his hand on the branch, afraid he'd draw attention to them if he let go of it.

The man in black jerked the gun. "Move."

Gumboots headed toward the exact spot where Jim and Melissa stood, swinging his machete.

Jim eased the branch back in place and motioned for Melissa to back out of her position.

Quietly, they moved several paces to their rear, then turned and hurried back the way they'd come.

"Hey, there's someone out here," Gumboots shouted behind them.

"Run," Jim urged Melissa, praying they got far enough away before the man with the gun could get a clear shot at them.

Melissa ran ahead of Jim, leaping over logs, slapping branches out of the way, running as fast as she could through the brush and bramble.

After several tense minutes, Jim realized they were headed the wrong direction. Somehow, they'd gotten off course and were running away from the boat instead of toward it. He picked up speed and came abreast of Melissa.

She ran, breathing hard, blood oozing from the cuts on her cheek and ear where briars had snagged her pretty skin. She wouldn't make it much longer.

From the crashing sounds behind them, the other men were catching up.

"Hide," Jim said. "I'll lead them away."

"No," Melissa said, her breathing harsh, her head shaking even as she raced past a tree and stumbled over a log covered in vines. "I'm not letting you go this alone."

Jim dodged to the other side of the tree and caught up with Melissa. "We can't keep up this pace."

"Neither can they." Melissa's face glowed red, sweat gleaming on her forehead and cheeks.

"The shooter is in good shape." The humidity and heat would soon sap Melissa's energy. "Just do it." He spotted a tree covered in kudzu vines.

Grabbing Melissa's hand, he yanked her behind the tree, parted the vines and shoved her between them.

A flash of black caught his eye and a loud bang sent him running again. Without Melissa, he was able to move faster, but not too fast that he'd lose his pursuers until he had them far enough away from Melissa's location.

Once he glanced back and noted only one of the men following him—the man in the black jacket. Fortunately, he was the one he was most worried about. If the other guy were smart, he'd bug out before his partner returned to take his anger out on him.

Another round popped off and Jim wished he'd brought a weapon. Having come straight from work at Stennis, he hadn't been able to swing by the hotel and collect his pistol from the lockbox. To stop and take a stand, he'd have to do so unarmed.

If the guy had any skill shooting a weapon whatsoever, he'd nail him before he could take him out with his fists.

Jim's best bet was to hunker down and hide. He couldn't afford to get shot and leave Melissa to fend for herself. She didn't understand the terrain as he did and she couldn't run as fast as the man in the black jacket.

Jim stayed low, zigzagging as best he could through the thick underbrush. Whenever he paused for a brief moment to listen, he could hear the other man crashing through the woods behind him.

Tired and running out of steam, Jim had to either make a stand or find a good place to hide. He leaped over a log before he realized there was no place to land on the other side. The log was the edge of a steep creek bank, where time and running water had carved the bank back into the dirt, creating an overhang of soft earth.

Jim landed in the creek with a soft plop and rolled under the overhang. If he was lucky, the man behind him hadn't seen him go over the log and wouldn't spot him where he was hidden beneath the overhang.

Still breathing hard, Jim pressed his body against the dirt, dug his fingers into the mud and smeared it on his cheeks and arms to cover his exposed skin.

The crashing sound in the woods slowed as it neared his position. Soon, he couldn't hear anything.

He strained to catch even the slightest sound. Until he knew for certain the man chasing him was gone, he had to wait and listen.

After a full minute, a twig snapped.

Thankful he hadn't moved, Jim froze in place and tried to breathe as softly as possible.

Another twig snapped, then another. Soon the man's footsteps picked up and moved away from Jim's position. He gave the man another two minutes before he emerged from the overhang and climbed the creek bank to see if the coast was clear. When he could see no sign of the man in the black jeans, he headed back the way he'd come, praying Melissa had stayed hidden in the veil of vines.

Chapter Nine

After James shoved Mel into the vines clinging to a tree, she adjusted them to hide all of her, hoping none of the green leaves were poison ivy. Her father had pointed out poison ivy when she was a girl. It had three leaves per stem. These vines had one big leaf per stem. But hell, who cared? These men were out to kill them! A little itch was better than a bullet.

No sooner had she closed the gap James had made to stuff her through than footsteps sounded in the brush beside the tree.

Mel froze and held her breath to keep from giving away her location.

"Damn," a voice cursed. "They split up. I'm going after the man. Find the woman."

Mel recognized the voice as the man in the black jacket with the gun. Her heart thundered as she balanced on her haunches, tucked into the dark shadows of the vines. She wanted to jump up and run to distract him from going after James.

But logic won out.

If she gave up her location to the two men, James wouldn't necessarily get away. She knew in her heart he was honorable and he wouldn't leave her in the clutches of the two men. He'd come back after her. He stood a better chance of eluding the gunman without her in the picture.

All she had to do was sit quietly and let the men pass. James wouldn't be slowed down and he'd easily elude their pursuers.

One man ran off in the direction James had gone. The other man stomped around in the brush, muttering curses, getting closer and closer to where she hid. Melissa eased her cell phone from her pocket and removed the plastic bag she'd wrapped it in to protect it should she fall into the river. She set it on silent and aimed it through a gap in the vines, hoping that if the man got close enough, she'd get a shot of him.

"Damn cocky, if you ask me. Thinks I'm some bumpkin to be ordered around like I got no brain in my head. Would serve him right if I left him stranded in this bugridden swamp. That girl's long gone. Ain't gonna find her in this." He stepped in front of her hiding place, kicking at the leaves and brush with his big, clunky gumboots.

Melissa aimed her phone's camera and took several shots of the man, praying he didn't find her.

"Hey, girlie, come out, and I'll think about letting you live."

Though Gumboots was large and could probably choke the breath out of her by clenching one meaty fist around her neck, he wasn't the man she was worried about. Black Jacket with the gun didn't seem to have any sense of humor or remorse for any of his actions.

Eventually, Gumboots moved away, leaving Mel on her own. At first she sat quietly, ignoring the creepy crawling bugs and flying insects buzzing around. The longer she waited for James to return, the more aware she became of her surroundings and all the possibilities it contained.

Every flutter of wings against her cheeks or brush of a leaf against her skin made her jump and think of the cool,

smooth scales of a snake or the hungry snout of an alligator. And she didn't even want to think about what insects
were crawling around on the vines and the ground she
crouched against. When she was moving at least she had
a fighting chance to outrun them.

Sitting quietly, she began to imagine all kinds of horrible creepy crawlies. Mel wanted to scratch her arms and
nose so badly she had to grit her teeth and close her eyes
for a full minute until the urge went away.

The sharp report of gunfire made her eyes pop open.

James?

He'd told her to stay put until he came back, not to
move.

As she sat there, biting her lip, sweat trickling down
her temples, she struggled with the need to check on him,
to see for herself he was all right. Images of him lying in
a pool of his own blood flitted through her head and tears
stung her eyes.

Please, James, be okay.

The crunch of sticks and branches breaking sounded
close by. She stared through the tiny gaps between the
leaves and vines, trying to determine whether the pass-
erby was friend or foe.

A flash of a black jacket and sunglasses had her holding steady in the shadows. Her breath caught and held in
her throat. For a brief moment, she got a glimpse of his
hand holding a gun. Had he used it to kill James? Was the
SEAL bleeding out at that very moment?

Mel raised her hand with the cell phone in it and positioned it to catch the profile of the man's face as he passed.
She snapped several pictures, hoping one would be clear
enough to help them determine who he was and why he'd
been so determined to kill her or James.

He paused for several seconds, his head cocked to the
side as if listening. Mel held her breath, willing the shooter

to move on and do so quickly. The sooner he was out of the area, the sooner she could find James and get the hell out of there.

Black Jacket performed a 360-degree turn, his eyes narrowed. After what felt like a very long time, he moved out of her sight.

When the swish of leaves and the crunching of branches ceased, Mel counted to one hundred and parted the vines, carefully.

She could see only what was directly in front of her. The shooter should be long gone. At the very least, he'd passed the tree she hid beneath. Slowly, and careful not to make noise, Mel shoved her cell phone into the plastic bag and into her pocket, then climbed out of her hiding place and stood next to the tree.

She leaned around the trunk, peering along the path she'd seen the shooter take. Movement about fifty yards away made her jerk back, her pulse pounding.

"I said I didn't find her. She's long gone," Gumboots said. "I heard gunfire. Did you find the man?"

"I took care of both of them. Get me out of this place."

"What about the man you came to find?" Gumboots asked.

"I'll look again another day."

"Good, 'cause it ain't easy finding yer way out of these parts in the dark and it's no fun running up on them alligators when you can't hardly see 'em."

"Then let's go."

A few moments later, Mel heard the sound of a motor as it sped away from where she'd been hiding and silence fell over the woods. Complete, utter silence.

Then one by one, the crickets, frogs and cicadas started up their evening song as the light faded into dusk.

Though it wasn't cold, Mel rubbed her arms and turned the direction James had disappeared.

He stood in front of her, his face covered in mud, a big smile gleaming white among the dark smudges. "Miss me?"

Mel squealed and clapped a hand over her mouth. Then she threw herself into his arms and clung to him, mud and all. "I thought he'd shot you."

"I'm fine. He never caught me in his crosshairs."

She leaned back, inspecting his body for signs of blood. "Then what was the shot fired?"

"I don't know. But let's get out of here before it gets too dark to see." He led the way back through the brush to where they'd tied off their boat.

Though the line was still attached to the tree, the boat was filled to the rim with water, the back end sunk to the bottom of the shallow inlet.

"I think I know where the bullet went," James said, his voice too cheerful for the circumstances. He inspected the ground, bent and, using a stick, lifted a bullet casing, dropping it into his pocket.

"What are we going to do?" Mel glanced around, darkness creeping in around them. "Better question is, how well do alligators see in the darkness?"

"They see pretty well. We just need to get this boat out of the water, plug the hole and head back down the river. Assuming the hole is just a hole." He grabbed the side of the small fishing boat and leaned back, dragging it up the muddy shoreline, inch by inch.

Mel moved to the other side of the craft and did the same, sweat pouring down her face by the time they got the boat out of the river enough to empty the water so that they could assess the damage.

"Not as bad as it could be," James pronounced. "It was a clean shot. The damage is limited to one somewhat small hole. All we have to do is plug it and bale as we go."

"Any idea what we can plug it with?"

James winked and pulled his shirt off.

Despite the gravity of the situation, she couldn't help her indrawn breath. The man was gorgeous. Well-defined muscles, tattoos on his shoulders and biceps and rock-solid abs. If she wasn't up to her neck in snakes and alligators…

James ripped a big square out of his T-shirt and used a knife to cut into a nearby tree. Sap oozed out of it. He rolled the wad of shirt in the sap, getting it good and gummy with the resin. Then he twisted the fabric and sap into a tight pointed wad and stuffed it into the bullet hole.

He straightened and planted his hands on his hips, studying the boat. "It won't stop it from leaking, but it will slow the flow."

"What about the engine? Will it start after being water-logged?"

"Probably not, but we have a paddle. We can get started back the way we came. At least we'll be headed down-stream."

Mel glanced at the little boat with the hole in it and out to the alligator-infested water. "You're kidding, right? That'll take forever. What if the boat sinks in the river?"

"The alternative is to stay here for the night and hope someone passes by tomorrow and we can wave them down to get a ride back."

Not liking either alternative, she stared at her cell phone. The words *No Service* glowed like a portent of doom. She shot another glance around at the lengthening shadows that could be at that moment hiding a hungry alligator. Drawing in a deep breath, Mel let it out slowly. "Okay, let's float this boat."

Together, they pushed the boat off the bank and back into the water. For the moment, the plug held with only a little water leaking in.

Once they were out in the water, James pulled the string on the motor several times before giving up. The engine didn't even rumble or make a sound during all the attempts. He shrugged. "I had to try."

He lifted the paddle and pushed it against the shore, levering the small craft out into the tributary, sending it sliding through the water toward the river.

"You don't think the men will come back to find us tonight, do you?" Mel asked as they cleared the low-hanging trees and floated out into the main part of the slow-moving river.

"No, it's getting dark. Most people who don't know this area are off the river by now. With luck, we should only run into fishermen."

"We can only hope those men are long gone," Mel said as water slowly covered the bottom of the boat.

James grabbed the cardboard cup full of worms, dumped them into the water and handed her the container. "If you want this boat to continue to float, make yourself useful."

While James paddled, Mel faced him, baling water from the bottom of the boat. Not exactly what she'd had in mind when they'd started out on this little adventure. But it beat being shot and left for the gators to scavenge.

A chill rippled across her skin as dusk turned to darkness and the sky lit with stars above.

"What made you quit the Navy?" Mel asked.

"I chose to leave for family reasons."

Vague, but interesting. Then a thought occurred to her that made her stomach roil. "Please don't tell me you're married and have a litter of kids somewhere." He'd kissed her and been so very close to making love to her.

His chuckle rumbled in the thick, humid night air. "No. I'm not married and I don't have any children. My father was dying of cancer. He and I have been close since my mother passed away when I was a kid."

Her roiling stomach dropped to her knees. "I'm sorry.

I didn't mean to be flippant. That must have been really hard."

"Yeah. He lasted two years after the diagnosis. We had a good run for those two years."

"So you were able to spend time with him." She nodded. "That's more than most people get when they lose a parent." Her parents had died in a car crash a month after she'd finished her training at Quantico. Her father had been so proud. She'd give anything to have them back or even to have had the time to say goodbye. "You were lucky."

For five more minutes, James kept rowing quietly, the small splash of the oar hitting the water the only sound competing with the frogs and bugs of the river and marshlands.

Melissa glanced up numerous times, unable to resist studying the way his muscles glistened, tinted indigo blue in the starlight. With every stroke of the paddle, the planes of his chest rippled.

Her pulse picked up and she ducked her head, bending to scoop the quickly filling hull. She pressed the plug in harder, but it wasn't doing much good. As fast as it came in, she was baling it out, praying they got to somewhere safe soon.

"What about you?" James asked. "Are you married with a passel of children tucked away in some small town?"

Mel jerked upright. "No." She hadn't met any man she could trust to stick around when she was away on assignment.

"I would have expected a beautiful woman like you to be married long ago."

"I love my job," she stated.

"And you haven't found a man who can love you and your job, right?"

Mel scooped water and poured it over the side. "That about sums it up."

"That happens a lot with SEALs. We love our jobs, but it sucks for family life."

"But you don't want to give it up," Mel added.

"Right. It's the hardest, best job I've ever had."

"It must be bittersweet to be back when you know it won't last."

"Yeah." He hesitated and then dug the paddle in the water again for several more strokes.

"Those two men back there…"

"What about them?"

"Sounded like they were looking for Cord."

"I think they were."

"I got pictures of them on my cell phone."

James's paddle froze in midstroke. "You got pictures?" He shook his head. "You could have gotten yourself killed."

She grinned and held up the cell phone in the plastic bag. "But I didn't. I'm not certain how good they turned out. If your boss really has some major firepower, does he have the ability to run the pictures against some facial-recognition software?"

"He does, as a matter of fact." James's white teeth shone in the darkness, lighting up his face. "You're an amazing woman, do you know that?"

Mel shrugged. "I had the opportunity to snap pictures with the sound off on my phone. I was quiet, and they never knew I was there."

"As soon as we get within cell-phone reception, we can shoot those off to Hank. Hopefully, he'll be able to run it and get us some answers. If we find out who else is looking for Cord, it might lead us to the man who has us all wrapped around the axles."

Mel laughed. "Or up to our ears in alligators?"

"That, too." James's teeth flashed in the near-darkness. "In the meantime, keep baling. I see a light ahead."

"A boat?" Mel twisted on her seat to glance over her shoulder.

"No, it appears to be a boat dock, and if I'm not mistaken, there's light in among the trees. Could be a house."

Mel shot a glance toward the light. By the time she returned her attention to the bottom of the boat, her feet were covered in water up to her ankles.

"I think our plug has given up," James noted. "Get ready to abandon ship."

"But we have a long way to go before we get to the dock."

"You can swim, can't you?"

"Of course I can," Mel said. "But I've never tried swimming with alligators, nor do I want the pleasure." To make a point, she baled faster.

James laid down his oar in the water and let it drift away.

"What did you do that for?" Mel demanded, baling as fast as she could, water up to her ankles.

"Because once the boat fills to a certain point, it'll sink like a rock and we'll be swimming. I'd just as soon be ready as not."

"But we still have a chance." She reached for the oar as it passed by, missing. "Here, you bale." Mel shoved the cup into James's hands. "Hurry." Cupping her hands, she splashed water out of the boat, a handful at a time.

In the next second, they reached that point James had described. The boat sank beneath Mel, dropping to the bottom of the river.

Mel was in the water up to her neck before her survival instincts kicked in, telling her to swim. She tried to touch the bottom, believing the river to be a shallow one, but when she stretched her toe out, there was nothing for her to step up on. Her head went under and she snorted a nose full of water.

IN THE MOONLIGHT, Jim watched as Mel's shiny hair sank into the water. Knowing the river could be tricky and have unexpected undertows, he swam toward the point at which she'd gone under.

Mel broke the surface sputtering and coughing.

Jim slipped an arm around her waist and steadied her back against his front. "You're okay. I've got you." He held on to her, treading water with one arm while kicking his legs hard enough to keep both of their heads above water. The lighted dock that seemed so close a moment ago appeared farther away now.

Melissa coughed again, then managed to say, "I've got this."

Still, he didn't let go, afraid she'd slip away from him in the murky water.

"Really. We'll make better time getting to the dock if we swim on our own. And I really don't want to tempt an alligator or snake to come along and see what's for supper."

Reluctantly, Jim loosened his arm from around her waist.

Melissa struck out using a breaststroke. "Last one there is gator bait!" She switched to freestyle and made short work of the distance.

Jim gave her a head start, then easily caught up and passed her, reaching the ladder to the dock in time to help her up the steps.

Melissa climbed the ladder, her eyes narrowed, her lips twitching as she breathed hard. "Show-off."

His chest swelling just a little, Jim was glad he'd kept in good shape. He'd been swimming many times in one of his favorite swimming holes on the ranch. Still, it had been a long time since he'd done any distance swimming, and his muscles and lungs were telling him about it.

But he wouldn't show it. Not to Melissa. She was one

tough cookie. If he hoped to impress her, he couldn't demonstrate any weakness.

Not that he was trying to impress her, but when she looked as she did…

Melissa stood dripping in the moonlight, her blouse clinging to her breasts and waist, emphasizing every curve and swell of her body.

Jim wanted to reach out and pull her into his arms and kiss her. Maybe even take one of the tight little nipples budding beneath her wet blouse between his teeth and nibble on it.

It took him a moment to realize that while he had been gawking at her, she was staring at his naked chest. Her eyes widened and she lurched toward the other end of the dock. Her foot caught on something and she pitched sideways.

Lunging forward, Jim caught her, smashing her against his chest to keep her from falling hard on the wooden planks.

Now that he had her there, he didn't want to let go. The moonlight shone on her wet cheeks. Even with her hair plastered against her scalp, it did little to detract from the beauty of her face and the long line of her neck. With her damp shirt against his skin, James could barely breathe and refused to move, lest he frighten her away.

Melissa's fingers curled into his skin, her short, clipped nails digging in slightly. Her lips parted and her tongue snaked out to swipe across them. "Sorry. I'm not normally so clumsy," she whispered in a ragged breath.

"I'm not sorry." He bent to capture those lips with his, sweeping his tongue past her teeth to caress the length of hers.

She leaned into him, her hands rising, weaving together behind his neck to pull him closer.

Soaked in river water, one of his shoes floating down to the gulf, Jim couldn't think of anything sexier or any other place he'd rather be than on that dock in the moonlight with Melissa.

"Thought I heard somethin'. Put your hands up where I can see 'em or I'll fill ya full of buckshot!"

off rip... text... and so close that... heart was... pounding loud...

"I thought I... moved!" Mel... hands up a few... inches from his fist. He shut... his eyes.

Chapter Ten

"Well, I'll be dad-gummed." Ronnie Boone chuckled as he sat across the Formica-topped kitchenette table from Mel while they waited for James to emerge from the tiny bathroom of the run-down shanty Ronnie and his wife, Wanda, called home. "Yer lucky ol' Nellie didn't get you before you made it to the dock."

Mel folded the long sleeves of one of Mrs. Boone's shirts up her arm so that she could see her hands. The woman had loaned her a blouse and a pair of her overalls that could have fit two of Mel inside them. But they were dry and clean and better than the sheer damp shirt she'd been wearing. "Nellie?" Mel asked.

"The twelve-foot gator what makes her home in these parts. She sits her nest in one of the tributaries nearby and comes out to hunt near the river's edge round here. I've known her to steal my string of fish from the side of my boat on occasion. One time, she 'bout took off my arm when I tried to get it back." Ronnie pushed his sleeve back to reveal a jagged scar on his forearm.

Mel shivered. "You argued with an alligator?"

The older man in the ragged overalls and scruffy beard blushed. "Yeah. Not too smart, was it? Just made me madder than a hornet. Been fishin' all day for that catch. My ol' lady weren't too happy when I come home empty-handed."

"Who you callin' ol' lady?" Wanda Boone plunked a chipped coffee mug in front of her husband. "You promised me fresh fish for supper. 'Course I was mad. Ended up havin' to take ya to the emergency room for stitches. Lucky that dang fool alligator didn't take yer whole dad-blamed arm." She nodded at the hallway. "Them jeans fit?"

"No, but the belt helped." James emerged from the hall in jeans that rose above his bare feet to midcalf and had a couple inches of loose fabric bunched up around his hips in a thick, worn leather belt. He'd stuffed his muscles into an old white T-shirt of Ronnie's, his shoulders bulging in the thin sleeves. "I can't tell you how much we appreciate your hospitality, Mr. and Mrs. Boone." He smiled at Wanda.

The charm practically shining out of his face nearly knocked Mel on her fanny. When the man smiled, it lit the entire room.

The older woman blushed. "Now, you go on there. 'Tweren't nothin' but a few old clothes. Ronnie, get on out of here and get these young folks back to civilization." She gave the chair Ronnie sat in a good shove.

Ronnie pushed to his feet. "We can go by truck or by boat. Although by truck will take twice as long. By boat, I can have ya to the marina in fifteen minutes. Tops."

Mel dreaded the thought of getting into another boat at night, but she had promised Eli she'd be at work by nine. Catching sight of an ancient clock on the Boones' wall, she groaned. It was already a quarter to nine. By the time she got back to her hotel, showered, changed and then to the bar, it would be closer to ten o'clock. "Boat would be great," she said.

Ronnie nodded and led the way out of the house and back to the dock. His boat, the same size as the one they had sunk to the bottom of the river, rocked as he stepped off the dock into the bottom.

James got in next and held out a hand to Mel.

She gladly accepted it and sat on the middle seat while James took the bow and Ronnie manned the tiller in the stern. A quick yank on the cord and the engine hummed to life.

The men talked over Mel's head as the little boat cut a smooth wake down the river to the marina. Stars and moonlight shone on the smooth surface of the river like so many diamonds on a field of satin.

By now, the marina had closed, and just as well. Mel didn't relish explaining to the owners what had happened to the rented boat. That could keep for another time, preferably after they found Cord. Alive.

As Mel stepped out of the little boat onto the dock at the marina, she leaned over and kissed Ronnie Boone's cheek. "Thank you for all your help. And be sure to tell Mrs. Boone we'll get these clothes back to her as soon as we can."

"No need to worry. They're just ol' rags."

"Thanks." Mel hurried toward her truck and climbed in.

James caught up to her as she turned the key in the ignition.

She hit the button to lower the window.

James placed his hand on the door frame and leaned in. "Where are you headed to?"

Even in his baggy, short jeans and too-tight T-shirt, he was irresistible. Mel had to lick her lips before she could get words past them. "I'm supposed to be at work already."

He frowned. "You're not going to the bar tonight, are you?"

"I am." When his frown deepened, she went on softly, "Cord's still missing."

"I don't like it. What if those two boneheads show up? They might be able to identify you."

"I was wearing a ball cap with my hair up inside it. Besides, it's a chance I'll have to take. I need to find out more about Cord's disappearance, and the only ones who might be able to shed some light are the members of the Pit Viper team."

"Then let me handle it. I'm the one on the SEAL team."

"Yeah, but you might be too close. If I get one of them drunk, they're likely to talk."

"Or attack you. These men are strong. You don't know how they'll react if they're too drunk to think straight." James shook his head. "It's too dangerous."

Mel rolled her eyes. "Sweetheart, I'm a federal agent. This is what I do."

He appeared as if he wanted to argue the point. Instead, his lips pressed into a tight line before he nodded. "You're right. And I need to give you the benefit of a doubt. Just because you're female doesn't mean you can't handle yourself."

"I couldn't have said it better myself." She liked that he worried about her, and liked it even more that he recognized the fact she could handle the situation. "Now, I need to get a shower and change before I report to work late."

"Right. See you at the hotel in fifteen minutes."

"Will do." She reversed out of the parking space and glanced in her rearview mirror.

James had climbed into his truck and was pulling out as well, falling in behind her.

Fifteen minutes later, she pulled up at the hotel and hopped out of her truck.

Before she could swipe her key card in the exterior door to the stairwell, James was beside her. They entered the building together, him holding the door for her. Rather than stop at his floor, he climbed the remaining flight to hers.

She laughed. "I can get to my room all by myself."

When she reached her door, she swiped her card and twisted the handle. "I'll be fine. You can go now—"

James pushed the door open and stepped in first. "Just want to make sure you don't have any unwanted visitors."

She frowned, irritated by his insistence on being one step ahead of her. At the same time, she couldn't help but feel the tug of attraction. James's big body filled the room. "I thought you agreed I could handle situations myself." The door swung closed behind her and she leaned against it.

James gave the room a quick glance and turned to her, his lips lifting in a wicked smile. "I know you can handle situations yourself, but it makes me feel better since I'm here." He headed for the door she was leaning on.

She should have moved, but her feet refused. "I need to get a shower," Mel said, her voice low and gravelly, her heart in her throat.

James's nodded. "Yeah, me, too. I smell like river water."

Her pulse quickened the closer he got, and leaped when he stopped in front of her.

"I'll let you get to that shower." He reached out to brush a strand of her lank hair behind her ear. "I just need to get by."

Mel leaned into that hand, her cheek brushing against his palm, everything that had happened that day rushing back at her. How he'd saved her by leading the black-jacketed man and Gumboots away, by fixing the boat enough to get them back on the river and helping her stay afloat when the boat sank.

Damn it, in the two days she'd known him she'd come to rely on him, something she rarely did. And darned if she didn't want him to leave. Her feet remained rooted to the floor, her body blocking the door. "Thanks for taking the heat off me out there. You could have been killed."

He cupped her cheek and repeated her earlier words, his lips curving upward. "This is what I do."

Her body, which was on high alert, ready for anything, wanting everything, took the lead while her brain manned the backseat to desire. "My shower can fit two." There, it was out there. She couldn't take it back. She raised her eyebrows in challenge, her breath catching and holding as she waited for his response to her blatant invitation.

His nostrils flared and the hand on her cheek froze. "It's been a long day. Don't tease me, Melissa."

Her name rolled off his tongue like a long, warm caress. Mel captured the hand on her cheek and moved it downward to slip one strap of her overalls off her shoulder. "I'm not teasing. And we need a shower."

James smoothed the other strap off her shoulder and the baggy overalls slipped down her body, whispered past her hips and pooled on the floor at her feet. She stepped out of them and turned toward the bathroom, unbuttoning her shirt as she slowly walked away.

"Are you sure about this?" he asked.

She shot a smile over her shoulder as she shrugged the shirt off. "Never more sure." The shirt drifted to the floor. Mel entered the bathroom, twisted the knob on the shower and stepped behind the curtain. She shook with anticipation, her body on fire. The cool water did nothing to chill her lust.

She stood for a moment letting the spray wash over her, taking with it the smell of the river and leaving her clean and wet, her nipples puckered, sensitized and aching. For a long moment she wondered if James would take her up on her offer. Perhaps he wasn't the kind of guy who went for one-night stands.

As for that matter, Mel wasn't that kind of girl. But for James, she'd make an exception. Not to be confused with commitment. She couldn't afford that commodity in her line of work.

She lifted her face to the spray, closing her eyes. What was taking so long?

She didn't see the shower curtain move or hear anything over the rush of water around her ears. But she felt the warmth of big, calloused hands as they curled around her hips and pulled her bottom against his hardness.

Warm lips caressed the curve of her neck. "My turn." Holding her against him, he turned her, placing himself under the spray.

Mel reached for the bar of soap and rubbed it until her hand foamed with lather. Then she turned in James's arms and smoothed her hand across his chest in slow, steady circles.

He lathered up and swept his hands across her shoulders and down her arms and up her back. Though they were both naked it was as though neither wanted to be the first to make the big move.

What was wrong with them? Mel usually wasn't hesitant when it came to what she wanted, and she doubted James was, either.

Taking the first step, Mel trailed her hand down James's chiseled, muscular torso to the line of hair angling toward the apex of his thighs and the stiff erection jutting out, hard, thick and ready.

Her hands circled him, sliding over his length. He felt so damned good, her core tightened and her blood pumped fast and hot throughout her body.

James's fingers rounded to her front and brushed across her breasts, stopping to tweak the nipples into tight little beads. He leaned back and let the shower spray the suds off the swells and then leaned forward to suck a nipple between his lips.

Mel let her head fall back, pressing the breast deeper into his mouth. The man was gorgeous and she was about to make love to him.

BEFORE JAMES HAD entered Mel's hotel room, he'd convinced himself he was tired and in need of rest, not another round of intense exercise. After PT with his old unit, testing his strength and determination, and then running through the jungle-like underbrush of the southern Mississippi Delta, he should have been exhausted.

Once he stepped through Mel's room door, all thoughts of rest flew from his mind. Even in her borrowed overalls and the oversize shirt, she'd been incredibly beautiful. Out of those clothes was even better. He'd had every good intention of checking her room and getting the hell out.

Oh, but the sweet Melissa had plans of her own.

Jim bent and hooked the backs of her thighs and lifted her, wrapping her legs around his middle and turning to press her against the wall.

"Protection?" she said, her voice catching as the cool tile touched her back.

"Damn." He let her legs down and reached out of the shower to grope in the pockets of the pants he'd hung on a hook on the back of the door. Removing his soggy wallet, he extracted a foil package.

Melissa closed the curtain and took the packet from James, tearing it open. Then she rolled it down over his staff.

"Better?" he asked.

She nodded.

Once again Jim scooped Melissa up by the backs of her thighs and wrapped her legs around his middle.

He pinned her arms above her head and skimmed the back of his hand down her front. "Your skin is so soft. I find it a delicious contradiction to your tough-gal persona."

Melissa laughed. "Thank you, I think."

His lips curled. "That was a compliment."

"In that case, thanks." She grinned and dug her heels into his buttocks, urging him to take her.

Still, he held back, kissing the sensitive area beneath her earlobe. "Why the hurry? I want to savor the moment."

"I have to be at work. I called and let Eli know I'd be in around ten. He wasn't too pleased."

"Call him and tell him you won't make it after all." He nibbled her neck and trailed his lips along her collarbone, one hand holding her wrists above her head, the other cupped on her bottom.

"I want…to…" she moaned, her breasts rising as she sucked in a deep breath. "But I can't. Please."

The woman had him tied in knots and ready to explode, but he understood her desire to make love and her need to find her friend. Jim didn't argue the point further. Instead, he thrust into her, driving in long and hard.

Her channel tightened around him, her muscles contracting and holding on to him.

Pulling out, he thrust in again and again, settling into a smooth, steady rhythm until the sensations built into a towering crescendo and launched him over the edge. One final thrust and his entire body exploded in a myriad of electrical impulses, shooting from his center to his outer extremities. He held her for a long time, buried as deep as he could get.

When he came down from his release, he eased her off him and onto her feet, completed soaping and rinsing her body and his, then set her out on the bath mat, dripping wet.

"You see?" Melissa smiled. "It doesn't take long when you put your mind—" her voice sank deeper "—and body to it."

Grabbing one of the towels, he tossed it to her and took another, quickly drying his body and then hers. When she started to slide her feet into a clean pair of panties, he grabbed them, tossed them to the counter and swept her up in his arms. "We're not done."

"But I have to get to work."

He shook his head. "Not yet you don't. I got where I wanted to go. You're coming with me." Jim marched from the bathroom into the bedroom and tossed Melissa on the bed.

"Really, you don't have to—" She edged backward, her eyes widening as he climbed up between her legs and settled over her.

"Yes, I do." He cut off any further argument with a searing kiss.

Her hands rose to curl around the back of his neck. When he broke the kiss, he continued his conquest of her body, blazing a path from her lips to her breasts, sucking first one nipple then the other into his mouth, rolling the bud around between his teeth, gentle, yet insistent.

Abandoning her breasts, he moved lower, kissing and nipping the tender skin of her torso and her belly. Finally hovering over her mons, he parted her folds and stroked his thumb and his tongue over the narrow strip of flesh.

Mel's heels dug into the mattress and she raised her hips to meet his conquest of the most sensitive part of her body. "Please," she moaned.

He chuckled, blowing a stream of air across her damp entrance. "Please, what?"

"Again."

Obeying her demand, he touched his tongue to her and she bucked beneath him, raising her hips and holding, her body tense, her muscles straining. Her hands smoothed over his shoulders and up to his head, digging into his scalp, holding him there as she rode the waves of her passion.

When at last she collapsed against the sheets, she let out a long, low sigh. "Wow."

James crawled up her body and lay down beside her, trailing his finger across one breast. "Ready to make that call?"

She closed her eyes and dragged in a deep breath, then sighed. "As good as that was…I need to get to the bar."

He pinched the tip of her nipple.

"Hey!" Mel swatted his hand. "Watch it."

"I'd like to but you insist on going to work." He rolled away from her and off the bed to stand naked beside it. "Get moving, woman. Eli will be champing at the bit."

Mel leaned up on one elbow, her gaze on his still-stiff member. "I'm tempted to play hooky."

"But you won't." James entered the bathroom and emerged with a towel around his middle, the clothes he'd come with bunched in his arms. "Before you leave, send those pictures to my cell phone. I'll make sure they get to Hank. Then I'll see you at the bar."

"Damn," she muttered.

He softened. "Look, we aren't getting any closer to finding Cord holed up in a hotel room having sex. As much as I'd like to."

"I hope like hell we find him soon." Melissa's eyes blazed. "I can think of a whole lot more interesting things to do than trudge around in the swamps or shoot the bull with a bar full of SEALs."

Chapter Eleven

Mel sent the photos to James via text and hurriedly dressed in her shorts, tank top and high heels. A quick blast from the built-in blow-dryer got her hair halfway dry before she pulled it back and wove it into a French braid down her back.

Fifteen minutes after James had left her room wearing nothing but a towel, Mel was ready for work. She grabbed her truck keys and purse and headed down the stairwell.

Part of her wanted to knock on James's door and take up where they'd left off. The dedicated agent and lifelong friend in her wouldn't let her dally any longer. She had to get to the bar and salvage what was left of the night for investigation.

After hopping into her truck, she headed for the Shoot the Bull Bar. The parking lot was packed and she could already imagine how mad Eli was she hadn't shown up on time for work. She parked in the back of the building and entered through the rear door.

Cora Leigh was hefting a box full of Jack Daniel's whiskey into her arms from a stack against the wall. "Thank God. I thought you were going to be a no-show. Here." She shoved the box into Mel's hands. "Get that out to Eli. He's all out of whiskey and hollerin' for tequila." Cora Leigh lifted another box and followed Mel into the bar.

Mel laid the case of whiskey on the floor at the bar owner's feet.

"'Bout time you showed up," Eli grumbled. "Table five needs this tray. Hustle up." He shoved the tray full of longnecks toward her, the bottles teetering precariously before they settled.

Melissa wove through the tables to get to number five, where SEALs from SBT-22 sat around in a big circle, making it difficult for her to reach the actual table. She stood back and handed the bottles to the individuals instead of setting them on the table.

"Hey, sweetheart." The man she'd identified as Duff from the previous night lumbered to his feet and swung her into his arms. "Come dance with me. Cowboy isn't here tonight. You got to be feelin' lonely."

With the big round tray braced in front of her, she managed to keep from being squashed in the SEAL's embrace. "I'm working."

"Didn't keep you from kissing Cowboy last night." The man gave her a sad-puppy look. "Aw, come on. Just one dance."

"Maybe later, big guy. I just got to work and my boss is giving me the stink-eye." Melissa nodded toward Eli, who at that moment was glaring her way.

Duff sighed heavily. "Okay, but I'll take you at your word. I expect a dance."

Melissa went back to work, serving shooters and mugs of beer to the thirsty SEALs until there was a lull in the orders and she was able to keep her word.

Dancing would be a good way to get to know the members of the Pit Viper team in a fairly safe environment. She wouldn't have to be alone with anyone and she could still ask questions to get to know them.

She spied Quentin Lovett and Sawyer Houston sitting in the middle of the big group. She imagined she'd have to dance with a couple of the guys in order not to single out the Pit Viper team. When she got the chance, she snagged Duff and pulled him onto the dance floor. Thankfully James hadn't made an appearance yet. She'd been watching for him, her nerves on alert.

"I thought you were Cowboy's girl," Duff said, swinging her around in an energetic two-step.

She shrugged. "I like him okay. But I'm not anyone's girl."

"In that case…" He spun her out and back into a tight clinch.

Melissa managed to extricate herself from his hold and dance out to a more comfortable distance. The music was loud and she wasn't sure how much she could ask without rousing suspicion, especially in a crowded barroom, but she had to try. Cord's life could depend on her.

"I imagine as a SEAL you go on some pretty dangerous missions," she noted on one of her spins back against his body.

"Yup. All the time." Duff's chest puffed out. "I eat danger for breakfast, lunch and dinner."

Mel laughed. "Gives you a pretty big bellyache, doesn't it?"

"Sometimes." He guided her into a spin under his arm and back out.

"Someone told me you lost one of your team members recently," she ventured.

Duff didn't respond, focusing his attention on the dance floor.

"That had to be hard," Mel continued. "Was it a particularly bad mission?"

"I wasn't there. I wouldn't know. Gosling was young. He left behind a wife pregnant with their first kid."

"I'm sorry to hear that. To lose your father before you

have a chance to get to know him isn't the way a kid likes to grow up."

The song ended and Melissa stepped away. "Thank you for the dance. I'd better get back to work." She hurried back to the bar and collected a tray full of liquor and turned to study the interior of Shoot the Bull. Where was James? He'd said he'd come to the bar, but he had yet to show and it had been over an hour since she'd last seen him.

A man in a cowboy hat stepped through the front entrance. The electricity in the air charged and Mel could feel his presence before she actually saw him.

James Monahan strode into the bar, scraping the cowboy hat off his head, his shoulders pushed back. The blue chambray shirt he wore barely contained the breadth of his shoulders, and his jeans fit snugly on his hips, emphasizing his narrow waist and thick thighs. He crossed the floor as though he owned the place.

Mel's breath lodged in her throat and her cheeks heated as she pictured the man standing in her bedroom naked, his member stiff and straight, his body glistening with a fine sheen of perspiration after making love to her.

"Hey, Melissa, get me a beer, will ya?" Sawyer Houston was saying.

Pulling her head out of James's naked image, she nodded. "Sure. Anyone else?"

Several other SEALs shouted out their orders. Mel struggled to remember them, her mind knocked off-kilter by James's appearance. She spun away from him and marched to the bar, feeling his gaze on her backside.

When she arrived at the bar, she gave her order and finally turned to face the man who'd made love to her an hour ago.

His gaze was on her, his lips curling in a secretive smile. Her cheeks burned and she turned her back on the

SEALs. How was she supposed to question his team with him in the middle of it?

"You feeling all right, honey?" Cora Leigh asked. "You're lookin' a bit flushed."

"I'm fine," Mel said, concentrating on the tray Eli was filling with drinks. She risked a glance back at the big group of SEALs crowding around the single table in the middle of the bar.

Cora Leigh's gaze followed Mel's. "Ah, the SEAL babies."

"I don't know what you mean."

"You fancy yourself in love with one of them, don't you?"

"Not at all. I barely know any of them." Mel bit her bottom lip. *Could Eli take any longer?*

She could practically feel James's glance burning a hole in her back. As Eli plunked a mug of frothing beer on the tray, Mel said, "Throw another one of those on the tray." When he'd done as she asked, she had no reason to continue to stand at the bar with her back to the room. She turned with her heavy tray and squared her shoulders.

As soon as her gaze met James's, her knees weakened and her heartbeat kicked up to double time. All this time she'd been wondering when he'd show up. Now that he had, she wished he would disappear. She'd had a hard enough job working the SEALs without him in the room. Now she'd be doubly conscious of him.

Marching across the floor, she quickly distributed the beers and whiskey shots to the men, noting that two of them were for Quentin and Sawyer. If she kept them coming, she might have a chance at gleaning information from them.

As she leaned in to place the shots on the table. Quentin grabbed her wrist. "Duff tells me you're not Cowboy's babe."

Mel glanced across at James.

James smiled. "Melissa's her own person. I have no claim on her."

Mel breathed a sigh of relief that James had gone along with her story. At the same time, a twinge of irritation hit her that he'd give her up so easily.

"Sure looked like it last night, all that kissin' in the hall," Duff noted.

Quentin's hand tightened on her wrist. "You danced with Duff. How about me?"

"I have to work." She tugged her hand free and winked. "But I'll see if I can fit you in."

Across the table, James's smile slipped and for a brief moment, Mel could swear his eyes narrowed. Good. Let him stew. After all, she was there to investigate Cord's disappearance, not make love to the cowboy of the group.

Mel busied herself getting caught up on all the other tables she was responsible for, as well as filling the empty glasses and mugs at the SEALs' table, sure to give Quentin and Sawyer several of the whiskey shooters. When she had another break, she hurried back to the table and snagged Quentin. "Come on, lover boy. Let's dance."

Quentin lurched to his feet, swayed a bit and then swept her onto the dance floor. "Now, this is nice. Good beer, better whiskey, live music and a beautiful woman to dance with."

"Thanks." Mel suffered being spun out a little too hard and dragged back to smack against Quentin's hard chest. The SEAL was a little too far into his cups. But then, that's where she wanted him to be. The song changed to a slow one and she leaned against him. "You're a big, bad SEAL. What's it like to be on an operation?" She glanced up at him and batted her eyes. "Have you ever been shot at?"

Quentin's hand tightened on her lower back. "Yes, I have."

"Really?" She widened her eyes, pretending to be an airheaded fangirl. "What's it like? Have you ever killed a man?"

"It sucks. And yes."

For the charmer of the group, he was less than communicative on the subject of his work. Mel leaned against him, pressing her cheek to his chest. "You must be very brave," she said, wanting to choke on her act. Far from being a vapid woman who couldn't take care of herself, she was strong. Playing a wimpy female grated her nerves. But it had to be done.

"Sometimes. Sometimes you just get in and get it done and watch your buddy's back."

She paused for a moment, then asked, "Have you ever lost one of your teammates?"

His fingers dug into her back painfully. "Yeah." Quentin stopped in the middle of the floor, his arms falling to his sides, his body rigid. "Do you want to dance or talk shop?"

She smiled up at him. "Dance, of course. I'm just fascinated by what you SEALs do. You're all so brave and strong. Come on. There's still more song left." She leaned her breasts against his chest and locked her arms around his neck.

He raised his hands to her bare midriff and soon he relaxed. After a while, he stopped again and shook his head. "I'm dizzy. Can I get a rain check on the dance?"

"Sure." Mel glanced up at him, concerned. "Are you feeling okay?"

"Yeah. Just a little too much to drink."

"Do you have a ride home?"

"I'm okay. I brought my vehicle."

"You're not driving." Mel took his hand and led him from the dance floor. "I'll get you home."

"Won't Eli fire you?"

"Screw Eli. I can't let one of our nation's finest drive

drunk. Come on. I just have to get my keys." She led him to the bar, reached behind it to grab her keys. "Eli, this man's in no condition to drive. I'm taking him home."

Eli frowned. "Some help you are."

Mel planted a hand on her hip. "Would you rather I let one of his drunk friends drive him home?"

"Ah, go on." Eli waved a dismissive hand at her. "I don't want a lawsuit on my hands. I'll get Cora Leigh to cover your tables."

Mel cut a glance back in James's direction. The man had a frown that would scare little children denting his brow.

Too bad, Mel thought. If Quentin was drunk enough, she might just get some information out of him. The sooner, the better. Cord's life might depend on it.

JAMES HAD SPENT forty-five minutes talking to Hank after sending the pictures Melissa had taken of the two goons in the bayou to his computer guru, Brandon. He'd filled him in on what had occurred on the river and the conversation they'd overheard. When he'd finally been able to leave his hotel room, he'd had to hold himself back to keep from speeding out to the bar, afraid Melissa hadn't made it there or was being watched or cornered by one of the men from earlier that day.

To find her dancing with Duff was enough to push him over the top. A man could take only so much. It was all James could do to stand by and watch Melissa dance with Quentin. Every nerve in his body screamed to go after the other man and pound him into the ground. What was Melissa doing? When she took Quentin's hand and led him to the bar, James came out of his seat.

Duff's hand came out to slap against James's chest. "Whoa there, Cowboy."

James's eyes narrowed and he cut a glance in Duff's

direction. "If you know what's good for you, you'll get your hand off me."

Duff removed his hand. "Melissa told me herself she's not anyone's girl. You have no right to go after her and Quentin."

Still halfway out of his chair, James paused, knowing what Duff said was true. Then again, Duff didn't know the game Melissa was playing. A game that could get her burned if the man was drunk enough.

Quentin Lovett was the charmer of the team. He had a girl in every port and he knew how to coax the panties off every one of them with nothing more than a smile.

Having just made love to Melissa a short time ago, James wasn't willing to risk Quentin letting things get out of control. But to leave now would show his hand. He'd have to wait a few minutes, make an excuse and then leave. Settling back in his chair, he stared at the mug of untouched beer.

"You gonna drink that?" Sawyer leaned across Duff, reaching for the full mug, his eyes bloodshot, his words slurred.

"No." He glanced at the other man. "Do you have a designated driver?"

Sawyer grabbed the mug of beer with one hand and backhanded Duff with the other. "Duff's my DD. He's always sober."

Duff snorted. "Someone's gotta be with you bunch of sots."

"That's me." Sawyer upended the mug, downing its contests in six big gulps, beer dribbling out the sides and down his neck. When the mug was empty, Sawyer slammed it on the table and wiped the beer off his lips with the back of his hand. Then he raised his fingers and snapped them. "Waitress! More beer!"

Duff shook his head. "You might want to slow down. We have PT in the morning."

"What's it matter, anyway? Gosling ain't gonna be there for me to run with. In fact he ain't ever gonna be there again." The man crossed his arms on the sticky table and buried his face on them, his shoulders shaking with sobs.

"Okay, big guy. You've had more than enough." Duff stood and tried to haul Sawyer to his feet.

Halfway out of his chair, Sawyer was no help and slithered back down to plant his face on the table.

"Here, let me help." James draped one of Sawyer's arms over his shoulder, while Duff draped the other. Together they straightened, bringing Sawyer up out of his chair, his head lolling to the side.

"Gunny isn't gonna be happy about this."

James headed for the door. "What's got Sawyer all messed up?"

"He ain't been right since they got back from their last mission."

"Which one was that?"

Duff's lips thinned as they stepped out into the parking lot. "The one Gosling bit the big one on."

"Pit Viper?" James asked, his gaze aimed ahead. He could see Duff's head turn toward him in his peripheral vision.

"What do you know about it?" Duff asked.

"Only that you lost one of the team there."

"I wasn't there, but I wish I had been. Maybe things wouldn't have gone so badly for Gosling." Duff stopped in front of an SUV and leaned Sawyer on the hood while he dug into his pocket for the key. "He was just a kid. With a kid on the way."

"You can't second-guess the work we do," Jim said. "You can only learn from it and keep moving forward."

"Yeah, but Gosling shouldn't have come back in a body

bag." Duff hit the unlock button on his key fob and the locks popped open. "Sometimes I hate my job."

Jim shifted beneath the weight of Sawyer. "Gosling knew the risks when he signed up."

"Yeah, the risks of the enemy." Duff lifted Sawyer's arm. "Come on, buddy, help us out."

"Collateral damage," Sawyer muttered, dragging himself into the front seat of the SUV.

"What was?" James asked.

"Not what. Who." Sawyer leaned his head back on the seat and seemed to have fallen asleep.

"Who was collateral damage?" James insisted.

"Gosling." Sawyer snorted. "Keep up with the sh-tory. Someone knew we were comin'. Goslin' got in the way. Shh. Can't trussst anyone," Sawyer whispered. "'Cept Duff. He's a good man." He patted Duff's cheek.

"Shut up, Sawyer. You're drunk as a skunk," Duff said.

Sawyer laughed. "Skunks don't drink."

Duff shut the door as Sawyer's head lolled to the side. "He'll be better in the morning."

"Need help getting him into his apartment?" James asked.

"Nah. If I can't get him there, I'll let him sleep it off in my SUV."

"I can follow you there."

"No need. I know you want to go find the girl before Quentin does something stupid." Duff grinned and rounded the front of the SUV. "For the record, Cowboy, I'm glad you're back."

James tipped his cowboy hat. "Thanks." Before Duff had cleared the parking lot in his SUV with a very drunk Sawyer, James had climbed into his truck and took off in the direction of Quentin's apartment, praying he'd be in time to stop Quentin from making an advance on Melissa that she wasn't prepared to fight off.

Chapter Twelve

Melissa helped Quentin out of his SUV. He'd insisted on her driving it, refusing to get into her red pickup, claiming it was a sissy color.

Rather than argue, she'd loaded him into his vehicle, driven him to his building and manhandled him up the stairs to his apartment. He fell only once on the pavement of the parking lot. Though the stairs had proved tricky, he'd managed to hold on to the railing, his arm draped over her shoulder as she assisted. Straining to keep the man upright, Melissa was breathing hard and ready for a very large pain-killer for her aching back by the time they'd reached the doorway. Leaning him against the wall and pinning his shoulder with one hand, she held out her hand. "The key?"

Quentin grinned, his eyes widening. "I lost it in my pocket. You'll have to go in and find it."

"Good grief!" Melissa fished in the man's pocket, feeling the hardness of his erection too close at hand. "Do you always drink this much?" she asked.

"Only when I'm trying to make a good impression on a lady." He draped his arm over her shoulders and leaned heavily on her. "How'm I doing?"

"Great. Just great," she said, her lips twisting as she shoved the key into the lock and pushed the door open. "Come on, Romeo. You could use some coffee."

"I'd rather have a kiss."

"I like my dates to be sober when I kiss them."

"Oh, come on. Jusss one little ol' kissss." He puckered up and aimed for her lips.

Melissa slipped out from beneath his arm and dived to the side. "I'm not that easy, Quentin." She nodded toward the couch, hoping he'd fall onto it and get sleepy.

Quentin lunged for her, faster than she guessed he could move in his state of inebriation. He caught her elbow and yanked her into his arms.

When he tried to kiss her, Mel turned her cheek and his lips slid across her jaw. "Calm down, Quentin. There's plenty of time for that later. I want to get to know you better. Why don't you sit, before you fall?" She gave him a gentle shove and the man backed into the couch. It caught him behind his calves and he sat hard. Unfortunately he still had hold of Mel's arm and he dragged her on top of his lap.

"Oh, yes, I can see where this is better." He nuzzled her neck and groped her breast.

Mel pushed one hand away from her breast, only to have another one find its way there. The faster she removed one, Quentin had another to replace it.

"I swear you're an octopus!"

"Thass right, baby."

"Please, Quentin. Let's talk for a few minutes before we do anything else. I barely know you."

He sighed, his hand falling to her waist. "Okay. Have it your way. Whaddaya wanna talk about?"

"I want to know why you didn't want to talk about your mission." She trailed a finger across his chest. "You know, the one you lost one of your friends on. What happened?"

His brows furrowed. "Not supposed to talk. Iss top secret."

"I know, but you can trust me. Besides, I already know

you lost one of your team. Gosling, wasn't it?" She hoped by saying Gosling's name, she'd trigger something in Quentin and he'd spill his guts.

"Damned shame, too. The kid was good."

"Obviously he wasn't as good as you." She traced her finger around his earlobe. "If he was as good as my Quentin Lover, he wouldn't have been killed."

Quentin grabbed her finger. "He was good, but someone leaked the deets. Whoever took that shot was aiming for the DEA agent, not Gosling. Gosling just happened to step up at that exact second. He shouldna died, damn it." Quentin pushed her off his lap onto the couch. "I couldn't stop it. Gosling died. Can't do anything to bring him back. Would, if I could. I don't wanna talk about it."

"Do you think one of your team leaked the information?"

"I don't know. If one of them did, I'd kill him." The SEAL staggered to his feet and swayed, grabbing for his head. "The room's spinning. Why do you care 'bout Gosling? You didn't know him like the res of us did. He wass a good man."

"Sit, Quentin. Before you fall." Mel stood and touched a hand to the man's arm. "I'm sorry if talking about Gosling upsets you. I'm just curious."

"And I don't want to remember. Gives me nightmares. All I want's to forget."

"Forget what?"

"That Gosling's dead. That we were set up. That someone set us up to get the agent out juss so they could kill him. That Gosling got in the way." Quentin grabbed her and hauled her up against his chest, his face red, his eyes blazing, his grip hurting her arm. "'Nuff talk. We came here to get it on."

"No, I only drove you home to keep you from driving yourself."

"You owe me a kiss." He bent his head to take her lips.

Mel put her hand up and the man's lips connected with her palm. "You're drunk. You need to sleep it off."

"No, I need a woman to bury myself in, to forget the look on Gosling's face as he died." He captured her hand in a vise-like grip. "Kiss me, Melissa. Make me forget."

"You don't want to kiss me."

"Oh, yes, I do. And a whole lot more."

"I don't want what you're saying. If you don't let me go, I'll be forced to hurt you," she warned.

"Just a damn kiss. Then we'll take it from there."

"Let go of me," Mel said through gritted teeth.

A loud pounding sounded on the door.

Quentin glanced toward the noise, taking his attention off Mel long enough for her to twist her arm, duck under his and bring his wrist behind him. She yanked hard, driving his forearm up the middle of his back.

The big SEAL yelled, "Damn it, that hurts."

"I told you to let go of me, or I'd have to hurt you."

"Melissa!" a voice shouted through the door.

Mel recognized it and groaned. James.

"Ouch! Let up on that arm so I can answer the door."

"You can answer it with one hand. Move." She guided him to the doorway, pushing his wrist higher up the middle of his back the more he fought to be free. He finally gave in and opened the door to his apartment to an angry James.

"What're you doing here?" Quentin demanded.

James leaned against the door, his eyes half-closed. "I came to get Melisssssa," he slurred. "She's *my* girl."

Mel could see the whites of James's eyes. The man was stone sober, playing the drunk. "Oh, baby. Are you drunk, too?"

"Damn right. When a guy sees his girl danssin' with another man…" He jerked his head toward Quentin. "Drives him to drink."

"And you drove here to tell me that?" She shook her head. "You could have caused a wreck."

"Yeah. I'm a bad boy. You can spank me, if you like." He winked.

"I'm done here, right, Quentin?" She let go of the man's arm, her hands shaking. If she hadn't gotten the upper hand in the situation, Quentin could have taken advantage of his heavier build and overpowered her.

"Juss wanna little kiss," Quentin grumbled, rubbing his shoulder. "Didn't have to break my arm."

"I didn't break it. You're drunk and I make it a point only to kiss a sober man." She turned him around and gave him a gentle shove toward the bedroom. "Now, go get a cold shower and go to bed, like a good little SEAL."

He spun and swayed, clapping a hand to his head. "Rather go to bed with you."

"It's not going to happen, sweetie. Besides, I have to get another drunk SEAL home." She hooked her arm through James's. "Come on, Cowboy. I guess I'm the designated driver of the night."

"Lucky bastard," Quentin muttered as Mel twisted the lock and closed the door between them.

"You had everything under control, huh?" James said.

"Shh. Wait until we get in the truck." She wanted to be angry with James for interfering with her interrogation of Quentin. But seeing him standing outside the door of Quentin's apartment had been too much of a relief.

Chapter Thirteen

"I'll need a little help…being drunk and all." He chuckled, leaning on her shoulder heavily.

"You want me to put you in the same kind of armlock I had Quentin in? Don't mess with me." Though her words were stern, her lips twitched on the corners. She was as happy to see him as he was to see her.

The thought made him grin.

Once they were both in his truck and she'd pulled out of the parking lot, she turned to him. "Much as I want to tell you which pier to jump off of…thanks."

He tipped his hat. "My pleasure. As drunk as Lovett was, I figured he'd be a little hard to handle."

"I swear the man had the arms of an octopus." Melissa laughed and shot a glance at Jim.

His lips pressed into a thin line. "Did he hurt you?"

"No. I just hope I didn't hurt him too badly."

"He'll get over it. The damage would be more to his pride than anything. He considers himself irresistible."

Melissa tipped her head to the side, her lips fighting a smile. "He's a good-looking man with muscles in all the right places, and that sexy voice could drive a lady wild."

A low growl rose in Jim's throat and he bunched his hands into fists.

Melissa laughed out loud. "Don't worry. He's not my

type. Too much of a ladies' man. But I can see why women would fall for him. Heck, I can see why women would fall for any one of the SBT-22 team. You SEALs are all built like brick houses."

Jim's chest puffed out and his chin tipped upward. "We are, aren't we?" To take the ego out of his words, he winked.

"Don't get a big head, Cowboy. I'm not going to fall all over myself over the Navy's version of a jock."

"Jock!" He shook his head. "Takes a lot more effort and training to be a SEAL than a football player."

Melissa reached out and patted his thigh. "Calm down. I just didn't want your ego to swell."

Electric shocks rippled from where she touched his thigh all the way to his groin. It was all he could do not to jerk the steering wheel to the right and force her off the road to take her there. Melissa was doing crazy things to his control.

"I need to circle back and collect my truck from the bar." She turned away from their hotel and toward the bar.

"Take it slow. I left Duff in charge of driving Sawyer to his apartment. They should have left the bar already, but they'll be on their way here. He had to stop and get gas. Gave me just enough time to get you out before they arrived." A pair of headlights shone in their eyes and Jim swiveled in his seat as the oncoming vehicle passed. "That would be them now."

"Good, I can get my truck."

"You could leave it there and let me take you by in the morning."

Melissa shook her head. "No, thanks. I know what five o'clock looks like, but I'd prefer not to get up that early unless I have to."

Jim wondered what waking up next to Melissa at 5:00 a.m. would be like. He'd have to wake at least by four-thirty if he had any chance of making it out the door in time for PT. He'd want to make love to her first thing and then start his day.

For the love of Mike, why couldn't he think of anything else but Melissa in bed? "What did you find out from Lovett?"

"That he's a flirt, he likes to dance and he thinks someone on the inside let it leak about their mission."

Jim's chest tightened. "I got the same from Sawyer."

"Do you think either one of them might have been the one to spread the word about the operation?"

"Not Sawyer."

Melissa glanced at him, her eyes narrowed. "What makes you so sure?"

"I've known Sawyer a long time. He's true to the core. He'd take a bullet for any one of the team. The last thing he'd do is leak information about a mission, knowing it could get one of them killed. And he's pretty upset about losing Gosling. Blames himself."

"What about Quentin?" Melissa posed.

James shook his head and stared out the window. "I don't know him well enough to guess."

"He seemed like he wasn't certain what had happened from what I could glean. Quentin was pretty upset about Gosling, as well. He said the same thing, that he thought someone had leaked information about their mission. That someone was waiting for them to get the agent out so that he could be killed."

"As far as I'm concerned, that doesn't rule out Lovett. He could be dealing with his guilt over getting Gosling killed."

Melissa nodded. "Could be. I hate to make a judgment when we still have two more team members to question. And we need more evidence."

Melissa pulled into the parking lot behind the bar, shifted into Park beside her red truck, climbed down and rounded the front of Jim's vehicle. "Nice truck, by the way," she said when she met him there.

"Thanks. It was one of the perks of the job with Hank."

Melissa's brows rose. "Nice." She pulled her keys from her pocket and hit the unlock button.

"Not going back to work?"

"No. Cora Leigh has my tables covered and Eli isn't really expecting me back. The sooner I leave, the less chance of him seeing me and dragging me back in."

"Then go." The urge to drag her into his arms and kiss her was strong, but he wanted her to avoid Eli, if at all possible. She could use a good night's sleep after the day they'd had on the river.

Melisa climbed into her truck and Jim climbed into his. He waited for her to back out and drive off before he followed. She might consider it unnecessary, but he liked knowing she made it back to the hotel safely.

As he followed her taillights, he went through what they'd learned from Sawyer and Lovett. It wasn't much more to go on than they had before. But it reinforced what Schafer had unearthed. Someone sent them in to get the agent out and set him up for assassination. Jim bet that whoever had given up the operation information had some connection to the arms deals. If not directly, he was commissioned by someone who did have a direct connection.

Ahead of him, Melissa picked up speed. The long straight stretch between the bar and the hotel had few crossroads. And those that were there were hidden by tall stands of cattails growing in the water-filled ditches along the sides of the road.

Melissa's truck jerked toward the center about the same time Jim noticed a large shadowy object erupt from one of the hidden side roads.

A large, dark SUV slammed into the side of Melissa's bright red pickup and sent it into a 360-degree spin. Tires squealed. Before Melissa could straighten the vehicle, it careened off the edge of the road and down into the ditch.

Jim jammed his foot to the accelerator, sending his own truck blasting forward, while he laid on his horn.

The SUV made a sharp turn onto the highway and fishtailed as the driver sped off into the night, no license plate, no taillights, just a disappearing shadow.

James skidded to a halt next to the point at which Melissa's truck disappeared into a deep ditch.

The truck's front tires were completely covered in muddy water, the entire vehicle pitched at a sharp angle.

Shoving into Park, Jim leaped out of his truck and ran to the side of the road, his heart pounding, his breath lodged in his throat.

Before he could drop down into the ditch to check on Melissa, the red truck lurched and crept forward, an inch at a time.

When the truck was fully in the ditch and leveled off— Melissa must have engaged the four-wheel drive—she gave the vehicle just enough of a tap on the gas that it surged forward, spinning up water and mud in its wake. She drove the truck up the embankment, tipping dangerously, but emerged safely onto the highway.

Jim released the breath he'd been holding and almost laughed out loud. The woman was a force to be reckoned with. A hit-and-run wouldn't keep her down long. Once the vehicle was on dry ground, the driver's door flew open and Melissa dropped down from the truck cursing like a sailor and waving her arms. "Who the hell can't see a vehicle coming from over a mile away? And don't tell me they didn't see me. I know they did!" She rounded to the passenger side and kicked at the gravel, more curses pouring from her lips. "My truck! That idiot ruined it. Look at it. Ruined!"

"That's why you have insurance." Jim stepped up beside her and slipped an arm around her waist, tugging her against his side. "At least it didn't roll and you're all right." He turned her toward him and pushed the hair that had fallen out of her ponytail back behind her ear. "You scared the bejesus out of me." He kissed her forehead and then her nose. Then his lips found hers, claiming them in a hard, desperate connection.

At first her hands lay flat against his chest, but after only a moment, her fingers curled into his shirt, dragging him closer. When they broke for air, she leaned her forehead against his chest. "I have to admit, if I'd had time to think about it, I'd have been scared, too." She laughed. "For that matter, my knees are shaking."

"Sweetheart." Jim smoothed his fingers along her cheek. "That was a deliberate hit-and-run. Whoever hit you knew you were coming and had time to hide their vehicle. When it pulled out, the lights were off. We need to get out of here."

Her brows knit in the middle, her jaw set in a hard, firm line. "But my truck—"

"Can be replaced. *You* can't be." He tightened his hold and lifted her chin. "Want me to drive the rest of the way?"

"No. I need to get my truck back to the hotel so that I can use it tomorrow. And you have things to do tomorrow, as well. I'll be more vigilant, I promise."

The rest of the trip to the hotel passed uneventfully. Melissa parked her truck under a light and got out again to inspect the damage, shook her head and walked away.

Jim fell in step beside her. "Whoever knocked you off the road meant to hit you."

"I know." Her full, pink lips firmed into a straight line. "The question is, why?"

That had been the one thought nagging him the entire way. If someone was onto them, that meant their questioning was getting too close to home. Melissa could be in more danger than being knocked off the road.

They entered through the side door, Melissa swiping her card to key the lock.

Without a word, Jim followed her up to her room and waited as she slid her key card through the door lock. Once inside, he gave the room a clean sweep and turned to her.

"Be careful." He lifted one of her hands and pressed a kiss to her palm, curling her fingers around it. "I'm worried that all our questions are raising red flags with the traitor. The more we push for the truth, the more nervous whoever is responsible will get. He'll want to keep us from discovering who leaked the information and who is supplying guns to the terrorists."

She left her hand in his. "Whoever is involved is already nervous. Nervous enough to send someone out to look for Cord in the swamp, and maybe to knock me off the road. Apparently, they think Cord knew too much. And they also think he's not dead."

"And if they've discovered that you and I were the ones out there looking for him as well and can identify them, they'll come looking for us." He didn't like the idea of someone stalking Melissa. "I suspect they already have."

"Did you have any troubles passing those photos to Derringer?" Melissa asked.

"No trouble, but he had a lot of questions. That's what took me so long getting to the bar this evening."

"Good. Hopefully some facial-recognition software can identify at least one of them."

"I don't like the idea of you out running around on your own, asking questions while I'm stuck with my unit. The man in the black jacket from earlier wasn't a member of SBT-22."

"Are you sure he's not someone new you haven't run into yet?"

"I'm pretty sure he's not one of us." Jim touched her arm. "If he knows you're investigating Pit Viper or Cord's disappearance, you're in danger."

"I can handle it."

"I know…" He smiled and swept the back of his hand along her cheek. "It's what you do."

She leaned into his palm. "It is."

"The point is that I won't be available to pull you out of a pinch. I'll be at my unit, training, working and most likely out of cell-phone range for much of the day."

"Don't worry about me. I won't ask specifically about Pit Viper or Cord."

"What else would you talk about?"

"I want to get a feel for who these guys are. What better way than to talk to the people they live with, like wives and girlfriends?"

"Okay. Just be very aware."

"I will. You, too."

He winked and raised his palms. "What could happen to me when I'm surrounded by people?"

Melissa's brows furrowed. "The same thing that happened to Cord."

"Good point." He wanted to stay with Melissa, but he sensed to do so would be too much, too soon. "Well, good night. If you need me, I'm only a stomp on the floor away."

Melissa hesitated for a moment. "Thanks again for saving me from the guys by the river today." She leaned up onto her toes and pressed a light kiss to his lips.

Jim tried to hold back, but when her lips collided with his, he felt his control snap. He gathered her in his arms and crushed her mouth with his. His tongue pushed past her teeth and slid along hers, caressing and teasing.

Melissa raised her hands to wrap around the back of his neck, her breasts pressing against his chest. He could swear he heard her heartbeat thundering in time with his.

But maybe it was his pulse pounding so hard in his ears that was all he could hear.

When he broke away, he leaned his forehead against hers. "I want so much more."

"Me, too."

"But it'll wait. We need to sleep." When he backed away, she refused to let go.

"Stay here."

His heart stilled and then thundered in his chest. He wanted to stay more than he could admit. But he was afraid. Afraid he was getting too close to her and that she was getting too close to him. If they weren't careful, one of them would end up falling in love with the other.

And that would be a disastrous trap neither wanted to fall into.

"I have to go." He pulled her arms from around his neck and set her back on her feet. "I'll see you tomorrow." Holding her hands for a moment, he stared down into her eyes. "And don't take any chances." He left before he could change his mind, before he could fall into the sensuous glaze in Melissa's eyes and forget why he was there.

Chapter Fourteen

Mel tossed and turned through the night. If she wasn't dreaming about making love to James, she was having nightmares about alligators and killers in the river. By six o'clock in the morning she was ready to cry uncle and rose from her bed.

As she prepared for the day, her thoughts went to James, who would have been up for an hour and was probably running PT or just finishing the SEALs' morning calisthenics. She could do with some exercise, and why not kill two birds with one stone?

Lillian had said she worked out at the gym or did yoga there at the same time every day.

Melissa could get in a workout and find out more about Gunny at the same time. She wished the other men of Pit Viper had wives. Waiting to question them at night at the bar left all day for her to wander around. Showing up at their unit would be far too blatant, and that was the angle James was handling.

So, yoga it was. Afterward, she'd take her photo of Gumboots around to the local marinas and see if they could shed light on the identity of the man in the black jacket's river guide.

Promptly at nine o'clock, dressed in bicycle shorts

and a sports bra, Mel showed up at the gym Lillian Petit frequented.

After a quick glance around, she found her in a spin class, hunkered over a stationary bicycle along with six other women and the female instructor at the front of the class. A screen on the wall behind the instructor depicted a mountain bike trail, the scenery speeding by at a simulated pace in keeping with the resistance and speed of the exercise equipment.

Mel climbed onto the bicycle beside Lillian. "Hey," she said softly. "How was your night?"

"You're back for more torture?"

Mel tilted her head. "If I want to look like you, I'd better get busy. Whatever you're doing seems to be working."

"Thanks." She smiled. "But everybody is different. I have a personal trainer I meet with twice a week. He sets me up with a plan depending on what I need or what area I should work on."

"Sounds expensive."

Lillian shrugged. "Expensive, but worth every penny. It's my husband's job to bring home the money and my job to be there when he gets home and look as beautiful as the day he married me."

Biting down hard on her tongue, Mel forced a smile. What century was this woman living in? She sounded like one of the stay-at-home wives of the late fifties.

Hello. It's the new millennium. We've come a long way, baby.

Rather than shoot the woman a biting reply, Mel gave her a stiff smile. "You sure take that vow seriously."

"Yes, I do. But sometimes I don't think Frank does."

"How so?" Mel asked.

"We've been married for three years and his raises have been pathetic. He's in one of the most dangerous jobs in the country. You'd think the government could pay him more. It's just not right that he puts his life on the line daily when he gets paid peanuts."

The woman obviously didn't understand the concept of service over self, or doing a job because you loved it, not because it paid well.

Mel chuckled. "Is this your first relationship with a man who is married to the military?"

"Actually, no. My father was a marine. Though, had I known we'd end up here, I might have reconsidered. I never pictured myself living in a hot and humid hellhole like this. I'd much rather live up north where they actually have varying seasons and cultural events and exhibits."

"You must love him to stand by him."

Lillian shrugged again. "That and my daddy wouldn't take me back if I went crawling to him. He warned me not to marry Frank." The woman spun faster. "I should have listened. Frank sure doesn't seem to hear me. You're lucky you're not married. All the sacrifices aren't worth it. I refuse to get fat on top of it all."

"You're far from fat. Like I said, I'm here because I want to look like you," Mel assured the woman, though Lillian Petit was the last thing she wanted to be. "What do you eat to stay so thin?"

Lillian went into detail about the protein shakes and vegetarian diet she ate, making Mel hungry just thinking about giving up steaks and hamburgers.

"If you're interested, I could take you to the little vegan café I found in Slidell. It's the only one between here and New Orleans. I'm surprised it's stayed open for more than a month."

"I'd love to. How about lunch?"

"I have an appointment with my chiropractor after this and I never know how long it will take. If we can make it a late lunch, perhaps," Lillian offered.

"I'd love that. Then it's a date. A late lunch at two?"

Lillian smiled. "I'm so glad there's someone who understands what hell I've been going through. Frank doesn't see it at all."

So all was not smooth sailing on the home front with Gunnery Sergeant Petit. His wife appeared to be a spoiled woman who wanted it all and didn't want to suffer or work for it.

Could Gunny have sold out to keep his wife in the luxury in which she wanted to become accustomed? In which case, why was she still in Mississippi? It was a far cry from luxury by anyone's means.

The spin class ended and Lillian left for her chiropractic appointment.

Mel staggered to her truck, wondering where those new muscles had come from that hurt so much. Back at her hotel, she showered, took two pain pills and dressed in jeans, a ball cap and a T-shirt advertising Slidell. Not exactly the vacation capital of the United States, but the shirt was one she'd picked up in the lobby and that she'd use as part of a disguise she hoped would keep her safe from discovery.

Armed with her cell phone and addresses of all the marinas in the area, she went on a manhunt for Gumboots.

JIM GRIT HIS teeth throughout the morning's calisthenics. Though he could run with the best of them, he hadn't done all the exercises this group was doing each morning and the muscles that had missed out were protesting. But he'd die rather than own up to being weak.

"What's the matter, Cowboy? Get soft on the farm?" Gunny stood beside him as he performed twenty pull-ups in a row, the last five slow and shaky.

"No, Gunny. I worked hard!" he yelled and dropped to the ground.

"Hard ain't hard enough." Gunny glared at him and

pointed to the ground. "Give me thirty good ones on my count."

Jim swallowed a groan. On Gunny's count meant he wouldn't be counting all of the push-ups unless they were perfect. Jim pumped out twenty-one for Gunny's fifteen, and stopped in the up position to catch his breath and to ease his burning muscles.

"I didn't say for you to stop. Keep moving."

Jim went down.

"Sixteen," Gunny counted. "I hear you've been asking questions about previous missions, Monahan. You forget how to be a SEAL while you were milkin' cows?"

"No, Gunny." He didn't refute Gunny's claim or affirm.

"Well, can it, or I'll have you out of here so fast you won't have time to pack your bags." Gunny leaned into his face. "Got it?"

"Yes, Gunny," Jim shot back.

The gunnery sergeant stared hard at him through slitted eyes. "Good. Then get to work."

As Jim walked past Gunny, he could see the older man's gaze following him. When a SEAL was lost in the line of duty, his teammates had to have a release. Talking was one way to handle the grief. If something went incredibly wrong on a mission, the team usually went over the tactics even if they didn't go into detail of whom they were extracting or where the mission had taken place.

Since rejoining his old unit, no one had reviewed the failed operation to discuss how it could have been handled better.

Jim dressed in his camouflage uniform. They were due to conduct riverine exercises that morning. The thrill of getting out on the boat filled him and gave him the charge of purpose and adrenaline he'd needed for a long time. Caring for his dying father had taken a lot out of him. To be back on a boat in the river was a godsend, acting like a wake-up shout to his mind and body.

As he stood in the locker room dressing, his cell phone vibrated against his thigh. He grabbed it before any of the other men noticed he hadn't turned it off. Stepping into a bathroom stall, he pulled his phone out and read the text message on the screen.

Several messages came in one after the other. The first had to do with Lovett. Quentin had amassed a pretty hefty gambling debt and was on orders to attend counseling until he got it squared away.

Gunny had a pretty big credit-card bill one month and paid it all off with one large lump sum. Further investigation revealed a couple of cash deposits made over the course of a couple of weeks, equaling up to the amount of the large lump sum.

The third message had to do with the man in the black jacket. With the photo and the fingerprint Jim had lifted from the bullet casing and sent via email, Hank was more than certain the man in black's name was Fenton Rollins.

A known mercenary for hire.

Prior Army Special Forces, Rollins had been discharged from the military after multiple infractions involving fights with members of his own team. His Army record indicated he was volatile and had issues with PTSD.

He'd hired on as part of a security detail with a large oil company in Iraq for several months and then returned to the United States to set up his own business training others how to shoot.

The business was nothing but a front to run his mercenary ops through. He'd been questioned on several occasions by the FBI about execution-style murders of suspected terrorists on US soil, but they hadn't found enough evidence to nail him for any of them.

Jim's hand tightened around the phone. If Rollins was

after Cord or Melissa, they were in a lot of trouble. The man was ruthless and an expert sniper.

Hank had sent someone to Rollins's business address, only to find it locked and that no one had been there for weeks. With no forwarding address and no credit cards to trace, they were at a loss for how to find him. Brandon, the computer geek, was chasing every electronic footprint the man had left, but Rollins seemed to have gone dark a month prior. About the time Pit Viper was deployed.

The last text from Hank was the name, address and a few details about Rollins's river guide, Dwayne Buck.

Buck had a criminal record for assault and battery from several barroom fights and for beating up his former girlfriend. He had an outstanding restraining order against him from the girlfriend and was on probation. The only good news in all of the information Hank provided was Buck's address. Maybe Buck knew where the mercenary was or how to contact him.

If Jim could find the mercenary first, he could stop him before he hurt Cord or Melissa. He had to be the sniper who took out the DEA agent and Gosling. And if he wasn't the man responsible for supplying the weapons to the terrorists, he would know who was or where to find him.

So many questions remained unanswered, but the texts he received from Hank gave him a direction to look. His first hurdle was to get out of training with his team in order to check on Buck and possibly find Rollins.

Until he found a way out of his unit, Melissa was in the open. Someone had tried to run her truck off the road the night before. It could have been the mercenary, or whoever hired him to kill the DEA agent and possibly Cord.

A sense of panic rose up in Jim. He had to get to Melissa before Rollins. And until then, he had to get word to her of whom to look out for and what to expect in the way of attacks. Standing out in the open would be dangerous. Hell, driving her truck at night had almost been deadly.

Now more than ever, Jim needed to be with her, to protect her. The best he could do for the moment was to forward the information on to her cell phone and hope she took precautions to safeguard her life.

As soon as he hit Send, he realized he might have made a mistake. Melissa would head straight for Dwayne and corner him with her questions. Jim sent her another message insisting she stay in her hotel room and wait for him to get off duty. Then they would go together to question Dwayne about Rollins.

The swinging door to the bathroom squeaked. "Monahan! You in here?" Gunny's voice echoed off the tiles in the head.

Jim pocketed his cell phone, flushed the toilet and stepped out of the stall. "I am."

"We're waiting on you. Didn't know we needed to send you a written invitation to the exercise."

"No need." Jim washed his hands and dried them on a paper towel. "I'm glad you found me. I just got word I'm wanted in personnel to finalize paperwork for my transfer in."

Gunny crossed his arms. "That can wait until we get back from training."

"I'm sorry, Gunny, but I was ordered to go."

The gunnery sergeant poked his finger at Jim's chest. "And I'm telling you, you're coming with us."

"The man ordering my appearance at personnel is a full-bird Marine colonel. You want me to tell him my gunnery sergeant pulled rank on him and told me to skip signing his papers?" Jim raised his brows in challenge, then shrugged. "I'll let you explain it to him."

Gunny's frown deepened, his eyes narrowing to slits.

Finally, he said, "Fine. Go sign your papers. The team will practice maneuvers without you."

"If you're certain…" Jim dragged out his words, giving Gunny the opportunity to call him on it.

Gunny snorted. "I expect you back here in one hour." He spun and marched away.

Free to leave, Jim hurried out of the building and climbed into his truck.

He hadn't gotten any response from Melissa and fifteen minutes to the hotel was fifteen she could be on the road to the address he'd given her for Dwayne. He could kick himself for sending it before thinking.

Then again, she needed to know what and whom she was up against in order to protect herself. Unfortunately, Melissa was just the kind of agent to charge into a dangerous situation without batting an eyelash.

For once, he wished she'd bat her damned eyes.

Jim floored the accelerator, picking up speed. The longer it took to get to Melissa, the more he felt he might be too late.

Ten minutes from the time he'd left Gunny, Jim got a phone call. When he saw it was from Melissa, he punched the talk button. "Where are you?"

"Near the Pearl River Marina." Melissa gave the name of the street she was on, her voice strained and wobbling.

Dread settled over James and he asked in a quiet, calming tone, "Tell me you aren't on your way to Buck's place."

"I'm not on my way. I'm here."

His hands tightening on the steering wheel, his foot floored the accelerator as he hit a long, straight stretch of road. "Are you in trouble?"

"No. When I got your text, I was in the neighborhood talking to a local marina owner only five minutes away from Buck's trailer."

"Don't go up to his door until I can get there. Stay out of sight."

She took an audible, shaky breath, the sound whispering against Jim's ear. "Too late."

His heart skipped several beats and his chest tightened. With the accelerator floored, he couldn't make his truck go any faster. "What do you mean, too late? Are you okay?"

"I am, but Buck isn't."

"And you know this because…?" Jim held his breath, waiting for her response.

Melissa's voice came across the phone, hollow and shaking. "I am standing in the doorway to his trailer. He's sitting in a recliner with a bullet hole between his eyes."

Chapter Fifteen

Mel had been talking to the owner of the Pearl River Marina, asking about the local man whose picture she'd taken with her phone. She'd made up a story about finding the man's hat that had blown off when he'd been in the boat in front of her. She hoped the owner would know him so that she could get the man's hat back to him.

The Pearl River Marina had been the fourth marina, her last option, she'd gone to with the photo. None of the other marina workers or owners had ever seen the man in the picture. The Pearl River Marina owner not only had seen him, but informed her that he was a regular who also had a card on the bulletin board for a charter fishing service.

He'd pulled the card off the bulletin board and handed it to Mel. Dwayne Buck. She'd been about to enter his name and phone number into her smartphone to find his address when James's text had come through with all the information Hank had sent.

Mel excused herself from the marina owner and went back to her banged-up truck in the parking lot to read through the information Hank had provided, concluding Dwayne was their only connection to the case.

When she punched the man's address into her smartphone, the map showed it was only five minutes away.

Knowing James would be tied up all day with his unit,

it was up to her to handle the investigation outside the SBT-22 team.

She drove to the small trailer park where Dwayne lived and parked her truck near the front entrance, tucked her forty-caliber handgun in her pants and covered it with her shirt. Then she'd gone into the trailer park on foot, searching for the address indicated on Hank's message.

It didn't take long to find the trailer. It was at the back of the park, the oldest, dirtiest place in the entire court. Beer cans littered the ground around the small wooden porch. The railing was broken and the beige paint on the aluminum siding of the trailer had long since faded to a dirty off-white.

As she neared the trailer, she noted the front door stood ajar.

Every nerve and muscle on instant alert, Melissa drew her gun and eased up to the structure, her ears perked, listening for any sound from within. When nothing stirred or moved, she inched forward. In her pocket, she could feel the vibration of her cell phone, but refused to respond to the call until she knew there wasn't someone inside the trailer ready to take her down.

No one accosted her or shot at her. After she'd climbed the steps of the porch and pushed the door inward with her pistol, she realized why.

Dwayne sat slumped in his recliner, a clean bullet hole through his forehead. At point-blank range, he had to have been killed by someone he knew.

Concerned his killer might still be on the premises, Mel entered the trailer and made a quick pass, poking her head through the two bedroom doors, noting the pigsty Buck lived in, the stench of unwashed clothes and dishes, and the piles of pizza boxes, beer cans and hamburger wrappers overflowing the trash can. Other than Dwayne's dead body, no one else was in the trailer.

From his waxy, gray appearance and the stage of rigor mortis, she'd guess he'd been shot sometime the night before. Probably by the man in the black jacket—Fenton Rollins. She'd been about to call the police to report the murder when her cell phone had buzzed in her hand.

Within five minutes, James's truck pulled up next to the trailer. Melissa had descended the porch stairs and met him as he climbed down from the vehicle.

He held open his arms and she stepped into his embrace. God, he felt good.

Big, solid and strong. Mel leaned against him, inhaling the clean, masculine scent of James. She hated that she'd come to rely on him, that his strength bolstered her when she was scared. What would happen to her on her next assignment with the FBI? James wouldn't be there. She'd be on her own, or with a partner who wasn't this man.

For a long moment he just held her, his heart pounding inside his chest, the sound reverberating against her ear, reassuringly.

"Didn't you learn anything at Quantico?" he said, his lips pressed to her temple. Then he set her at arm's length.

She laughed. "A few things. Why?"

"You never go into a situation without a backup." He shook her gently and then pulled her into his arms again, holding her tight.

"I didn't want him to get away." She snorted softly. "He's not getting away now, is he?"

"No."

"Do you think the man in the black jacket did this?"

"I'd bet money Rollins is behind this."

She leaned her cheek against his chest, her fingers bunching his military uniform shirt. "Do you think he killed Cord?"

"Until a body turns up, we won't know. I think Cord is holed up somewhere recovering from a gunshot wound."

Melissa sucked in a deep breath and let it out. "I have to admit, I wasn't ready to see Gumboots dead."

"Gumboots?" James grinned.

"Buck. He wore gumboots out on the river." She nodded toward the trailer.

James gripped her arms. "Look, it's not safe standing out here."

She knew that, but she didn't want to leave the comfort of his arms.

"Unfortunately, I have to get back to my unit. Gunny gave me exactly an hour to take care of my in-processing. I want to follow you to the hotel to make sure you get inside safely."

"I'm not going back to the hotel."

"Yes, you are. It's too dangerous for you to be out in the open with an expert sniper loose in the neighborhood."

"Someone has to report this murder."

"You didn't touch anything, did you?"

She shook her head. "I know not to disturb a crime scene any more than you have to. However, I did check inside for the shooter."

James's lips thinned. "You scare me, Bradley." He kissed the tip of her nose.

Mel liked the way it felt to be worried about, but she had a job to do and they still didn't know where Cord was. "I also have a lunch date with Lillian Petit at two o'clock."

"Given everything that's happened, you'll have to call and cancel."

"I could make an anonymous call to report this murder, but I can't miss my lunch date. I think Lillian needs to know I'm there for her. She's a very unhappy woman and the more she trusts me the more likely she will open up about Gunny. I'll be careful and not stand in one place too long."

"I'd rather you went back to the hotel and stayed in your room until I can cut loose from my unit."

Her brows rose challengingly.

James's lips twisted. "I don't suppose there's any chance you'll do that, is there?"

She shook her head. "I can't sit around and do nothing. Lillian isn't a threat and she might know something Gunny let slip. If it makes you feel any better, I'll take our lunch indoors, out of rifle range."

Nodding his head, James said, "Okay. I don't like it, but it's better than standing out in the open with a target hanging around your neck. Promise me that when you are done with lunch, you will take a very public road back to the hotel and stay put until I get off."

She smiled. "Okay. I'll do that. Hopefully, you won't be too late getting off. I haven't had a chance to check out Raines's and Sawyer's apartments."

"I can tell you already, Sawyer isn't in on this."

"Then we can start in Raines's apartment."

"I'll also see what I can do on my end while I'm at the unit."

"Deal." Mel glanced again at the run-down trailer. "Whoever shot him didn't mind pulling the trigger."

"Exactly. Be careful out there. I can't be there to back you up."

"I don't need backup for lunch."

"I hope not," James said, his face set in grim lines.

"Can you drop me off at the front of the trailer court?" Mel asked. "I left my truck there."

"Sure, hop in."

Mel climbed into his truck and ignored the seat belt for the short ride to the front of the complex.

As she reached for her door handle, James's hand shot out to grab her arm. "Wait."

He jumped out and opened the back door of the truck and leaned the backseat forward.

Mel climbed out as well and rounded the truck to peer over his shoulder.

James dug through a canvas bag, setting aside what looked like a headset to a two-way radio, night-vision goggles and a GPS tracking device. He frowned, unzipped a side pouch and grinned. "There they are." He pulled out a small plastic bag with a contemporary pendant necklace inside.

"Jewelry?" Mel asked. As soon as the word left her mouth, she realized what it was. "It's a tracking device?"

James grinned. "Hank has all the latest. His computer guru, Brandon, loaded the pack and mentioned this. Since I was being sent off to watch over a female, he thought it might come in handy."

"Remind me to thank Brandon and Hank." Mel reached for the necklace, but James held it out of her reach.

"Allow me."

She shrugged and turned her back to him, holding her hair off her neck.

His work-roughened hands brushed her neck as he slid the band around her throat.

The round pendant containing the tracking device settled between her breasts, sending a warm surge of blood straight south to her core.

Securing the catch in the back, his fingers skimmed the back of her neck. She leaned against him.

"Be careful out there," he whispered, pressing his lips to the sensitive skin at the base of her hairline.

"I will," she responded, her words breathy.

He squeezed her shoulders and let go, stepping back. "See you later."

James waited for her to get into her truck and pull out onto the road and then fell in behind her. He turned toward Stennis when Mel turned for Slidell and her lunch meeting with Lillian, though she had little appetite after finding Gumboots dead in his trailer.

Several minutes after two o'clock, Mel stepped into the delicatessen Lillian had selected to introduce her to its fabulous vegan menu.

"I'm so glad you got here." Lillian met her at the door. "I'm so hungry I could eat an entire head of lettuce by myself."

Mel laughed. "I could, too, but then I'd be hungry five minutes later."

Lillian smiled and waved to a seat beside her. "I took the liberty of ordering for you since you've never eaten vegan."

"Good. I wouldn't know what to order, and I'm sure they don't serve hamburgers here."

Gunny's wife held her hands up in horror. "Good God, no."

"Sorry, I couldn't resist." Mel settled into her chair. "How does that work with you being a vegan and your husband a SEAL? Surely he isn't a vegan."

"No, he most certainly is not. The man could eat an entire side of beef in one sitting. It's disgusting. And the more I try to get him to eat healthy, the more he eats out. I don't cook for him anymore." She unfolded her napkin and delicately spread it across her lap.

Mel felt gawky next to her. Sure, she had table manners, but being an agent in the FBI made her feel more empowered and a little less feminine than women like Lillian. *Arm candy* was the term that came to mind when she thought of the gunnery sergeant's wife. How he'd hooked up with her, Mel didn't know. Theirs seemed a match doomed to failure. Opposites attracting went only so far, then it ripped people apart. Couples had to have something in common to keep them together.

Take her and James. They were both warriors, used to

carrying and using guns. They knew the value of a well-planned operation and teamwork.

Not that they were a couple. One night of sex didn't mean anything, other than a great release between two consenting adults.

While Mel was thinking about James, Lillian jabbered away. "For that matter, I barely see Frank anymore. He gets up well before I do in the morning, and I don't see him until after I've gone to bed on most nights. I wonder if they're conducting more extended training operations in preparation for another deployment. Or maybe he has a mistress he's meeting on the side." Lillian shrugged. "Whatever his excuse, I'm alone most of the time."

Mel made a mental note about the late nights. James had gotten off duty in the afternoon of the previous day and hadn't mentioned getting off earlier than the others. What was Gunny up to in his off-hours?

"Anyway, I'm about ready for a vacation from this hell."

"How so?" Mel sipped her water and let Lillian ramble on.

"I'm going back to Boston in a couple weeks. I hope to stay for an entire month. Maybe when I come back—if I come back—Frank will reconsider and get out of that stupid unit of his."

Mel bit hard on her tongue to keep from telling the woman what she thought of her. SEALs underwent some of the toughest training of any military outfit. If they made it through, they were SEALs for life. Most preferred to do what they were trained to do, not sit around corporate offices in air-conditioned buildings.

"Anyway, it'll be a nice break from the humidity of southern Mississippi. I can't get my hair to do anything." Lillian patted her perfectly coiffed hair with her manicured fingertips.

Melissa nearly barfed, but managed to hold it together

while Lillian talked all about herself and the disaster her marriage to Gunny was.

By the time the waitress came to collect Mel's untouched tofu, she'd had her fill of Lillian's complaining. "I've always wondered what it was like to be a SEAL, to go on dangerous missions and be shot at."

"Sounds filthy, if you ask me. All covered in paint and sweat."

"Does Frank ever talk about his missions?"

"No, not really. Sometimes he talks in his sleep. But it rarely makes much sense to me."

"Really?" Mel leaned forward. "That's fascinating. I wonder if he's reliving a particularly dangerous operation. Haven't you ever been curious about what he does?"

"Not really, until this last mission. Something must have really shaken him. He nearly knocks me out of bed when he's dreaming about it."

"How do you know he's dreaming about it?"

"He mentions some kind of snake every time. Pit something."

"Pit Viper?"

Lillian shrugged. "I suppose. Whatever it was, it gives him nightmares and he wakes up yelling. If he's not shoving me out of the way, he's yelling 'No!' in my ear." Lillian rolled her eyes. "I'll be glad to get a good night's sleep in Boston."

"Did you ask him what bothered him so much about that mission? Maybe you could help him work things out."

Lillian looked at Mel as if she had grown two heads. "I can barely tolerate the Navy and the SEALs. Why would I ask him about a mission when he'd tell me he couldn't talk about it anyway?" She patted Mel's hand as if she were a not-so-bright child. "You'd understand if you were the wife of a SEAL. They're a tight-lipped lot."

"I suppose," Mel said. "But if you overheard him talking in his sleep, you might be able to help him."

Lillian tilted her head. "He did say something that indicated the mission didn't go as planned. Well, obviously. One of their teammates died on that one."

"Fascinating. What did he say?"

Lillian frowned. "I don't know why you think it's fascinating."

"I just do." Frustrated with Lillian's ramblings, Mel pressed, "What did he say?"

"Something to the extent of it wasn't supposed to happen that way. I don't know, it was all garbled and he was snoring and I couldn't get any sleep."

Mel sat back. What did that mean? Was Gunny involved in the death of the DEA agent?

The Navy anthem played in tinny tones nearby and Lillian glanced down at her designer handbag. "That's my ringtone for Frank. I'm sorry, but I should take it."

Mel smiled and waved her hand at Lillian. "By all means, please do."

Lillian dug in her bag for the cell phone as the Navy anthem continued to play. On the fourth iteration of the anthem, she unearthed the phone triumphantly and hit the talk button. "Frank, darling, I'm at lunch with my friend. What do you want?" she snapped.

Mel couldn't help but wonder what kept this marriage together. Lillian wasn't happy and if she was as snappy with him at home as she was on the phone, Gunny couldn't be happy, either.

"What? Seriously?" The more she listened to her husband, the deeper her frown grew. "Today? I can't possibly…Okay, okay. Don't get ugly with me, Frank Petit. I'll do the best I can…Okay." She hit the end button, threw her phone into her purse and slipped the handles over her shoulder. "He's insane."

"Something wrong?" Mel asked.

"He just moved the date up on my trip to Boston. I'm happy to leave earlier, but he doesn't realize it takes time to pack."

"When does he expect you to go?"

"Tonight!" Lillian snorted delicately. "I apologize for the short notice, but I have to leave and see what I can do to catch a plane in three hours. What does he think I am? A magician?" She stood and held out her hand. "Well, it was nice having lunch with you. I hope you're still here when or if I get back in a month."

Mel shook her hand and the woman darted out the door. What the hell had just happened? She pulled her own cell phone out of her pocket and entered James's number and waited for him to answer. After five rings, she pressed the end button. She'd promised to go to the hotel after her lunch meeting with Lillian. Part of her wanted to follow Lillian and stake out her house to see who showed up and when she left.

Gunny had to have played a part in betraying the unit. Mel could feel it in her gut. Though she wanted to witness the drama unfolding, Mel kept her promise and drove back to the hotel. Lillian had said she had to be ready to fly out in three hours. Hopefully, James would call her soon and they'd come up with a plan together.

At the hotel, she took the staircase to the third floor and slid her key card into the door lock. Even before she pushed the door open, she knew something wasn't right. A chill slipped down her spine and set her nerves on edge. She pulled her pistol from her purse and eased the door open. The curtains had been drawn and the room was dark. She reached out, flipped the light switch and gasped.

The room appeared as though a small tornado had flown through, tossing the contents of her suitcase, the bathroom and linens from the bed, including the mattress.

The drawers had been pulled out of the dresser and lay on the floor, the dresser shoved away from the wall and turned on its side. Someone had been looking for something.

Thankfully, the package she'd collected from the post office in Biloxi was still stowed in her truck's door panel. One thing she knew for certain—she couldn't stay in the hotel room, knowing whoever had gained access could do so again.

Chapter Sixteen

Jim didn't like going back to his unit while Mel was out in the open. Five times on the way back to Stennis, his foot left the accelerator and hit the brake. Five times he had to talk himself out of turning around and heading back.

Mel was an experienced FBI agent. She wouldn't be an agent if she hadn't been trained in how to defend herself and the importance of being completely aware of her surroundings. She could handle herself for the day. Especially if she did as promised and returned to the hotel and stayed put until he got off work.

By the time he pulled up at SBT-22 headquarters, he had gone through two dozen potential excuses for leaving again. He got out of his truck with the best one he could think of poised on his lips when Gunny came barreling out of the building, heading straight for his SUV.

"Gunny!" Jim called out.

The man barely glanced his way, continuing to his vehicle.

Jim loped over to the man, determined to get clearance to leave so that he could go back to Melissa as soon as possible. "I have a request."

"See the commander." Gunny jumped into his SUV and would have shut the door if Jim hadn't gotten there first and stood in the way.

"Is something wrong?" he asked.

The gunnery sergeant glared at him. "You should know. Get the hell out of my way."

"I should know?" Jim refused to move.

Gunny shifted into Reverse. "Move or be moved."

"What's the problem, Gunny? Tell me. Maybe I can help."

"You're the problem. You're in my way and if you don't get out of it, you're going to get hurt." He pressed the accelerator.

Jim jumped away from the SUV before he could be carried backward by the open door.

Gunny slammed into Drive and peeled out of the parking lot, leaving a black trail in the pavement. The scent of burnt rubber filled the air.

"What got his shorts twisted?" Montana appeared beside Jim.

"I'm not sure." He had a vague idea and he didn't like the way it was shaping up.

"That man hasn't been right since we returned from Honduras," Sawyer said.

"None of us have been right," Montana admitted. "That mission should have been a no-brainer. In, out and on the plane back home."

"I saw Gosling's wife yesterday," Sawyer said. "She's packing up and taking the baby back to Kentucky to be with her mother."

Montana shook his head, his eyes sad, his fists clenched. "Shouldn't have happened."

"I think Gunny is taking it personal," Sawyer said. "I tried to talk to him yesterday. I said he couldn't blame himself. He got angry and told me to get the hell away from him."

Lovett stepped out of the building. "What's going on?"

"Gunny tore out of here like his hair was on fire," Sawyer said.

"Really?" Lovett frowned. "Maybe it had something to do with the text he got when I was in his office," Lovett said.

Jim pinned Lovett with his gaze. "What text?"

Lovett shrugged. "I don't know. One minute he was telling me about the afternoon's riverine exercise and the next he kicked me out of his office and closed the door. Before I know it, he's tearing out of the building like he left the iron on at home."

Staring around at the men surrounding him, Jim made a decision. "I think what's happening with Gunny and what happened to Schafer has something to do with Operation Pit Viper. If any of you have anything to say that might have a bearing on what's happening, say it now. Otherwise, I'm going after Gunny to find out what spooked him."

Sawyer's eyes narrowed. "What do you know about it? That was a top secret mission."

Jim nodded. "I know. Cord sent for me before he disappeared. Apparently he got hold of more information and someone was trying to shut him up."

Lovett crossed his arms. "Montana, Sawyer, Rip and I all discussed it the day we got back. There was something off about the entire operation. We got in too easy."

"Yeah," Montana said. "We didn't meet any resistance until on our way out. And then only two shots were fired."

Lovett's jaw tightened. "The one that killed Gosling."

"And the one that nailed the agent," Sawyer finished.

"Come to think of it—" Montana's gaze narrowed as if he was thinking hard, trying to remember every detail of that day "—Gunny insisted on carrying Gosling."

"Yeah." Sawyer nodded. "When I reached for Gosling, Gunny yelled at me to stay put, he'd get him. But he didn't move until after the second shot was fired.

"Once the DEA agent was down, Gunny grabbed Gosling and slung him over his shoulder. Cord got to the agent first. I think he spoke to him, but I can't be sure. The shots alerted the people sleeping in the camp and we had to leave in a hurry."

"Cord carried the agent to the boat," Montana said. "By the time we were all loaded in the boat, the agent was dead. I checked Gosling first. He was hit in the neck and bled out immediately. The agent was hit lower. From what I could tell, it scrambled his internal organs. He didn't last long."

"Long enough to pass on information," Jim said. "I suspect that's why someone wanted him gone."

"Why didn't Cord tell us he'd gotten information from the agent?" Sawyer asked.

Jim's gaze took in the three men standing in a semicircle around him. "He suspected someone on the inside was part of the setup."

Every one of them stiffened. Lovett spoke first. "I may not like my teammates all of the time, but I'd take a bullet for every last one of them—any day, any time."

Sawyer nodded. "Including Gosling."

Montana's lips thinned. "That goes for me, too. I would gladly have died in Gosling's place. Thinking about his wife and kid going it alone because someone sold out makes me sick." He shook his head.

"It's not right," Sawyer agreed.

"Damn." Lovett's eyes narrowed. "You think Gunny was the traitor?"

"I don't know," Jim said. "But I'm going to find out."

Sawyer stepped forward. "We're going with you."

Montana and Lovett spoke as one. "Yeah."

Jim held up his hand. "I'd rather do this alone. If all of us go barreling in, Gunny might clam up or run. The sniper who killed Gosling and the DEA agent is still out there. If he thinks anyone is onto him, he might disappear."

"What can we do to help?" Sawyer asked.

"Be on standby. If I call on you, be ready to move."

"Wait a minute." Lovett's gaze narrowed. "Why should we trust you? You've been out to pasture for two years."

"I worked too damned hard to become a SEAL." Jim pushed his shoulders back and stood proud. "Once a SEAL, always a SEAL."

"I can vouch for him," Sawyer said. "Jim's as red, white and blue as they come."

Montana snorted. "I always thought Gunny was, too."

"Getting to the point you don't know who you can trust anymore," Lovett said.

"I suspect that's why Schafer wasn't willing to talk to anyone on the team," Jim pointed out.

"Why didn't he take it to the feds?" Sawyer asked.

Jim hesitated, unsure of how much to reveal to the team. "Rather than give it all away, let's just say what was happening in that camp had further-reaching implications."

"Like a traitor among the feds?" Lovett asked.

Jim nodded.

Sawyer shook his head. "I begin to wonder just who we're fighting for."

His jaw tight, Jim answered, "For now, it's Schafer."

"You think he's still alive?" Montana asked.

"I hope so." Jim opened his truck door. "I'm counting on you all if the crap hits the fan."

"We got your back," Sawyer assured him.

"In the meantime, tell the commander something came up at personnel and I had to take care of it. I won't be back the rest of today."

Before Jim could close his door, Sawyer grabbed it and held it open. "We mean it. If we can help you or Schafer in any way, call."

"I'm counting on it." As Jim pulled away from the SBT-22 headquarters building, he felt reassured, knowing he had the support of his team behind him. He might have been there only a day, but they'd back him as if he'd been there with them all along.

God, he'd missed the camaraderie of the military. When the time came to make the decision to stay in the Navy or work for Hank, he'd have some serious soul-searching to do.

For now, he needed to follow Gunny and make sure he wasn't leaving the country. Jim suspected he knew more about the attack on his men and about Schafer's disappearance than he'd let on. If he wasn't directly responsible for the sniper, he could have been the one to reveal the location and time of the attack to whoever had contracted the killer.

From what Hank's intel had indicated, Rollins was a gun for hire. He didn't have any connection to his victims. If he could catch him, he might convince him it was in his best interests to reveal his employer. The problem was finding the man.

Jim entered Gunny's address in his navigation system, whipped into Reverse and left the parking lot. Once off Stennis and on his way to Gunny's, Jim pulled the GPS tracker scanner from inside the duffel bag and flipped the on switch. For the first five seconds, the screen remained blank. Jim held his breath until the backlights came on. Pale outlines of roads, streets and buildings appeared and a little blue dot indicated where Melissa was located.

He stared at the dot on the tracking computer and glanced at his GPS built into the dash of his pickup.

Damn. She was on her way to Gunny's.

Jim floored the accelerator as he fumbled with his cell phone and dialed her number.

The phone rang five times before going to her voice mail.

He left a message. "Don't go near Gunny's house, Mel.

I think he might be involved in Gosling's and the DEA agent's deaths and Cord's disappearance. Stay. Away."

Jim tried to call her three more times. Why wasn't she answering her phone? She'd promised to go to the hotel after her meeting with…

Hell. She'd been meeting with Gunny's wife, Lillian. What if they'd gone to lunch at Lillian's house or were stopping there afterward?

If Gunny suspected he'd been found out, he'd get desperate. If he was responsible for two deaths, what was one more?

Every possible scenario blew through Jim's thoughts on the way. He hoped and prayed Melissa's FBI training served her well and that she didn't land in the middle of a disaster.

Jim couldn't get there fast enough.

WITH HER HOTEL ROOM trashed and nowhere else to go, Melissa drove toward Gunny's home, debating whether or not to contact Jim and let him know what had happened and where she was going. He'd likely be out somewhere on the river training, his cell phone stashed in a bag or locker at the unit. Still, if he wasn't, he'd want to know what was going on.

She glanced down at her cell phone briefly. When she looked up, a car had pulled out in front of her to cross the road, only it paused in the middle, the teenage driver fumbling with the gearshift.

With just a split second to react, Mel yanked her steering wheel to the right, swept over the shoulder and down an embankment, coming to a stop in a water-filled ditch. Her heart thundered against her ribs and she braced her hands on the steering wheel to catch her breath and get her bearings.

She shifted into four-wheel drive and pulled forward

slowly, leveling out in the ditch, before attempting the climb back up onto the road. Stiffening her backbone, she steered into the steep slope and eased her foot onto the accelerator. As the truck climbed out of the ditch, it tipped sideways sharply.

Mel was glad for her seat belt keeping her in place as everything loose in the truck slid to the right.

By the time she reached the road, her arms shook. She shifted into Park and leaned her forehead on the steering wheel to pull herself together.

Stupid, stupid, stupid. She knew better than to take her attention off the road while driving. She could have died, or worse, killed someone else.

When she had her pulse back to normal and her chest wasn't so tight, she pulled out onto the road.

The teenager had managed to get his car in gear and took off.

Shaken by her near miss, Mel headed for Lillian Petit's house.

Not until she arrived on the Petits' street did she realize she hadn't called Jim. For that matter, she couldn't find her phone. She parked against the curb a block and a half away from the Petits' house. Lillian's car was there. Other than that, nothing stood out as off or not quite right.

Mel unbuckled her seat belt, her shoulder sore from being thrown against the restraint during her second trip into a ditch in as many days. After a good three-minute search, she located her cell phone under the passenger seat wedged against the metal tracks used to adjust the seat's forward position. The phone's face had a long, jagged crack in it and the screen was dark.

Great. Her carelessness not only nearly cost her life, it had probably cost her a cell phone. She hit the button to restart and waited, praying the phone would revive and come back to life.

While she waited for signs of life in her phone, an SUV pulled into the driveway at the Petit house and a man in uniform leaped out.

He had to be Gunnery Sergeant Petit. The man disappeared into the house and the door closed behind him.

Mel glanced at the clock on her dash. It was too late for lunch and too early for him to get off work. What was Gunny doing home at this hour when James had said he had to hurry back to his unit to go out on a training exercise?

Mel's phone beeped and the screen lit up. She had four missed calls and two text messages.

The calls had all been from James. Damn, he might be in trouble. Tempted to hit the redial button, she hesitated and pressed the button to listen to her voice mail first. Maybe he'd left her a message as to why he was calling.

The first message was from James. "Don't go near Gunny's house, Mel. I think he might be involved in Gosling's and the DEA agent's deaths and Cord's disappearance. Stay. Away."

She winced. "A little too late for that, don'tcha think?" she muttered to herself and stared down at her phone, bringing up the screen for her text messages.

As she brought up the messages, a scream ripped through the air.

Mel's head tipped up and her gaze shot to the Petit house. Lillian Petit ran across the yard and out into the street, screaming hysterically, tears streaming down her face, dark streaks of mascara making tracks across her beautiful skin.

Mel shoved the door of her truck open and ran toward the woman.

When Lillian spotted her, she sobbed and ran toward her. "Melissa, oh, thank God, you're here." When she reached Mel, she sagged against her.

Wrapping her arms around the woman, Mel asked, "What happened? What's wrong?"

The woman continued to sob, her tears soaking Mel's shirt. "It's horrible. Just horrible," she moaned, hiccuping between each word. "Frank. Oh, dear God, Frank." Her body shook with the force of her sobs and she blubbered against Mel's shoulder.

"What about Frank, Lillian?" Mel asked, pushing the woman to arm's length. "Where is he?"

"Sweet Jesus, he's been shot."

"Lillian, who shot him?" Mel worried that Lillian with her deep dissatisfaction of being married to the man for so long and living in substandard conditions, according to her parents' standards, had gotten to her.

"Some man was in our house. Oh, dear Lord. He was waiting for Frank to come home. I'd been there for a while and I never saw him." She sagged against Mel again. "I couldn't stop him. He pointed his gun at Frank and shot him! I couldn't stop him." Lillian shook, holding herself around her middle, rocking in misery.

"Where is he now?" Mel asked.

"He's dead. On the floor in the kitchen. Dead," Lillian sobbed.

"Not Frank. Where's the man who shot him?"

"I don't know," Lillian wailed. "Before he started shooting, Frank told me to run." She looked up at Mel, her eyes wide, her fingers pressed to her lips. "I couldn't. My feet were stuck to the floor. Then that man shot Frank. I don't know how, but I made it out of the house, to you."

Mel's hand tightened on Lillian's arms. "Listen to me."

Lillian looked at her through tear-smeared eyes.

"My truck is a block that way." Mel pointed to where her truck sat against the curb. "Go there and stay until I get back." She shoved her phone into Lillian's hands. "When you get there, call 9-1-1 and report the shooting."

When Lillian stood, unmoving, Mel shook her gently. "Do you understand?"

The frightened woman nodded, but still didn't move.

"Go!" Mel said sharply and gave Lillian a nudge, sending her in the right direction.

Mrs. Petit stumbled at first and then ran as fast as her well-toned legs could take her.

Mel patted the gun in her waistband reassuringly, leaving it hidden until she got closer to Gunny's house. If the Navy SEAL wasn't dead, he needed medical attention ASAP. She crossed the street a house down from Lillian's and eased along the bushes, hunkering low.

She didn't have time to call for backup. Lillian would have to manage that. Gunny didn't have the luxury of the time it would take. A man could bleed out faster than an ambulance could deploy and arrive.

Getting to him might be the challenge. If the shooter was still inside the house, Mel might become another victim. She grit her teeth. *Victim be damned.*

She edged up to the house and leaned close to one of the windows to the kitchen. Nothing moved within her view. She ducked below the window and peered in from the opposite corner. She could barely see the lump of uniform on the floor and it wasn't moving.

As much as Gunny needed her help, she didn't dare rush in when the whereabouts of the shooter was still unknown. She wouldn't be of much use to Gunny if she joined him, injured on the floor.

Hunching over, she moved to the next window. This one overlooked the living area. The room was neat, almost too neat, with perfect furnishings that had interior designer written all over them. Nothing was out of place, and nothing moved.

Making her way around the house, staying close to the bushes and low to the ground, Melissa looked through the windows she could see through until she came to the back door. It stood wide open, leaving the impression the shooter had escaped that way. And if he wasn't in the house, he could be pointing *at* the house, at her.

Melissa crouched close to the ground and peered at the backyard, at the rear of the neighbor's house and the bushes and shadows in the surrounding landscape.

A dog barked and a black cat slipped in and out of the bushes near the back of the house behind the Petits'.

Feeling exposed, Melissa drew her gun and slipped through the back door, into a mudroom that served as the laundry room. No mud dared touch the clean tiled floors. Moving quickly and quietly through the house, she searched for the intruder, finding no one but Gunny lying on the floor of the kitchen, his belly soaked in blood.

A lead weight settled in Mel's gut. Foraging through the drawers, she found the one containing dish towels. She grabbed a handful of cloths and knelt on the floor beside Gunny. She pressed her fingers to the base of his throat, feeling for a pulse.

At first she didn't feel anything. Then the soft, re-assuring thump of a pulse bumped against her fingertips.

She let go of the air she'd been holding, ripped open the camouflage uniform shirt the man wore and eased his T-shirt up to expose the wound. It appeared to be a small hole, but the amount of blood on the floor beneath him and oozing from the injury indicated much more internal damage and an exit wound on his backside. Dragging from her memory the self-aid and buddy-care lessons she'd learned at Quantico, she laid the wad of cloth over the wound and applied pressure.

"Hang in there with me, Gunny," she whispered. "Hang in there. We'll have help here soon."

The man lay still, his eyes closed, face pale.

A noise made Melissa jump, her hand leaving the wound.

When she spun toward the sound from the front of the house, a hand reached up and grabbed her wrist in a tight grip.

A low, guttural sound came from Gunny.

"What did you say?" Mel asked, leaning close to the injured man, even as she strained her ears for the sound coming from the front of the house.

"Wasn't...supposed to...kill...Gosling," he gasped in little more than a whisper.

Melissa bent her head close to the man's lips, barely able to catch all his words. "Who wasn't supposed to kill Gosling?"

"Mercen—" The man gurgled and coughed, bloody spittle dripping from the side of his mouth.

"Mercenary?" Melissa prompted.

The man nodded, his eyes closing.

Melissa touched his cheek to get his attention. "Did you hire him?"

Gunny shook his head, the movement so slight, Mel almost didn't catch it.

"Were you the one who leaked the details of the mission to the mercenary?"

A single tear squeezed out of Gunny's left eye and ran down the side of his face. "Gosling...good man. I made... mistake."

"Why did you share the information about the operation?"

The man's lips pressed into a thin line and he snorted softly, setting off another bout of coughing and more blood trickling from his mouth. He opened his eyes and stared up at the granite countertops. "Bills."

Melissa followed his gaze. The granite was clean and polished to a glossy shine. She couldn't begin to guess how much it cost to remodel an entire kitchen and to make the countertops granite, but it couldn't have been cheap.

"What do bills have to do with killing a federal agent?" she pressed.

"Didn't know."

"You let a mercenary know about the operation and didn't think he would kill the agent?"

"Told to get agent out in open. They'd take him from there."

"Take him where? And who is they?"

"Shooter and…man who hired…him."

"What about Cord? Did you have anything to do with his disappearance?"

Gunny shook his head. "Tell him…"

Mel's heart leaped. "He's still alive?"

"Tell him, I'm sorry." Gunny's words released on his last breath, like a sigh.

Mel felt again for a pulse, but knew she wouldn't find one. Too much internal bleeding. No amount of CPR would bring him back.

The loud bang of the front door being slung open so hard it hit the wall made Mel grab her gun and leap to her feet, her heart thundering, her nerves taut.

"Melissa?"

The sound of James's voice was like a balm to her ears and she ran toward it.

James burst through the kitchen door in time to catch her in his arms. "Sweet Jesus, Mel." He crushed her to his chest, pressing his cheek against the top of her head. "I think I lost two years off my life."

"Why?"

"When I heard Gunny was on his way to his house and saw that you were headed the same direction, I couldn't get here fast enough." He pushed her to arm's length, his eyes widening. "Oh, my God, did he shoot you?"

"No, he didn't." Mel stared down at all the blood on her hands and shirt. "This is Gunny's blood."

"I saw Mrs. Petit at your truck bawling hysterically. That must have been why. She shoved your phone at me, but I couldn't get a coherent word out of her, so I left her and came straight to the house."

"James, Gunny's dead." Mel turned toward the man on the floor.

"Did you—"

Mel shook her head. "I didn't kill him. Someone else shot him. When I got here, Lillian came running out of the house screaming that he'd been shot."

"I told you not to leave the hotel. You could have been shot, too."

Mel stared up at him. "I couldn't stay at the hotel. Someone had been there and ransacked it, tearing everything apart, including the mattress on the bed."

James's lips thinned. "Looking for the packet."

"That's my guess. When I had lunch with Lillian, she got a call from her husband and she said she had to leave to pack to go to Boston in three hours. Before that, she'd said she wasn't leaving for two weeks."

"Gunny was going to run. He left out of the unit in a big hurry after a text message he received." James bent over the dead man to fish in his pocket, unearthing the man's cell phone. He hit the key to turn it on. A password screen popped up.

"What are the chances Lillian would know his password?" James asked.

"Slim to none. The woman is—was arm candy. As far as I could tell, she didn't know anything about what her husband was up to. I do know she has expensive tastes." Mel glanced around the kitchen with its granite countertops and stainles-steel appliances. What she'd seen through the windows of the living room had appeared to be furnishings from high-end stores, placed beautifully as if by a talented interior designer. "I think Gunny sold out his unit to pay off the credit-card debt his wife ran up. When I asked him why he gave out mission information, he said bills."

"Makes me sick to think Gosling died because Gunny couldn't get his wife's spending habits in check."

Mel's cell phone chirped. She glanced down at the cracked screen and frowned. "What the hell?"

Bring the packet to me at midnight. If any of the information has been copied, destroy the copies. Schafer's life depends on that information going no farther.

The message concluded with Coordinates will be forthcoming.

A surge of joy ran through Melissa. "Cord's alive."

"Or so he says."

Another text followed the first.

Your boyfriend comes with you.

"What's it say?" James leaned over her shoulder and read. "Good, I wouldn't have let you go alone, anyway."

Melissa's heart sank to her knees. "The fact he wants both of us to bring the packet tells me one thing—this guy isn't planning to make an even trade, Cord for the data. He wants the data and to kill all three of us."

Chapter Seventeen

James opted for a speedboat instead of the small fishing boat they'd used the last time they'd set off up the river. The coordinates they'd been given were very close to where they'd almost been caught before by Fenton Rollins.

More than likely it was Rollins, the mercenary hired to kill the DEA agent, who'd sent the text and planned on killing James and Melissa at midnight.

When the ambulance and the police finally arrived at the Petit house, Mel had been the one there, holding Lillian up and answering the hundreds of questions for the homicide detective. Lillian had been too distraught to be coherent. When they'd been released, Mel had taken Lillian to a hotel and got her into a room, telling her to stay put until she'd gotten a good night's sleep. Melissa promised to check on her the next day.

Assuming they survived the night.

Jim had spent the better part of the rest of the day trying to talk Melissa out of going. She'd insisted. The message clearly stated she was to bring the package.

During the hours they had to kill until midnight, he'd been on the phone with Hank, trying to determine how to get into Gunny's cell phone, hoping to get a trace on the text message he'd received that had him running scared for himself and his wife. He'd also hoped Brandon, the computer geek, could trace the texts to Melissa's cell phone. Unfortunately, the texts had come from a disposable cell phone, which would take a considerable amount of time to trace and with no guarantee it would help. Time was something they didn't have a lot of.

Jim and Melissa had cleaned their weapons and packaged the packet of data in a watertight plastic bag. Melissa showered in Jim's hotel room, refusing to stay any longer than she had to in her own room. She'd grabbed her clothes and moved in with Jim. Every chance he got, he hugged her, pulling her into his embrace to reassure her that everything would work out okay.

Melissa was strangely quiet and tense, dismantling her pistol three times, sitting at the desk in his room.

The coordinates didn't come until an hour before they had to be there. When Jim determined the location was on the Pearl River, he'd had to scramble to find a boat at the last minute. All of the marinas had already closed.

He'd called Sawyer and asked if any of the men in the unit had a speedboat. Luckily Sawyer did. He used it to travel the tributaries and intracoastal canals when he had time off.

He and Melissa had met Sawyer at the marina where Sawyer kept his boat.

"Cowboy, you know you can trust us to help you if you're in a tight spot." Sawyer handed him the keys to his boat. "What happened to Gunny..." He shook his head. "Hate to see that happen to you and the girl." Sawyer tipped his head toward Melissa walking across the dock to them, carrying the plastic bag with the packet of data.

"We might have a chance to find Schafer."

"Then let us help," Sawyer insisted.

"I don't want anyone else hurt. The situation is highly dangerous."

Sawyer grinned. "Yeah, well, that's what we do."

Jim's chest tightened as he steered the boat upriver toward their assignation with a killer. SEALs had teamwork drilled into them from the time they hit the ground in BUD/S training to the time the final few graduated. They had each other's backs.

With only minutes to spare, Jim rounded a curve in the river, barely slowing.

Another boat burst out from beneath the low-hanging branches of a willow tree, headed straight for them.

Unable to get out of the way fast enough, Jim turned the boat away from the oncoming one, placing the rear between the attackers and Melissa.

The other, larger vessel crashed into Sawyer's speedboat. The bow launched into the air and rolled to the starboard.

Jim held on to the steering wheel as long as he could, until his body was flung off the boat, ripping his grip loose. Somewhere beside him, he heard Melissa scream and she flew past him, splashing into the murky river water.

Helpless to get to her, he hit the water hard, sinking beneath the surface. As soon as he got his bearings, he started kicking, fighting the momentum of his downward trajectory. The sooner he got his head above water, the sooner he could locate Melissa and make certain she was okay.

As he came up, the boat that had rammed theirs blasted past him, barely missing him by a couple of inches. Churned beneath the wake, he didn't realize they'd stopped until he came up for air and tread water, spinning in a circle while searching for Melissa.

A bright moon illuminated the night, but didn't help him find Melissa. The boat that had run them down floated several yards away. A shout went up and a scream rent the air.

Jim kicked out, swimming with all his strength toward the boat and Melissa.

As he neared it, he saw two men drag Melissa out of the

water by her arms. Kicking and screaming, she landed a heel in one captor's gut. She twisted and kicked the other one in the face.

One of them loosened his grip, but regained his hold and they landed her on the boat.

Within two yards of the boat, Jim yelled, "Let go of her!"

Once they had her on board, one of the men reached out with a large fish net and scooped up the plastic bag containing the information Schafer had sent Melissa to recover.

With the woman and the information on board, the boat driver shifted into gear and blasted forward.

No matter how fast he could swim, he'd never catch up with them without a boat. His pulse racing, he looked around for Sawyer's boat. It drifted in the water near the shore several yards downstream.

Striking out, Jim swam hard and fast for the boat. He dragged himself up the back, using the motor for a toe-hold. Once on board, he surveyed the damage. The other boat had clipped the back corner and the outboard engine on Sawyer's boat. The craft was taking on water and list-ing to the starboard.

Jim shifted into Neutral and twisted the key in the igni-tion. Encouraged by the sound of the motor turning over, he continued to turn the key. The engine sprang to life, but as soon as he shifted into gear, loud, grinding, metal-on-metal sounds ripped through the air and the engine shut down.

He tried again, hoping to at least limp along to keep the distance between him and Melissa from becoming too great.

No matter how often he tried, the engine wasn't going to run with the damage to the propeller.

Jim slammed his palm against the steering wheel,

chances of finding Melissa slipping away with each passing minute.

The still of the river night surrounded him. One by one, the frogs resumed their song, the cicadas chirped and the other insects of the night chimed in.

Buried in the din of nature, Jim heard the distant hum of an engine. Not the engine of the boat carrying Melissa away, but the sound of another coming from the south, closing in on his position. His heart thumping hard in his chest, he grabbed a paddle from the side well and desperately paddled toward the middle of the river to flag down the boat headed his way.

Moments later, the SBT-22 Special Operations Craft-Riverine (SOC-R) whipped around the bend in the river, spewing a heavy spray of river water out the sides. Aboard were the special warfare combatant craft crewmen of the Navy SEALs Special Boat Team 22.

Never had Jim been more proud or more relieved to see his team speeding toward him, guns mounted, dressed in camouflage and full combat gear.

Jim dug in the dash compartment of the boat, searching for a flashlight to hail his comrades. His hand closed around the cylindrical shape and he yanked it out, switched it on and waved it slowly back and forth.

The SOC-R slowed and slid in sideways, bumping gently against the damaged boat.

"My boat!" Sawyer cried out.

"Sorry, buddy." Jim leaped into the SOC-R. "I take it you have the tracking device I gave you?"

"That I do." Sawyer held it up. "The dot is still moving. What happened?"

"I'll fill you in as we go. Let's move!" Jim stood beside Sawyer, the acting boat captain. "And I don't want to know how you commandeered government property to participate in this mission."

"We're counting it as black-ops training. Hang on." Sawyer shifted the gear into forward, spun around and headed upriver, following the blinking dot on the tracker.

"Where's the commander" Jim asked.

"We didn't—" Sawyer coughed into his hand "—invite him. Better he didn't know what was going down. That way he can't be court-martialed."

Jim understood the degree to which these men had sacrificed themselves and their careers to help him. He'd do no less for any one of them. As he was for Schafer. And Melissa.

He filled in the team as they went, praying the men who'd taken Melissa and the information packet didn't kill the woman now that they had what they wanted.

MEL KICKED, BIT, kneed and struggled against the hands that held her, but the men were stronger and there were more of them than of her. As soon as she was brought on board, someone zip-tied her hands behind her back and another slipped a dark bag over her head, cinching it around her throat.

The little bit of light the stars had provided was cut off, leaving her disoriented in a black abyss. The boat shot forward and she slid off the seat she'd been pushed into, slamming into the bottom of the boat. Unable to slow her fall, she hit her head on the fiberglass, pain shooting through her temple.

Lying still, she pushed aside the headache and concentrated on the sound of the motor, the rush of the wind across her skin and each turn they made on the river. She hoped that something about the small bits of information she gathered would help her to find her way out of the maze of tributaries and canals when she managed to escape her bonds. And she would escape. Failure wasn't an option.

She had to get back to where they'd left James. He could

be injured. While fighting for her freedom, she'd seen a shadowy figure swimming toward the boat. Had it been James? Had he tried to get to her to rescue her from her kidnappers?

She hoped it had been him and that he'd gotten back to the other boat safely, before an alligator got to him. If he did manage to get back to the boat and if the craft was still operational, he'd come after her, following the tracking device she'd wrapped in a small plastic bag and tucked into her bra.

A terrible thought crossed her mind. If they'd been tossed from the boat or the boat had capsized, the tracker would be lost. James wouldn't be able to find her. The device in her bra would be all for naught.

Mel couldn't let herself dwell on whether or not James would be able to follow her. She had to be proactive, keep calm and come up with her own escape plan. Even if James came after her, it might not be soon enough. The men had fished the packet of information out of the water. When they realized it was everything they were after, they'd have no use for a prisoner.

The Mississippi Delta was a vast and complex ecosystem of canals, tributaries and bayous. Finding her would be difficult even with the tracking device. If she wanted to live, she'd have to get herself out.

After what seemed like hours, but was probably only thirty minutes of curving, weaving, turning and skimming along the water, the boat slowed and eventually stopped, bumping up against something hard.

The craft rocked as someone got off and footsteps sounded across wood, probably a dock. Muffled voices murmured from a short distance away.

Then hands grabbed her arms and jerked her to her feet, half lifting, half dragging her through the boat and up onto a wooden dock.

Mel debated fighting for her freedom then, but the bag on her head and her hands tied behind her back gave her pause. If she fell into the water, she wouldn't know which way was up and couldn't get her hands loose.

She'd bide her time until they at least untied the hood and she could see again.

Once they stepped off the short dock, the ground was rough beneath her feet and she tripped over bramble and sticks. It wasn't a well-worn path, whatever it was.

A door creaked open and a male voice carried to her from inside a cave or building. "Good, you got her. Did you get the information packet?"

"We did."

Something thwacked against a surface. Mel assumed it was the packet wrapped in plastic.

One of the men holding her arm shoved her in front of him.

Her knees hit something hard and she fell over, landing partially on a mattress and partially on a lump both hard and soft.

A groan rose from the lump and Mel realized it was a person. The tie holding the bag around her throat had loosened in transit. She shook her head, tipping her chin upward to give her the best view of what was directly beneath her.

It was a man, his hairy arm caked in dried blood.

He moved and moaned again.

Mel scooted up his body, her heart skipping several beats as she neared his head. The chin was first to come into her view, then a bruised cheekbone.

Excitement flared when the corner of an eyebrow appeared in the narrow window of her view. The eye beneath it opened to a decidedly green eye, the whites tinged yellow and bloodshot.

Cord!

Mel had to bite down hard on her bottom lip to keep from shouting out his name.

She'd found Cord.

Her best friend from her home in Ohio was lying on a nasty mattress in a shack in some godforsaken hellhole of a swamp.

And he was alive.

Now, more than ever, she knew she had to escape. And she had the added complication of getting an injured SEAL out with her.

The rustle of plastic behind her indicated the men in the room were going through the packet.

"Is this all of it?" a man demanded, his voice direct, clear and unsympathetic.

"Yes," Mel answered. "Everything I collected from the post office in Biloxi is in that packet."

"Oh, God. Mel?" Cord whispered, his voice cracking, coarse and dry.

"Shh," she responded softly, hoping their voices wouldn't carry across the small room to the men gathered at the other end.

"It's just a bunch of pictures and an after-action report." Mel recognized that voice as belonging to the man in the black jacket from the day before on the river. Rollins, the mercenary sharpshooter.

"It's enough to get people snooping where they don't belong," said the man with the I'm-in-charge voice. "It's what got the DEA agent all wound up. We can't afford to let anyone connect the dots."

"Where's Monahan?"

Mel froze, her attention riveted to their leader's voice.

"When we rammed their boat, both of them fell in the river. We found the girl and the packet." Rollins cleared his throat. "I thought that was what you wanted most."

A loud bang sounded, like a fist pounding a tabletop.

"Damn it! I don't pay you to think. I pay you to do what you're told. Get back out there and find him. He's as deep in this as the girl. If you have to use the girl as bait, do it. I want all three of them dead before morning. Do I make myself perfectly clear?"

"Yes, sir," Rollins replied.

Wood scraped against the wooden floor, like a chair being scooted across. "By sunup, I expect to hear nothing less than my orders were carried out to the letter." The man in charge's voice sounded farther away, as if he stood near the door.

"You'll hear it, sir," Rollins said.

"I'd better, or your body will be the one found floating in the river. You've screwed up this operation from the start. Don't do it again."

"Yes, sir."

A door squeaked on its hinges and the room seemed to empty of occupants except for Mel and Cord.

"Mel, you have to get out of here," Cord said, his voice weak, strained.

"I will. But you're coming with me."

"Can't," he said. "I was wounded during the live-fire exercise."

"How badly?"

"Bad enough I can't get myself out."

"I'm here to help."

"I'd have died if Rollins hadn't found me today and given me water and food." Cord snorted softly. "Ironic that the man who injured me saved me only to be ordered to kill me by sunup."

"Not happening." Mel leaned over, placing her head close to Cord's hand. "Can you pull the bag off my head so I can see?"

"I think so." Fingers curled into the bag and held on while Mel backed out of the bag.

A single battery-powered lantern sat on a filthy wooden table in one corner of the room, lighting the small shack in a soft yellow glow.

Mel stared down at Cord, joy tempered with fear at the bloodstains on his uniform shirt.

"How bad?" she asked.

"Not terrible. No major organs, but the river water did me no good. The wound is infected."

Mel laid her cheek against Cord's. His skin was hot and clammy. If she didn't get him to medical care soon, Rollins wouldn't have to kill him. He'd die on his own.

"I need to break this zip tie." She crawled around the room on her knees searching for something jagged to scrape the plastic against. She found it in the rusted metal bedframe. Squatting with her back to the frame, she rubbed the plastic tie against the corroded metal, the effect like sanding the plastic, scraping her skin.

The voices outside grew louder and the door to the shack slammed open. Rollins strode in, his brows drawn together in a menacing frown. "You and your boyfriend have been nothing but trouble. I've got a good mind to finish you off now."

"Don't be a fool," Cord croaked. "She's your ticket out. Use her as bait to get Monahan to come to you."

"Already thought of that. Which is why I'm not going to kill her, yet. But what about you? I have no reason to keep you around, now that I have the girl and the packet."

Mel glared at Rollins. "If you kill him, I'll kill you."

"Big talk for a little girl."

"Says the man who had to have backup to capture me," she spat back.

Rollins's arm snapped out and he backhanded her across the cheek, sending her flying across the wooden floor.

Pain made her head spin and brought tears to her eyes, but she refused to let one fall. She ran her tongue across her lip, coming away with the coppery taste of blood. "You're nothing but a coward. A big man who beats up on a woman who's tied up and can't fight back. Let me loose. You and me—one-on-one."

"He's not worth it," Cord said. "Save your strength."

"What for?" Rollins laughed. "She'll be dead by morning."

One of the men who'd chased Melissa in Biloxi poked his head through the door. "Boat's ready. We need to get back down the river and find Monahan. Are you going to bring the girl?"

"No, he'll come on his own as long as he knows we're taking him to his girl. Shorty can stay and guard her and the SEAL."

"Sure he can handle both?"

"If Shorty can't handle a girl and a man who's near death, he deserves to die." Rollins chuckled. "Eh, Shorty?"

"No problem." He waved his gun. "If they give me any trouble, I'll shoot 'em."

Mel ground her teeth, wanting to stop them from going after James. She hesitated, knowing it was hers and Cord's chance to make a break for it. First she had to sever the bindings around her wrist. Then she'd take out the single man left to guard them.

As Rollins left, Shorty stood in the doorway, watching them go.

Mel scooted across the floor to the corner of the bed with the rusted leg and continued to saw at the plastic binding.

The noise of the boat engine outside helped mask her attempt to break her ties. A little…bit…more…and…

Snap!

Her wrists flew apart, the zip tie broken.

Shorty chose that moment to close the door and turn to face her and Cord. "No funny business. I'd kill you just as soon as look at you." He held a nine-millimeter pistol in his hand as he sat in the only chair at the wooden table.

Mel remained seated on the floor, keeping her hands hidden behind her back. She searched her surroundings for a weapon of any kind and came up with nothing. The odds of overpowering him were slim considering he had at least a hundred pounds on her. But she had to try. For her own sake and for Cord's.

If she could find a way to divert Shorty's attention for long enough to get across the room, she might have a shot at disarming him.

Cord moved his knee, bumping her head.

Casually, she turned to glance up at him. Slowly, he winked his eye.

Mel braced herself, ready to spring into action.

Cord coughed, a racking, gurgling, horrible cough. The coughing went on for a full minute. Cord wheezed. "Can't breathe."

"Shut up," Shorty demanded.

Cord coughed more, again and again, the sound filling the small room.

"I said shut up!" Shorty lurched to his feet, crossed the room to the bed and pointed the gun at Cord's head. "Shut up."

Mel pulled her feet under her and launched herself at the man, hitting him in the side like a football player going in for the tackle.

The gun exploded, the bullet veering wide of the target.

As Shorty regained his balance, Mel cocked her leg and let loose with a sidekick, hitting the man's gun hand. The pistol flew across the room and clattered against the wooden floor.

"What the hell?" he shouted and turned a confused expression toward Mel.

She kneed him in the groin. When he bent double, she

brought her knee up, crashing it into his nose. The man went down.

Mel leaped across the floor, grabbed the gun and aimed it at Shorty.

The man writhed on the floor, blood pouring out of his nose, his eyes squeezed shut. Mel ripped the hem of her shirt into a long strip, yanked the man's arm up behind his back and grabbed the other. With her knee pressed firmly into the small of his back, she tied his wrists together and knotted the cloth firmly.

Leaning over Cord, her heart squeezed tightly in her chest. Her friend was in bad shape and needed a doctor. He wouldn't have much energy or stamina once they got moving, if at all. "I'm going to check out the situation. I'll be back."

Cord grabbed her wrist. "Get yourself out of here. Leave me."

She shook her head. "Can't. You're all the family I have left."

"Leave me," he begged. "Save yourself."

"I'll be back," she insisted and left the shack, stepping into the night, praying for a miracle.

Chapter Eighteen

Jim glanced down at the tracking device and then back up, peering into the darkness. Melissa's dot had stopped five minutes before. At the rate they were moving, they'd be there soon.

He held up his hand.

Immediately, the boat slowed, the bow dropping until it was on an even keel with the rest of the craft. The roar of the engine settled into a tempered hum.

Though he wanted to blast into the kidnappers' camp like John Wayne with all guns blazing, Jim knew it would be more dangerous for Melissa. Stealth and patience were what was needed to extract her without bringing harm to her.

Jim leaned forward, the rumble of the engine behind him. But then he heard something that sounded like the roar of another engine coming around the bend in the river.

"We've got company!" he yelled.

Trained for any situation, the men of SBT-22 stood ready, manning their weapons.

The speedboat Melissa had been carried away in blew around the corner, sending a rooster tail of spray high into the air, the starlight glancing off it, making it shine like a diamond rainbow.

In lights-out conditions and hugging the bank, the

SOC-R would be difficult to spot and the enemy wouldn't be expecting it.

When the other boat neared, Jim yelled, "Take 'em!"

Sawyer shoved the throttle forward, sending the craft on a path to intercept the kidnappers' boat. At the last minute, he turned sharply, sending a towering plume of spray over the other boat, enough to slow them down.

Jim glanced down at the handheld tracking device. Melisa was not on board the boat. Either that or they'd found her tracker and left it behind somewhere.

The pop of rifle and pistol fire echoed against the night sky. Someone on the rear of their craft let loose a barrage of .50-caliber bullets in an attempt to warn the shooters they were outgunned.

The warning went unheeded and the men on the other boat fired again.

Sawyer swung the craft around and headed straight for the other.

The enemy boat turned in the opposite direction.

Jim aimed his weapon at the rear of the boat and squeezed the trigger long enough to send twenty bullets toward the stern, hoping to hit the engine and put it out of commission.

Tracer rounds helped guide his efforts, but the other boat had moved out of range, and the engine continued on, driving them away.

They fired rounds back at the Navy team.

Sawyer slowed the boat enough their bullets would fall short.

It seemed that now the race was on to get back to where they'd left their prisoner.

"We have to cut them off," Jim shouted over the roar of the SOC-R engine. "We can't let them get back to Melissa first."

Sawyer kicked up the speed.

The distance between their boat and the one ahead closed. A sharp bend in the river hid the other boat from sight for a few long seconds. When their craft rounded the tight bend, Sawyer pulled back on the throttle.

Jim braced himself. It would be a good location for their enemy to turn and engage.

As their boat made the turn, the river stretched before them.

Empty.

The speedboat had disappeared.

Jim leaned over the bow and stared at the water. A cloud chose that moment to block the light from the moon.

"Where'd they go?" Montana called out.

"Don't know." Jim waited for the cloud to release the light of the moon, praying it wouldn't be too late.

At last the cloud shifted and the moon shone bright over the water, and the remnants of a wake disappeared beneath a thick drape of Spanish moss hanging over the water from a cypress tree.

"There!" Jim leaped to his feet and pointed to the moss.

As he took his position behind his weapon, Sawyer eased beneath the moss into a hidden channel. Moonlight shimmered off the ripples of the lead boat's wake.

Sawyer pushed the throttle forward and the SOC-R's bow lifted high as the propellers dug into the water. As they gained speed, the bow leveled out on the water and they were flying forward.

Jim held up the tracking device. "Getting close."

An S-turn in the river forced them to slow.

As Sawyer pulled through the final curve, Jim spotted the speedboat moored to a rickety wooden dock, its occupants jumping out.

Sawyer didn't slow. He blasted up to the shore, beside the dock, running the bow up onto the bank.

The enemy ran toward a shack.

As the Navy SEALs ran up onto the shore, the kidnappers turned and fired at them.

Rifle fire greeted the team as the enemy turned to defend.

"I'll cover!" Montana yelled from on board.

Jim dropped out of the boat, hit the ground and raced forward, hunkered low, bullets flying around him. One nicked his arm, tearing through his shirt.

He ignored the stinging pain and pushed forward. Melissa was somewhere nearby. Jim prayed she was safe and out of range of the bullets flying all around.

Someone kicked open the door to the shack.

Jim held his breath. This was it. If they brought Melissa out with a gun pointed at her heard, the shooting match would be over. Jim would lay down his arms before he let anything happen to her. In the short time he'd known her, he'd come to love her fierce determination to find Cord and her refusal to give up no matter the odds.

"Put your guns down or I'll shoot the girl," someone yelled.

"Show me the girl and we'll think about it." Jim motioned to Lovett and Duff to swing around the sides of the shack. He'd keep the shooters entertained from the front.

"Throw down your guns and I'll show you the girl," the bad guys said.

Lovett and Duff slipped into the shadows, headed to the north side of the shack.

Jim gave them sufficient time to get into position. "I want to hear her voice before I commit to giving up my weapon."

His query was met with silence.

Jim's heart stopped while he listened for any sign of Melissa.

If the men in the shack truly had Melissa, they would have paraded her out for them to see their bargaining chip.

Unless she'd been injured or killed during the kidnapping.

His heart pounded as Jim fought to keep from charging forward to find Melisa.

"I'm gonna shoot her," a voice warned. "Throw down your weapons!"

"Okay, I'm throwing mine down," Jim bluffed.

"No, James, don't!" Melissa called out from somewhere in the brush on the south side of the shack, away from where Duff and Sawyer were headed.

His relief was overwhelming and short-lived.

"Grab her!" said the man near the shack.

Jim leaped forward at the same time as a rush of shadows converged in the area from which Melissa's voice had come.

He was too far away. Chest tight, adrenaline racing through his veins, he charged ahead.

The sharp report of gunfire made him drop to the ground, roll to the side and come up on his feet running.

A scuffle ensued in the underbrush. Men grunted and one yelled out, "Damn you!"

When he reached the melee, one man was on the ground and another man had a tenuous hold on Melissa's hair.

Jim grabbed the man from behind, yanked him around and punched him in the nose.

Melissa's attacker crumpled to the ground, blood rushing from his nose.

"Watch out!" Melissa shouted.

The other guy, who had been on the ground, raised his arm. In his hand, he held a gun pointed at Jim.

Melissa cocked her leg and landed a sidekick on the man's hand.

The gun went off before it flew from his hand.

The man with the bloody nose grunted and slumped forward, a dark stain spreading across the front of his shirt.

A shout went up behind Jim. He spun in time to see Lovett and Duff take out the leader of the threesome.

Jim flipped the man on the ground over onto his stomach and bound his wrists with a zip tie he carried in his back pocket.

He straightened. A hand on his arm made him spin.

Melissa stood there, slipping her fingers into his hand. "Thank you for coming after me."

"Thanks for living long enough for me to get to you." He dragged her into his arms and crushed her to his chest. "When they left with you…" He held her for a long moment, his cheek pressed to the top of her head. Then he tipped her face up and kissed her. "You're growing on me, you know that?"

She smiled up at him, the moonlight making her teeth glow a bluish white. "Ditto."

"What are we going to do about it?"

"I don't know. But whatever it is, I know this…I want to get to know you better. Preferably somewhere other than a swamp." She laughed, the sound ending on something of a sob. "In the meantime, come with me. I need your help."

She led him through the brush to a point where Spanish moss trailed from a cypress touching the ground. She parted the coarse moss and held it to the side. "Look who I found," she called out softly.

A shadowy lump lay hidden in the moss. "Cowboy?" a man's voice called out weakly. "That you?"

His chest swelling, Jim dropped to his knees. "Yeah, it's me."

"About damn time." Cord coughed. "I thought you'd never get here."

"I almost didn't, buddy."

Cord struggled to sit up, his body swaying with the

effort. "What are you waiting for? Let's blow this Popsicle stand."

Melissa laughed out loud and bent to help Jim lift Cord from the ground.

As they emerged into the clearing around the shack, Jim was happy to see three of the four men who'd taken Melissa trussed up like the pigs they were.

Sawyer called out, "Holy hell, Cowboy, what have you got there?"

"It's Rip!" Montana rushed forward and took over from Melissa, looping Cord's arm over his shoulder. "Where the hell have you been hiding? We all thought you were dead."

"I think death would have been easier," Cord said.

"Let's get him to the boat," Jim said. "He can fill us in later."

Sawyer stood back, his cell phone pressed to his ear. "I'm placing a call to the skipper."

The other members of the team shot concerned glances his way.

Sawyer held up his hand. "He's going to find out anyway. This way he can get the ball rolling and have an ambulance meet us there." He made the dreaded call that could get the entire team in hot water for appropriating government equipment and using it for personal purposes.

Jim and Montana scooped Cord beneath his legs and carried him the rest of the way to the SOC-R, settling him on a bench near the back.

Melissa sat beside him, slipped an arm around his waist and let him lean most of his weight on her.

"Thanks, Mel." Cord slumped against her. "Thanks for looking for me. I love you, babe."

"I love you, too, Cord. I wouldn't have stopped looking for you."

Jim overheard their softly spoken conversation, and

something sad and painful ran through him. He stared hard at the two on the bench.

From the beginning, Melissa had been doggedly determined to find Cord. For a moment he wondered if there was more between them than just friendship. He balled his fists, wanting to lash out at someone. His anger centered on the two sitting on the bench, leaning on each other.

Hell, why was he angry with Melissa and Cord? He barely knew her, and Cord was his friend. That didn't stop him from wanting Melissa to wrap her arms around him and hold him as she was holding Cord. What was it about Cord that drew Melissa to him?

Jim shoved a hand through his hair and turned away to man his gun near the front of the boat. If he were anyone else, he'd suspect he was jealous of Cord. But he had nothing to be jealous of. Melissa didn't belong to him. Their lives were destined to go in different directions. She had the job she loved with the FBI. He had either the SEALs or CCI, both of which would guarantee he'd be gone more than he'd be home. Not that he really had a place to call home. Since his father's passing, he didn't have roots. Didn't have anyone else in his life.

As they sped down the river back to the boat's mooring at Stennis, his thoughts drifted back to the hotel room where Melissa had lain naked in his arms.

He wanted to get to know her better, to date her to have the opportunity to find out if they belonged together. His father had once said he'd known from the day he met Jim's mother that he would love her forever. When his mother died, Jim's father hadn't remarried. He'd loved her so completely he couldn't see himself with any other woman. He'd known from the first day.

Had that been what had happened to Jim? Had he fallen for the FBI agent from the moment he'd seen her walk through the door at the post office in Biloxi in her dress and big sunglasses?

He wasn't sure if it was love, but every fiber of his being screamed for him to take a stand. If he stood by without telling her how he felt and she left, he'd forever regret having let her slip through his fingers.

Jim glanced toward the back of the boat several times on the ride back, his gut so knotted when they neared the dock he hurt. Now that they had Cord back, Melissa would leave to return to San Antonio and her job with the FBI.

Jim had one shot at this—one chance to let her know how he felt. What she did with that knowledge would be totally up to her. But he had to let her know or live with regret for the rest of his life.

As the SOC-R boat slid into the slip, they were met with a crowd of people, two ambulances, the local police, county sheriff and state policemen.

"Great. The gang's all here," Montana muttered.

The team clambered off the boat. Sawyer and Montana carried Cord to the waiting EMT, settling him onto a stretcher. Melissa walked alongside, talking softly, soothingly to Cord the entire way.

Duff stopped next to him. "It's good to see Rip back."

"Yeah," Jim agreed. No matter how jealous he was of his friend, he was happy the man was alive and had a shot at staying that way, with the proper medical attention.

"Funny thing, but I thought Melissa was *your* girl."

Jim's gaze never strayed from Melissa as she climbed into the back of the ambulance with Rip. "Melissa is her own girl."

"I remember Rip telling me he had a sister, only his records show he's an only child." Duff nodded toward the two as the EMTs shut the ambulance door. "Suppose he was talking about her?"

Jim shrugged. "All I know is Rip's my friend."

"And a good SEAL doesn't poach another man's girl, right?" Duff nudged him with his elbow. "Seems to me you'd better find out which way the tree falls. That Melissa is one tough cookie. Worth a second look and a little chasin'."

"Who said I was in the market for a woman?"

"The way you're lookin' at her…well, I'm not blind. But they say love is. Take the blinders off and find out if she's available. Don't go on appearances. They can be deceivin'."

Jim's lips twitched and he turned a glance toward his old friend. "Since when have you become the philosopher?"

Duff shrugged. "A man can change."

"Don't change too much. You're a damned good SEAL."

"Yeah. I'll never change that part of my life, but a good woman doesn't come along every day. If she's what you want, don't let her slip away without trying."

Jim nodded. "Thanks for the advice." With the ambulance pulling away and the skipper headed toward him, he didn't see much of a chance to follow Melissa and Cord anytime soon. Besides, his truck was back at the marina where he'd borrowed Sawyer's boat. If he wanted to see Melissa again, he'd have to catch a ride to his truck.

An hour later, Jim had given his statement on what had happened. He'd also taken the commander of SBT-22 aside and filled him in on his real reason for being there.

Commander Paul Jacobs had listened with a poker face, never once showing surprise or anger over Jim's revelation.

"We know Fenton Rollins is a mercenary for hire, but we still don't know who hired him or who paid Gunny to leak information about Operation Pit Viper," Jim said. "The man who hired me will continue the investigation until he finds the source of that funding."

When Jim had finished, the commander nodded. "I suppose we have some decisions to make, then."

"Yes, sir." Jim stood at attention.

"Right now, though, I'd like to get to the hospital and see how Chief Petty Officer Schafer is fairing."

"Me, too, sir."

"Do you have a ride?" the commander asked.

"No, sir."

"Then ride with me. We can discuss your future on the way."

His heart pounding, Jim took a deep breath and nodded. This was it—the time for him to decide whether or not he wanted to remain on SBT-22 or stay with CCI and work for Hank Derringer. He marched with Commander Jacobs to his SUV, images of the past couple of days flashing through his mind. By the time he climbed into the passenger seat of the commander's vehicle, he was calm, his pulse back to normal, his decision made.

MEL PACED THE FLOOR of the waiting room. Cord had been in surgery for the past forty-five minutes. How long did it take to dig out a bullet and sew him up? The longer it took, the more convinced she was that he'd suffered more internal damage than she'd originally thought.

Not one for praying much, she found herself closer to God than at any other time in her life. Cord was like a brother to her. With no other family left in her life, he was it.

And where was James? Yeah, the tough female FBI agent needed someone to lean on. No, she needed James. In the short days since she'd met him, she'd come to rely on James and to really look forward to seeing him.

Her heart thudded slowly, her belly churning at the realization that her mission and his were over. They'd found Cord and he was alive. At least she hoped he was still alive.

What was taking them so darned long?

"Excuse me, miss?"

Mel spun to face a young nurse standing in the doorway of the waiting room.

"Are you a relative of Cord Schafer's?"

She didn't hesitate with her answer. "Yes. I'm his sister."

"Melissa?" the nurse asked.

"That's me."

The nurse smiled. "He's been asking for you. If you'll follow me, he's still in recovery, but he's coherent."

Mel hurried behind the nurse, whose rubber-soled shoes didn't make a sound on the tiled floors.

"He's doing well. They were able to remove the bullet and clean up all the scarring and infection. He's on a good antibiotic and the doctor says he'll heal well."

Melissa let go of the breath she'd been holding and smiled after what felt like years of intense drama. "Thank you."

The nurse led her into a room where Cord lay on a gurney, hooked up to an IV.

Taking his hand in hers, she whispered, "Hey."

Cord's eyes blinked open. "Hey, yourself," he replied, his voice hoarse, but stronger. "Can you fill me in on what happened after you decked the guard? I seem to be missing a few details."

Mel told him about the SEAL team coming to their rescue and taking down the four men who'd held them captive.

Cord nodded and grinned. "Glad I got to see you in action. I thought all those FBI agents were just glorified security guards."

Mel frowned. "Watch it."

Cord raised the hand not hooked up to the IV. "I stand corrected. If I'm in a battle, I want you on my side. You're a formidable opponent."

"Yeah. More determined than anything. I didn't plan on you or me dying in that shack."

"Well, thanks, kid."

She smiled. "You'd do the same for me."

"Damn right. That's what family's for." He closed his eyes, his face pale behind the tan.

For a moment Melissa thought he'd fallen asleep.

Then he said, "When are you going to marry me, Mel?"

He'd asked this question a thousand times before. And she had the same answer for him every time. "You don't want to marry me. It would be like marrying your sister. I don't love you that way."

"So you say. But you're everything a man could want in a woman." His eyes opened. "You're tough, sassy and beautiful."

"Yeah, and you're not bad yourself. But I know there's a woman out there perfect for you. You have to wait for her to come along. Don't shortchange yourself with someone who will only ever love you as a brother. Besides, if I married you, you couldn't be my brother. I'd have no one to give me away."

"You have a point." He smiled, his eyes drifting shut again. "What about Cowboy?"

"James?" Her heartbeat kicked up a notch. "What about him?"

"Even through a fog of pain on the boat, I noticed him glaring at us. Is there something going on between you two? Do I have to give him the talk, since your father isn't here to do it?"

Melissa's cheeks burned and she turned away. "We worked your case together. And now that you're back, he'll be headed back to wherever he's from, and I'll be on my way back to San Antonio once I know you're okay. There's nothing going on between us."

"Bullshit."

Mel spun at the sound of a voice in the doorway.

James stood tall in his damp uniform pants and T-shirt, his face drawn into a tight frown. "There *is* something special going on and I'm not going anywhere until we figure out just what it is."

Mel's pulse pounded and her body lit up like a firecracker at James's sudden appearance. "What do you mean?"

"You said it earlier, you want to get to know me better. And I want to get to know you better, as well."

"I thought you'd want to be on your way back to your unit or to Texas to your next assignment."

He shook his head and closed the distance between them. "First, I want to know, are you and Rip a thing?"

Rip snorted softly and groaned. "Don't make me laugh. It hurts too much. I've asked Mel to marry me a hundred times. She always says no."

James turned to her. "Is that right?"

Mel straightened her shoulders and narrowed her eyes, her chin rising. "What's it matter to you?"

"A lot. I don't poach in a teammate's territory." He held himself stiff.

"She's not in my territory." Cord waved his unattached hand. "She's all yours."

"Hold on just a minute. I'm not anyone's unless I say I'm someone's." Mel didn't like that her statement sounded silly, but her head was spinning from what James had said a moment earlier. "And what do you mean, you don't poach?"

"Since Cord says you don't belong to him, I guess you're free to do whatever."

Mel refused to get her hopes up. James wasn't being all that clear on his intentions and she couldn't get excited about anything until he did. "So, are you planning on hunting illegally or something?"

"No, I'm planning on, as you put it, getting to know you." He gathered her hands in his and pulled her close to him. "Then, if we find that we like each other, I might consider doing some things to you that should perhaps be illegal. Deliciously illegal."

Mel's blood heated and her nerves burst into flames as James's hands circled her waist and drew her close.

"So what's it to be? Will you go out with me? I might be able to work with my boss and get a few days off."

"But you just got here. Won't your unit expect you to stick around and train with them?"

James shook his head. "I've decided not to re-up with the SEALs. As much as I loved being back, I think I can do a lot of good working with Hank and Covert Cowboys Inc."

Her heart beating out of control, Mel realized the implications of having him in Texas. "So what you're saying is you'll be within driving distance back in Texas?"

"Even better. I can be within shoutin' distance. Working for Hank, I can live anywhere."

She stared at his chest, her pulse pounding with emotions. What could be more perfect? He could live in San Antonio. Her heart stuttered and galloped ahead.

As good as it sounded, Melissa couldn't bring herself to hope. She loved her job with the FBI, and San Antonio might be only a temporary assignment. She could be relocated to somewhere else in the United States. In the meantime, he could be close by.

James touched a finger beneath her chin and tilted her head upward. "Yes, even San Antonio." His lips curled in a slow, sexy smile. "As for getting to know each other… what do you say we start with a date on the River Walk?"

She nodded. "Yes, please."

"Just to set things straight…I know what your work with the FBI means to you and that you could be gone on assignment. I won't like it, but I'll understand and respect you for your dedication."

"Thank you." She lifted his hand and pressed his palm to her cheek. "Not many men understand."

"I'm not many men. I sat with my father while he was dying of cancer. I learned that you can't be afraid to love, even if you stand the chance of losing that person you love. With what happened to my father and Rip, I realized you have to grab for what life has to offer. You might not get a second chance."

"You're right." She pressed her lips into his palm. "I've learned that family is everything. Even if you're only family by what you feel in your heart."

James stiffened. "And Cord?"

"Is like a brother to me."

"Good to know."

"In the meantime, Cord is concerned we didn't find the man responsible for the weapons shipments to Honduras."

"If Hank holds true to his actions, he'll find the man and bring him to justice. He might even assign me to the case."

"Does that mean you'll have to be away?"

James nodded. "Could be."

"Well, I won't like it, but I'll understand and respect your dedication," Mel said, repeating his words.

"It won't be easy?"

"Hey, you're a SEAL. And don't you have a saying about that?"

He chuckled. "The only easy day was yesterday." Then drawing her close, he leaned close until their lips were a breath away. "Can we start our date now? I can't seem to resist you."

Mel wrapped her arms around his neck and smiled. "A wise man once said, you have to grab for what you want. You might not get a second chance."

A soft snort came from the bed. "Could you two take your second chances out into the hallway? I could use a second chance at some sleep. And when I'm up to it, I'm going after the man who sold the goods to the terrorists."

Mel laughed. "One step at a time, Cord. One step at a time."

* * * * *

MILLS & BOON®

It's Got to be Perfect

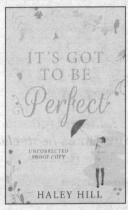

When Ellie Rigby throws her three-carat engagement ring into the gutter, she is certain of only one thing. She has yet to know true love!

Fed up with disastrous internet dates and conflicting advice from her friends, Ellie decides to take matters into her own hands. Starting a dating agency, Ellie becomes an expert in love. Well, that is until a match with one of her clients, charming, infuriating Nick, has her questioning everything she's ever thought about love…

**Order yours today at
www.millsandboon.co.uk**

MILLS & BOON®

The Thirty List

* cover in development

At thirty, Rachel has slid down every ladder she has ever climbed. Jobless, broke and ditched by her husband, she has to move in with grumpy Patrick and his four-year-old son.

Patrick is also getting divorced, so to cheer themselves up the two decide to draw up bucket lists. Soon they are learning to tango, abseiling, trying stand-up comedy and more. But, as she gets closer to Patrick, Rachel wonders if their relationship is too good to be true…

Order yours today at
www.millsandboon.co.uk/Thethirtylist

MILLS & BOON®
INTRIGUE
Romantic Suspense

A SEDUCTIVE COMBINATION OF DANGER AND DESIRE

A sneak peek at next month's titles...

In stores from 15th May 2015:

- **To Honour and to Protect** – Webb & Black
  and **Navy SEAL Newlywed** – Elle James

- **Untraceable** – Janie Crouch
  and **Security Breach** – Mallory Kane

- **Cornered** – HelenKay Dimon
  and **The Guardian** – Cindi Myers

Romantic Suspense

- **Cowboy of Interest** – Carla Cassidy
- **Colton Cowboy Protector** – Beth Cornelison

Available at WHSmith, Tesco, Asda, Eason, Amazon and Apple

Just can't wait?
Buy our books online a month before they hit the shops!
visit www.millsandboon.co.uk

These books are also available in eBook format!